I0642238

And Then
There Was
Silence

Drifters, Book Six

SUSAN RODGERS

Copyright © 2015 Susan Rodgers

All rights reserved. This book or any portion thereof may not be reproduced or used in any manner whatsoever without the express written permission of the author or publisher except for the use of brief quotations in critical articles or reviews.

Cover design by Alanna Munro. All rights reserved.
Edited by Kathy Gillis and Stephen Reaman.
Book design and formatting by Valerie Bellamy, Dog-ear Book Design.

ISBN: 978-1-987966-04-6

This is a work of fiction. Names, places, businesses, characters and incidents are either the product of the author's imagination or are used in a fictitious manner. Any resemblance to actual persons, living or dead, actual events or locales is purely coincidental.

For Siomon, Erin, Keira, Jane and Lana
The best nieces and nephew a gal can have
Go create, write, dance and sing
And, above all, make the world a better place

Contents

"7:29—crap! Kids, wiggle your butts!"

Tossing a green striped cotton dishtowel over her shoulder, Sara Lawrence hustled from the perimeter of her living room back into the kitchen and, as if she didn't believe it the first time, glanced again at the time on the microwave clock.

She called over her shoulder, her voice a quickly rising crescendo, "Ren, Mark, you never want to eat because your food is always cold by the time you get to it. Leave the friggin' computer alone and come eat your breakfast. Do you want to be late for school?"

Whipping open an oak cupboard, she grabbed a juice glass and deposited it on the counter, then she clutched a carton of orange juice and hauled it out of the fridge. She filled the glass in such haste drops spilled onto the counter, and then Sara grabbed a second glass and quickly dumped juice into it as well. When both glasses were on the table and her kids were still nowhere nearby, she tossed the towel on the sink and strode hurriedly back into the living room.

Running fingers through bobbed bottle-red hair, she stormed up behind the kids and stole the computer mouse from under her oldest son's small hand. Immediately he straightened and frantically grabbed at it.

"Mom, you made me get eaten by a shark!" He tossed his hands into the air in frustration as his game made its low dying *wh-wh-wh-whir* 'you lose' sound. Mark sat back, frustrated.

Sara cursored over an 'x' at the top of the screen and closed her kids' game. "I'll show you 'get eaten!' Get out there and get your egg eaten before it's cold!" She swatted his longish surfer-mojo locks lightly, then gripped her younger son's shoulders and pointed him towards the kitchen as well. "You too, monkey. Go! Now!"

Heavy footsteps on the stairs announced the arrival of the kids' dad. Stocky but not too beer-bellyish for a forty-something dad, or so he told himself, Kevin Lawrence pulled a chair out from the round table and dropped his ample frame into it.

"Do I get an egg?" he asked, tucking a royal blue work shirt into his jeans as he mobilized his butt and feet to situate the chair more comfortably. Kevin looked up at his wife expectantly.

"I'll give you an egg," Sara muttered sarcastically, spinning around and cracking an egg into a frying pan. She stood there, one hand resting over pink flannel pajama pants on a comfortably generous hip, and watched the egg bubble up quickly in the heat.

At the table, Ren poked Mark in the ribs.

"What'd you do that for?" hollered the older boy. He was eleven, in grade six at St. Catherine Catholic Elementary School, which made him, in his opinion, too big to be poked at by his nerdy younger brother at the breakfast table. Besides, the girls at school told him he was cute. Not only was Mark too big, he was also too *cool* to be bothered by his kid brother.

Nine-year-old Ren sat back on his haunches and pouted. "I want my dinky car," he whined.

"I don't have your stupid dinky car. Dinky cars are for babies."

"Mark, you know Ren's car is special. Kevin, can you do something about those two?" Sara's voice was high and edgy. She didn't bother turning around. Instead, she flipped the egg she was frying for her husband. It skidded across the pan with one edge folded underneath. "Shit," she intoned under her breath, trying to work the folded part back out so it would fry flat.

In a patient voice Kevin asked, "Mark, where's the Jag? Ren, is that the one you're missing? The 60's Jag, the red one your great-grandma gave you?" He was reading the Peterborough Examiner—the paper version—and didn't bother looking up.

"I don't have it!" Mark, on the defensive, yelled unnecessarily. "Stupid baby takes it everywhere and he left it at Bobby's."

Sara turned half around, then back to the stove. Her quick peek at the table was enough to discern that her husband either had seemingly no interest in the kids' dispute, or else he was just immune to their squabbles. She looked back at the egg and folded it over so it was all yolk with the whites layered on top. She let it fry for another moment before hoisting it out of the pan with a spatula and dropping it onto the plate at her husband's place, where it lay ignored underneath his newspaper.

Mark and Ren were now poking each other openly. Biting one corner of her bottom lip, Sara watched them until the inevitable happened—Ren exploded in frustrated tears.

"Honey, I'm seeing Bobby's mom tonight at hockey. I'll text her and ask her to be on the lookout for a little red sports car." Silently, Sara fought a wave of irritability as it coursed through her veins. Fighting the urge to speak loudly, she added under her breath, "Seeing as it's likely the only red sports car any of us will ever own."

Bending down between her sons, Sara soothed strands of sandy-blonde hair away from Ren's face. She spoke to Mark, slapping his knee gently to accent her point.

"Mark, ease up on your brother. You're eleven and he's nine. Antagonizing him is only going to get you cooties in your Kool-Aid when you're fourteen and he's twelve."

Kevin chose that time to fold up his paper and pull his plate towards him. "Thanks for the egg, Sara." He shot her a grateful look, which she disregarded completely, almost annoyed that he didn't complain about the way the edges of the whites had flipped and fried underneath the egg.

"What are cooties?" Ren inquired between choking sobs, wringing his fingers together.

"I'll show you after school," Mark answered, sneering. "I'll put them in your chocolate milk."

"Mooommm!" Ren was outright wailing now.

"He won't have time, honey," Sara bit off to Ren while frowning at the grinning Mark. "We have hockey right after school. First your practice and then your brother's. Don't worry. Now, finish your juice and go brush your teeth." She glared at Mark, who laughed outright at the obvious success of his cootie joke.

3

"He'll get you back one day. You just wait," Sara told him, before standing up and grabbing a tattered baseball cap off a hook on the wall by the nearby mudroom. A faded plum in color, its edges were ragged and its *Peterborough Petes* logo was smudged with dirt. She plonked it on Mark's head, yanking it roughly down over his ears.

"Ouch!" he yelped. "Mom! Geez!"

Sara scowled outright at her husband, who was wolfing down his egg between bites of toast. "Kevin, if you had as much interest in reffing the kids' fights at home as you do coaching their games on the ice, you'd be a helluva lot more use to me."

"Huh?" Her hubby looked up, dazed. "What?"

"Lord help me," she muttered, spinning around and grabbing the frying pan off the stove. She shoved it in a sink already filled with water and foamy soap. Some of the bubbles plopped up onto the counter, leaving big wet lumps here and there.

"Mom." Ren was tugging at Sara's pajama pants.

She looked down. "Hmmmm? You brush your teeth that fast? What, you just choose to do one tooth a day, Rennie?"

"You cursed. I heard you. You said hell."

"Actually, I said helluva." Grabbing a handful of dish soap, she swiped his lips with it, to great exclamations on his part. "And if I hear you say hell again, kid, you'll get that soap on the inside next time. Hmmm?"

Groaning, he skipped off towards the door. Sara followed him and grabbed a matching ball cap to Mark's, which she pulled down over Ren's ears. She yanked a coat off a hook and wrapped it around him, and he poked his skinny nine-year-old arms in the sleeves. Zipping it up carefully so as not to catch Ren's chin, Sara stared down her nose at him. "Mind your teacher and don't aggravate Douggie Jones."

"Douggie Jones spits food out of his mouth when he eats. Everybody picks on him."

"Not my kid," was Sara's warning response. "My kid sees a kid who other kids pick on, and my kid takes the kid aside and makes friends with said kid. Capiche?"

She tucked his lunch into his Teenage Mutant Ninja Turtles backpack and gave the schoolbag an extra check for his lunch and homework. "Okay," she mumbled, exhaling. "One down. Two to go." She eyed her husband warily.

By the time she got the kids out the door with Kevin, who promised not to speed to get the kids to school on time, and himself to work at a big-box store lumberyard, she was ready to go back to bed. Instead, she dug her elbows into the rest of the dishes, which didn't take long. She eyed the microwave clock again. *Two hours before I have to be at work,* she considered thoughtfully.

Hurrying into the living room, Sara adjusted the kids' chairs at the computer so that one was directly in front of the old monitor. Sliding into the chair, Sara clicked on the monitor's email icon. A quick scan and she isolated the more important emails, deleting anything that looked like junk mail. An email in the middle of the pile caught her eye. Her heart rate picked up.

She double-clicked on it and inhaled slowly before reading.

Hello Sara,

I hope this finds you and your family well. Evelyn tells me you have two boys who play a lot of hockey. That must keep you very busy!

Sara guffawed at that, making a little choking sound in her throat. She rolled her eyes before continuing to read, inching forward in the uncomfortable white wooden kitchen chair.

Thank you for agreeing to see me. My husband Josh will be shooting a new television series in Toronto that starts up in a few weeks. I'm wondering if I can come down then? I understand Peterborough is about an hour and a half from Toronto?

Let me know what works for you. I'll just stay a few hours the first day. We'll take it slow, okay? I'm just really looking forward to meeting you and your family and, of course, Martha. Our grandmother. Wow. And maybe I can take in a hockey game?

I'll email when I know for sure exactly when I'll be in Ontario. We can pick a time then, if that's okay.

All the best,

Jessie

Sara sat back and stared at the screen. *Jessie Wheeler is coming here. Jessie. My sister.*

An immediate nauseous ripple seized her at the thought of it. For one thing, how would this work? For sure the woman would have an entourage, which would consist of what, exactly? How many people would a big star like Jessie Wheeler have with her? Security, bodyguards, the like...also, Sara knew Jessie was expecting her first baby. She'd Googled her—Jessie's due date was officially around the first of December. It was now October 21st. Likely she wouldn't stay long, at least, because she probably wasn't feeling super comfortable at this late juncture in her pregnancy.

There were two more troubling aspects about the singer's impending visit. One, their grandmother, Martha Kilfoil, was 89—a bright, energetic 89 who still baked for bake sales, thank God, otherwise Sara's kids would show up at half their fundraisers with store-bought cookies. Still...she was older, and fragile in some ways, especially relating to the disappearance of her daughter more than three decades before. Sara herself sure as hell wasn't keen on any reminders of those horrible old days, either, when Emily Wheeler—Martha's daughter and Sara's mom—climbed down a ladder outside a bedroom she'd been locked in for more than a month, and disappeared. When she was pretty much almost nine months pregnant, at that.

Sure, Aunt Evelyn screwed off herself eventually, too, and even lived for a time in P.E.I., near her sister Emily and the sordid lover. Occasionally the women reported back, sending pictures of the new baby and all, but Sara's mom never darkened the Ontario doorways again. She'd made it very clear she was not interested in her Peterborough family—not her dad, not her mother Martha, and not the daughter Emily deserted when Sara was just the ripe old age of fourteen.

Sighing, Sara let her shoulders sink as she pondered the second troubling issue concerning Jessie's visit. A few months ago, a number of nude photos of Jessie were released online. The first, back in April, was tragic enough, showing the star with a devastating single tear on her cheek, but now—well, Sara refused to look at the newer photos, although she sat with her cursor over one for quite some time before choosing not to click. She did spend a few hours reading about Jessie, though, and getting a feel for all the controversy surrounding the release of the scandalous pictures. The Huffington Post featured a number of bloggers on the subject. The biggest consensus was that Jessie had posed for them as an adult, so it was her choice to do so and therefore they shouldn't be held against her. Instead, the real scandal lay in the person who chose to release the photos online against the singer's wishes. The other prevalent note in a lot of the blogs was, of course, advising folks not to look at the pictures. But people did…Sara knew this, because she was a hockey mom, and a soccer mom too, and besides, she worked at Boston Pizza. The old hens liked to gossip, and Sara was intrigued enough to listen.

Did her co-workers and the other moms know Jessie Wheeler was Sara's half-sister? No. Absolutely not. Neither Sara nor her grandmother ever disclosed that rather shocking fact. They hadn't paid much attention at the beginning of Jessie's career—Martha mostly listened to country music, and Sara just went with pop tunes without really caring to learn much about any singers' pasts, and she purposely avoided the rag bags.

The women knew Emily's daughter's name, and they were well aware the man Emily ran off with, David Wheeler, was a bar singer. But they didn't make the connection right away. The last photo Evelyn sent to Peterborough was Jessie at age thirteen—a sad, lonely waif, loose hair streaming over wide frightened eyes. But then, the child lost her father just over a year before the photo was taken, so of course she would be pale and drawn.

Then, according to Aunt Evelyn, when Jessie was fourteen she disappeared from her home in P.E.I. She just packed up and ran away. Soon after, Evelyn, too, lit out for higher ground. Supposedly Emily met someone else after her husband died, and Evelyn would rather eat dog shit than sit at that man's table again. At least that's what she told Martha in one of her few letters.

So what was the chance Emily's daughter Jessie would one day hit the world stage as a singer and actor? Well, in the sad, dark hours when Martha and Sara let themselves ponder Emily's runaway daughter, they sure as heck didn't think much more than *I wonder if she's even alive*. The girl was fourteen when she left. What were the chances she would survive on her own, period? But then one day years ago, Sara got wind of the fact that singer and actor Jessie Wheeler was from P.E.I., when one of the gals from Boston Pizza mentioned passing Jessie Wheeler's old Bedeque Village home during a visit to the island. The woman was visiting relatives in Summerside, who took her and her kids out to the popular Chelton Beach, which scooted right by the singer's old one-and-a-half story century house. Sara thought *the name is the same, but what are the chances...?*

As it turned out, on a day when she felt strong enough to bring it up, Sara admitted the 'coincidence' to her grandmother, who knew Emily raised Jessie in a small village called Bedeque. So one day when Sara's baby Mark was napping, she and her grandmother studied the famous Jessie's photos online. They read her bio. They were dumbstruck.

Over the years Sara made it a point to see most of her half-sister's films and the well-loved *Drifters* series. But she watched them alone, without her redneck husband in tow. Because, despite the odds of this famous girl being Emily's Jessie, in the end there was no doubt. And that just drove the dagger in deeper, as far as Sara was concerned. And she didn't need dopey Kevin aware of her pain.

And then...the Shawna Coupland interview. That was the first time in years—since Martha's husband died, in fact—that Sara saw her grandmother cry. When they finally reunited with Sara's Aunt Evelyn recently, Martha admitted to an interest in meeting the granddaughter she didn't know. The singer was just someone Sara and Martha had rarely discussed after that long ago day spent stalking Jessie on the Internet. But the sorrow unleashed in the Coupland interview—the girl suffered so much. Martha and Sara were family. Evelyn was family. It seemed Jessie needed...family.

Now...Jessie wanted to come to Peterborough. But what good would it do to reopen old wounds? Sara's eyes flitted around her home...there was dust on the rads and the blinds, and smelly hockey gear strewn in one corner, airing out. Her intestines clenched. Never mind the crap about being left behind so many years ago, about the infernal ache of abandonment... what was worse was the curse of inferiority. Sara's sister was a big star. Why the hell was she coming here? To placate some moral obligation to herself? To ease her conscience? To give the dagger a twist?

Sara couldn't see anything good coming of this visit. How would she keep her kids out of the fray if somehow it got out about Jessie's nude photos? Mark was eleven. He was computer savvy. And he didn't need to see his aunt in all her birthday suit glory. Sara looked down at her own round midriff. Jessie likely had a personal trainer and a well-defined gym regimen. Another reason not to let the girl in her home…or in her life.

Well, if I have to do it, Sara told herself, *the only solution is to keep the visit quiet, behind closed doors, and as much on the down low as possible.* She hoped the entourage would be manageable.

"But," she muttered between clenched teeth as she closed the email, "be damned if I'm gonna clean my house from top to bottom."

Shoving back her chair, she trotted upstairs to have a shower. She had to work. At freaking Boston Pizza. She grimaced as she wriggled out of the pink flannel pjs. *I wonder what Jessie wears to bed. Likely a silk negligee from stupid Paris.*

Stepping into the shower, she closed her eyes and lifted both hands so the hot spray could caress her. She thanked God for the simple luxury and told herself she was grateful for the blessings she had.

But Sara was glad she closed the email without responding right away.

Writing back to spoiled rich-girl Jessie Wheeler could wait.

Chapter One

"Josh, make sure Jon has a GP lined up for this show. I don't want you getting sick and having to wait while the production hunts around for a doctor."

Josh only had to peek over at Jessie to know exactly what she was thinking. Those worried sea-pearl eyes telegraphed her every thought and emotion as clearly as his Harley Sportster's low chug-chug announced its arrival. He smiled affectionately at her, sitting there on the front steps of their home on this unusually warm fall day, fingers linked behind her knees, watching as he checked the oil on the King Ranch.

Her baby belly protruded enough that Josh wondered how she could even sit comfortably, but during this pregnancy he was discovering Jessie to be genial and easygoing, never a complainer of any ills (well, maybe the constant urge to pee, of late). The only real issues from last summer were the constant worries about how the release of the photo album Matt first read about in the Globe and Mail during Charles and Dee's Anniversary dinner would affect Jessie's career. Surprisingly, it seemed most people understood her right as an adult to pose nude (Josh still had his own feelings on *that* subject, given her fragile state upon arriving in Vancouver), and most also knew Jessie's story thanks to the Shawna Coupland interview. So the fallout had risen and fallen and then, for the most part, thankfully disappeared. And at this juncture no films had been released, but their invisible shadow clung to Josh with every breath. He prayed Caryn, with the release of the nude photos, got the revenge she sought for whatever ills she figured Josh and Jessie caused her, and that the films made featuring Jessie in the black box studio on East Hastings would never see the light of day.

What lingered in the fallout were the sad eyes Josh often saw on his wife's face, at odd times like when she was supposed to be reading, or sun tanning by their pool with music from her iPhone earbuds supposedly protecting her from the world. And, regretfully, the tension between himself and Charles and Dee also remained, at least to a point. It had eased to a certain level of civility and comfort, but Josh honestly felt it would likely never be fully alleviated. He'd screwed up when he went off on a lonely crusade digging into Jessie's past. Now, despite Charles' big speech at the UBC neighborhood home before the craziness of summer had dispersed the made-up family in all directions, Josh knew there was still a lot of unspoken anger floating around regarding the release of Jessie's photos. And he knew the blame for their release was—deservedly—directed at him.

He slammed the hood of the truck closed and sauntered over to his wife. Plunking down next to her on the top step, Josh wrapped an arm loosely around her shoulders. Placing his other hand flat against his wife's belly, he shoved away the bad memories of his stupidity, and smiled broadly.

"Well, little Emily-Grace, your momma is still worrying about me. Will you please come soon so you can take care of her and let her know I will be fine?"

"What if it is a boy, in the end?" Jessie asked Josh, eyebrows knitting together. "And we've messed him up by calling him Emily-Grace all along. He'll think that's his name."

Laughing, Josh leaned in and brushed his lips against his wife's earlobe. "It's a girl," he answered confidently. "I had that dream again last night."

"The one with the little golden blonde girl running through the field?"

"That's the one. So I'm assuming she's just saying hi before officially arriving."

"All right." Jessie smiled. "Anyways, we'll know soon enough."

"Not too soon, Jessie." Josh frowned.

"Now who's worrying?"

"I just wish you were resting more instead of working."

"Hey, years ago women gave birth in the cotton fields, bundled up their babies, and kept on picking cotton."

"And that was barbaric."

11

She poked him. "You'd spoil me rotten if you could," she said lovingly, wrapping both arms securely around her husband's waist.

"Damn straight I would," Josh replied, kissing the top of her head. "You deserve it, little one." He felt a chill run through Jessie at that, because they both knew he'd omitted a word—*after*. *After* all the crap they'd both endured and, especially, Jessie. The first large photo to be released online—the one of her with the tear on her cheek—arrived unbidden and stuck itself to Josh's retinas. He pulled his wife close.

"Josh?"

"Mmmhmmm?"

"What if I can't do this?"

"What, give birth?" he teased, relaxing his hold on her so he could see her eyes. He wiped a loose strand of hair off her forehead. "Like it or not, that baby's coming out of there one way or another."

"No, dork, not so much that." She waved a hand in his face. "No, the… the mother thing." Jessie looked down and dug two fingernails of her right hand into the bottom of her left thumb.

Josh's voice was gentle once he found the words. "Of course you can do it. You're gonna be a great mom, Jess." He squeezed her shoulders.

"Yeah, to a point, maybe."

"Hey, what's this I'm hearing? Doubt? From a woman whose music heals people? Who is such a softie that last week she spent an entire afternoon on the floor playing dolls with little kids in a playroom at the B.C. Children's Hospital?"

"Yeah, I woulda liked to take a few of those kids home," she murmured, before adding mournfully, "some of them won't ever be going home."

"Your hormones are in overdrive today, little one," Josh cautioned.

After Jessie's time at the hospital with the children, she had been hard to break through to for the remainder of the day. Josh made the executive decision to try to steer her in other directions in terms of charity and community involvement. Children suffering from cancer were heavy subjects for a sensitive singer who often wrote songs filled with pain.

She cut into his solemn thoughts. "Stop blaming everything on my hormones! No, it's just…" Jessie looked off to the side, away from him, as she reined in her feelings. "I've got problems, you know? I'm not exactly Mrs. Oh-come-over-I-baked-chocolate-chip-cookies." Jacob flashed across her mind. He and she often baked cookies 'in the old days.' But this crazy life, with Josh by her side, didn't leave a lot of time for such simple luxuries.

"Jessie. Little one. Look at me." Josh touched her cheek and urged her to face him, which she did, reluctantly. "Being a parent is mostly about love. The rest you can get from mommy blogs." He smiled. "And I don't know anyone who has more of a capacity to love than you do."

"I shoulda started with a plant. Not including the petunia in P.E.I. Since it got all brown and spindly and kinda died and all."

He laughed outright. She was sitting next to him on the hard concrete step, shoulders hunched over, a light sweater over a pretty floral maternity top, leggings underneath, and her hair in a messy ponytail. Not exactly the international superstar the world so desperately loved. Her eyes were luminous in the new morning light, and they swept themselves right inside Josh and into his heart and soul, all worry and angst.

"Ask me if I love you," he whispered to her, laying a palm against her cheek. It drew a small smile, and she placed her hand over his without losing his loving gaze. "C'mon, I dare you," he whispered, leaning his forehead against hers, "ask me."

She was all smiles then. Jessie closed her eyes and reached out a hand to tug Josh's T-shirt and pull him closer. She brushed her lips against his and spoke without moving back, which tickled him. "Josh Sawyer. Do you love me?" she complied, her voice small and quivery.

"Always and forever," was his response, as she thought it might be.

They sat there together, unmoving with the exception of a few soft murmurs and sweet kisses, until Josh eased her worry a little more, on a practical level.

"We've got lots of support, Jessie. Our baby's going to have so much love. Our biggest worry is going to be raising her without spoiling her rotten. And if…if someday you're tired and it's all getting to be a bit much—the feedings, the lack of sleep, the crying…well then, I'll take over, or Dee and Carlotta will help. You know they'll pitch in."

"And Jane," she added helpfully. "She's got the momma thing all figured out."

"Then you can pay it forward."

At her raised eyebrows he tossed in, "You know Steve is a competitive kind of guy. No way are he and Sophie going to be far behind."

"I can't wait," she breathed, relaxing into her husband's arms. "Sometimes, though…sometimes this is all a dream. You know? I just never thought I'd ever be this happy. It…it scares me. I can't completely give into it. I just keep worrying."

"No," Josh said, insistent. "No, Jessie. We are not worrying about the future. Trudy taught us to take this thing one day at a time. No worrying allowed. No unreasonable worrying, anyway. Worrying about learning lines, fine. Stage fright? Okay. But let's draw the line there, okay?"

Nodding, she fixed her gaze on a crack in the bottom step.

Josh changed tack. "Maybe we should get a nanny."

"We've talked about this."

"You're going to be on set before—and then likely within a month after—this baby is born, Jessie, despite my desperate attempts to convince you otherwise. You know how that goes. Long days. And sleepless nights."

"Dee'll be around some of the time. And I've agreed to a sitter while I'm working, but I don't want some strange woman living in our house. Other people raise their babies alone—we can do the same. Heck, in P.E.I. a lot of the men have gone out west to find work and their women are raising two and three kids alone! Single parents, too…although I don't know how they do it."

She pondered her and Josh's circumstances. Money was never a concern anymore, and hadn't been for a long time. But Jessie well remembered a gnawing ache in her belly that started the day after she left home at age fourteen. Food was very sporadic for the next two years, and after she fled Charleston as well, until Caryn and Eric took her in. And now, with more money than she would ever be able to spend, and reams of it coming in every day from music and acting revenues, she and Josh could spend wildly. But they didn't. Neither of them saw the need. They didn't lack for anything, but they didn't need a fancy mansion or slick sports cars. They were living in Josh's modest UBC neighborhood home, he had his Harley and his fancy pickup, and she had her vintage Mustang for the summer, and the BMW SUV for the colder months. And Jessie was eternally grateful.

"Fine, then," Josh responded almost agreeably, the nerve on his cheek twitching just a little. "We'll see how things are in Miami after the baby comes, and go from there, okay? One day at a time, little one." He leaned in for another kiss and then eskimo-kissed her on the nose, which achieved the desired effect. Jessie giggled.

"Any other worries you'd like to air and then chuck away for a while?" he asked light-heartedly.

"Well, Josh," she responded, sighing, "so much for our promise of staying together as much as possible. Me in Miami and you in Toronto…and our baby coming soon… I'm not impressed."

"Jon's got things figured out, Jess, so I can be home with you for a few weeks, at least, when Emily-Grace comes along. Then we'll set you up in Toronto for a bit until you go back to *Mystic Nights* to finish the season. You'll have lots of time to get to know those Peterborough relatives. And you can grab Charles for a few dashes to P.E.I. to see George and your mother, and to sort things out for the hockey film."

"Our little girl will be quite the hardened traveller at the ripe old age of a few weeks." Jessie frowned. "Newborns need a schedule, Josh." She eyed him wisely. "I got that from the mommy blogs."

"She'll adapt," he responded, brushing his lips against her forehead and breathing in the lavender scent he cherished; a scent that sometimes lingered in a room after Jessie left, thankfully, so Josh could keep her essence close. "Listen, Matt's going to be here in a few minutes. I'm gonna go grab our things."

"I hate this. I really really hate this."

Josh was saddened to see tears moisten the surface of his wife's eyes. He lifted her chin and peered into her soul. "I'll see you this weekend, Jessie. It's only five days."

"Six, really. Counting today, Sunday."

"Go have fun with Kelly and," Josh cringed, "golden boy Jacob. And keep Matt close by in case you need him. Michael too, I know he'll watch out for you."

"If nothing else, it'll be interesting to see how they shoot me in water-buffalo mode." Jessie took Josh's outstretched hand and he eased her up.

"Oh, they'll just use After Effects to digitally draw in someone else's body." He grinned.

"Ach, that's disgusting! God, I hope they can't do that," Jessie replied half seriously, wrinkling her nose.

At that, Matt pulled in, the Audi purring happily to be escorting both Josh and Jessie to the airport that day.

Josh waved a greeting and disappeared inside to grab their suitcases while Jessie wandered over to say hi. She and Matt embraced warmly, as had become their custom since the proverbial shit hit the fan back in April, when she was in desperate need of his calm wisdom and presence.

"You okay there, kiddo?" Matt held his superstar charge at arms length and frowned.

"Nope. I'm really not." Jessie's voice was thick, all hurty and sorry.

"I see that."

"I want Josh. Now and forever. For always."

A small smile ignited Matt's kind eyes. "Um-humn."

"How do you do it? Leave your family all the time? To come hang out with the likes of me?" She grimaced. "I don't deserve you."

"Julie acknowledges my need for speed. To keep the earth moving under my feet. And she likes having control of the remote. When I'm not around, she gets to order pizza and watch her chick flicks. For us, a little space works."

"Absence makes the heart…" Jessie sighed, and tried to spy her toes beneath her large baby belly. She had to strain to see them.

"Don't go there, Jessie. You'll see Josh in less than a week. You have phones and you have texting."

"It's not the same. I want him with me."

"You have friends in Miami, Jessie. They'll help pass the time. And first off is a big party to celebrate Kelly and Michael's marriage. Most of the cast and crew's back, right? It'll be like old times."

She cringed. "Not quite, Matt. The last time I saw most of those people I was screaming at Josh. It's gonna be a little awkward."

"They're good people, Jessie. They'll be fine." Matt cocked his head at her and shoved his hands in his jeans pockets. "I'm sure you're looking forward to seeing Jacob?"

She pursed her lips and shrugged. "Yeah. But it'll be weird." The big eyes were luminescent, albeit a little hopeful. "I've talked to him a few times since the press junket, but that's it. No emails, even. A few texts here and there. He's been at his dad's writing songs."

"Ahhh. There's the rub, huh?"

She sighed. "It's all good. We needed some space. But Matt…it'll be crazy for him to see me this pregnant, don't you think?"

"His problem," Matt answered with enthusiasm, winking at Jessie.

She swatted him. "You cow! Since when did you become so cavalier and uncaring?"

He eyed her carefully and shot her a look that said *since that fight in the studio*. But his response was kind. "He's a lost puppy around you, Jessie. And may I add it's obvious there are still strong feelings on your side as well. I'd just prefer not to see you hurt…anymore."

"Gad, I wish everybody would stop worrying about poor Jessie and her stupid feelings!" She softened. "Things are good with me and Josh now, Matt. We've been really blessed to have these last months together. The film in New York was a blast and Josh's career is just skyrocketing. It was surreal to connect with Maggie, Sue-Lyn and Carter again…we're going to make it a tradition, try to meet once a year at the very least in New York. But I think all that time together is making today's parting even harder."

A low rumble caught their attention. Josh was careening around the corner dragging both his and Jessie's suitcases, hauling one in each hand. Matt launched forward to help.

Josh gratefully gave one suitcase to Matt. "Jessie, I don't know what you've got in here, but I'm not looking forward to the day when you also pack a suitcase for our baby."

"A suitcase?" Jessie pressed her lips together thoughtfully. "Plus a diaper bag, a stroller, maybe one of those foldy travel playpen thingies, and lots more!" She paused and cocked her head sideways before adding with a wide smile, "Mommy blogs, Josh."

"Okay, I take the mommy blog thing back. Stay off the damn things! Oh Lord," Josh said, lifting up her suitcase to slide it into the trunk beside Matt's and his own. "We'll be taking the truck to the airport after the baby comes." All business now, he looked at Matt. "Speaking of which, I checked the oil and it's good to go. So anytime you want to use it, you're welcome. After Miami, I mean."

"Thanks, Josh. It's just that one time, though, I think. I like how Julie volunteers us to help her friends move, but it's me who ends up doing the grunt work."

Jessie pinched his bicep. "She just wants to see you using those muscles, Spike. Sexy man."

"Hey!" Josh grinned. "No flirting with security." He came around the car and swooped Jessie up in his arms and flung her around. She squealed, delight crisscrossing her features as the gentle breeze tossed the curls in her ponytail. When he set her down, though, Josh didn't let go. Instead, he held her tight, arms around her big waist, and he pressed his forehead against hers.

"I hate this part," he groaned.

She swallowed, eyes misting again. "Not yet, Josh, we're not even at the airport yet."

But in twenty minutes they were, indeed, at the airport. Matt pulled over to Domestic Departures and discreetly removed Josh's suitcase from the trunk while the couple said their goodbyes. Once Josh left them, Matt and Jessie would cruise around to the private wing of the airport where they'd climb aboard the Keating jet for the trip down south.

"Josh, text me as soon as you find out about the GP. And if Jon doesn't have one lined up, tell him I'm coming to Toronto to strangle him."

"It's been ages, Jessie. The risk is getting smaller and smaller as time goes on."

"But you could still get sick, Josh. God, I can't stand the thought of being away from you. I hate this!" Inhaling deeply, she snuggled in closely and stuck her nose in the hollow of his neck.

He held on, too, and then pushed her gently away from him. "Look at me, Jessie. I'll see you Friday night. We'll get takeout from the Noodle Box and watch old Audrey Hepburn films, okay?" His eyes were moist, too, but he didn't want her to see him being emotional, so he tried to stay calm. She was sad enough for the two of them.

"Hi to Steve," she whispered. "Tell him I miss him like crazy. Sophie too. Tell them to get started on that baby."

"You'll see lots more of them since his series in L.A. was cancelled and he signed on permanently to Jon's 1920's show."

"Thankfully. I need his stupid jokes in my head. I hope he's not too disappointed about L.A." She changed beats. "I wish Jon was shooting this in Vancouver, though."

"His producing partners are in Toronto. We've been through this, kid."

Lifting her chin, his heart ached when Josh saw a single tear slide down Jessie's cheek. He thumbed it away, but not until after a modicum of ill-concealed shock traversed his spine and landed on his face. *That old photograph is going to haunt us forever,* he thought.

"Jessie, baby," he begged. "Please don't do this. Don't leave crying."

"Uh, Josh, not sure if you've noticed but I'm a whale right now. Remember that stupid hormone word you brought up a while ago?"

"I thought you said not to blame everything on hormones. And I thought it was a water-buffalo." One corner of his lip curved up in a lopsided smile, and he leaned in for a kiss on those soft pink lips he loved to caress with his tongue. "Love you, little one."

"I can blame things on hormones. You can't. It's one of those husband-wife rules." Both hands on his waist, she kissed him back. "I love you too, Josh. I'll see you Friday night, okay?"

Suddenly unable to speak past the knot in his throat, he nodded.

A scratchy timbre colored Jessie's voice. "Noodle Box, remember? You promised me."

"Yeahhh," he managed. "See you soon."

And, with a wave to Matt, he was gone.

Matt eased himself around the car and, always aware of those who've noticed the celebrities in their midst, he scanned the area. He opened the passenger door for Jessie and gave her an arm to help her ease into the seat. Closing it gently behind her, he smiled softly at the tears she was swiping away from her cheeks.

"Here," he said, after sliding behind the wheel. He handed her the iPhone she'd left on the dash. "I think you're going to need this."

She pulled earbuds out of her purse's side pocket and, without responding to Matt, selected the music icon and her 'favorites' list. After untangling the earbuds, Jessie hit 'shuffle', placed the mini-speakers in her ears, and closed her eyes.

For Jessie Wheeler, there was no better healer than music, and Matt knew this well. He put the car in gear, did a shoulder check, and cruised around to the private area where he and his charge would be boarding the Keating jet.

He could hear the song blaring out of her ears, and he cringed, thinking he ought to get her a better set of headphones to save her hearing. But then he relaxed, and settled further back into the seat. The song the iPhone chose—on the shuffle setting, Matt had noticed—was everyone's favorite—*Josh's Song*.

See little girl, he thought to himself with a satisfied smile. *Everything's going to be just fine.*

Chapter Two

*A*t was a strange feeling.

After all those months of hanging out together, suddenly he and Jessie were apart again. Josh threw his smaller second bag on a lime wingback chair in the hotel suite's living space, wandered into the adjoining bedroom, and collapsed onto the king-sized bed. He told himself to suck it up, that lots of men were often separated from their families. But that word—family—suddenly there was a new little Sawyer to consider. He couldn't wait to introduce the new baby to Zach and Hilary, and Kayla and Paul. *Kayla will be over the moon*, he said to the ceiling, a huge smile on his face. Butterflies erupted in his belly. Josh sent a silent prayer to the universe. *Please God, let this go well— Jessie, the birth, the baby…and then after. Let us be good parents to this beautiful new child. Let his—or her—life be filled with grace and peace.*

A hard, loud few knocks erupted at the door, and Josh jumped.

"Geez!" He vaulted up and sprang for the door, which he threw open with gusto. "You could give a man a heart attack! You couldn't just knock like normal people?!" The insistency of the knock had Josh's heart racing at warp speed. "You scared the shit out of me!"

But he was grinning widely. His good friend Steve was standing there— well, leaning actually—on the doorframe, one arm extended upwards, one on a hip, and ankles crossed.

"You're a big star now. I figured your quarters on shows are likely getting bigger and bigger. You could be lost somewhere in the depths of this gargantuan…" Stephen peeked around Josh to see just how big his suite was, "…Uh, not so gargantuan accommodations." Standing back, he eyed Josh quizzically. "What's the matter, Sawyer? Not used to fame and fortune yet? You're supposed to ask for BIG. Who do you ask, you ask?"

Steve sauntered into the suite and dropped down on the wingback chair's matching sunny sofa. He laid his head back on a cushion, folded his arms behind his head, and swung his ankles up over the opposite armrest. "Well, you ask the Executive Producer, of course! Oh, wait. Let me think about this. That would be your...daddy?"

Josh grabbed a second cushion from under Steve's legs and swung it at him. "Jonathon's got bigger fish to fry. The guy doesn't need me at his feet begging for favors." After removing the bag he'd tossed on the wingback chair earlier, he eased himself down and faced his friend.

"Uh yeah, he does. In fact, I'm sure he wants that." Steve sobered. "He is your dad, Josh. He's got your back."

Josh shrugged. "He's always had my back, Steve. Sorta. I come from good stock, apparently."

"Don't tell Wes that."

"Don't plan to." Tossing his feet up on an ottoman, Josh regarded Steve. "Where'd you leave Sophie?"

"In Vancouver. She's arranging our household move from L.A." The pronouncement came with downturned lips.

"Sucks the sitcom didn't go. Sorry about that, Steve."

"Whatever. We can't all be as famous as the Josh Sawyer types of the world. Spoiled little rich kids with famous dads. Two...famous dads, that is."

"Lighten up, Steve!" Josh's cheeks bloomed pink. "I work hard."

"So do I. And you and I are going to rock this show." Steve eased his feet down off the armrest and sat comfortably against the cushion, one ankle over the opposite knee. He grabbed the ankle and settled into the conversation amicably.

"You have your wardrobe fitting yet?"

"No, I just got here."

Steve watched him for a minute. He narrowed his eyes. "What is it, Sawyer? I know you."

Josh shifted uncomfortably in his seat and then pressed his lips together. "I just hated leaving Jessie today, that's all. And our baby-to-be, y'know?"

"I get that," Steve answered honestly. He brightened suddenly. "At least you don't have to worry about Jacob trying to get into her pants at this late stage of her pregnancy."

"Damn it, throw me back that cushion so I can smother you with it!"

Chuckling, Steve tossed Josh the cushion, who threatened to throw it, but instead just threw Steve a lopsided look. He laid the cushion in his lap and abstractly fingered the edges of it.

Steve regarded him curiously. "She'll be fine, Josh. Matt's with her, isn't he?"

"Yeah, I know, it's just that…well…" Josh shifted again, and gazed at the large gauzy curtain covering the window. Then, he turned his focus back to his friend. "Do you think there's anything to all this…" He waved an arm in the air as he searched for the words. "Psychic stuff? Or…intuition… dreams?"

"New baby's got you a little freaked?"

"No, I can't wait, *we* can't wait," Josh corrected himself before leaning forward over the ottoman, moving his legs to the floor and resting his elbows on his knees. "But I've been having this weird dream. It's a…recurring dream, actually. Not something I normally have."

"And? What's the dream about?" Steve removed his hand from his ankle and leaned an elbow on the armrest.

Josh hesitated. Steve could see the slide show playing on his friend's mind before he started to speak.

"It's Jessie, walking through a field of, I dunno, grain or something. Bearded barley, I think. But behind her is a little girl, all blonde curls and… and wearing this little white dress. She's about three, maybe."

He glanced up at Steve to see if he was listening. He was, intently. Josh continued, staring at the floor as he spoke. "Sometimes behind the little girl is a boy, a toddler, maybe, although at other times in the dream Jessie's carrying a baby that somehow I know is a boy. She turns around to see the little girl, and she's got this gorgeous smile." He smiled himself as the image of the woman he loved most in the world crossed his heart. "And she holds out her hand to the little girl who, for some reason, I know is our daughter, Emily-Grace. I'm watching them, and so I wave. I'm super, super happy, feeling really blessed, you know, but when I wave they just ignore me. It's as if Jessie and the kids don't even notice me standing there on the edge of the field watching them."

Looking up again, his nose wrinkled as Josh considered the dream and whatever hidden meanings it might hold. "The other thing is the whole dream is, like, bathed in gold. Like really bright gold, like a Heavenly gold kind of thing. I feel so peaceful and we are all so happy...until I realize they can't see me. And then I'm devastated, and I wake up in a pool of sweat, trembling. I feel like I'm going to lose my mind at that feeling of emptiness, of loss, of being alone." He was speeding up now, as he finally emptied this latest fear onto the shoulders of his best friend. "You know that feeling, Steve, we both know it, and I sure as hell don't want to feel it again."

Josh didn't have to say *when Jessie was gone*. He could tell by Steve's somber expression that he quite clearly knew what Josh was referring to.

Steve was quiet as he pondered the dream. "What's your gut telling you it means, Josh?"

Choking a little, Josh voiced the fear that had been in his mind since the dream started coming in the wee hours of the mornings. He stared straight at Steve, hands loosely folded in his lap. "I think it's supposed to be Heaven."

"Well, that makes sense to me. You've got a gorgeous sweet wife and a new baby on the way. How can that not be Heaven?"

"You don't understand, Steve. They can't see me."

The shock value of that statement threw Steve. He recoiled. "Geez, Josh, don't even go there." His breath caught in his throat at the thought of...

He looked hard at Josh. "Who is in Heaven? You...or..." He couldn't say it. The thought of a man, any man, losing his entire family in one fell swoop, was unmentionable.

"Maybe it's me," Josh said. "This whole no-spleen thing, you know? If I get sick...Jessie's always worrying about that."

Steve exhaled slowly, pinching his nose abstractly as he did so. The result was a high-pitched whistle as Steve let out his breath, but neither man noticed. He straightened suddenly, and looked at his friend. "You know what I think?"

"No, but I want to." Josh waved at him. "Talk. Tell me I'm not losing my mind."

"I think you and Jessie have been through hell, and that being in the spotlight with a quickly advancing career—and I'm not jealous, by the way, although you suck—is adding a lot of pressure. Partly because you're both working in different parts of North America. You've got a new baby on the way, and you're stressed. What man wouldn't be?"

"You think that's all it is?" Josh looked worried, but anxious to have those worries lifted through Steve's friendship and understanding.

"Yeah, man, I do. Look, Josh, there's no way you're going to get sick and not get past it. You've made it this far. And believe me, on this set there will be eagle eyes on you. A sniffle or a cough in this damned frigid Toronto climate and both myself and Jon will have you at the hospital. And you know Matt's got eyes on Jessie at all times in Miami. That dream was all about stress. Dreams are never literal, anyway."

But as they stood and he grasped Josh's shoulder and pointed him towards the door, Steve couldn't shake the niggling sense of fear that crawled inside his stomach when Josh mentioned Jessie and the kids not being able to see him, and that it felt like Heaven. He walked behind Josh, and thought of Jessie alone—heck, him, Steve, alone—on the planet without this man who once had a lot of old demons to fight, but who was now a respected and talented actor, and also a good friend and a loving husband (and about to be father).

They went down to the bar and ordered dinner, but despite the excitement and adrenalin rush of starting on a new television series, neither could get past the fear that settled into their veins at the telling of Josh's recurring dream.

Thankfully, Jonathon arrived and sat with them, and it was his animated conversation about the new series that lifted the uncertain gloom, and that later enabled the guys to fluff pillows behind their backs against the headboards of their beds, settle into some mindless TV, and think about their gals.

Soon the pink sunrise of a new uncertain dawn would urge Steve and Josh towards another day, but for now, perhaps because of Josh's spooky dream, both men were wise enough to treasure the gifts of today.

Chapter Three

"You suck, Jacob!" Jessie couldn't help but laugh when she saw Jacob for the first time after the *Mystic Nights* between-season hiatus mid-summer press junket. Her co-star and good friend had just admitted to Googling Jessie's nude photos.

"What?!" He threw up his hands. "It's not like I haven't seen you in your birthday suit before, Jessie."

"I hope you didn't look at the pictures with your dad." Frowning, Jessie sat back on the high chair and eyed him suspiciously. She picked at a nacho covered in cheese, removed a jalapeno, and dropped it between her lips. "Not like the whole world hasn't seen me in my birthday suit now, anyway," she mumbled, silently sending telepathic switchblades to Caryn and Eric.

"Awww, Jess, it's not like that," Jacob said in his usual pouty tone, reaching out and taking one of the nachos on the big platter they were sharing. "You have a beautiful body. Those photos were very tastefully done. You're gorgeous, girl."

"My body's changed a bit in the last few months, Jacob." She looked up at him from underneath long eyelashes.

Shrugging, he sat back, unapologetic. "Let's just not go there right now, okay?"

"Kinda hard not to notice, hon." She was being a little sarcastic. *Just a little*, she told herself.

His stare told her what he was thinking, which was *I wish that baby was mine*. Jacob frowned but didn't speak.

"Anyways," Jessie added, forking up some of the gooier cheese, "I can't believe you haven't found a woman yet. A guy like you? Big star now, songs bursting up the charts, and a new television show about to premiere? You're on fire, Ryan!"

"I've found lots of women." He raised his chin in defiance. "Just not any I like enough to hear the woes of PMS from."

Biting her bottom lip, Jessie stopped scooping up nachos and eyed him with a defensive scowl. "I never got all PMS'ey," she attested strongly. "I still don't."

He mimicked her in a high-pitched voice. "Jacob, oh Jacob, you left your socks on the floor again, and the rice is overcooked, and oh would you please get me some chocolate?" With a wry grin, he resumed his regular voice. "Oh, let me just get some cheese to go with that wine, Jessie."

Laughing heartily, she tossed her head back. "I'm never like that! I could care less about where you leave your dirty socks, you dork!" She winked. "Anyways, I don't think you minded the hormonal changes at certain times of the month, Jacob."

"Depends on which ones you're referring to," he winked back.

Jessie shook her head and shot him a sweet smile he wanted to grab and hold onto forever. Her eyes twinkled. "Jacob Ryan. I'm a cow. Eight months pregnant, and still you're flirting with me."

Jacob was saved from answering by the ring of Jessie's cell. Her cheeks flushed pink when she glanced at the display and saw it was Josh. She peeked up at Jacob, who rolled his eyes, looked away, and took a big swig of Guinness. But he didn't leave, as Jessie kind of hoped he would, and she felt too big and bulky to slide off the high seat without assistance, so Jacob got the gist of the conversation at the same time Jessie did.

"Hey, Josh. How's TO?"

Licking two fingers, she tilted her head so the phone would stay close to one ear while she wiped the fingers on a napkin.

"Lonely. I'm counting the seconds 'til 'Breakfast At Tiffany's.'"

"And Noodle Box."

"And you."

Jessie eyed Jacob timidly, and smiled wistfully at him. Crossing his arms, he sat further back in his high seat and moped at her. She turned her body slightly away from him.

"You're not just gonna watch it because I want to?"

Josh's laugh was loud enough for Jacob to hear. Jessie frowned at Jacob's thinly disguised scowl when her dinner mate threw his linen napkin down by the plate of nachos.

"Actually," Josh was saying, "I thought it was the other way around."

"Yeah, so, she's got style. I'm good with that. And you have to admit Audrey Hepburn is every man's vision of the perfect woman, despite the fact she's long gone and, even if she were alive, she'd be three times—or more—your age." She tapped a finger absently on the table and smiled bashfully. "I'll try not to be jealous."

"She was a classy lady, Jessie. And there's a lot we can learn from those old films."

Truthfully, sometimes Josh and Jessie chose to watch classic cinema simply because it was a departure from their everyday lives. And these days, with so much CGI and green screen utilized in filmmaking, sometimes they just craved something real. Audrey Hepburn films were real. And 'Breakfast at Tiffany's' was a lesson for all kinds of reasons. It was a favorite.

Jessie switched gears. "How're Steve and Jonathon?"

"Steve's bummed about L.A. but he's adjusting. I told him to gear up with some mukluks and a parka. Jon's running at light-speed trying to micro-manage the production. Giselle flew in this morning so she's making sure he sleeps. Or not," he chuckled. "How's golden boy?"

"Jacob says hi. He's as gloomy as ever." Jessie's eyes glinted sideways at her co-star across the table, noticing, as she did, that Jacob had downed his Guinness.

The object of her gaze cut in. "I didn't. I didn't say hi."

"Eeyore," she mouthed at him, eyes alight, as Josh's voice came over the cell again.

"What great wisdom is your orgasmic hero trying to impart?"

She groaned. "Geez, Josh." To Jacob as well she added, "We're in this sandbox together. Mightn't you try to get along?"

Jacob stuck a toothpick in his teeth and rocked back on his chair. He squinted his eyes and stuck his tongue out at Jessie.

"I'll call you from my room in a bit, okay Josh? Jacob's being an ass. I'd better go stroke his drooping ego."

"Don't go stroking his anything, Jessie."

"You can stroke my whatever, Jess." Jacob's eyes danced and he straightened his chair and leaned forward so Josh could clearly hear him. "Any time!"

"Especially anything droopy. Jesus, girl!" Josh cut in loudly.

"Take the phone, Jacob," Jessie laughed, cheeks full-flamed red now. "Make friends, little boys! I have to pee. I'll call you in a bit, Josh."

"Don't—Jessie?"

"Ha," Jacob chortled, accepting Jessie's cell with one hand and helping her slide off the high chair with the other. He turned his head away from her warning glare as she wandered off to the bathroom, glancing behind her until she bumped into a server and had to look ahead. "Shove your jealousy in a drawer, Sawyer, I can barely get two words in edgewise with her anyway. All she does is pee."

Josh's amusement was genuine. "Tell me about it. But I guess we can't complain."

"Some of us can't. Some of us just might anyway."

"Ryan, in some ways I'm just glad you're there to keep an eye on her. I mean it." The ennui in Josh's voice almost touched Jacob. *Almost.*

He sighed and started picking at his teeth with the toothpick again, then looked up at the door through which Jessie just disappeared, despite the knowledge she would be at least a few minutes before he could lay eyes on her again. "She's easy to keep an eye on. If you know what I mean." Jacob allowed one corner of his sagging lips to curl upwards, just a little teensy bit.

Josh wisely chose to ignore Jessie's co-star's last comment. "Is she feeling okay?"

"I guess so," Jacob put in. "As much as I can tell, anyway. The producers seem reasonable. Everyone's already watching out for her."

"Good. Because she's gonna hate me."

Jacob paused, suddenly on high alert. "Why do I feel like I am always picking up the pieces for you, Sawyer?"

"You wouldn't be my first choice, Ryan. But you're there and I'm not, so—"

"Yeah, yeah, same shit, different pile. What have you gone and done to her now?"

"Nothing, nothing, it's just…Jesus, Jacob…I hate this as much as she does. But after this weekend I'm on a two week run, that's all."

"No break."

"No break."

"In Toronto."

"Yeah, in fucking Toronto."

Jacob could hear Josh exhaling deeply. He pictured him ensconced in some big lonely chair, likely anxiously rubbing his hands over his face.

Josh's next words were an addendum, laced with frustration. "We've got that Sunday off but Jon's asked Steve and I to do some community PR. There's some big convention or…or conference or something. He wants us to make an appearance. Anything to start pushing the new show forward, you know."

"Why don't you just do a concert like the rest of us?"

"Yeah, well, not all of us want to stand under hot lights and wail out hopeless lyrics."

"Damn, Sawyer, you want to tell Jessie what you really think of us?" Jacob glanced back towards the washroom door, where he could see Jessie just coming around the bend. "Sometimes I wonder what the hell the two of you have in common at all. Besides sex," he added sarcastically, as he took in Jessie's baby belly.

In Canada, Josh's own belly clenched. "Damn it," he muttered. "Ryan, don't be an ass. Any more than you already are, that is."

Jacob grinned at Jessie, who grimaced and narrowed her eyebrows at his smug self-satisfied expression. He stood and pulled her chair out, and helped her into it. Then he smirked diabolically and said into the phone, "Okay, Josh, no problem, I'll rub her back for you. And I'll snuggle her and sing to your baby."

Jessie lunged across the table for the phone. "Jacob! Stop it!"

Jacob slid back up into his own chair and held the phone away from Jessie. "Come to think of it, I should probably sleep in her bed, too. Just to keep an eye on her. In case she gets cold. Do you mind? Does she still like being spooned?"

"You little shit!" Jessie gave up fighting for the phone and clenched both hands tightly in her lap.

"What's that you say, Sawyer? Stop yelling, I can't make it out."

Josh, in fact, wasn't saying a word. He was hanging his head in agony, missing his wife and wondering what the hell they were doing, breaking their promises to each other by not working in the same town. He, for one, was lonely as hell. Thank God at least for Steve, to lighten things up and to ease the pain of separation.

The silence on the phone was enough to mellow Jacob a bit. That and Jessie's somber eyes touched him. So did memories of a deep sadness and an endless aching noose around Jessie's neck, in the form of a ring, one he noticed Jessie was not wearing tonight, so swollen were her fingers from the pregnancy.

"All right, Josh. I'll watch out for your girl. But she's fine, so stop worrying. Your baby is fine. Already cute, and he's only a bump. A cute bump," he said wistfully, smiling woefully at the downcast Jessie.

"Thanks, man," Josh said quietly. "I mean it."

"I know ya do, loser. See ya around." Jacob handed the phone to Jessie, who sulked at him as she accepted her cell from his outstretched fingers.

"Hey babe," she said into the phone. "We're just finishing up here. Call you soon, okay?"

After she disconnected, Jessie regarded Jacob carefully. "What? You look far too happy. What'd he say to you?"

Jacob reached for a last clump of now cold nachos, popped the gooey things into his mouth, and leaned back in his chair. He shrugged. "A week from Friday," he said.

"What about a week from Friday?"

He pointed to his chest and then extended the same finger towards Jessie. "You and me, kid. In the Robson studio. It's time to get started on your new album."

"Oh no," Jessie warned. "I told you. My weekends in Vancouver are exclusive for the time being. You've got me during the week, Josh at least gets the downtime."

"Not next weekend, he doesn't." Jacob waited until Jessie got the message.

Her reaction satisfied him immensely, despite the slight guilt that crossed his face when she figured it out.

"What the hell?! Jacob—"

"He has to work."

"No! He can't!"

"Some PR thing—"

"Fine, then. I'll fly to Toronto."

"No point, Jess. He's booked for the weekend."

"Jonathon is all of a sudden on my shit list."

"It's one weekend. Let's you and me make some music. Come on, Jess, we haven't played together in ages."

"Damn." Jessie laid her head in her hands. "I guess Josh and me better make this weekend count, then, huh?"

"Maybe you should just skip the Audrey Hepburn, then. Spend the weekend in bed."

"In the bathroom, you mean," groaned Jessie, making a motion to slide off the chair again. "I might as well just park there. And get an intravenous caffeine drip."

"And by that you mean an orange juice drip, obviously."

"Obviously. That's exactly what I meant. I miss coffee more than I miss..." She eyed his empty Guinness. "And how was the great Irish Stout?" She licked her lips.

Jacob smiled slyly and wiped his greasy fingers on the linen napkin he'd discarded by the nacho plate earlier. "Come on, Mizz Daisy," he urged easily. "Let's get us some kale smoothies and go snuggle up and watch us some Hepburn. Light entertainment before our long day tomorrow."

"Can't watch Hepburn, Jacob. I'm sorry," she snapped a little too harshly than the remark demanded. "Some things will indeed remain sacred between Josh and me. Deal with it. Audrey is one."

"I meant Katherine," Jacob chided gently. "The other great Hepburn."

"All right then. Fine." The server brought them their bills so they could sign them and assign the charges to the production, and then Jacob draped an arm loosely around Jessie's shoulders. She reached up and took his hand as they strolled casually towards the lobby of the hotel.

"Daisy?" she asked curiously.

"That's what my grandmother called one of her pet cows when she was a kid. The other one was Clover. I thought you'd prefer Daisy."

"You nerd!" Punching Jacob lightly in the ribs, Jessie howled. "For the record, I'm the only one allowed to refer to myself and Emily-Grace here as a cow. Watch your p's and q's, Ryan."

While they waited for their kale smoothies at the bar, they chatted with Kelly and Michael, who'd just wandered in seeking sustenance and who were both excited about the little celebration the production had held for them that afternoon. Then, with the green drinks in their hands, Jacob and Jessie headed up to Jacob's room to snuggle and watch TV before hitting the sack early.

It wasn't until Jessie awoke the next morning that she checked her cell and saw messages from Josh.

"Darn it all," she moaned inwardly. "I told him I'd call him back." She perched on the end of her bed, twiddling her phone in her hands, and contemplated calling now. Instead, because she was running late to meet Matt and Jacob downstairs in the lobby for her 5 a.m. ride to the studio, she texted instead.

Hey babe sorry I didn't call u back

After a moment she paused and typed in a second text.

Jacob & I were watching Hepburn

Guilt sliced across her belly like a hot knife through butter, but she shoved it away. They'd promised each other to try to work in close proximity. They had a baby on the way, in about five short weeks, in fact. She was hormonal and pissed about Josh's upcoming no-show on his second weekend in Toronto. Tears misted across her ice-pearl blues. Jessie swiped a hand across and underneath both eyes. It came away moist.

"Damn it, I hate these stupid five a.m. calls," she complained to the dust motes floating on the light from her bedside lamp. "They suck. They just suck suck suck!"

Pushing her heavy body off the bed, Jessie stomped off into the shower and turned on the faucet.

In Toronto, where the time was in fact the same as in Miami, Josh, too, was stepping into the shower. But he heard the phone chime and so he left the water running and hurried out to check his message. After reading Jessie's terse notes, the nerve on his stubbly cheek went into overdrive.

"For fuck's sake, Jessie," he snapped before throwing the phone onto his rumpled pillow. "Why don't you give the goddamned knife a little twist while it's in there? Jesus."

Absently, he ran a few fingers over the large scar on his side, wishing he was running them over his unborn baby's little feet, which were comfortably ensconced in the belly of the wife he ached to hug and touch. He forced out of his mind the image of Jessie snuggling with Jacob in some king-sized hotel bed the night before. Josh trusted her—and Jacob, for that matter, wisely or not—but he couldn't stand the thought of them together in such an intimate manner. With Josh's own unborn child between them, and maybe even—

He shoved the thought of Jacob's hand on Jessie's belly away. But that was the first thing they fought about when they both stumbled home, exhausted, that Friday night in Vancouver.

Chapter Four

"You let him touch you?"

"Why not? He's never felt a baby's foot move like that before."

"And he likely won't, as long as he keeps mooning over you, Jessie!"

"That's old news, Josh. Stop whining about Jacob."

"He's not old news, Jess. He's on your fucking back again! All the time, it sounds like!"

"Can you maybe try not swearing around our baby for once?" She moved a hand protectively over her large belly.

Josh was moping around the kitchen counter sorting out dinner while Jessie sat contritely at one of the island's stools watching him. He wasn't making much progress, though. Their Noodle Box take-out had sat too long and so was soggy. Josh was trying to warm it up in the microwave, but was only succeeding in further mushing the supposedly crisp bean sprouts. He was starving, and not just for mediocre food.

The microwave beeped and Josh flipped open the door. He reached for the take-out box, which immediately burned his fingers. The result was an upside down take-out box on the counter, its contents leaking out into a sodden puddle.

"Oh for Pete's sake," he muttered, licking the sore fingers and helplessly watching the puddle expand.

"Thank you," murmured Jessie from beneath long eyelashes. "For not swearing, I mean. Not for depositing my dinner on the counter."

He whipped his head around to glare at her, but then Josh caught the sad defeated aura his wife was giving off. He sighed, and leaned one hand on the counter and the other on the kitchen island.

"C'mere," Jessie said softly, nodding towards her area of the kitchen.

Silently, Josh padded around the island over to her, a puppy with its tail between his legs, as, behind him, the spilled food remained untouched. She took the burnt fingers in her hand and lifted them towards her mouth. Jessie licked his fingers, placed them inside her mouth, and closed her lips over them. Sucking quietly, she teased them with her tongue and eyed him all the while. Josh couldn't help himself. He let the corners of his lips curl upwards, and then ran his second hand through his layered hair.

"No more swearing," he told her apologetically.

She shook her head solemnly from side to side, never losing his gaze, then removed his fingers long enough to say, "Not with a baby in the house."

"Nope." Moaning slightly, Josh wished said baby would soon arrive.

"We'll make ourselves a swear jar."

"A swear jar?" The dreamy ecstasy was easing its way into his groin. Sighing, Josh shifted his feet.

"You know what I mean," Jessie mumbled, closing her eyes and licking the sides of one finger at a time. "One of those jars where you put in money every time you swear. It's supposed to teach you not to swear."

"Okay."

"Okay?"

"Whatever you want." He whimpered and closed his eyes. "Anything."

"Anything?" Jessie stopped her ministrations and looked up.

"Anything. Want to skip dinner and go to bed for a bit, little one?"

"No." Dropping his fingers suddenly, Jessie frowned at her husband. "I want you to stop picking on Jacob. Once and for all."

Josh's eyes snapped open. The languorous stupor disappeared as quickly as it had come. "I know," he started, a nasty sarcastic tone exacerbating the tension between them, "Every time one of us says *Jacob*, we put money in the swear jar."

"You suck," Jessie muttered disagreeably, crossing her arms over her belly as Josh went back to the messy pile on the counter and started scooping it into a ceramic bowl with his fingers.

"We'll charge twice for the word *Jacob* when you say it," Jessie decreed. "It'll be a double-swear."

"Oh, fuck off."

"What? What'd you say? That'll be ten bucks."

"Expensive swear jar."

"*Jacob*'ll be twenty."

Jessie slipped off the chair and waddled towards a nearby storage closet. Josh whipped his head around to watch her.

"What're you doing?"

"I'm getting us a jar." She turned around and held out an empty clean spaghetti bottle she'd pulled from the recycling bin. "That'll be twenty bucks."

Josh put the Noodle Box food in the microwave and set the timer for two minutes. Frowning, he grabbed his wallet from his jeans pocket and fished out a twenty. Jessie wandered over with the bottle in one hand and the lid in the other, and Josh shoved the bill inside. She replaced the lid, but his icy stare didn't cool, despite the small smile tickling Jessie's lips.

'There," Josh stated definitively. "That's just about where Jacob belongs. In his own little fishbowl where he can't touch you."

"Done with your little tantrum? Can we eat now? Emily-Grace's belly is rumbling."

A muted mumbling, which Jessie ascertained as a yes, accompanied the microwave's bleep and Josh's subsequent handing of the bowl to Jessie. They settled into a quiet evening eating in front of their small in-home theater in the downstairs media room, but neither made it to the end of the movie. Five a.m. calls were too early, and both were beat. Josh woke Jessie at midnight, and helped her toddle up to bed.

The remainder of the weekend was spent peppered with little fights over nothing, that were, in essence, fights over the larger picture of an impending two-week separation. Then, early Sunday evening, Matt escorted the couple to the airport with Jessie clinging tearfully to her husband, and they parted yet again.

～～～

The next weekend, on a crisp, cool, starry evening, Jessie stubbornly reclined on the black leather couch in Charles' large recording studio in the downtown Vancouver Keating Building on Robson Street.

Jacob stood before her with one arm outstretched. He was holding the Gibson out like some kind of sacrificial offering.

"If you would stop pouting, we could make some progress here, Jessie."

"Duh, if I had a place to put the guitar, we could make some progress here, Jacob. This belly's epic. I luv it. But Emily-Grace is not at all about the guitar right now. She's all about chillin' in her little baby cave."

They were alone, and had the run of the Robson Street studio. It was Saturday night, and Jacob was fired up to work. But Jessie was exhausted, as evidenced by the dark circles under her eyes and the slump of her shoulders.

"Fine. I'll play, you hum." Jacob nosed the Gibson back into its case as Jessie pondered what part of her tired brain had even considered bringing the treasured guitar in the first place. Its message to her was *you've been ignoring me. I'm lonely.* A little ache nudged its way into her heart as she watched Jacob close the top of the case and lock the clasps in place. Shifting her bum on the couch, she sucked on a lip with displeasure.

"Ouuccchh. There." Sighing, she settled. "That's better. I need to sleep, Jacob. Why don't I just close my eyes and listen to you play for a bit? Maybe the song will make its way into my blood by osmosis."

She closed her eyes and rested her forehead on one hand, which was propped up on an elbow on the arm of the couch.

Jacob frowned at her, concerned. His songwriting partner's Acai berry smoothie sat virtually untouched between her knees, one hand roughly balancing it.

"Are you feeling okay, Jess?" With his foot, he nudged the guitar case to the side of the couch so Jessie wouldn't accidentally trip over it when she finally found the energy to stand. She seemed so sleepy and out of it that it wouldn't surprise him if she didn't notice the case, and he wasn't about to be responsible for any accidents that might potentially harm either Jessie or her and Josh's baby.

"Nope. Can't say that I am, Ryan. Not so great today."

"Okay then…just rest. I'll go over the new tune and you can throw down some thoughts on it when you're ready." He turned to go, to pad over the oriental rugs lining the studio floor to grab his own guitar, but then Jacob stopped and flipped halfway around again. "Can I get you anything, Jessie? Water? Or do you want me to order you something?"

"Nauseous," she complained, eyes still closed. "No food. Food not good. Talk of food not good either. Silence good."

"Uhhh—" Jacob hesitated, and then looked over at his guitar, which he'd left snuggled upright in a padded stand by his favorite wooden stool.

"I take that back," Jessie read his mind and uttered quietly, as if it hurt her to speak. "Music good. Soft music. Jacob kinda music." The diaphanous eyes flitted open and she smiled timidly up at him. "Play me something beautiful, Ryan. Take my mind off how awful I feel right now."

Her gentle words warmed him the way the peaceful buzz of fat honeybees soothed wilted petunias on a perfect summer day. Jacob wasn't feeling his and Jessie's old magic here today, but there was definitely some consolation in her quiet encouragement. He wandered back over to her, leaned down, placed a hand on one side of Jessie's head, and brushed his lips across her forehead.

"You got it, Jessie," he said amiably. "Music coming up. Just for you and Baby Bear hiding away in the cave."

"Thank you," she smiled, grabbing his hand as Jacob started to move away. "For everything, Jacob."

"Aw, don't get sentimental on me, Jess. Just sit back and rest, okay? And help me out if I get stuck."

"It's not sentiment, you nerd. It's hormones. I get all weepy when I see stooped old men stumbling all alone through the grocery store, for God's sake."

"Geez, good thing you're taking me out to Bob Likes Thai later then, if you're still up for it. You'd be a puddle in the Deli section of Whole Foods."

"Yeah, I see a guy with his hand wrapped around a little paper wrapped single serving of black forest ham and I'm toast."

"You must find the salad bar painful."

"It's bad. Utter woe. Heartbreak. I take the tongs right out of their hands and walk them through it. I'm pretty steady when it comes to adding Kalamata olives."

"And the feta, if I do recall."

"The worst part is the greens. Trying to explain arugula versus romaine to a lonely bachelor is like trying to clarify the difference in milk foam between a latte and a cappuccino."

"Or like trying to explain the subtle differences in all the new craft beers, apparently." Jacob let go of Jessie's fingers, finally, and grinned at her twinkling eyes. "I thought we were talking about lonely *old* guys."

"No, I leave them to figure out salad greens on their own. But sometimes," she pointed a finger at Jacob, "I can get *you* to eat spinach."

"And walking me through the Whole Foods salad bar makes you cry?"

"Your lack of respect for milk foam makes me cry."

"Well, your lack of respect for my new tune makes me cry."

"All right then!" She chuckled half-heartedly. "Go. Play. Make magic."

"Go. Rest. Dream." Grabbing a small cushion from the opposite end of the couch, Jacob placed it under Jessie's neck. He pulled an ottoman closer and settled her feet on it.

"Are your ankles supposed to be this big?" He scowled playfully as he reached for a throw blanket bunched up at one end of the couch and tucked it over Jessie's legs and around her big belly.

"Go play already," Jessie groaned lightheartedly, snuggling lower on the couch. "I had a check-up last week in Miami, everything's fine. I'm fine."

"And the doctor said…?"

"Soon, that's all she said. And I'm seeing Dr. Wyatt here tomorrow just to be sure we're ready to go. All is well."

Momentarily, Jessie closed her eyes again, after she watched Jacob mosey back over to his guitar, settle on the stool across from her, and start to strum softly. His gaze had briefly met hers as a shared smile passed between them. Both knew this time in the studio was sacred, that it was a respite from the world, from the ache each carried for the other, and for the long summer apart without the comfort of playing music together to ease the moments when they, even just as friends, plainly and simply missed each other's company.

Jessie did drift off, not quite to a place of sleep, but at least to that plane where an 'almost-sleep' carries folks, where the eyelids get heavy with the sandman's gold dust and where strange images flit across one's mind. She could hear Jacob trying out different chords and finger-stylings and, at one point, someone came in—one of Charles' recording engineers, she thought drowsily—to borrow some cables for his Saturday night gig, but she was in that sedate 'far-off' pre-sleep state, and so Jessie tuned out the brief conversation the tech shared with Jacob.

Until...

When the pressure on her bladder was too much to bear, and reality cut into Jessie's blissful thoughts of touching Josh again at the end of the next week, she muttered uncomfortably and rather ungracefully maneuvered her hulk of a body off the couch. With a sudden quizzical expression crisscrossing her face, she stood facing Jacob, who was still on the stool humming and working out the melody to his new tune.

"Um, Jacob?" Jessie asked, her voice a little higher-pitched than usual.

He looked up from his own dazed state, lost still in the creative aura of music making. Upon seeing Jessie standing there regarding him strangely, though, Jacob bounded off the stool and almost dropped his guitar into its protective stand.

"What? Are you okay, Jessie? You're a little..." He pondered a moment before completing his thought with one simple word. "Green. Like...Kermit the Frog green."

Then he looked down. Confused, his eyes drifted back up to Jessie, who, he noticed, was suddenly near tears. A small puddle of liquid was forming at her feet.

She was standing there unmoving, one hand supporting the right side of her back, the other now pointing at him. Accompanied by knitted eyebrows and downturned quivering lips, Jessie's threatening expression was a sign to Jacob that demanded only one thing. *Silence.* He chewed his bottom lip and waited.

"No, you nerd," she started. "This has nothing to do with me not making it to the bathroom."

He clued in rather quickly at that, although the realization started from the bottoms of his toes and worked its way up Jacob's body. "N-no," he demanded of the universe, shock soaking his torso in a sudden clammy release of damp chilling sweat. "No way."

Her shoulders were slumping even further now, and Jessie had to reach deeply to even out her breathing. She employed one of Trudy's techniques and found a place to focus on, on the opposite wall. It was a framed vinyl album cover of Jacob's first full-length release, which still featured singles soaring up the charts. So while her water broke and she stood with a thousand wild random thoughts echoing around her brain like some deranged Ping-Pong ball, she used one of her favorite images to keep her calm—Jacob, three-quarter profile view, head down, curls teasing his shoulders, muscled forearm and fingers posed over a bar chord on the guitar. She counted, "1—2—3—4…"

The real Jacob was frozen in place, his cobalt eyes locked into Jessie's frightened baby blues. She breathed deeply while steadfastly avoiding his gaze by focusing on the album cover image of him. They were having the same thoughts, a jumble of odds and ends roller-coasting here, there, and everywhere, bouncing from one side of their brains to the other, laying reality out for them in a frank and decisive manner.

Oh shit all of a sudden there's a baby coming; Charles and Dee are in Paris; Charlie and Jane are in L.A.; Matt's around, good, we'll call him; Steve's in Toronto, but Sophie's gotta be around somewhere, or maybe Trudy's in town; oh shit one of us oughtta call the hospital and tell them we're coming, or maybe we should call Matt first; what about this puddle on the floor, how much more fluid is there gonna be? Maybe one of us should get a towel…

And then the most incredible realizations of all struck the two. They hit Jacob about a minute later than they hit Jessie. He knew he was late to pick up on those, because by the time the thoughts crossed Jacob's mind, Jessie had already lost the battle with her emotions and had given up counting and staring at Jacob's album cover, and instead was swiping viciously at the tears now pouring down angry, blotchy cheeks.

The first thought bolting out of the blue to accost Jacob's baffled mindset was voiced by Jessie at about the exact same time he thought it.

"It's too early, Jacob. It's almost a month too early."

The second was worded more in subtext, by Jacob's stunned dusky voice rising to the surface in the acoustically friendly space.

"You've got to be fucking kidding me," he bellowed, as reality hit him between the eyes, speaking more to the puddle at Jessie's feet than at her piqued face.

He didn't have to say it twice. But he did, anyway, after realizing exactly where Josh was at the moment—*in fucking Toronto.*

And guess who's going to be holding his wife's hand while she's in labor, sky-rocketed through Jacob's mind. The second time he spoke aloud, he fixed his eyes solidly on Jessie's scared expression, and clenched his fists at his sides. He said it slower this time, with emphasis on each unbelievable word.

"You've—got—to—be—fucking—kidding—me. Oh, Jesus."

"Jacob," Jessie managed, gulping hard to remain in control of the terror overtaking her at the idea of having this baby without her husband by her side, "did you hear me? It's—too—damn—early—to be having this baby!"

He didn't move. Jacob didn't know shit about having babies, and there were a lot of scattered thoughts fluttering around his addled brain at the moment. Blinking, he simply stared at her, which motivated Jessie to action.

"Oh, for God's sake! I'm calling Matt. While I do that, do you think you could possibly make a little trip into the change rooms by the gym and grab some towels? Jacob?"

Still, he stood immobilized, afraid to move, the blood pounding in Jacob's ears now as he contemplated where the next few hours were going to take him—them. He swallowed painfully, finally, and nodded haplessly, but he didn't move. Jessie was terrified, obviously, and likely too afraid to voice the *why* as far as Josh's whereabouts were concerned. Yet Jacob knew the *why*, and the truth rather sickened him.

"Jacob! Goddamnit!"

Jessie's petrified (or was it angry) voice startled Jacob into action. In the end, he did what he always did—he took the high road.

"Jessie," he said urgently, ultimately, needing her to understand. "I know I'm not what—who—you want right now. But you need to know—I won't be leaving you alone through this."

At that simple declaration, a whole new waterfall opened up, this one tears of a deeper intensity accompanied by gulping sobs Jessie tried to still by covering her pretty mouth with her hands. Jacob was by her side in two quick steps, and he took her into his arms and rocked her just a little.

"All right," he said, finally taking charge. "Back to the couch. I don't need you falling and getting hurt while I'm a few floors down looking for towels."

He placed her safely back on the couch on top of the earlier coverlet, which he wrapped securely around her legs again. "You'll be fine, the baby will be fine, and Josh will get here as soon as he can. You'll see. And soon you'll have that beautiful child in your arms, and all will be well. Jessie, look at me." He took her cheeks between his palms. "I'm leaving you your cell, call Josh, I'll call Matt, okay? I'll be back before you get off the phone and we'll make our way downstairs, okay? Together. Come on, some day we'll laugh about this, I swear. Okay? Think about the baby. Okay?"

She smiled then, a weak, limp attempt, but it was enough to assure Jacob that she would be all right while he ran for towels. Jessie was speed-dialing Josh before he'd even left the studio and, despite the feeling that the situation was under at least some modicum of control, Jacob couldn't help it. One last time, by the elevator, he hung his head and cried to the universe, "You've got to be fucking kidding me!"

Pounding the side of the wall with a closed fist, he groaned loud enough for Jessie to hear him down the hall. Then the elevator beeped and, as he disappeared inside, Jacob grabbed his cell phone from his pocket. He prepared to speed dial Matt the second the elevator spit him out on the floor where he'd find the gym, along with a pile of soft, welcoming, soothing towels.

Chapter Five

"You've got to be fucking kidding me!" cried Josh in absolute dismay when he answered his hotel suite's door at midnight, bare chested and still yanking up his jeans. He leaned one suddenly trembling outstretched hand on the doorframe for support, and stared hard at Steve while he digested the news. "Jessie's in labor? Now?"

Steve held out his phone. "She just called. She's been trying to reach you. What the hell did you do with your phone? Drop it in the toilet?"

"I fell asleep! It's fucking midnight! It's here…somewhere…" Inside, as Steve followed, Josh sorted through a pile of clothes occupying a chair in his suite. He pulled the offending phone out from underneath a pair of discarded denims. To his dismay, the screen lit up with alerts from Jessie and, he noticed with a growing unease, Matt and…*oh shit*…Jacob.

"Oh, Jesus," he groaned, as a disheartening panic escalated in his belly. "I have to get a flight!" Whipping around, he made a dash for his laptop, which sat contentedly on a nearby desk.

Steve halted him with an outstretched hand. "Stop. Josh, stop. I called the concierge—I tried Jacqueline from the production office but she must be screwing her new A.D. boyfriend because she's not answering. The concierge downstairs is booking us a flight."

At Josh's quick, thankful glance, he added, "You're welcome. And of course I'm going with you. The other cast can do the event tomorrow. Jonathon will get over it—he's about to have his first grandbaby."

"Baby. Yes, oh Jesus Steve, I have to get back to Van." A sudden thought constricted Josh's throat. Steve saw the fear pass over his face.

45

Josh stared wide-eyed at his good friend. "It's too early, Steve. It's too god-damned early." He ran a hand through his hair, dropped down on the end of the bed, and hastily pulled a white T-shirt over his rumpled layers of chest-nut locks. "Jessie and her stupid swear jar. I'm going to be shit broke after tonight," he muttered pointlessly to no one in particular. "Jacob. Seriously. Fucking Jacob. Jacob Jacob Jacob! God, I hate that stupid guy and his fuck-ing puppy-dog eyes!"

He jumped up off the bed and reached for his brown boots while Steve nosed around for a duffel bag. Falling backwards, Josh shoved his feet into the boots one at a time, cursing and muttering under his breath.

"Call Jessie, Josh. She was beside herself on the phone. Calm her down, don't aggravate or provoke her, and for God's sake leave Jacob out of it. I'm going back to my room to pack. I'll check in with Joey at the concierge's desk and see if he's had any luck with a flight. I'll call Jonathon and then I'm call-ing Sophie. It's only nine o'clock in Vancouver, so she won't be in bed yet. Get your shit packed and meet me in the lobby in ten. There's got to be a flight west sometime in the next few hours. Capiche?"

Josh groaned one last time and started literally throwing things into his bag. Steve grabbed the cell phone off the bed where Josh had tossed it, and he speed dialed Jessie's number. He held it out to his friend and grinned widely. "Talk to your baby mama, Josh. You lucky bastard." He placed a calming hand on Josh's shoulder, which served its purpose and eased Josh's rapidly growing angst. "A baby, Josh. You and Jessie. A new little person. Tell Jessie you love her and that you're on your way. I'll see you downstairs."

He held the phone a moment before Josh reached out and grabbed it, a worried grin now replacing the anxious frown. Steve left him with a smile when he heard Jessie's voice come across the line.

"Josh?"

"H-hey," Josh answered, his voice cracking, his stomach sick with worry. Josh collapsed backwards onto the bed and laid his left palm on his forehead. "Where are you, Jessie? Are you at the hospital?"

"Almost." He could hear her gulping on the other end, struggling to remain composed. Josh didn't know it, but Jessie's left hand was now firmly wrapped up in Jacob's. She barely noticed it herself, but Jacob was silently gloating, although his emotions were, overall, a frayed mess of *this sucks* mixed with generous helpings of *how freaking cool is this.*

Jessie continued. "Matt picked us up on Robson rather than us taking the SUV. I'm not up to driving and Jacob hasn't driven since Scotland. He'd likely have us on the wrong side of the street. So…" She looked around for landmarks. "We're almost to Broadway. We'll be there in about ten minutes."

Us. Josh grimaced, but ignored the debilitating ache in his chest and the urge to curse audibly, although he did so under his breath, rather rapidly and fairly expensively, in fact, should Jessie's swear jar be considered at all.

"Are you okay, Jess? Like…what's happening exactly…you were fine when we talked a few hours ago."

"Fine is relative," she answered glumly. "I haven't really been feeling good all day." She heard a muffled *pppffffttttt* vibrate through the phone. "Just nauseous, Josh, that's all. But then…at the studio…my water broke. So I guess it's all happening, you know?"

"Oh. Shit. Okay, so this is the real deal."

Jessie inhaled deeply. "Yeah, babe. I guess it's the real deal." New tears started and she tried to squish them away, to no avail. "And you're halfway across the goddamned country." She squeezed Jacob's hand tightly but couldn't look at him. Still, she was glad he was there, and the squeeze affirmed it.

Josh caught the angst in her voice when her last few words cracked mercilessly, like hot flaming arrows, through his heart. "I'm on my way, Jess. Steve's got the concierge booking us a flight. Just tell our kid to hang on, okay? I'll be there before you know it. In the meantime…"

This time it was his voice that caught, that couldn't force the next words through strained lips.

Jessie finished his sentence for him. "Jacob's here. I'm not alone. And I've got Matt, too," she added, glancing upwards towards the rearview mirror to catch Matt's sympathetic smile.

"Steve's calling Sophie. You can send golden boy on his merry way."

"Calling him golden boy is thirty bucks, Josh. Cause it's kind of cheating. In a way. And I'm not sending him anywhere."

A slow exhalation reverberated across Ontario, Manitoba, Saskatchewan,

Alberta, and British Columbia. "Calling him golden boy is about the nicest way I can refer to your ex right now, Jessie. I have a whole store of colorful names at hand but somehow I don't feel this is the right time to educate you about the finer details of those. Not at this particular moment, anyway."

"No, and it's not exactly the right time to waste your precious breath calling Jacob down, either, Josh. Cuz like it or not, he's here and you're not, and one thing's for sure, he's not any happier about it than you are. So deal with it." She glanced at Jacob, who simply added a little more pressure to her clammy fingers while avoiding both her eyes and Matt's, which he knew were fixed on him in the rearview mirror. "You should be home this weekend, that's what, and you're not, and I'm rather pissed about that!"

Geez, thought Jacob, *she's on her way to have their baby and they're fighting.* He gloated a little more effusively. Matt frowned at the slight upturn of Jacob's lips, and then ran a yellow light on West Broadway.

"All right," Josh offered quietly, "we've established that. And believe me, Jessie, this sucks for me too."

"Oh, does it now, like, you're the size of a whale, dripping amniotic fluid all over Matt's super-ultra-clean Audi, and about to launch a human through your body? While your spouse is across the country? Yeah, it really sucks for you, Josh. Jesus."

Josh hung his head in his hands and closed his eyes. He was still sitting on the end of the bed, his waist button undone from when he'd swiftly pulled on jeans to answer the door in a hurry, and he was wearing a smelly wrinkled T-shirt yanked from his laundry pile. Moonlight snuck in through a crack in the drapes, and settled on a one-inch tear just over the left knee in his jeans. He stuck a finger in it and poked at it, fighting his own wild emotions at this strange evolution in his and Jessie's—and apparently Jacob's—lives.

He could hear Jessie struggling, sniffling and breathing heavily. Finally, he found his voice. "Put him on, Jess."

"What?" came the surprised response.

"Put fucking Jacob on the goddamned phone."

"I swear, Josh, this is not the time—"

"Put him on the goddamned phone."

Swearing noiselessly, Jessie sucked in a breath and hesitated before fearfully passing her cell across to Jacob. She peeked out the window and studied the street signs. They were about five blocks from Oak Street, where they would turn right to head towards the hospital. She stared at the swift flying streetlights and brightly lit store and restaurant windows as they passed by, oddly noting that the Thai restaurant where she and Jacob had planned a late dinner was amongst them.

"Yeah," Jacob grunted into the phone on her left. Jessie strained to hear her husband speak to him.

"Ryan, I swear to God—"

"Cool it, Sawyer. Someday I'll expect you to return the favor."

"I just mean—" Josh was struggling, and Jacob heard him suck in a breath.

A man of few words, he helped his adversary out. "I know what you mean, Josh," he cut in.

Even Jessie picked up the slow exhale coming their way from Toronto.

"Okay then. All right. Jacob?"

"Yeah."

"Just call me, okay? I mean, you can't while I'm on the plane, I know that, but call anyway and just leave a message, you know, or messages, I mean, so when I land I'll know what the hell's going on. Okay?"

"You got it, Josh. I'll call. You'll be sick of my voice."

"I'm already sick of your stupid voice."

Jacob laughed. "Yeah, ditto, man. Get yourself to an airplane, will ya? I'd rather she breaks your fingers instead of mine. Your wife's got a helluva grip."

Josh swallowed. "Yeah, well, I wish to hell it was my hand she was breaking right now, Ryan."

"That makes two of us. Or maybe three. I'll see you in a bit, Sawyer. I'm giving you back to Jessie now."

He handed the phone over to Jessie, treating her to a wide smile as he did so. "He's a mess," he mouthed. "Go easy on him."

She smiled back and would have laughed at the unexpected rapport between the two men, had Josh not been stranded in Toronto for the time being while she suffered increasing knife slices through her abdomen.

"Josh?" she said into the phone, unable to disguise her angst but no longer edging it with frustration and anger.

"Okay, little one," he said softly. "Break his fingers if you need to. But think of me, okay? Think of me going crazy up there in the big blue sky aching to be with you." He sighed helplessly. "I'll be there as soon as I can."

"I know you will be, babe." She pawed a fist at one last tear streaking all lonely-like down a pink cheek.

"And be strong, Jessie, okay? You can do this. You're the strongest person I know."

"Not so much," she mumbled. "Not always."

"We've been over this. You know what to expect. And Jessie? This is our baby. Our sweet beautiful gorgeous loving little baby you are bringing into the world tonight." *With Jacob by your side*, he added silently, painfully.

"It's too early, Josh. It's too early."

"It'll be fine, little one. You're going to be in one of the most advanced hospitals in the world. They'll take good care of you and the baby."

"I know, Josh. Get your ass onto a plane, will you?" Jessie cared about the carbon footprint, but that night she would have given anything for Charles and Dee to be parked in Toronto, their jet close at hand. But the Keating jet was in gay Paris at the moment, likely fueling up for the trip home, if Matt had anything to do with its schedule. Jessie figured rightly he had already called her pseudo-parents.

"You got it, baby girl. I love you."

"I love you back." It was a whisper. Jessie met Matt's eyes again in the rearview mirror. The car was stopped and Jacob was opening his door. They were at the emergency entrance of the hospital. It was time.

"See you soon, Josh."

"Real soon, Jessie."

And then, after a few moments of an anxious hovering silence, Jessie tapped *end*, and the connection was broken.

Chapter Six

"Oh, God," Jessie moaned many hours later in the dark of night while Jacob groaned and lifted her hand to his damp lips so he could brush them across her sweaty knuckles. "Sweet Jesus, Jacob," she panted. "Don't ever get pregnant."

"It's not in my immediate plans, Jessie," he managed to murmur nervously. "D'ya want some more ice chips?" He glanced over at Sophie, who rushed over to a pitcher and filled a paper cup with fresh ice chips. She handed the cup to him and wiped a moist cloth over her friend's forehead at the same time. Jessie looked up at her gratefully and leaned to the other side to accept the refreshing ice chips from Jacob, who placed a hand behind her head to support her while she sucked some up between her lips.

"Sophie," Jessie urged between crunches and gasps, "it's not as bad as it looks. Really." Grimacing, she moaned loudly as another contraction sliced her abdomen in two. "Geez Louise! God in Heaven!"

Across the bed from each other, Jacob and Sophie exchanged concerned looks. The kindly but businesslike and efficient Dr. Wyatt had been in for a check only about five minutes ago. Jessie's contractions were coming more quickly now and, as far as her friends knew, Josh's plane was somewhere over the prairies. He was still at least a good few hours away.

"Jessie," Sophie broke in quietly, "honey, why don't you let them give you a little something for the pain?"

"Nope," Jessie insisted bravely. "I can do this. I can do this. I can—do—oh Jesus! Jacobbbb....!!!!" She twisted around in the bed and, despite her attempts at bravery, a few sobs escaped from between the parched lips.

51

"I want him here," she cried. "I'm sorry Jacob, I am, but damn it he got me into this mess and he oughtta see me out of it!"

Jacob fought the urge to get up and walk away, to leave her here with Sophie, and his downcast eyes telegraphed that across to Sophie but Jessie was in too much discomfort to realize just how deeply this whole situation was hurting her good friend and ex-lover. He willed himself to deal with the absurdity of the situation, including the weird good fortune that he got to be there for her, and he kissed the tired knuckles again.

"Beautiful girl," he said, his eyes misting over for the thousandth time that evening for her pain as well as his own, "listen to me. I've got your back here. And Josh's too, apparently. I love you like crazy, and so that's what you get right now—me. Stupid love struck Jacob. Not your first choice, I know, but it's all we've got to work with. You're stuck with me, I'm your person right now, and believe me I cannot even imagine how much this sucks for you. But like it or lump it, it's me you're stuck with for the time being, so suck it up and let me be here for you, Jessie. Okay?"

"Jacob," Sophie chided, more mouthing the words than actually saying them. "Harsh. Chill, honey."

"Not harsh," he shrugged somewhat dispassionately across to Sophie while Jessie leaned forward and cried out again. "Just the truth. I know where I fit in, but right now even her cowboy is riding the skies hoping I'm helping her. I know he is, because that's what..." He gulped. "That's what I would want, if things were different. I'd want him here with her if it was my kid and I couldn't be around. Because I know...I know how he feels about her, the same damn way I do, in fact, so I know he'd do whatever it takes to help her through this. And besides, he asked me. In the car on the way here. So," he said again, to Jessie, letting his gaze drift away from Sophie's chiding stare and downwards to his ex's flushed cheeks, "this is what you get, Jess, this stupid lovesick musician right here, at least for the time being."

Leaning forward, he whispered in Jessie's ear as she sat, panting heavily, back on the two pillows Sophie re-fluffed for her. "You can curse at me all you want, Jessie. Under the table. I won't report it to Josh. I promise."

"Jacob?" came a small voice from the snowy pillows.

"Um-humn?"

"I don't remember telling you about the swear jar."

"Josh told me."

"Huh?" She eyed him quizzically.

"The last time we talked, just before he boarded the plane. I'm feeling quite honored to be your biggest money-maker."

She laughed outright at that. But then another contraction seized Jessie's gut and with it came another stream of tears. White knuckles gripped the sides of the birthing bed instead of Jacob's red raw fingers, but he placed his hand over hers anyway.

"Yes," she gasped afterwards. "I've made a lot of money off your name already, Jacob."

"Somehow that appeases me. I'm not sure why." He wrinkled his brow.

"You know why," Jessie smiled weakly, wiping strands of damp matted hair off her cheek. "So stop your whining, Ryan. You know I'm glad you're here."

"I know *I'm* glad I'm here," he smiled sadly. "Sort of. In a fucking strange way. For now, at least."

At that, Dr. Wyatt breezed back in. Her soft-soled runners squeaked on the clean floor, which sounded odd in the silence between contractions. She picked up the chart at the end of the bed and had a good look at the data recorded there, comparing it with data displayed brightly on an iPad in her hand.

"Dr. Wyatt, are we doing okay here? Really?" Jessie asked soberly, squeezing her eyes tight and panting hard to endure another searing pain.

"The baby's heart rate is fine, Jessie," the kind doctor assured her. "We've got a team standing by if anything changes but so far everything looks just fine." She bent over her patient and adjusted the fetal heart rate monitor attached around Jessie's swollen abdomen. "Now, give me an update on your husband's whereabouts. What's his ETA?"

"I'm not telling," Jessie moaned while Jacob frowned. "It doesn't matter anyway. I'm just gonna hold my breath and not push until he's here."

"I see," the doctor smiled. "Are you."

"Damn straight I am." Jessie looked up at Jacob, pleading. "That's like, only fifty cents."

Jacob threw his hands up in the air. "What happens in the delivery room stays in the delivery room."

Grabbing his hand again as another powerful contraction seized her belly, Jessie tried to laugh. A quick grimace followed, and she added, "Geez, doc, tell me this is as bad as it gets."

The doctor reached for the cool cloth in Sophie's hands and gently wiped a few more stray wafts of hair off Jessie's pinched cheeks. "You're doing fine, honey," she said firmly. "You just keep right on doing what you're doing, and before you know it you'll have a gorgeous brand new baby in your arms. Now let's have ourselves another little check, shall we?"

She handed the cloth back to Sophie, who herself was now white as a ghost, and then she settled herself at the foot of the bed, pulled some gloves over her fingers, and checked Jessie for dilation.

"Oh, fuuu….." moaned her patient. Then, between her teeth, Jessie hissed at Jacob. "That doesn't count. It's only a partial swear word."

"It should be worth at least a dollar," Jacob whispered conspiratorially to Sophie.

The good doctor grasped the cuffs of her gloves, peeled them up over her fingers, and tossed them in a nearby bin before grasping Jacob's elbow and taking him aside. "She's having this baby with or without her husband, Jacob. Soon. I suggest you step outside and fill in your security so he knows what to tell Josh when he lands. You'll be busy. All right?"

"Really?" Jacob asked sheepishly. He shook his head wordlessly. "This is too weird, like, I can't even tell you how freaking weird this is for me right now."

Jessie cried out again, and Jacob shuddered. "I guess soon is good, right?"

"Yes. Soon is good." The doctor started to walk away.

"Dr. Wyatt?"

She stopped and turned. "Yes?"

"So the fact this baby is early…ummm…"

"There are things we won't know until the child is born, Jacob. But there's no point in worrying. So far the baby is holding up just fine. You can tell your security friend that." She gestured to the doorway. "Now would be a good time."

"You got it," Jacob nodded. He moved back to Jessie's side. "Jess, I'll be right back. Sophie's here. I'm off to have a little chat with Matt, okay?"

Her pale eyes frightened him but Jessie responded with a tiny smile so Jacob pushed his fear aside. He resorted to the knuckle kissing again. It was fast becoming his nervous reaction to the extreme angst of guiding the woman he loved through the natural agony of labor.

"Hurry back, please," she moaned.

Jacob couldn't resist the urge. Sophie shook her head at him and pursed her lips and the doctor raised her eyebrows curiously when Jacob leaned forward and pressed his lips to Jessie's. "I will," he agreed softly. "Just give me a minute."

Outside, he found Matt pacing the hallway, his wife Julie seated nearby. Katy, their little girl, was at her cousin's for the night. Matt lunged forward when he saw Jacob appear. Down the hall, another woman in labor was having a harder time of it than even Jessie. She was crying openly as the pain cut her in two. Jacob squeezed his eyes shut. "Well, I think I'll adopt," he grimaced. "Although Jessie's a tough one. She's refusing any meds, at least. Although if this continues for much longer I might have to find a sturdy twig to stick between her teeth."

"How much longer?" Matt asked, his pretty petite wife coming up behind him and tucking her smaller fingers into his. "The plane lands in an hour and a half."

"I don't know exactly," answered Jacob. "The doctor just said to come out and tell you things are happening. That I likely won't be out again. So maybe you should just hit the airport, Matt, so you're there when the guys get in. Maybe their flight'll come in early," he added rather hopelessly.

"Good then, Julie and I will head out." Matt paused before leaving. "Tell Jessie we're rooting for her, okay? We can't wait to meet this new little baby. And comb your hair, you look like shit." Affectionately, Matt reached out a hand and tousled Jacob's hair.

"Matt, I am not gonna tell you what you would do if I did that to you."

"You don't have to." Matt grinned. "Seriously, Jacob, I'm glad you're here. Somehow you always seem to be…" His words faded into the ether.

"What, in the right place at the right time? Something like that?"

"Where Jessie's concerned, yes. I suppose that's what I mean."

"What about where Josh is concerned?"

"He should be here. But nobody thought this baby was in such a damn hurry to make its entrance."

"He'll never get this back, Matt."

"I know," Matt said quietly.

"Yet another reason for him to hate me, I guess. Not that I care." Jacob shrugged.

"If you feel that way, then I'm guessing you really don't know Josh all that well, Jacob."

"No," Jacob replied stoically, raising his shoulders and shoving his hands in his pockets. "I guess I don't."

"He's good for her."

"Apparently. Just listen to how good for her he is."

Jessie was hollering pretty good now as her contractions intensified.

"But then again," Jacob added softly to himself as Matt patted him on the shoulder and strode off down the hall hand in hand with his wife, "what's love without pain?"

He turned on his heel and stepped heavily into a nearby washroom for a piss. Down the hall, the second woman's birthing cries completely disarmed him. Yet when Jessie's cries reached his ears, he smiled inwardly. This baby wasn't his, but somehow, he was a major part of the whole experience. And whether Jessie or Josh knew it, or cared—and really, he doubted they cared at all, or would, in the end—he knew it was one more thing he and Jessie would always share, that had already become their own special experience.

Jacob took his leak, washed his hands, and headed back inside to settle at Jessie's side.

"Okay there, girl," he murmured gently to her as he took her hand. "You're doing great. And just how much more do we owe the swear jar?"

～～～

Josh was losing it. He and Steve were in first class on this flight, and he had watched every damn drop of liquor get poured into the glasses of first class passengers, yet none made it into his own glass. His knuckles were white and he'd been to the bathroom at least six times on the five-hour flight, sometimes just to lean his head against the wall and moan. He couldn't stand the not knowing—the waiting and the wondering. What was happening at the hospital? Was Jessie okay? Was the baby okay? He had pictured every last scenario—even the bad ones—and in the end he knew that, despite all, Jessie would have to be okay. Not that he would ever want to have to choose between his wife and child but, if he did, if the universe ever played that terrible card, well then he would choose his wife. He knew it. He needed her. He could not live without those pale blue eyes searching his, loving his, diving into his, having a soul connection…with him. He'd done it before, for far too long, and the hell he would ever do it again.

Steve was losing it, too, but for an entirely different reason.

"Damn it, Josh, just settle, will you? Disrupting your friend and co-star when he's trying to sleep is not going to get you on his good side!" Steve was snuggled up in a blanket, his feet stretched out in front of him. He was in the aisle seat, which he'd quickly realized upon boarding was perhaps not one of his brainiest ideas, since Josh was up and down so many times.

"Yeah, I'll be happy to remind you of this little trip when it's your turn to be a dad-in-waiting, Steve," Josh griped back at him.

"Harrumph," was Steve's genial response. "Take a chill pill, Sawyer."

"I can't," Josh groaned. "This is torture. I can't stand it."

Steve gave up on the effort to sleep. He tossed off his blanket and sucked back the water at his side. "Soon. We're like an hour away, Josh. Think about something else."

"Like what, Steve? Something other than my wife being in Jacob's arms right now? Or the fact he's in all likelihood gonna see my kid before I get to? It's kind of hard to erase that tender loving scene from my mind, in case you're wondering."

"I wasn't. Wondering, that is. Just…look, let's run some lines."

"I'm not there yet. I can't focus."

Steve reached into the saddle-leather messenger bag at his feet. Pulling out a script, he tossed it onto Josh's lap. "Here. Focus."

So they ran lines until the plane was no longer airborne. Matt was at the gate waiting for them with news the birth was imminent, so they piled into the back of the Audi and were driven to the hospital, which was a good twenty minutes away.

Sophie was on the phone to Steve the second he landed, and in his arms when they reached the hospital. She gladly gave up her place in the birthing room to Jessie's husband and, when Josh finally ran in, Jacob felt he had no choice but to vacate his spot as well.

～～～

When Josh rushed in, still knotting the waist of his surgical greens, his heart was pounding bloody murder. He was so grateful to finally be at Jessie's side that he almost dropped to the floor in prayer. Instead, he simply whispered a few silent words of thanks. Fixing his eyes first on his exhausted wife, he did a quick scan of her sweaty face and pale knuckles before letting his gaze drift over to Jacob.

Jacob had been versed on Josh's imminent arrival. He'd spent the last twenty minutes whispering good-byes to Jessie. When he sensed Josh's eager presence in the birthing room, he felt the air around him shift. He knew if he met Josh's eyes the spell would be broken, that magic spell he was under from the time Jacob finally realized he would be Jessie's labor partner; when he realized he would be the one holding her captive in his eyes while he was lost in hers, while her baby made its way into the world.

If he looked up now? Well, laying his eyes on Josh would burst that bubble. It would send the dreamlike night scuttling away into the corners like fairy dust from a dream.

But then the baby's father spoke, and so Jacob had no choice but to look away from his girl. Jessie broke his gaze first—she'd been buried in Jacob's eyes trying to control her breathing while he led her, coached by a Doula she and Josh had consulted and who finally arrived about halfway through the night.

Now, though, Jessie too sensed her husband's presence. When she heard Josh simply whisper her name, she had to let Jacob go, even though by now she was completely under his spell, transfixed by the adoration in the blue eyes, and by the gentle voice that coached her so patiently these last many hours.

Her fingers slipped from his first, and then Jessie's tears started anew when she spotted her husband making his way to her in messy surgical greens, his cloth cap askew, and his moist eyes afraid, expectant and hopeful.

Jacob backed away, remembering another time when Jessie cried for this man, and he couldn't help but wonder yet again if he had met her first, would things be the other way around? Would she love him more? Was it possible? Jacob was so inextricably wound up and in and around her now, again, after their summer apart, that he felt he would explode then and there. He was doing okay, he knew he was getting better, hanging out at his dad's and writing music, and learning to let go, until…until he and Jessie were back on *Mystic Nights* again. Until they were singing again. Until…until this long special surreal incredible night, where he was the one holding Jessie's hand, counting with her while she focused on her breathing. Where he was the one in whose eyes she was lost, trusting and loving and hoping and praying and, well, at times sobbing.

And now she was sobbing again, but this time it was from relief. Relief that her man was here, finally—not Jacob, no, but Josh, the guy who almost walked away from her last spring in Miami the night the first semi-nude photo—the one with the searing, lonely tear—trended on Twitter.

Jacob let her fingers slip away, he had to, what choice did he have? And he stood back and watched as, without a goodbye or a thank you very much, Jessie leaned into Josh's arms and cried while he held her and whispered to her.

Cocking his head curiously, Jacob felt completely detached as he watched. Around them, Doctor Wyatt and her nurses were hustling about, preparing for the same birth Jacob was prepared to see—no, had *planned* to see, had accepted that he would see, would witness firsthand—but they were like fuzzy ants in Jacob's peripheral vision. He was entirely focused on only one thing, and that was the reunion between Jessie and Josh.

Josh was holding her and she was crying out now, her body almost jackknifed on the bed as another powerful contraction contorted her. But he was whispering, and consoling, and kissing and touching and holding and loving, and even Jacob could see the magic floating on some invisible current between them as their baby made its way into the world loved by two incredible parents who, now, were so lost in each other's eyes nobody could come between them. Not the doctor's gently urging voice saying *push now, Jessie, push* nor the Doula who had left a rousing party to attend the birth and who, now, was sliding ice chips between Jessie's lips; and certainly not Jacob, who before was only invisible on a certain level but now was invisible altogether.

He thought about backing out and leaving them alone for the birth of their daughter—and it was a daughter, indeed, as Jessie and Josh both intuited so many times during the pregnancy—but he couldn't. Jacob was rooted to the spot, lost in the soul of the woman he loved and in the downright intoxicating spell she and Josh were lost in, buried so deep they could never get out; and so he stayed, and, unnoticed by anyone, Jacob was one of the first to see that beautiful baby girl come into the world.

Afterwards, when the child was on her momma's belly and Jessie's tears had turned to joy at her safe arrival and good health despite the baby's haste to partake of the joys and pains in the world, Jacob finally tiptoed outside. He needed a minute to compose himself, but he didn't get one. Upon exiting, he was immediately deluged by Matt and Steve, and so he had to wipe his own tears away and accept that this entire experience was his and his alone to worship and to cherish and to remember with fondness and love, and that Jessie had Josh and now they had gorgeous little Emily-Grace, and he, Jacob, had no one.

He was alone again, and so he delivered the news of the baby's safe healthy arrival as best he could, in a voice born of exhaustion and defeat.

And then, while Matt and Steve were rejoicing in the over lit hallway, Jacob ripped off his surgical greens, dumped them in a bin, and stole silently away.

Chapter Seven

When Kevin's old Dodge rumbled into the driveway, Sara was sitting on the family's ancient floral chesterfield, pondering what she would change first about her home décor if she could, in fact, afford to change anything. But hockey registration and gear was expensive, their mortgage was pricey, and sometimes they needed heat, and food for their two growing boys, not to mention that new alternator on the old Dodge Dakota last spring, and then of course they'd spent all that money taking the kids to Canada's Wonderland twice last summer…

She heard the slamming of truck doors, accompanied by muffled voices as Kevin and the kids rattled on about today's practice. Sara knew they were grabbing their large duffels out of the bed of the pickup as they chatted, and would be one big excited rumbling mass of *Mom this* and *Mom that* when they got inside, so she took one last glance around the room, trying to see it through superstar Jessie Wheeler's eyes. She absently tapped a silicone oven mitt on her thigh while she did so, sucking in tense breath after breath, sitting forward on the couch, her eyes darting here and there like a baby bird, with about as much power and funds as said baby bird at her disposal, in fact.

Their television was a small screen, about fifteen years old. Beside it was a few game systems they'd managed to fund for the kids over various Christmases. Her coffee and end tables were plywood, seventies style, with the legs painted white by her thrifty husband, who insisted new coffee and end tables were less important than the new roof he and a few handy friends hammered onto their home three summers ago. In the master bedroom, their curtains were blue, her duvet cover pink. The curtains were original to the two-story townhouse, which was built in the early 80's. Sara had washed them a few times but never seemed able to make it a priority to buy new ones. She sighed wearily. *At least Jessie isn't likely to go in there*, she thought. *I'll just keep the door closed.*

At that, the front door opened. A shocking *whoosh* of cool air made its presence felt all the way to Sara's hunched shoulders in the living room at the back of the small townhouse. She shivered. Stamping feet trooped in, supplemented by a guttural swashbuckling of noise as the kids emptied their big hockey bags of sweaty helmets and pants, and pulled out skates to give the blades a second wipe before laying them out to dry by the boot bench in the small entryway. Coats were unzipped and boots thudded off. One hit the wall when it was unceremoniously kicked off a foot. Sara groaned when she pictured the mud she'd have to wipe off the wall later, but she knew it was a common occurrence and not worth the ire it would raise in her older son's eyes if she nagged him about it. *Choose your battles carefully*, she intoned under her breath, heaving herself up off the couch and wandering out to the kitchen to pull steaming homemade lasagna out of the oven.

"Mom, I almost got my finger cut off today." It was Ren, the younger boy, always dramatic. He shoved a forefinger in Sara's face, and she bent over, grabbed his wrist and stared at the finger, searching it up and down for any sign of bandage or, heaven forbid, blood. There was none. Dropping it, she rolled her eyes at him, but he was non-plussed.

"My glove came off and I landed on my butt and Owen Radfield almost skated right over it." The nine year old stood facing his mom, feet squared a hip distance apart, and arms now crossed adamantly over his small chest, which he thrust out like a puffed up peacock.

Sara reached up into the cupboard for plates. "And how did your glove come off, Ren?"

Mark marched in then, and plopped himself into a chair at the round table. The boys were always famished after hockey practice, and generally rather cranky until they balanced their bellies with hearty nourishment. "He got into a fight and threw his gloves off like Dion Phaneuf does."

"Well, I guess we'll just have to stop watching Hockey Night in Canada, then," Sara stated matter-of-factly as she handed the plates to Mark to distribute around the table.

"And the Peterborough Petes," remarked Kevin, coming into the kitchen and wrapping his arms around his wife's hefty waist.

She huffed and threw him off. "Kevin, I need to get this meal on the table. It's already almost seven, and the boys both have homework."

"What can I do?" he asked amicably.

"Slice the garlic bread," she instructed. "Mark, Ren, sit. Eat. And then homework."

The boys hashed over their practices while they ate, but Sara mostly tuned out, only adding the occasional *um-hum* and *is that right* here and there to punctuate their debates and to give the impression she was listening. When they left the table, she couldn't help but toss a question at her husband, who carried their plates and cutlery to the dishwasher while she filled the sink with soapy water for the lasagna pan.

"I was thinking we could use a new couch, Kev," she started carefully, intentionally not meeting his eyes.

Now it was his turn to mutter *um-hum*.

When no other answer was forthcoming, Sara glanced over one shoulder at her husband. "I'm serious," she maintained, eyebrows rising as she studied him for signs of resistance.

He straightened. "What brought that on? I thought we agreed to save for a new furnace next. Or a new truck."

Planting a hand defiantly on one hip, she faced him. "The furnace will last a few more years. And I thought you were trying to make it to 300 000 km on the truck. Just for fun, you said."

"Sara, I hit 300 K in August. Mark's about a year from a growth spurt. We won't be fitting him and Ren in the cab together for more than another winter."

"So get another job."

"You want a new couch? You get another job. That's a luxury item. The old one's fine. We sit on it, we watch TV on it. I'll rent a carpet cleaner, it'll spruce right up."

"Kevin, we've had sex on that couch. I don't particularly want—"

"First of all, we haven't had sex at all in the last six months, and we seem to be living with the couch just fine." He narrowed his eyes at her and closed the dishwasher door. "Why a new couch all of a sudden, anyway? Does this have anything to do with Jessie Wheeler's visit?"

"It has everything to do with Jessie's visit," Sara declared, boldly raising her chin. "Only I can't seem to decide which is most important to get, a couch or a new TV."

"I can answer that for you. Neither. We're not getting either."

"We'll put it on a payment plan. We can swing that."

"We're maxed out, Sara. I've already got creditors calling me about the Visa card. We couldn't get more credit if we tried."

"This sucks," she mumbled, turning back to the sink and grabbing the Caesar salad bowl. As she rather furiously washed it, her shoulders sagged.

"Hey," Kevin said, reaching for her, but she brushed him off. "It's not always going to be like this."

"No, it's going to get worse," she told him, wiping a hand across her forehead and inadvertently leaving a soapy trail as she did so. "We're about to have teenagers, which means more road trips and more clothes and more food and more—everything!"

"The boys will get jobs. Sara, we'll figure it out."

"That's what you always say—we'll figure it out! Kevin, what exactly do you intend to figure out, and when? Would you mind illuminating me?"

"Geez, will you *start* already?" he muttered under his breath, but she caught the gist of what he said.

She threw a handful of soapy water at him. "Will you stop blaming everything on PMS?"

"Then stop acting like you're always PMSing! Sara, if this is about Jessie Wheeler's visit, you can relax. She won't likely be here for a bit. She had her baby early. I don't expect she'll be travelling anytime too soon."

"What?" This threw Sara—she stopped fretting and leaned back against the sink.

"She had a baby girl. Yesterday. You didn't hear it on the radio?"

"Apparently not! I didn't think she was due for a month."

"She wasn't. They're saying apart from being a little on the small side, the baby's just fine. So's the mom. But I doubt she'll be travelling for a bit."

"Oh."

"What's this? Disappointment?"

"No, not really, I just…" Sara turned back to the dishes. "I suppose I'm curious. That's all. And I kind of want to get this visit over with."

"Yeah, me too," Kevin frowned, "if it means constant PMS until she's been and gone. I don't think our marriage can survive that."

"We've made it this long."

"One of us must be a saint." He grinned and grabbed the dishtowel off the oven door, where it was hanging over the handle.

"Don't flatter yourself, Kev," responded Sara, but she managed a small strained chuckle.

"Well, what about that sex thing…there's only so long a man can go, you know. I think that almost does qualify me as a saint." His crooked grin tickled her cheek when he nuzzled up against her, but she pushed him away again.

"Oh, go stick it in a hole in the wall."

"Sara, I—"

"I'm serious, Kevin. Go stick it in a hole in the wall. I'm exhausted." She couldn't meet his eye, but his silence and the sudden stillness in the room hurt. Sara didn't hear him leave but she was too wound up and beat to care. Plunging her hands deeper into the dishwater, she finished wiping the last few dishes. She left them in the second sink to air dry, and then gave the table and stove a wipe.

When she was done, she turned off the light, and headed out to the living room to see about the boys' homework. Kevin was there, however, leaning over Ren while Mark worked close by, kneeling on the floor, math spread out over the ancient coffee table. For some reason, the silhouette of her family diligently working away, Kevin's hair as mussed up as her kids', touched her deeply. Sara was separate, apart from them, watching unnoticed from a doorway, and her stance and thoughts unknowingly echoed Jacob's from the night of Emily-Grace's birth.

She was on the outside looking in. She was the matriarch of this little family, and she felt she was the glue holding it together. Yet Sara could feel herself unraveling. It had been coming for a long time now, since she was fourteen, in fact, since the days she had to be strong for everyone else around her when her mother climbed down a ladder and took her leave of them. Sara's father was a devastated, angry mess—he went to his grave a bitter, desperately sad man. Her grandmother and grandfather fared better, but only because they had each other, and could talk each other through the clouds of despair at the emotional loss of a daughter and grandbaby they did not know, nor— at the time—welcome.

Now, Sara had to clench her gut together to keep from screaming. Kevin would never understand. Her crappy furniture echoed her mental state. And now, her family was hunched on and around that crappy furniture, toiling away at the everyday stuff that had to get done but which seemed sense-less, some days, given the battles that often ensued when it came time to slog over homework. The image in her mind was confused, muzzy. *That's my family*, Sara thought, *so why do I feel like I am always ten thousand miles away from them?*

Kevin…he was her rock, and she wasn't stupid enough not to know that. He fixed things. He dealt with rust and snow tires and stuck garage door openers. He wasn't jumpy when it came time to light the barbecue, like she was, and he was always game for church despite his adversity to Catholicism (he was raised Pentecost, after all, and couldn't understand why altar boys had to wear dresses and hold the heavy Bible for the Priest). Kevin was a good man. And he needed Sara, in the Biblical sense, in fact, but she felt help-less to give him what every married man deserved. Why? She couldn't even answer that question herself, at least not on any deep level. But on the sur-face she recognized that it had to do with how she felt about herself, about her life, about her surroundings, and about…her past.

Was she ready to welcome Jessie Wheeler? Her *half-sister*? No. But she and Martha had discussed it, and they'd agreed to at least meet the woman. But that wouldn't make the visit any easier to bear.

The news that Jessie had already given birth settled into Sara's bones. She started towards the stairs but paused at the bottom step.

"Kevin?" she asked.

"Yep?" her husband answered affably, their earlier brief discussion appar-ently lost in the abyss of boys and homework.

"What did they name the baby?"

Kevin straightened over the top of his younger son's head and regarded his wife judiciously. He knew more about her than she would ever in a million years understand or give him credit for. He swallowed before answering.

"Oh," he said, his voice cracking a little. "Well. She actually called her Emily-Grace, Sara."

"Oh. Of course she did." And this time Sara did scream. But she waited until she had turned around, went to the door, threw on her puffy black Mark's Work Wearhouse coat, forced her feet into a pair of old rubber boots, and went outside and around the corner of the house to their beat-up shed in the backyard. Once there, she sat on a pile of stacked moldy lawn furniture, and she let the universe have it, albeit with both hands clamped tightly over her mouth.

Then, Sara reached under Ren's lifejacket from his swimming lessons three years ago, pulled out a stash of cigarettes saved for nights such as this, and chain-smoked until she saw Mark and Ren's bedroom light get switched off.

Shivering, she plodded heavily back inside and hung up her coat, agreeing with Kevin's earlier statement that one of them was, indeed, a saint, when he simply put his arm around her on the ratty old couch. There were no complaints about her absence while he put the boys to bed, nor were there any over the fact that she stank like cigarette smoke, nor over the fact he already knew tonight he would not be getting laid. Kevin even made microwave popcorn for the two of them, put butter and salt on it for her, and let Sara eat most of the bowl.

She laid her head on his shoulder, and they watched *So You Think You Can Dance* before turning off the old TV and the downstairs lights. Upstairs, they kissed both of their sleeping children good-night, and slid into bed beneath the faded old blue curtains, which hung stoically and bravely over a patient moonlit window.

Chapter Eight

Jacob's phone rang at exactly five minutes to nine Miami time. He was just settling into his suite again—his home away from home—when the iPhone's caller ID flashed *Jessie Wheeler*. He hesitated before answering, staring at the familiar letters and feeling a small sense of satisfaction that she hadn't completely switched her name to Jessie Sawyer, or even Jessie Wheeler-Sawyer (although she occasionally used both).

Grabbing the phone from its resting place on the end of the bed, he hit the answer icon. "Hey, Jess," he started, apprehension cracking his voice, before Josh cut him off.

"Yeah, uh, it's Josh, actually," came the unexpected dusky voice from Vancouver.

"Oh." The disappointment in Jacob's single syllable was palpable. Then he hit the panic button. He jumped in quickly. "Is everything—"

"She's fine, Jacob. Jessie's fine. The baby's great, too, well she's smaller than we would have liked—just over six pounds—but she's already dazzling everyone with her long eyelashes. Like her mom."

Josh's voice was low and throaty. Jacob figured rightly he was well fatigued after the previous night's long flight from Toronto. Somehow he doubted the guy got any sleep on the plane.

Josh was continuing. "Emily-Grace had a few tests but she's got the all-clear for handling now. Gramps and Grandma are already fighting over who gets to hold her the longest."

"Charles and Dee finally got there, then. That's good." Jacob struggled to put together thoughts that made sense. He scratched his head idly while reaching for some reason why Josh would be calling him on Jessie's phone. In the end, he simply scratched it up to his number being in her Contacts list.

"Yeah, the eagles have landed," Josh harrumphed with a grin. "We might have to go hide somewhere to get time with our own baby."

"Good luck with that. The great Charles Keating can be a brick wall."

"You don't say!" Josh's quiet chuckle was husky and tired. From his vantage point in the hall he peered inside Jessie's room to spy 'the great Charles Keating' oohhing and aahhing to an adorable little person less than a day old. "But right now his wall is all putty. Emily-Grace already has him wrapped around one of those tiny little fingers of hers."

"I bet," Jacob answered softly, rather wistfully, in fact.

Josh switched gears. He wandered off down the hall a ways, the phone to one ear and his free hand shoved in the back pocket of his black jeans. He stared at the toes of his boots as he walked. "Look, Jacob—I feel like I'm always indebted to you these days."

"My broken fingers will recover." As if to prove the point, in Miami Jacob opened and closed his hand a few times.

"No, it's more than that. I just—I don't know why I'm calling. I think it's just that I get it, you know. And I want you to know that. About me. That I get it. That I know it sucks." Josh stopped and leaned back against the wall. "I know how hard it must have sucked for you last night."

The connection was silent for a few beats. Then Jacob said abruptly, "I appreciate what you're trying to say, but I don't need your pity, Sawyer. Or your gloating mug in my brain tonight. Uhhh, I know, why don't you take a long hike off a short pier?"

"Just listen for a sec, okay? You musicians are all the same, a fella can't get a word in edgewise." Josh lifted his head, turned towards the end of the hall, and stared out a window. He had a nice view of the mountains despite the cloak of fog surrounding their snowy peaks with mystique and mystery. "I just want to say I get it. That's all. You know? Jesus, you're not easy to, like, sort of apologize to. You know that?"

In Miami, Jacob dropped down into his comfy sofa and propped his feet up on a leather ottoman. A wry attempt at a grin creased his face. "Apologize?" He was incredulous. "Man, I'm the one that got to hold her hand all night, loser."

From Vancouver came a deep sigh imbued with a heavy lack of sleep. "Ouch, that hurts."

"It's fucking supposed to."

"Jesus, Ryan. Give a fella a break. I'm trying here."

"Bullshit. You're calling because you want to know what it was like. Cause you fucking missed out on one of the most important nights of your life."

"Not the most important part."

"Yeah, you cut and run for the work part, then show up for the climax. That's your deal, Sawyer. You do the sex thing like that too? You know, skip the foreplay?"

"Christ, you can be an asshole, Ryan. I fucking had to work."

"You want the truth, then? You won't like it."

From Josh's end of the line came silence. When a small *pfffttt* entered the fray, Jacob took it as a sign to continue.

"It was surreal, Josh. You know? I mean, yeah it sucked on so many levels, but we hit this, well, zone. I think the pain got so bad she had no choice but to just go with it. And if it's the truth you want, by then my mind was either gonna snap too, or I could just go with it too, so I did, and…well, Sophie was in the room, and other people, like the Doula, who finally got her ass there, but for a while it was just me and Jessie, you know?" His voice got quieter. He could hear Josh's solemn breaths on the other end. "She knew you might not make it on time. She knew the second her water broke at the studio. At like 4 a.m., she finally stopped crying for you."

A small *uhhhh* caught Jacob's attention but, rather callously, he marched on. "Yeah, she cried for you, don't be a dick about it. But then we were just in this little bubble for a while and it was like we were in this crazy mystical dream. I'm sorry, but that's the truth." Jacob didn't add *until you got there and burst it with your last ditch whispers and your touch.*

The line was silent for so long that Jacob actually pulled the phone away from his ear to see if the timer was still going on his cell. It was.

Josh spoke slowly. "It's like the two of you are always in some kind of dream."

"What'd she say about it?" Jacob's heart quickened.

"You helped her with her breathing. You fed her ice chips."

Jacob heard Josh emit another *pfffttt* before continuing. "If you and my wife had a magical night, somehow I don't think she's going to share it with me, Ryan. She holds any cards with your name on them pretty damn close to her chest."

Her heart, you mean, thought Jacob with smug satisfaction. Out loud he said, "I just did the grunt work, Sawyer."

"The grunt work. Huh. The surreal grunt work, you mean."

"You would have liked me to lie?"

"No. I just—I don't know, it's like all of a sudden you and me are even more connected. And I'm grateful, I'm so damn grateful, for everything, but—ahh-hhh—" Josh stretched and groaned at the same time. Then he dropped his free arm from rubbing his already well-ruffled hair, and he completely deflated. He sighed. "I don't want to be connected to you, Ryan. I don't want to be grateful, I don't want to be thankful, I don't want to apologize for being so fucking jealous of you, I just want to get on with my life. With Jessie and our baby. But it looks like you now hold the key to a good chunk of the memories I should have about *my* baby's birth. You and Jessie. It's your thing. But it should be mine."

After a moment, Jacob spoke. "You hold the key to Jessie, Josh."

Considering his words, Josh answered pensively, "Sometimes. As much as a person can, I guess, with her."

"Josh…?"

"Yeah."

"She was amazing. You would have been real proud of her."

"I bet." The tired voice was quiet now, accepting. "She's quite the gal, Ryan."

"Yeah. Don't fuck it up, Sawyer."

"Why do people keep telling me that?"

But Jacob detected a hint of amusement coloring Josh's voice. He jumped in. "Because as much as I hate to admit it, I don't think she would survive losing you a second time, Josh."

"A third, actually," Josh said quietly. "Although the first time she really still belonged to Charlie."

"Ha!" Jacob couldn't help guffawing loudly at that comment, which he found totally inane.

"What?" came Josh's somewhat alarmed and mystified query.

"Well, it's just that…Jesus, Sawyer, are you ever gonna fucking get it?"

"Get what, damn it?"

Again, Jacob hesitated before answering. He dropped his feet off the ottoman and back onto the carpet, and then leaned forward and, both elbows resting on his thighs, studied the geometric pattern on the beige carpet. He was tired of having this thought constantly bam around his brain, and now he'd got himself into a corner where he had to say it. *Hell, I might as well,* he thought. He dove in, and the sorrowful words were clearly perceived thousands of miles away from where they were voiced. "From the moment she met you, she was yours, Josh. She's never been anybody else's since. Ever. And she never will be."

In the hospital hallway, Josh paused. "Okay."

Jacob knew it was all Josh could likely manage after his emotional and likely restless night and day. And now Jacob didn't see a whole lot of point in egging Josh on, too deeply, at least. Apparently the guy was already suffering enough after missing most of his wife's night of labor. He'd missed the zone, the bubble. He'd missed the magic, but Jacob hadn't. He would never, ever forget the way Jessie's pale eyes were lost in his as he counted for her, and how she responded to his coaching through the breathing exercises, and how her skin felt when he brushed his knuckles over hers…and when he let his lips linger on her forehead, or on her cheek, or on her soft, needy fingers. It was like when they played music together, or acted together on *Mystic Nights.* Regardless of Josh's presence in Jessie's life, Jacob knew there was a part of her soul that only he had access to. And he damn well knew that was why Josh was on the phone to him tonight.

But he had one more thing to say. "Doesn't mean I'm ever giving up on her, though, Josh. Ever. Don't matter if I'm always second in her eyes. She'll always be first in mine." *Take your pity and stuff it. You might need it for yourself some day.*

"You could have had her. That night at the concert—"

"Not like that. Not as your seconds. She has to come to me. I have to be her choice. Even if it means she's grieving for you. " *And,* he added to himself, *some day I will be her choice.* He didn't always admit it to himself, but Jacob felt it, intuitively. *Or maybe it's just wishful thinking*, he grimaced to himself.

Again the line was silent momentarily. "I call you to say thanks, to see what I missed out on, which, by the way, I feel shitty enough about, and you tell me she loves me and then you threaten me. Nice." Josh sank to the floor and absently scratched an itch on his cheek. "Who dropped acid in your Cheerios?"

"It was unbelievable, Josh. Last night. What you missed. The thought that I…that I might never feel that again…" Jacob didn't finish. He couldn't. Sure, Josh was tired and sorry for what he missed. But Jacob was exhausted. Of everything.

"Jacob?"

"Yeah man."

"I'm chalking this acid trip you're on up to some weird drug or lack of sleep. And I'm ending this bizarre conversation with thank you. Again."

"I'll take that kind of magic with your wife any time, Sawyer."

"I really hate you, you know. You suck."

"And by that you mean you want to hate me. But you can't. I know your type. Feeling's mutual, Josh."

"Yeah. That's what I mean."

"Tell her I say hi. Get her to call me when she's alone."

"Sure, I'll get right on that." But there was no amusement in Josh's voice. Jacob allowed himself a tiny flicker of a rueful smile.

"The gang's all arriving," Josh said definitively, "so you know, you might just have to wait." He didn't even try to hide the anger—or was it fear—in his voice.

"Then I guess I'll just take a number and get in line."

"You just do that."

"Take care of your girls, Sawyer. While I deal with the shit hitting the fan down here." Jacob's voice faded as he added an afterthought meant for himself. "Wonder what magic the writers will unleash with their messed up shooting schedule this time around."

'They'll sort it out. They always do." Josh's slurred thoughts were barely registering in his muddled brain. He was robotic, barely there.

"Good thing us guys are reliable," Jacob was muttering. "The women on *Mystic Nights* kinda suck."

In a half-hearted attempt at being amiable, Josh asked drily, "How is her highness?"

"Kelly? Happy as a clam. Michael must be a genius in bed."

"Is that the secret." Josh scowled.

Jacob stretched and yawned loudly. "He's doing something right. Kelly's been downright awesome to work with so far this season."

"I guess she just needed to get laid a few hundred times. You should try it. Just not with my wife."

Jacob ran a thumb and forefinger over the fuzz on his chin. He considered thoughtfully before replying. "I could use some cheering up."

"Jessie says you're seeing one of the female grips on the show."

"Not seeing. Sleeping with. On occasion. Is she jealous?"

"Jesus, Jacob. Go get laid already."

They signed off then, and both men paused and reflected before Josh went back into Jessie's room to snuggle his newborn and kiss his wife, and while Jacob considered texting his lady friend in the grip department of *Mystic Nights*.

The boys' tenuous relationship was odd, fraught with a dual jealousy as well as a modicum of sadness on both parts. But something had changed since the night of Emily-Grace's arrival. Josh hoped it was nothing more than a lingering ennui over Jacob's obviously surreal experience in the birthing room with Jessie, and that it would pass, and the two would settle back into their weird friendship. He didn't like Jacob's seemingly cock-sure statement that he would one day win Jessie back of her own accord. It was like the dream that kept haunting Josh. If he died…well, that would fit right in with Jacob's affirmation that Jessie would go to him, but that she would never stop loving her husband.

He shook the aberrant thought away. With the current level of exhaustion Josh was feeling, it only served to dig a bigger hole of blind white fear.

In Miami, Jacob tapped the cell absently against his cheek and considered his ability to hurt Josh when the man was already down. The guy had a new baby, with a woman who was so desperately in love with him she couldn't seem to face the man's weaknesses. So Jacob knew Josh wouldn't stay down for long—he could handle Jacob's weird thoughts. Was Josh worried? *Nah,* Jacob said to himself as he looked back at his cell and punched in his password before texting his lady friend, the grip from the show. *Not a chance. I wish.*

He felt a little bad. Just the tiniest bit. But not enough to keep him from contorting his lips into a bitter smile.

Chapter Nine

Jessie shoved a place setting aside and set Emily-Grace's carrier directly down on the table in the hotel's restaurant in Miami. She grinned at Jacob, who hadn't noticed her enter, and who jumped at the interruption to his web search for Christmas gift ideas for his dad while he waited for the enchiladas he'd ordered to arrive.

"You scared the crap out of me!" he gasped, his heart suddenly racing at breakneck speed. "What the hell were you thinking, Jessie?"

Then he eyed the carrier. Tucked sleepily inside was a perfect little bundle of joy—Emily-Grace. He leaned forward for a closer look while Jessie delicately fingered a bottom corner of the carrier and pushed it around to face him head on.

"Huh. She's a tiny little thing."

"She's a newborn. They're known to be small, you goof. But you should hear those lungs." Jessie slid up onto a high chair. "In fact," she added wryly, "I'm sure you will, eventually."

"Small but mighty, huh?" Jacob had yet to look away from the baby. He wasn't sure, but he thought he could see Jessie's pretty sea-pearl eyes peeking up at him, fringed with lovely miniature eyelashes. "You got her singing already?" He finally looked up at his good friend and co-star, only to have his heart jump again. Having a baby was good for her. Instead of the tired, over-wrought woman he left behind in Vancouver, was the peaceful, joyous Jessie whom Jacob loved deeply. She was glowing; an aura of calm bliss surrounded her and the light halter-necked tank top she wore with a rose-petaled sweater overtop. Jacob swallowed.

76

Jessie caught the look. She smiled warmly and reached out to take his fingers, before sliding off the chair and pulling him into her arms entirely. "Thank you," she breathed into his neck. When she leaned back, her eyes were misty. "You are without a doubt my best, best friend, Jacob Ryan."

His belly clenched, but the lavender scent imbued in her presence lingered, and so Jacob sucked up his usual Jessie-related angst and simply smiled back. He glanced past her.

She caught the curious look. "Josh isn't here this trip. He had to go back to Toronto. I'm just staying a few days to get the scenes they really need in the can, then I'm off to Toronto as well. And then…" She took a deep breath as she slid back into her seat and nudged her daughter around so both she and Jacob could admire her. "Then we're going to go to Peterborough, finally, to meet the long-lost family. After that, it's off to P.E.I. It looks like we'll finally get that hockey movie in the can sometime in the spring."

Frowning, Jacob watched Jessie's glow extend to the baby.

She reached out and let Emily-Grace grab one of her fingers.

"Sounds like EG will be a jetsetter at the ripe old age of…" He considered thoughtfully.

"Three weeks. Well, four by the time we get to P.E.I." Jessie grinned up at him from across the gurgling baby. "Don't tell me you've already forgotten that insane night?"

"Ha." Jacob drew a circle in the condensation puddling underneath his beer. His face flamed red. "Not likely to. I just suck at math."

"Jacob," Jessie breathed, "do you have any idea what it meant to me to have you there? Despite my screaming and hollering?"

"Hey, it wasn't me you were calling a bastard asshole for getting you into that mess in the first place!"

She laughed wholeheartedly. In a few tiny, stuttery movements, little Emily-Grace turned her miniature face towards her momma. "I did no such thing! And don't you go telling Josh that I did, either."

"How much of that night do you actually remember, Jessie?" He was teasing now, so she swatted him and grinned.

"All of it, shit-for-brains." Her smile said it all. Jessie reached across her daughter and took Jacob's hand in her own. She emitted a gentle pressure on his fingers, which he returned without losing her gaze. For a moment the magic came rushing back—not just the ethereal night at the hospital, but all of it. For both of them.

Jessie's eyes softened. "I love you like crazy, Jacob, you know that, right?"

"Course I do," he answered, lifting her fingers to once again brush his lips across them. "Hopefully enough to help me out with that new tune I want you to learn, at least."

"Emily-Grace is already a fan. We listened to your album on the jet on the way here. Let me order some dinner and then we can chill in my suite, okay?"

"Who's with you on this trip? Just Matt?"

"Heck, no. You think Deirdre would let me fly Emily-Grace out here without her? She's floating around somewhere. Charles is here too. They were meeting Martinique for dinner at some swanky place across town."

"Good, well Kelly and Michael are meeting me, so I hope you're training your daughter to handle fans. She's about to get real spoiled."

At that, Jessie glanced a little anxiously around the restaurant. Sure enough, there were folks watching them, straining for glimpses of the new little Sawyer. Jessie smiled nervously at them, and lifted a hand in greeting. Matt chose that moment to wander in, and they changed over to a larger table so that five grown-ups and one baby would have a little more space to share a meal and stories.

Matt flipped Emily-Grace's carrier around so prying eyes couldn't take photos, then he draped an arm loosely around Jessie and leaned in to remind her to be aware of her surroundings, to try not to let random people photograph her or the baby.

Somehow knowing she was the topic of conversation, Emily-Grace blew a few bubbles, accompanying them with feeble cries.

"Hmmmm," Jessie mused brightly. "Someone's saying 'attention me!'" She looked up at Jacob. Shyly, she asked, "Do you want to hold her?"

Matt watched Jacob's expression change from simple pleasure at the presence of Jessie and Emily-Grace in Miami, to one of outright fear.

"Hell, no. I don't hold no babies." The singer/actor sat straight up in his chair and leaned back, as if that slight movement could create more distance between he and this new little creature.

At that moment, Michael and Kelly wandered in arm-in-arm. Kelly ran the last few steps and stood beside Jessie, one hand on her friend's shoulder, exclaiming in awe, "She's so tiny! You couldn't even get nail polish on those fingernails, they're so small and delicate!"

Jessie laughed and lifted her daughter's arm. "Hold out your finger, Kelly."

Kelly did, and Emily-Grace wrapped the tiny aforementioned fingers around the proffered larger—and well-manicured—finger.

"Oh my Lord," Kelly exhaled. "I can't breathe. She's simply beautiful, Jessie." Glancing up at Michael, who stood quietly beside her, Kelly's cheeks turned an interesting shade of pink. She fluttered her eyelashes at him.

From the other side of Jessie, Matt grinned at his brother. "I know that look, bro."

But Michael, although obviously enchanted, was silent. He placed a hand underneath Kelly's elbow. "Come," he urged. "Sit. I'm starving."

Kelly peeked up at Jessie, a flicker of sadness creasing her face.

Jessie smiled sympathetically. They all knew Michael's own daughter was long gone, the victim of a tragic car accident, and so, if Kelly wanted children, it might take some gentle encouragement to get Michael on the same page. Jessie pictured a few interesting girl-talk chats coming her way sometime in the next few days. She whispered to Kelly before her friend eased her way around the table to sit with her husband, "He'll come around. We'll get Emily-Grace on it."

Truly, the newborn was a porcelain doll. Her tiny eyes and crinkled nose, button mouth and soft down of light hair, were enchanting. So far, Jessie and Josh found her to be even-tempered and an easy baby to care for. Even the numerous nighttime feedings were quick and almost effortless. She wasn't colicky, and liked to coo softly between gulps, so that her baby voice charmed all around her. She was getting a little frisky now, though, enough to let Jessie know she was hungry. Glancing a bit nervously in Jacob's direction, Jessie pulled a small baby blanket out of her bag and covered her chest and shoulder. Reaching up to her halter, she undid a button, and then gently brought the baby to her breast.

By the time Jessie finished feeding her infant, Jacob, too, was done his pre-ordered enchiladas. But the others were just starting on their dinners, and Emily-Grace was still a bit fussy. When Jessie's salad was placed before her, she eyed Jacob from beneath long eyelashes. She smiled, slid off the chair, and placed the baby in his arms.

"Just for a few minutes," she cooed, either to him or to the baby no one was quite sure, but he didn't protest this time and, instead, held Emily-Grace as if she were indeed a breakable porcelain doll.

Jacob lost himself in those perfect little eyes, which seemed to search his curiously. "Hey there, baby," he whispered softly, unable to look away from the sweet face he had helped nudge into the world a few short weeks ago.

Everyone at the table watched him, Matt with a restless unease because he had a sense of how Jacob would feel about this tiny child in his arms, Kelly wistfully, Michael silently and diffidently, and Jessie…well…lovingly. She couldn't help herself. Her daughter was spellbound in Jacob's arms and he, too, fell immediately in love with another Sawyer gal.

"Do you sing?" he was asking Emily-Grace as she clutched his finger and gurgled noisily up at him. "Has your momma taught you any tunes yet?"

Breathless, Jessie just watched. A moment before, her baby was fussy and unsettled. But something about Jacob had quieted her child.

"She knows your voice," she murmured, and the others at the table fell absolutely still. No one moved, and no one ate. They just watched the interplay between the three. "Emily-Grace recognizes you."

Goosebumps flitted up Jacob's arms and legs and, to his utter mortification, he felt a moistness fill his eyes. Without looking up at Jessie, he blinked it away.

Jessie continued, her eyes reflective and lips upturned slightly, thoughtfully. She tilted her head and watched the completely entranced Jacob with her and Josh's baby. "Probably from *Mystic Nights*," she suggested simply. "Or maybe from you counting her into the world, Jacob. It doesn't matter how. But she definitely knows you."

"It's the three day whiskers," Jacob managed with a croak, which almost brought Kelly to happy tears.

"It's your voice," Jessie whispered. "So gentle."

Clearing his throat then, Matt brought the table back to attention. He lifted his beer and toasted the friends gathered there. "To Emily-Grace. May she bring light and love to those around her, always."

And forever, thought Jessie, her eyes transfixed on her daughter's obvious connection to Jacob, and his to her. Josh flashed across her mind, desolate and lonely when they said goodbye earlier in the day, and Jessie absently touched her phone, which sat by her plate. She thought about texting her husband but, instead, she lifted the phone and selected the camera Ap. She aimed it at Jacob and her daughter, and froze their introduction in the annals of time.

Chapter Ten

Four days later, Matt accompanied Dee, Charles, Jessie and Emily-Grace on a commercial flight to Toronto. Charles had graciously loaned the jet to one of his producing partners, who had a sudden family emergency to attend to in Texas.

Upon arrival in Toronto, since Josh was on set, the family split up at the airport so Charles and Dee could check into their hotel and take naps before they gathered as a group for dinner, while Matt—who needed his own vehicle—took Jessie to set. Jonathon had arranged rental of a vehicle for Matt, Jessie and the baby, whereas the Keatings gratefully climbed into one of Jon's production vehicles, which he'd wisely arranged to be driven by his most dependable driver, a silver-haired hippy draft dodger from the States.

Upon meeting Charles and Dee, the man, whose name was Marco, had tipped his finger to a grungy blue bandana he wore wound around his head and over his ears, and moved to escort his tired charges to a waiting SUV, but he had to stand back and exercise patience until Dee was ready to let her new pseudo-grandbaby go off with her momma.

"We'll see you both in a few hours," Jessie was saying. "We're fine, we'll meet you at dinner."

"Don't let that baby get cold, Jessie, keep her bundled up. Don't let Josh take her hat off." Dee was adamant. In her experience with babies, which was in fact based almost entirely on Carlotta's lone grandson, certain rules applied. One was that babies must be bundled up against the cold at all times, and one was that it was okay to rock them to sleep, which worked against Jessie and Josh's attempts to create some kind of schedule for their jet setting little one.

Charles' rules were even worse—he liked to give honey or jam to small babies, applied either on the end of a finger or on a pacifier. Josh was more determined than Jessie to challenge the man on this practice, but so far the two men rarely spent time in each other's presence. Instead, Jessie had meekly reported her angst to Josh about the two times she caught Charles giving the baby honey which, she was certain, would erode the baby's teeth before they even had a chance to break through the tiny gums. The hostile reaction she got from Josh at reporting this was not something she cared to repeat, so she decided to let Charles do his thing, and not create a federal issue over it. They rarely had the opportunity to be together as a big extended family anyway, so why create unnecessary friction?

Once Charles and Dee went off in the safety of Marco's care, Jessie heaved a sigh of relief that emptied her soul right to her toes.

"Matt," she started as he grasped the travel handle on her suitcase for her while she pushed Emily Grace in the stroller, "I love them, and I know they mean well, but sometimes grandmotherly and grandfatherly wisdom—I'll just say it—gets on my nerves. Especially when it's *don't let Josh do this*, or *don't let Josh do that*. Sometimes I think I should just leave them all in one big room and let them duke it out, you know? Lock all the doors and not let them leave until they're really and truly on the same team."

"Charles and Dee are doing their best, Jessie. They know Josh always means well. They're coming around."

"Why do I sense a 'but' in there? As in 'but he better never screw up again?'"

"Because there is."

"Et tu, Brute? Jesus, Matt."

"What's done is done, Jessie. And may I remind you that what gets put on the Internet stays on the Internet. Forever. In perpetuity."

Jessie ducked around a family laden with bags on a silver cart. A young teen eyed her excitedly, and tapped her mother's arm. They approached Jessie and goggled the baby, but Matt shook his head at photos. Jessie made a face at him and posed anyway. Afterwards, they moved on down the wide hall, and Jessie rather glumly apologized to her security chief and friend.

"I'm sorry, Matt. But they looked harmless enough. And you may note

I am actually fully dressed. And, may I add, I know too damn well what happens with photos that get dumped onto the Internet."

"I know you do, Jessie, and for some reason I would think that hard lesson would help you understand that not everyone has your best interests at heart."

He stepped forward and spoke to a clerk at the car rental agency where Jonathon had reserved their vehicle. Jessie waited patiently and then, as Matt accepted the keys and signed the appropriate documents, she continued her earlier conversation with him.

"Why do I get the feeling you're not just talking about people snapping our pictures?"

Matt's stubborn silence pissed Jessie off further. In later years the two had grown close, and sometimes she even felt he was a big brother of sorts. She respected his wisdom immensely, and she worshipped Matt's gentle manner and kind heart. But sometimes her celebrity got to her, and Jessie, despite a lonely summer under the thumb of a stalker, still often went rogue and did her own thing.

"Spike," she called to Matt's back as he opened the back hatch of their rental, knowing as she did so that the nickname would irk him further, "talk to me. We're going out to Peterborough to meet an old lady and her daughter. My sister. We'll be fine."

He turned to face her, and helped her take the baby, in the carrier, off the stroller's base.

"The problem, Jessie," he declared with his Matt-like acumen, "is that you seem to forget you are no longer one. You," he nodded at Emily-Grace, who was sound asleep at the moment, "are now two. Or even three, if you want to include Josh. Which raises another point. He'll be working when you make the trip to Peterborough."

"And Charles and Dee and yourself will be at a fundraiser with Jonathon and Giselle."

"Let me correct you there, Mrs. Sawyer. Charles and Dee and myself were not invited on the Peterborough excursion."

A pout creased Jessie's lips. "I can't very well show up at my grandmother's house with Deirdre Keating in tow now, can I Matt?"

"That's fine, Jessie, I understand you're trying to keep the peace here but—"

"I'm always keeping the damn peace, Matt! Between everybody! Between Charles and Dee and my husband, for God's sake, and between Josh and Jacob, and Kelly and Jacob, although thankfully that's improved, and—"

He raised a hand to her. "Stop. I'm well aware of your role as peacekeeper. But would you mind explaining why you won't let me accompany you to Peterborough?"

"Because, Matt, I don't want them thinking I'm some sort of…well…" Her shoulders slumped, and Jessie actually stomped her booted foot and crossed her arms. She stared at Matt and willed him to understand. They were standing outside the rented SUV now, trying not to notice the stares of people wandering by, but a passing couple called out to her.

"Jessie! We love you! Congratulations to you and Josh on the baby!" Thankfully, they didn't break the rhythm of their pace, instead they strolled on by at a brisk walk, hand in hand.

Jessie looked up shyly and waved, her face blooming pink. "Thanks, guys. That means a lot." After they passed, she looked back at Matt, petulant. "I don't want them to think I'm anybody special. I'm just Emily's daughter when I'm in Peterborough. I can't show up with security."

"Jessie, you blow me away," Matt replied, aggravated and even a little cross so that his words were pitchy. "You cannot possibly expect that anybody is going to treat you anything other than like the celebrity you are."

"They're my family, Matt!"

At his incredulous, disparaging look, she cried out angrily, "Don't say it! I don't need judgment from you regarding my long-lost relatives! Or the fact I was birthed by a woman who climbed out a window to run away with the love of her life and left a teenaged daughter behind! Okay? I know what I am descended from, at least in the short term. And anyways, Evelyn is flying in tomorrow so she'll be there as well, and you've met her, Matt, and I'm sure you've run all of them through some fancy computer database back in Van, so just chill, will you? I'm going to Peterborough to meet my family, and with the exception of Emily-Grace, I'm going alone!"

"You are one stubborn—"

"Bitch? Is that it? Is that what you were going to call me, Matt?"

"Jesus, Jessie! No, for God's sake, will you relax?" He eyed the surrounding area. All seemed clear, but Matt motioned roughly for her to get in the car. She refused for the moment. She was still too riled up, and was shifting her feet and harrumphing at him. Matt added in a clipped tone, "I was going to say hormonal mother, but I suppose you can define that any damn way you want!"

"Listen, Spike. Sometimes I am amazed that you even stay on my team. Seriously. I know I'm not the easiest person to watch over. But there are limits as to how much watching over I can handle. Plain and simple."

"What, am I boring you, Jessie? You want to move to the back seat again and pretend I'm not here?"

"Oh, for God's sake! Now who's acting all hormonal?"

He pointed a quavering finger at her. "You—are not alone anymore, Jessie. You have that precious little girl to keep safe now. And you may or may not have noticed, but your husband is now a huge star. You've already got me keeping Ulysses, Dan and Susanne at arms length with the exception of big events, and now you want me to back off too!"

"Not as a friend, Matt, geez, I just need a little space here, that's all. Just so I can meet these relatives and get some sense of what kind of people they are. That's all."

"Why do I feel like you have some kind of secret agenda, Jessie?" His voice was quieter now. Matt stretched one arm out and rested it against the car's window.

Once again, she slumped. From inside the car, Jessie could hear little Emily-Grace making tiny adorable wake-up sounds, gurgles interspersed with the odd little cry.

"I just want to see what their lives are like, Matt. That's all." Extending both arms out to the sides, she started to back away. "That's all. No biggie."

His words were spoken so quietly Jessie hardly heard him. But Matt didn't look away. He held her gaze and she felt powerless to break it. Jessie swallowed and stopped backing up. Matt was saying, "You want to see what your life might have been like if you were your sister. Instead of you being you."

Shocked that he was so perceptive of her, that he knew her that well,

Jessie froze, and cocked her head before answering. A bitter taste, like blood, formed in her mouth, and she tried to swallow it down.

"Something like that," she whispered.

Matt glanced in the back seat at the baby before he spoke again. Emily-Grace was still in that not-quite-awake-but-I'll-be-hungry-and-screaming-bloody-murder-soon stage. When his gaze drifted back to Jessie, his eyes were moist and soft. "Stop trying to be someone you're not, Jessie."

"That's it? Those are your words of wisdom, Matt? I'm so moved I just wanna puke."

A hard mask washed over his face. "Get in the car," he demanded. "We'll work something out. I can follow you in another vehicle."

"No, Matt." Jessie shook her head slowly from side to side. "You're not coming."

"There's no way Josh will go for this."

"He knows me. He doesn't stand a chance. Anyways, he'll be working."

At Matt's raised eyebrows, she cut in with, "No, I'm not going to lie to him. But he won't be around to stop me now, will he, Matt?"

Their standoff ended with the baby's first real howl. Jessie closed her eyes in frustration.

"Damn it, now she's awake and we're what, forty-five minutes from the set? I'll have to feed her, Matt."

Grumping, he nodded and turned his head while Jessie climbed into the spacious back seat of the SUV and prepared to breast feed her baby. Matt flipped on the ignition and cranked up the heat to about mid-range. Jessie hollered once more to him while Emily-Grace was latching on.

"Matt, will you text Josh, please? Just let him know we're running late. Hungry gums here will be a much more amenable baby for her daddy if she gets to chow down first."

Matt didn't answer, but Jessie saw him pull out his cell phone and type in a message she presumed was to her anxiously awaiting husband. She settled in to feed her daughter while Matt stewed outside the vehicle.

He got it—he knew where Jessie was coming from, but that didn't mean he had to like it or go along with it. Matt learned his lesson the hard way the year Jessie was stalked and exited their lives for a year and a half. In those days he often got a little sulky when she pulled her disappearing acts, but after the whole Deuce McCall terror, Matt knew he could no longer let Jessie run him. Especially now, with crazy women sending Josh tweets and blogging about his 'sexy brown bedroom eyes,' and with Emily-Grace in their lives. No, Matt knew he had to plant both feet firmly on the floor when it came to Jessie's desire to run around the country without security. It was his job to protect the Sawyer family. The hard part was trying to figure out how.

After a bit, Jessie stepped out of the car and rocked Emily-Grace gently. She held the tiny child upright against one shoulder and moved slowly back and forth, singing softly to the baby in order to encourage a few good burps. Then, calling *success* to Matt, she eased Emily-Grace back into the car seat, checked to see it was secure, tucked a blanket warmly over her, and closed the back door before climbing into the front seat.

Matt slid in behind the wheel and turned the heat back down a notch before backing out of their parking space and steering the vehicle out of the airport's Parkade. Alert and cautious on the busy multi-lane Highway 401, he guided Jessie and her daughter safely to their anxiously waiting husband and father.

Chapter Eleven

"Josh, just chill! I'm not having the same argument with you that I had with Matt. And what's going on with your voice today? You're all husky."

"You know Jessie, I used to think this whole 'wanna be normal' kick of yours was kind of endearing. Now I just think it's stupid. And my voice is fine. I'm just tired. I'm not sure how much our little munchkin likes this whole hotel living thing. She's missing her view of the ocean. And late nights and early mornings and not much sleep in between makes for one tired daddy."

Josh was reclining on the lime green window seat in his suite, with his tiny daughter resting comfortably on his thighs. His hands supporting her back and neck, he couldn't take his eyes off her. She was a perfect little baby girl, all cherubic sunbeams and kitty kisses and satin ribbons and lace, just the way he pictured a baby daughter should be. Minus the frustrating lack of sleep, perhaps.

"Hey," he called to Jessie, who was pacing the room with her arms crossed and a sullen frown darkening her usually sunny countenance. "Jess. Come see. She's smiling at me."

"I don't think so, Josh. I think it's gas." Jessie wandered over, and her frown fell away. She slid down next to Josh on the wide seat and tucked one arm behind his waist. "I don't think babies really smile until they're about six weeks old."

"Who says?" He nudged his butt over to make room for his wife and spoke to his daughter in a happy voice lit from within by pure joy. "Show momma, Emily-Grace. Show her your pretty smile."

At that, lo and behold, the baby's perfect round mouth twisted a little. Her eyes lit up too, or so Josh declared to his wife.

"Whaddaya say to that, little momma? Looks a lot like a smile to me."

Jessie laughed and leaned her head against her husband's broad shoulder. She reached out to brush the back of a finger against her baby's soft cheek. Her sour mood did a turnabout as quickly as it had come on.

"She's so beautiful, Josh. Look at how unbelievably perfect our baby is."

"You got that right, little one," he agreed amicably, the earlier worries temporarily shoved aside. "We done good, you and me." He smiled at Jessie, and she rubbed her hand across and up and down his strong forearm, soaking up his energy and his essence.

"Sometimes I can hardly believe it, Josh," she murmured quietly as Emily-Grace's eyelids seemed to get a bit heavy. "There were times it seemed we would never get our shit together. And now here we are, with this amazing little bundle of beauty keeping us awake all night—"

"Stealing all our press—"

"Pooping and peeing like it's nobody's business—"

"Making your nipples red and sore—"

They shared a laugh then, and both decided they wouldn't change a thing if it meant the world wouldn't be as perfect now. After a moment, Jessie took her daughter from her husband's grasp and placed her in the carrier. She strapped her securely in so the baby could drift off to dreamland, and walked softly back to the window seat where she crouched over her husband's lap, facing him. She placed her palms on his cheeks and implored him to look at her. He had no problem complying. Josh's face lit up like a schoolboy's on Christmas morning.

"Josh, I feel like I never see you anymore."

"We were only away from each other a few days this time, Jessie."

"Well, it feels like forever. I miss this face." She smiled and leaned forward to plant kisses on his neck and to feel his hair tickle her cheek as she did so. Inhaling deeply, Jessie mumbled from beneath the layers of chestnut hair, "You smell like the man I love more than life itself."

"Little one," he murmured back, strongly approving of the tender kisses now landing on his cheek, "I've been missing you too. Come visit more often."

"I could kill Jonathon for shooting *The Wyatt Boys* here. He should be making this show in Vancouver." The series had finally received name approval from the network.

"It'd be kind of hard to shoot out the mountains, Jessie." Josh grinned as his wife's kisses landed on his lips for a few sweet moments. Then he moaned as she lifted his shirt and gave the same attention to each of his nipples in turn.

"Can we have sex yet?" he begged. "Please?"

"What's the rush, big boy?" Jessie teased as her kisses went lower. "Wanna make us another gorgeous baby?"

"Let me get some sleep tonight and then I'll think about it," was his tongue-in-cheek response. An image of the recurring dream flashed across his mind, and Josh shivered. There were two children in that strange mystical dream.

"What?" Jessie asked, letting his shirt fall back over his chest and sitting back on her haunches on Josh's lap.

"It's nothing," he said. "Just got a chill, that's all."

She eyed him suspiciously, one eyebrow raised and the frown returning. "Babe, you're not sick, are you?" She leaned her cheek in and pressed it against his. Josh smiled at the cozy feel of Jessie's face against his skin. He pulled her closer and she adjusted her position so her knees were up, toes against the wall. She held her man close to her heart. "Oh God, I love you," she whispered. "Josh, I love you so much it scares me."

Now it was his turn to frown. "No being scared allowed," he said in a guarded tone, placing one big hand against her head and drawing her lips to his. He sucked on her bottom lip, eliciting a tiny giggle, and kissed her tenderly. Josh literally ached to love her properly, but for the next few weeks Emily-Grace's birth was still playing that trump card. Jessie's body wasn't quite ready yet, although her spirit was more than willing. She unbuttoned his jeans.

"One of us can have sex," she murmured as Josh shivered again, this time in glorious anticipation.

Then a hard knock jarred them away from each other. It was accompanied by a loud bellow.

"Sawyer, git yer ass in gear! The sooner we shoot, the sooner we get home!"

"Oh, Lordy," Jessie giggled again, yanking Josh's zipper back up as far as she could. "That'd be your co-star at the door waking our finally sleeping little baby."

Josh groaned and gently pushed Jessie aside by using both hands to manipulate her biceps sideways. He leap-frogged to the door and swung it open. "Steve, you sunuvabitch, if you wake Emily-Grace you can be the one staying up with her all night cause she's off schedule."

"Oops!" Steve oozed loudly, marching into the room and leaning over the baby carrier to spy the infant snoozing contentedly away. "I still forget. Damn, she's something."

"Shhh! Damn it!" Josh kicked him lightly in the back of the shins. "Keep it down. Church voices. Like on set, y'know?"

Striding over to the sofa, he grabbed his vintage green leather jacket while Steve hopped over to Jessie and pulled her into his arms on the window seat.

"Hey, baby momma," he whispered gleefully, "this guy's cranky as hell when you're not around. Did you service him yet? I can't think of any other reason for him to be such an ass."

"Put it this way, Steve," Jessie said, giggling uncontrollably as he tickled her, "your timing is impeccable."

"Oh geez," Steve complained. 'Too damn much information, girl!" He hoisted her off his lap and bent over and kissed and hugged her affectionately as Josh stood back and took in the happy vista of his best friend, wife and new baby daughter, all in the same frame in his vision. It would have been one of life's perfect moments, should he not have to leave the two most precious of the bunch behind with the knowledge they were leaving for Peterborough imminently.

He issued his wife one last warning. "Jessie," he tried, "please reconsider. Take Matt with you, at least as a tail for you and Emily-Grace."

She stayed seated on the window seat, facing him, her hands folded delicately in her lap. "Just this once, Josh," she answered. "I swear. Okay? We'll be fine."

"Matt's got me by the balls on this one, Jessie. I can't agree to you going alone."

"I know how to drive. I GPS'd it, I know where I'm going. I'll pee before I go and not get coffee on the way. I won't stop until I get to Sara's."

"Please, Jessie. Please."

She stood then, as Steve wandered back over to the baby so he could pretend he wasn't totally eavesdropping. He bit his tongue, but he agreed with the rest of them. He supposed it was one of Jessie's charms, that she didn't realize who she had become, really, and that she might be at risk in a strange province, a strange city, and with people she really didn't know.

"I need to meet them on my own," she was saying to Josh.

Grimacing, he pulled her close to him. "Just this once," he breathed as her body sighed into his. "I would lose my mind if anything ever happened to you. Or to Emily-Grace. Even though she spits up and pees a lot. And keeps me awake."

'That won't last." Jessie's eyes twinkled. "Soon she'll be calling us names and telling us we're old-fashioned."

"Can't wait," Josh murmured adoringly, at the thought of this tiny baby growing into a petulant teenager with ideas and notions of her own. "Go pee, then. Steve and I will walk you to the car, at least."

When she ran into the bathroom for one last pee before hitting the road, Josh avoided his friend's eyes. But Steve spoke anyway.

"Put your foot down, Josh. Don't let her do this by herself."

"It's okay," Josh said quietly. "Matt and I had a chat."

"And?" Steve eyed him warily. "Doesn't look to me like it solved anything."

Josh glanced over at him then, a little red in the face. He shrugged knowingly. Steve caught on.

"Oh shit," Steve inhaled. "You're putting Matt on her anyway."

"Damn straight," Josh replied, one eye on the closed bathroom door as he picked up the carrier with his little daughter tucked safely inside. "No way am I letting her go off to some strange people's home without Matt at least eyeballing her. He rented a beige Toyota Corolla. Everybody and their dog has one of those. She won't know he's anywhere around, and if she gets into trouble he can help her out."

"You better hope she doesn't find him on her tail or both he and you will be in more trouble than anyone can help you out of."

The bathroom door opened then, so Josh was off the hook in terms of answering Steve, but in his heart he knew he and Matt—and Charles and

Dee were in on it as well—had made the right decision. Jessie was an international superstar with more eyes and long lenses on her than normal, now that she had Emily-Grace in the public's curiosity as well. He could handle the after effects if Jessie caught on and her temper flared, even if it meant the silent treatment for a bit. What he couldn't handle was losing his wife or child.

They left her in the underground parking area with hugs and gentle admonitions to be careful, and then Josh and Steve climbed into a production vehicle for their ride to set. Josh gripped his cell phone firmly in one hand, and heaved a sigh of relief when a message from Matt popped up almost immediately.

I have eyes

Interpreting that as Matt having Jessie and the baby in sight, Josh texted back.

Stay in touch when u can

He knew Matt could only text when stopped at a light, so he accepted there would be long breaks before he heard from him. Peterborough was about an hour and a half outside Toronto, maybe a bit more, depending on traffic. Emitting a low nervous whistle, Josh laid the cell phone on his lap and clutched it with one hand. His good friend clapped him on the shoulder, and the boys settled in for their ride to set.

Chapter Twelve

"Okay, little baby, let's you and me rock a little adventure."

After Jessie eased the SUV out of the hotel's underground Parkade, she pointed it towards a side street that would take her to Highway 401 east. She cranked her neck for the telltale 401 directional signs. Fingers tapping nervously on the steering wheel, she gulped a few times but relaxed when the first posted sign she saw actually seemed to put her on the same track the GPS did when she reviewed the route earlier.

"Okay GPS, I'll try to trust you," she told the automated voice of Siri, her weird iPhone vocal guide for this trip. "But don't screw up. This is not a city I want to get lost in."

A quick peek in the rearview mirror assured her that baby Emily-Grace was well secured in her carrier. Glances out of the side mirrors revealed no imminent followers, although a delivery truck for some bakery annoyed her, as it was parked on the side of the street with its four way flashers glaring rhythmically at her. Jessie had to flick on a blinker, do a quick shoulder check, and deftly dodge around it.

"Okay, baby girl, we're good," she breathed after she tucked the SUV safely back into its own lane. "No need to be nervous, just follow the signs and for the most part stay in the middle lane once I get to the 401. We'll just cruise along and listen to Jacob's album again. No hurry."

She stepped a little harder on the accelerator, leaned back in the seat, wiped a sweaty palm on her jeans, and reached over to adjust the volume on the car's entertainment system. Her iPhone was plugged into the auxiliary port, and Jacob's voice rang out.

"Oops, a bit too loud for little baby ears, huh, Emily-Grace?" One finger deftly tapped on the volume and Jacob serenaded them a bit more quietly.

The song was a rare type of ballad now taking over radio airwaves in droves. Jacob's dusky voice and soothing melody, combined with Charles Keating's flair for the sneaky extras in production—like sweet escalating violins and soothing, punctuating auxiliary percussion—resulted in immediate and gratifying Top 40 success. As a songwriter and singer herself, Jessie appreciated the finer details of the recording, with which she'd had some input in terms of guitar nuances and background vocals, but it was Jacob's lyrics that held her hostage every time she got the chance to listen to the song in private, or away from Josh.

Jacob's music was real; he sang about the truths in his life, one of which was his time in Scotland with his Annie, and their friends John-Paul, Charlene and Katrine. This particular ballad was Jessie's favorite on the album. It referenced a sacred time together in simple, perfect harmony, and even mentioned her small flat in Edinburgh, and 'you' who was now nothing more than 'a wistful trail of smoke'. Jessie actually laughed when she heard that lyric for the first time. She'd had to clap a hand over her mouth and give pouty Jacob an extra big hug. They'd had many arguments over their bad smoking habits, weed included, and although in that old life it seemed like she was a whole other person (and, in many ways, she was), she found the reference to their smoking rather amusing. It certainly wasn't what she would have chosen to remember about Annie Hayden and the intense searing passion of loving Jacob Ryan.

She did get a kick out of how Jacob, in the song, referenced Jessie giving her flat to someone new. He was eulogizing and memorializing their treasured time—which was also a sad time, filled with longing and deception—in Edinburgh. Through the ballad, he was trying to let go. In reality, when she left Charleston after her concert there, with Josh's engagement ring finally twinkling happily on her left hand once again, Jessie paid the rent out on the flat for five years. And she gave the lease to Charlene.

At any rate, Jessie mellowed when she listened to Jacob sing, and the touching ballad served to steer her safely out onto the 401 and towards a new chapter in her life, one which would also include new-olds yet again, for better or for worse.

As she cruised along, she lost herself in memories of the past, chiding herself for listening to Jacob's beloved love letter ballad over and over again, but she couldn't help herself. Each time it ended, with a honeyed woeful definitive final chord, her finger darted out to the iPhone, and she hit the 'back' arrow so the song would have no choice but to repeat.

～ ～

In Peterborough, Sara was sitting in the stands at the rink with a Venti Starbucks caramel macchiato clutched in one gloved hand. She was sipping at it fretfully, and when it was gone, she tipped the paper cup up until it was completely upright, and pretty much sucked out the last drop. She held onto the cup until her youngest son Ren scooted by during one of his trips around the rink looking for stray hockey pucks, and then she grabbed his arm and deliberately handed it to him.

"Ren, drop this in the compost on your next trip by, please."

"Okay, Mom," he answered agreeably before proceeding to drop two cold black rubber pucks in her ample lap. "Hang onto these for me."

He was about to take off, when he remembered something. "When's your sister coming? After lunch or before?"

"Hush, Ren. She's supposed to be here at two."

"Is that before or after lunch?"

"After, if we're quick. During, if your brother's slow getting his skates off. And if your dad talks too much after practice."

Ren seemed happy with that news, so he skipped off down the row of seats with his mom's empty white Starbucks cup. Sara cocked her head and listened to him hum his way down the row until he was out of range. He was small for his age, and hockey, especially as he got older and had to play against larger boys, was often a tough and unforgiving sport. Maybe music would be more his thing…she shook her head and the thought immediately fragmented and disappeared.

"You've got a sister coming to visit?" The friendly query was spoken by Sara's best friend, a quickly diminishing 'because-I-just-joined-a-gym' rather perky bleached blonde, Crystal. Who had a ways to go in the diminishing department, but whose commitment and positive self-esteem Sara unequivocally admired.

Sara bristled at the question, which was spoken freely and casually. "A half-sister," she responded tightly, not offering any further information on what she considered a taboo subject, even with a good friend who brought you wine when you were obviously depressed, and you were ready to slit your throat with your son's 'for decoration only' samurai sword.

"I didn't know you had a sister."

"Half-sister," Sara repeated with more emphasis than was necessary. She strained her eyes towards the ice surface, where her coach husband was genially pulling a couple of tussling eleven-year-olds apart. "They all think they're Dion Phaneuf," she said idly, trying to throw Crystal off the scent of what would surely be the gossip of the year, should the famous Jessie's presence in their small city become inadvertently known. "Practice must be intense today if they're fighting each other." She squinted. One of the boys was her older son. "Hmmm."

"Where's she from?"

"Huh?"

"Your sister."

Sara closed her eyes in frustration. "My *half-sister* lives in Vancouver. She's in Toronto with her husband, who's here on business."

"You must be excited! Let's have a girls' night. I'll bring the wine."

"She's only staying for a few hours, and not likely drinking these days anyway. She has a newborn."

"A baby! It's been ages since I've seen a newborn. Come on, Sara, invite me over."

"The thing is, Crystal." Sara fidgeted in her seat and glanced across the ice to the opposite bleachers where Ren's butt was stuck up in the air as he bent over a seat apparently trying to reach for something, likely another stray puck. "I've never met this woman. My aunt contacted my grandmother and myself ages ago, saying she wanted to meet, but neither of us was really up for it. But apparently today's the day."

"Why wouldn't you want to meet a sister?" Crystal asked in her forthright manner, eyebrows knitting together in curiosity. "Who wouldn't want more family? And a new baby?" She elbowed her friend, who jumped. "Think of it. More birthday and Christmas presents."

"You know the old saying, every family has skeletons in their closets. Well, she's ours."

A tinny laugh reverberated throughout the stands. "You make it sound like she's connected to the mafia or something! What is she, an axe murderer?"

Sara sighed hopelessly. "We're just not exactly running in the same social circles, that's all. And besides, our mother chose her years ago. Not me. So why would I want to meet someone I've pretty much hated from the time she was born? I was fourteen. Don't bother doing the math, Crystal. Let me just say there have been hard feelings for what feels like a lifetime."

Crinkling her pretty rose-colored cheeks, Crystal thought hard. "We definitely need to have that wine. Why is all of this suddenly a surprise to me? Your best friend?"

"Some things are better left swept under the rug for the mice to munch on, Crystal. Can we just leave it alone now?"

And they would have left it at that, at least until the next occasion which would have seen Crystal bring a bottle of wine to Sara's door, when Ren ran back up towards them.

"Here's another one, Mom." He deposited his latest treasure on his mother's lap. Leaning both hands on her knees, he searched Sara's eyes. "Is the baby a boy or a girl?"

"Ren, honey," Sara glanced sideways at Crystal, who was listening intently. She sighed and gave up. "It's a girl."

"What's her name?"

At this, Sara sucked in a breath. It resulted in a low whistle. She exhaled slowly and maintained eye contact with her son. Her words were almost inaudible, and were spoken with a measured caution. "Her name is Emily-Grace, Ren."

"Emily-Grace?" asked Crystal, searching her brain for where she'd heard that rather unusual name before. "You're not talking about Sophie Gregoire, are you? Justin Trudeau's wife?"

"No," corrected Sara. "Their daughter is Ella-Grace. And she's not a newborn, Crystal. Do you ever listen to the news? Or read Chatelaine?"

"Her name's Jessie," jumped in Ren, helpfully. "My mom's sister. She's a singer. And she's on TV, too."

At that declaration, Crystal almost fell off her seat. "Jessie? Jessie Wheeler? Who is married to Josh Sawyer? You've got to be kidding me!"

"Would you mind for once keeping your voice down?" Sara spit between clenched teeth. "I don't need the whole goddamned rink showing up at my place today!"

"How could you keep this from me? Were you even going to invite me over to meet her? And, like, the most famous freaking baby on the planet right now?"

"Mom, you swore." Ren was downcast.

"I'm sorry, honey. I did. That was careless of me." Sara gathered her youngest in her arms and breathed in his little boy scent of post-hockey practice sweat and bubble-gum.

To her friend, she said, "Crystal, I have no idea what to expect from Jessie. For all I know she'll sweep in with some huge entourage, wave a few manicured fingernails at me, get a picture for Entertainment Weekly, and basically just suck the life out of me. All, may I add, in my 1100 square foot townhouse with its loose stair rail and moth-eaten couch. We eat in the kitchen, or haven't you noticed."

"Honey," Crystal responded kindly, touching her friend's elbow as Ren took in his mother's seedy impression of the only home he knew, "lots of people eat in their kitchens. At least we're not eating on mud floors. Or haven't *you* noticed?"

"I know, Crystal. I know. I appreciate what I have, I swear, but sometimes..."

"Sometimes you just want more."

"Does that make me a bad person?"

"I think it makes you a very human person. Whose kids adore you, by the way. Moth-eaten couch and all. Don't you, Ren?"

The little guy, who was still wrapped up in his mother's arms, looked up at his mom with a big, wide, toothy grin. "I love you, mom." He squeezed her as tightly as he could, which elicited a joyful laugh from his stressed and worried mother.

"Thanks, buddy," she chuckled, delivering a kiss on top of the messy hockey helmet hair. "I love you, too."

The buzzer went, then, ending the practice, and the women watched in silence as the ice surface emptied its players through a door someone yanked open in the boards. Ren ran along the row and hopped down the stairs to join the older boys, as well as his dad, in the dressing room.

"You can come by if you want to," offered Sara softly, putting her hands in her pockets as, on the ice, the Zamboni started up with a loud roar of its engine.

"Why, so you can hide behind me?"

"What are best friends for?" asked Sara with a small smile. She looked at her friend. "I mean it, Crystal, there's a whole history here that I had hoped to just not dredge up, but all of a sudden it's staring me in the face, and all it's succeeding in doing is reminding me how much I hate my life. Myself, in fact."

"Oh, honey," Crystal soothed, wrapping an arm around Sara. "You just need to put your record on a new loop. You're such a good mom to those boys. And your husband worships you."

"That would explain why he's always lost in conversation with Lorraine Allevante. Because he worships me so much."

"All of our husbands are always in conversation with Lorraine Allevante." Crystal gestured comically towards her own generous bosom. "If I wore these girls in the kind of low cut sleazy slingshots she wears, they'd be wanting to chat me up too!"

Slowly, the women extricated themselves from their seats at the rink. "You'd better give me about an hour with Jessie first, okay? If she stays that long."

"Is your grandmother coming over?"

"No, I'm supposed to take Jessie and the baby over to her sometime in mid-afternoon. My Aunt Evelyn is visiting with her today. They haven't seen each other much, either, so I guess they're having their own little reunion first."

"So is, uh, Jessie, is she, uh, coming alone? Besides the baby, I mean?"

"I'm sure she'll have her whole kit and caboodle with her, Crystal. But if you're asking about Josh Sawyer, I honestly don't know. I think he may be working, which is why she's taking the time to come out in the first place."

At her defeated look, Sara laughed lightly and loosely hugged her friend. "Don't worry. If I ever hear that he's decided to come around, I'll be sure to invite you over. You can crush on him, but I suppose it'd be a little weird for me to, huh? To crush on my half-sister's husband?"

"Happens all the time, hun!" Crystal winked. She elbowed Sara again lightly. "You think you've got it hard. What must it be like to be married to a man the whole world wants in their bed?"

Sara glanced down the stairs at a cluster of people gathering below, one of whom was her husband, Kevin, who was now standing there chatting with the father of one of the players. Kevin's hands were resting gently on his and Sara's sons' tousled heads.

"I think it would actually suck," she agreed in a subdued voice.

"Yes. So do I," concurred Crystal. "And that, my friend, is what you need to have running around that dim-witted head of yours when you greet this long-lost sister at your door."

"Crystal?"

"Yep?"

"Half-sister," Sara reminded her. "She's only a half-sister."

The women stepped lightly down towards their waiting families, and then, all too soon in Sara's books, it was time to go.

Chapter Thirteen

Matt managed to find a parking space before Jessie pulled into the driveway of the cute townhouse on Eagleview Drive. There was a strip mall not far down the road. He could see Sara and Kevin Lawrence's home from his discreet spot behind a large blue metal waste bin. He watched as Jessie drove slowly up in front of the house, overshot the driveway, and backed up on the quiet street. She turned the wheel to the left then, pulled in behind an ancient Dodge truck, and apparently sat for a minute before opening the door.

The mostly residential area was quiet. Nobody rushed to greet Jessie, even though she was expected.

Matt was relieved to see only a usual number of vehicles in the area. He had already driven out to Peterborough to scout the neighborhood. His reconnaissance mission was carried out early that morning before Jessie was likely even out of bed; the area didn't appear any different now than it did at the time, other than the number of middle class vehicles parked in driveways, whose owners mostly had them parked securely at work now, or were off running errands in them.

Leaning back now, watching Jessie, Matt was interested to note that she seemed so intent on this meeting she appeared to have forgotten to look around her for signs of him, or anyone else for that matter who may be suspicious or curious or just plain simply following the rented SUV.

At the house, Jessie took a deep breath and wiped both sweaty palms on her jeans. The townhouse was cute—grey brick on the bottom and cream vinyl siding on the second level, with a garage to the left of Sara's home, which was mirrored by her corresponding neighbor's home on the far right.

A short ceramic block walk led to the center front door, which was reached by two cement steps and bordered by skinny iron rails with decorative twisted posts. Wooden flower boxes adorned the main floor windows, albeit they were overflowing with the crispy remains of some kind of colorless long-dead flower, since it was now December.

It was cold, and Jessie'd shrugged off her thin fall leather bomber jacket in the car, not that it was very well equipped for this kind of cold anyway, although she found it useful on her shuttles between the moderate climate of Vancouver and the hotter, dry Miami. Regardless of its lack of warmth, she reached in, pulled it out, and zipped it up. Glancing nervously at the now waking baby, she fought the urge to drive away and feed Emily-Grace before the hungry demanding 'feed-me's' started. Instead, double-checking to be sure she had her keys, Jessie gently closed the driver's door and strolled cautiously towards the house door she figured the family used most often, the one between the garage and the main part of the home.

Tentative, she knocked.

A young boy instantly pulled the door open and grinned at her. He raised a hand in greeting. "Hi," he said amicably.

Jessie inhaled. Both hands were now moving just a bit up and down her hips, clammy and anxious. "You must be Mark," she managed, eyeing the cute pixie nose and happy eyes. "Aunt Evelyn told me about you." Inside, she thought, *oh shit, he's blood related. To me.* It was a rush.

"Nah," the boy answered. "Mark's my brother."

"Ah. So you're Ren. Hmm?" She smiled. The kid was leaning against the exterior storm door, with one foot on its bottom edge that made it move and creak. Jessie's breaths were all in the top part of her chest. She purposefully tried to exhale more deeply so her words wouldn't come out sounding all weird and scared.

The little guy helped her out. Opening the door wider, he looked towards her car. "I'm just wondering if you brought the baby."

"Ah. Do you like babies?"

"I don't know. Maybe. I don't really know any."

"Well, I did. I brought the baby. I should maybe go get her. It's cold. Ummm…" Jessie looked past him inside the house where she could hear low muffled voices punctuated by the clanging of dishes. "Is your mother home?"

Just then Mark came skidding up behind his brother. He was a handsome kid topped with longish surfer hair and two dimples that framed a curious mouth, also supremely confident, it appeared. He reached out a hand to Jessie.

"Hey," he said in a friendly welcoming way as she accepted the smallish but strong hand and shook it with a smile. "My friends at school want me to ask when you'll have a new record out."

"Mark!" griped Ren with a sudden downturn of bossy small boy roguish lips. "Mom said you weren't supposed to tell anybody she was coming!"

"They don't believe me anyway," Mark rebutted, grinning playfully. "But I guess I wanna know."

"I'm not sure right now," Jessie answered him honestly. "I'm just doing music on a TV show right now." Shivering, she tossed a look back over her shoulder at the cooling car, where her baby was likely starting to wail.

"Yeah, *Mystic Nights*," pronounced Mark. "We're not allowed to watch it, but our mother does."

"Um, Mark, is your mom—" Jessie heard footsteps behind the oldest of Sara's boys. Looking up, she spied a man whom she figured rightly was Kevin, the boys' dad and Sara's husband.

At Jessie's rather anxious look, he smiled apologetically. "I'm sorry. Sara insisted on making sure the lunch dishes were cleaned up and stashed in the cupboards before we allowed you into our humble castle. You are quite obviously Jessie. It's a pleasure to meet you."

The man had kind eyes. Jessie's tense shoulders lowered a bit.

Kevin peered over her shoulder. He wrinkled his eyebrows. "I'm not sure what I expected, but I thought you might have some kind of entourage with you." Straightening, he looked at her curiously.

"I do, actually," Jessie answered.

"Hmm, thought so," Kevin responded, peeking over Ren's head to gaze up and down their street. "Your clan must be hiding."

"It's an entourage of one," Jessie declared, wiping both palms on her thighs. "And she's likely screaming bloody murder right now. It's just about feeding time. She's a rather demanding little thing."

105

"The baby's in the car?" Kevin didn't hesitate. He went right out in sock feet, followed by his boys, and stared into the tinted window of the SUV. He looked over at Jessie. "Can I get her for you?"

"Can you feed her?" Jessie laughed. "No, I guess not. Feed her, I mean. Sure, go ahead." She smiled at the boys and raised her hands to cover both ears. "You might want to protect your hearing."

As the guys fiddled with the baby, Jessie heard quiet footsteps land behind her. She turned, and stared into the pretty pale green eyes of her sister. Neither woman had a clue what to say or how to react. Finally, they just resorted to a simple handshake.

"Hi," offered Jessie, shoving her hands in her pockets and trying to tune out her baby's high-pitched wails.

"Hi," responded Sara, not smiling. She looked over at the car. "Someone's hungry?" She, like her husband, also glanced up and down the street. Down the street, she spotted the beige Corolla, but immediately dismissed it as having anything to do with Jessie. "Where's all the hype? Photographers and such? I thought you celebrity types always capitalized on dreary real-life drama."

"Sara," chided Kevin gently as he passed by her with the baby carrier in one hand and a diaper bag in the other. The brothers followed, silently eyeing their mother in confusion.

Jessie's heart sank. She hadn't expected miracles, but she was hoping for some level of genial cordiality, at worst. This woman was defensive and, apparently, somewhat hostile.

She raised and lowered both shoulders slowly. Still standing outside the home, she was starting to shiver. "I just wanted to come alone, Sara. I wanted to keep this on the down-low, you know?" Searching her sister's eyes for some sign of reticent truce, she quickly realized, as her heart sank, that it wasn't forthcoming.

"I see," bit off Sara. Shrugging, she stood in the middle of the doorway, blocking Jessie's access to both warmth and to her crying infant. "Better to keep us in the shadows. It's my understanding you have enough scandal to deal with."

Jesus, Jessie mumbled under her breath. *Well, won't this be fun?* Josh's voice echoed through her brain. *You might not like what you find, little one.*

"What's scandal, mom?" Ren peeked out from underneath his mom's elbow. "Dad says let her in, her baby's giving me and Mark earaches."

Swallowing past her fear and a growing unease, Jessie clenched her belly and forced threatening tears to dissipate or, if not go away altogether, at least not release their fury and hurt in the presence of this small family and its unwelcoming matriarch.

Sara moved aside, and Jessie slipped indoors.

Kevin, at least, was a gracious host. He had already removed Emily-Grace from her carrier and was holding her gently against his body, moving rhythmically, which seemed to have at least temporarily eased the infant's desperate cries. At the defeated expression inherent in Jessie's pale eyes and crushing her earlier hopeful discourse, he smiled genuinely. "She's beautiful," he said, nodding at the baby's light downy hair. "So I know where the name Emily came from. How about the Grace part?"

"Josh's mom," answered Jessie gratefully. "Her middle name was Grace."

"They sound pretty together," Kevin remarked truthfully, eyes drifting up to his wife who, he noted, was still not engaging in any polite social graces.

"And your boys are Ren for—" Jessie struggled to maintain conversation, although she really just wanted to grab her baby and slink back to Toronto to face everyone's *I told you so's* with some modicum of apologetic grace and dignity.

"Ren is for our first movie date, when we were kids," offered Kevin.

"Footloose. Lucky kid."

"Kevin Bacon," came a cool voice from behind Jessie. "I suppose you know him."

Jessie twisted around. "Only in passing," she mumbled to Sara.

"And Mark?" she asked Kevin over her shoulder while eyeing her half-sister. "I can't think of any famous Marks right now."

"No, you wouldn't know this one," cut in Sara hotly.

"Sara, easy," was Kevin's easygoing warning to his wife.

"Mark was named for my father."

At that, Jessie's lips curved downwards as she straightened her hips to better face Sara square on. "Sara," she started, finally finding some energy with which to battle this obviously pissed off woman, "I need to feed my daughter. Then can we maybe have a cup of tea and a chat? Please?"

Sara's cheeks flushed pink, and she bit her bottom lip. Then she stared hard at her guest. It was at that precise moment that she caved a bit, and saw at least part of Jessie's side of this whole weird equation, an equation that, essentially, neither had procured for themselves. So she did what Jessie always did. She recognized a woman in pain, and responded to that growing awareness.

"You can feed her in our bedroom," Sara said quietly, her feeble attempt at some kind of meeting-in-the-middle. "Up the stairs and to the right. You'll see it."

"Thank you," Jessie breathed. She bit her lip too, before turning and accepting the baby from Kevin's arms. She couldn't help but smile at him. "She likes you."

"All the girls do," he snapped off amicably, grinning, although the grin quickly faded with the death ray glare sent his way from his wife.

Tucking the diaper bag over one shoulder, Jessie made her way upstairs for some privacy to feed and change her daughter, while Sara turned to the kitchen and the boys to their PlayStation.

As Sara filled the kettle, she palmed her forehead.

"What?" queried Kevin, coming up behind her and wrapping his arms around his wife's round waist. "She seems sweet, Sara. Give her a chance, will you?"

"I forgot about the stupid curtains," she moaned in response.

"What curtains?"

"In the bedroom. We never got new ones. The ones on the window are the ones that were here when we moved in."

He paused before answering. "Somehow I doubt she'll even notice, Sara."

"Kevin." Turning, she pushed him away. "They don't match. They've never matched. They look awful. Now go keep your boys quiet and let me get through this god-awful day, okay?"

Whipping back around, she finished filling the kettle, then plugged it in. When Kevin left the kitchen, Sara was standing at the sink with her back to him, head hanging down, one arm on the edge of the sink for balance, the other trembling on the handle of the kettle.

Chapter Fourteen

*I*n the upstairs bedroom, the first thing Jessie noticed was the mismatched curtains. Did she care? Nope. Something about them warmed her heart. In fact, something about the entire townhouse warmed her heart. Maybe it was the distressed wooden *faith, hope, love* signs on the living room wall downstairs, maybe it was the Toronto Maple Leaf comforters on the brothers' beds (she couldn't resist peeking in on her way by), or maybe it was the way Kevin seemed to rest his hand on his boys' heads when they were standing at the door. *It certainly isn't Sara, at this point*, Jessie told herself under her breath, before quickly scolding her brain for thinking such a thought about the half-sister she just met.

"Yes, yes, little nipple monster, I hear you, momma hears you. The whole neighborhood hears your fiery little temper. Give me a second, okay?"

Dropping the diaper bag on Sara and Kevin's queen bed, Jessie laid the baby gently in the middle of their duvet, and gently tugged off the baby's warm one-piece Sherpa bunting. All pink, with pop up ears and embroidered feet, and lined with jersey fabric, the tiny outfit was toasty warm but maybe a bit too much for the house, although Jessie half considered leaving it on her daughter in case they had to make a quick exit.

Underneath, Emily-Grace was dressed in a matching peach and grey jersey print dress and cardigan, which Jessie had fastened that morning at the neck. Her little white tights and leather slippers capped off the outfit, which Jessie thought was adorable on the baby and perfect for meeting a whole new part of her family.

"Half the fun of having you is all the cute little clothes, isn't it, Little Miss

Sawyer? Although your daddy would say the fun is in trying to make you smile, I think." She took Emily-Grace's tiny feet in her fingers and tapped them together, which did seem to make the baby almost smile in between wails. "Okay, let's feed you. And then I can text your daddy and tell him we are doing just fine on our own."

The bedroom was large enough for a white wicker rocking chair in one corner. Scooping up her precious bundle and tiptoeing over to it, Jessie settled on its edge and arranged Emily-Grace against her breast. Leaning back, she let out a breath and looked around.

The room was tidy and rather pretty despite the mismatched curtains. The duvet was a light beige but was covered in tiny pretty pink and green flowers. There were teddy bears leaning on the pillows; Jessie's heart lurched at one, which resembled her own battered armless Tedsy. She wondered if both bears were gifts from their mother, Emily, although Sara's appeared newer and certainly wasn't missing any important appendages.

On the nightstands were the usual accouterments of living—clock radios on each, books on one, and a messy pile of magazines on the other. The larger dresser was obviously Sara's, it contained earrings and rings and brooches; the smaller one must be Kevin's. A family picture rested on it, surrounded by lots of odds and ends like change and packaged soaps and, oddly, what appeared to be a cute white-chocolate sheep in a sheer plastic boxy package.

When Emily-Grace was settled, munching and gurgling in contentment, Jessie pulled her iPhone from the pocket of the leather bomber, where she'd placed it earlier, and she balanced it in one hand while she texted Josh.

Safe and sound ur baby has crazy vocal range

In less than ten seconds, her phone bleeped. "Ha. Daddy must have been practically sitting on his phone," Jessie told her precious daughter. She read the text:

We're keeping her out of the biz glad u got there ok

Jessie chuckled at Josh's response. *I agree, no biz for EG I kinda like this whole normal family thing* was her text back to him.

In a moment her screen lit up again. *R u ok*

Softening at her husband's worry, she wrote back *Sara not so happy but hubby & boys sweet, feeding EG now will see how it goes*

She waited a moment before sending a second note. *C u soon luv u will text when I leave for TO*

K Jess luv u back drive safe precious cargo

When Emily-Grace finished feeding, Jessie burped her before changing the baby's diaper. Sara ducked in once, her eyes trying not to dart towards the mismatched curtains.

"Have everything you need?" She wasn't exactly Miss Congeniality, but she was kind enough to check in, was Jessie's interpretation of the quick visit.

"I'm fine Sara, thank you so much," Jessie said kindly in response, before finishing her duties with the baby.

Downstairs, she handed her daughter over to Kevin. "Go wild," she suggested, resisting the urge to hug him for his simple acceptance of her as well as the warm reception he was offering in contrast to Sara's reticence. Then she ducked into the kitchen to see about this half-sister of hers while Kevin sat on the carpeted floor with his kids, the baby on his lap and the boys ogling her closely between the driving game they were manipulating on the PlayStation.

"I have chamomile, lemon zest, and green tea," was Sara's way of offering Jessie a choice of beverage.

"Lemon zest," answered Jessie quietly. "Thanks."

Once the tea was poured, the women settled on the edge of chairs at the round table in Sara's kitchen. An awkward silence reigned until Jessie finally said, "It's pretty here, Sara. Your house."

Sara chose not to respond to that comment. Instead, she eyed a stain on the floor she'd missed when she mopped it early that morning before the family's trek to the rink.

She looked up. "Jessie, I admit you're not exactly what I expected, but I still think you should know I'm not all that interested in getting to know you."

"Ouch," replied Jessie, wrapping both hands around the steaming cup. "Don't hold back, Sis. Tell me how you really feel."

"I'm pretty certain you can take a stab at how I really feel. And please, let's leave the sister thing out of this. Shared blood in one's veins does not make you any more my sister than Katy Perry. I think Emily made that decision for us."

"Sara, do you ever think Emily had reasons for doing what she did?"

"Leaving a fourteen year old behind? Sure. I was a bitch."

"You were fourteen," Jessie offered in an attempt at understanding. "But your dad—"

"My dad's heart was broken. The woman he loved was in love with someone else. Someone who got her pregnant. He knew he was losing her."

"That's no reason to confine someone against her will."

"Look, Jessie. I don't want to get into the ins and outs of why Emily left us, my dad and I. And I can't say that having one of the reasons here in my kitchen—hell, on the radio, on TV, in the news, staring me in the face from behind her $ 23 000 engagement ring and $ 5 000 jacket—helps in any way to eradicate a past I'd just rather forget." Sara's voice was steady, but her fingers were trembling against the teacup. She glanced out to the living room, where the men in her family were quite happily playing with the baby, who was cooing delightedly back at all the attention.

Jessie followed her gaze. Shuffling in her seat, she switched gears. "Kevin's great with kids."

A heavy sigh preceded Sara's remark. "Yes, as I often hear." At Jessie's curious look, she added, "He coaches their hockey teams. Both of them."

"You're busy, then."

"We are, yes. We live at the rink in the winter, and on the soccer field in the summer."

"Oh. That's nice." A wistful tone edged Jessie's voice.

"What?" asked Sara. "Not exciting enough for you?"

"Um, no," responded Jessie, confused at the hostile tone aimed in her direction. "I just don't know if that's something Josh and I will ever get, you know? The regular stuff. Like him coaching our kids in sports, or hanging out at the rink."

"Oh, so you're not counting the Keating box at the Vancouver Canucks games?" Sara's bitchy side was escalating again.

Regarding her closely, Jessie melted a little. "That's not really fair, Sara." Her voice remained even, and it still contained genuine warmth. She swallowed. "You have no idea what my life is like."

"Sure I do," bellowed Sara then, waving an arm in the air to accentuate her point. "The whole world does! Uh," she started to count on her fingers, "pot smoking, glamorous parties, designer gowns, Tiffany jewelry, Oscars, let's not forget those, um, jetting around the world, hanging out with the rich and famous…what's not to know?"

"Hard work, egos and princess tempers, constant security—"

"Speaking of which, I do admit I'm surprised you're here alone."

"I had to beg everyone to let me come alone. My life isn't my own, Sara. It's all at the beck and call and management of others."

"Yes, others, and by others I assume you are referring to the Keatings, is that right?"

In a subdued voice, Jessie responded with a solo, "Mostly. Yes."

"So this Deirdre I've read about is, like, your adopted mother or something. And her husband is not only your producer, he's, like, your adopted father."

"They've been good to me, Sara. For a long time now. And I haven't always reciprocated their kindnesses. I'm lucky to have them."

"I'll say. You traded up. Good old Emily must be thrilled."

"Jesus, Sara. Is this really necessary? Why can't we just get to know each other? Start from scratch?"

"Because, Jessie. Because we can't. Because there is no starting from scratch for us. I see you as a spoiled princess, right from the get go. From the time our mother conceived you, in fact. With some low rate starving musician."

"Owww. Fuuuccck, Sara. Really."

Sara's chair scratched eerily as she backed it up and stood. "You got her, Jessie. You got our mother. In fact, you got everything. Money, fame, success…the perfect rich and powerful pretend parents, you got—"

"Yes, I got everything, Sara. But what did our mother bring me? What did success bring me? Obviously you saw the Shawna Coupland interview. What did I get by being Emily's daughter? I got a step-monster replacement father. And then I got a stalker who—. I don't want to go there with you, not right now, Sara. But suffice it to say I got a Charleston snake by the name of Deuce McCall. And right now, less than outstanding photos of me are all over the Internet. You know something else, Sara? For a long time I had nobody. No friends. Until *Drifters*, until…until I met Josh. So you should rethink how great it was that I got Emily. Because, believe me, she was no picnic, and she sure as hell didn't lead me to any greater glory. What I have now, I got on my own. And through the pure luck of being in the right place at the right time. *Not* because of her."

Jessie was standing now, too, and despite her wishes to remain civil and calm during this first auspicious meeting between sisters, she lost control. Her bullets were aimed right back at the contentious Sara, at a volume which startled the happy gamers and baby googlers in the next room.

Kevin made his way slowly into the kitchen, and handed Jessie her daughter.

"Ladies," he reprimanded. "Big ears on small pitchers." He nodded towards the living room.

"Oh shit, Kevin. I'm sorry." Jessie pressed a palm to her forehead, then snuggled her daughter close. "I just—I get this a lot, you know? The whole, 'God, it must be great' thing. But I never chose this life. I want—what you guys have."

"What we have? You've got to be joking." Sara refused to look at her husband, which was good, because if she did she would see a great hurting shadow flit across his kind face. "What we have is debt up the yin-yang, old furniture, and a truck about to disintegrate into a pile of rust!"

"Seems to me you have two amazing kids and a husband who cares enough to be involved in their lives."

"Humph." Crossing her arms, Sara trained her gaze on the kitchen window. Kevin looked too, in time to see Crystal's Mazda sedan pull up and park on the street in front of the house.

"Boys," he called to his kids. "Time for us to go get ice cream." Shooting Jessie an apologetic look before leaving the kitchen, he didn't meet his wife's eyes.

The jovial Crystal was a handful of 'don't-get-me-started' and 'tell-me-everything.' Jessie actually enjoyed bantering with her, and in some respects they connected in the way Jessie hoped she and Sara would. But Sara remained quiet and watchful, although the bitterness edging her voice earlier was now relegated to the occasional *hmmmpfh*.

Crystal no sooner admired the baby and had her tea than she hit Jessie with the first question, which was fired upon Jessie just as its object sent Jessie a text.

The question was not disguised in any way. It was a plain and simple, "What's he like?"

The text was more curious. It read *so who all is there?* Jessie narrowed her eyebrows as she stared at the small screen.

Crystal jumped in, with a hand on Jessie's elbow accompanied by an apology. "Oh, I'm sorry. That's a bit too forthright, isn't it, hun? I'm just curious. We all are. He's so damn sexy."

Her face blooming red, Jessie texted Josh back while, at the same time, smiling widely at the vociferous Crystal. The text read *boys left, Sara's friend Crystal arrived.*

Unbeknownst to Jessie, Matt, in the beige Corolla down the road, was soon momentarily appeased. He relaxed again, and texted Josh back *tks.*

Jessie had to answer Crystal. But it was easy. She loved to talk about her husband, and it showed. Thoughtfully, she ran a finger over her top and then bottom lip, and touched Crystal's arm the same way the woman had touched her. Somehow, the gesture seemed cozy and appropriate here at a small kitchen table in Peterborough.

"Josh, huh? Well, he leaves the toilet seat up in the middle of the night, which drives me crazy."

"Tony does that," threw in Crystal while Sara disdainfully watched the easy rapport between the two women.

Jessie continued, eyes aglow. "He is actually a good cook but he loves getting takeout. We eat a lot of Thai food, um, he is sexy as hell on his Harley, hmmm, I agree with you…and on a horse."

"I knew it!"

"He likes all the old black and white films."

"What, like *It's A Wonderful Life*? The Christmas one?"

"Yeah. Like that. Um, what else? Let me see. His hair drives him nuts. It gets in his eyes. But I won't let him cut it unless he has to for a part, because I love the way it tickles my cheek when I kiss my favorite place on his neck."

"You really love him."

"Of course I do! He's my guy."

"What kinda stuff do you fight about?"

Jessie's nose wrinkled. "Fight?"

"You know, knock 'em down drag 'em out the door send 'em to the couch for the night kind of fights."

"Em…" Jessie resorted to her old Scottish ponder with that one, instead of the North American *um*. "We don't, really. I mean, we have heated discussions sometimes, but we don't really have fights."

Crystal sat back, a tad confused. Sara cut in with another acerbic declaration. "Bullshit. I saw the video on YouTube."

Jessie opened her mouth to speak, but no words came out. She juggled Emily-Grace to her other shoulder. "Which video? The one taken on Cambie?" Bad memories came flooding back. She had to mindfully keep herself from shuddering.

"The one outside, when you and this man you supposedly love so much were hollering at each other with his girlfriend standing there watching!"

"Easy, Sara," cautioned Crystal carefully. "Cut her some slack, will you?"

"It's okay, Crystal," responded Jessie, her voice now even and controlled again. To Sara, she said, "We only fight about the big things. The big drama. And for the record, she wasn't his girlfriend."

"No, she was yours, apparently. I thought maybe you, like, shared her around after, like you big Hollywood types tend to do."

"I don't live in Hollywood. I only go there when I have to. And no, Josh and I don't share lovers. We're happy enough with each other."

"But that woman was your girlfriend."

"In a manner of speaking. She took me in when I was homeless and sick. Years ago."

That shut Sara up for a moment. Crystal took up the conversation, a little less boisterously this time. "So you really don't fight?"

"He likes to tease me about dishes and stuff but we usually just end up hugging and laughing. No, Crystal, we're really pretty happy." Jessie didn't bother getting into the whole Jacob swear jar thing with these women she hardly knew, one of whom was just stargazing, per se, and the other who was simply jealous and sad.

Sara butted in again. "You've only been married a year. Wait til it's been twelve. Then talk to me about fighting."

"I hope not," was Jessie's simple response, with a confused look to Sara. "It's so precious, what we have—the snuggles, the kisses, the touching…the sex…we fought hard to get here. Why would we waste any time fighting? Especially over things that don't really matter."

Her remarks silenced the two. Then Crystal took Jessie's hand. "It sounds to me as if you're pretty blessed, Jessie."

"It was a long, hard road, Crystal." Jessie tossed a nervous glance over to Sara. "But yes, now it seems like it was all worth it."

Sara stood again, then, and took her teacup to the counter. "We should go see Martha and Evelyn," she stated. "And then you should probably be heading back into Toronto before traffic gets insane."

With that, the reunion at Sara's house was over. Next, it was time to face the grandmother.

～ ～

In Toronto, Josh checked his cell phone for the umpteenth time. He had a message from Jessie saying she was off to see her grandmother, and one from Matt, which confirmed Jessie and the baby were on the move.

He shoved his phone back into the pocket of his leather jacket. "Geez, I'll be glad when she gets back," he told Steve. The guys were still on set but were shooting an outdoor scene near the studio. It was freezing, and Josh had thrown his vintage jacket on over his 1920's costume suit jacket, but the cold air still whipped in and through his prohibition era flannel pants. "Damn, it's cold." He shivered. "I hope Jessie's keeping Emily-Grace bundled up."

He and Steve were both leaning against the studio's exterior wall while the crew's grips and electrics tweaked the lighting under the creative tutelage of the show's Director of Photography. Steve hailed a gal from wardrobe as she scooted by on her way to the production's big red wardrobe truck to grab a hat for the female lead.

"Marci, can you bring a jacket out while we're waiting? One of the down filled ones?" He nodded at Josh. "For him."

"What?" Josh asked, surprised. "I'm fine," he said to Marci, who kindly rushed off for a jacket anyway.

"Jessie would never forgive me if I let you get a chill. Which, may I add,

I think you already have. Either you've just started your teen years or you have a cold. Your voice is suddenly deeper today."

"It's nothing. I'm fine. Everybody needs to stop worrying."

"You have no spleen, Josh. You're down one defense that the rest of us take for granted. Why don't we go inside and wait instead, huh? I'll let Greg know so no one has a shit fit when they can't find us. But I'll get the jacket from Marci anyway, for later."

"Fine, I'll go inside, but only because it's cold enough to freeze the tits off a cow out here. Not because I'm worried about being sick."

"You have a beautiful wife and a gorgeous dreamy new baby. Don't be a selfish bastard, Josh. Stay healthy."

"You forgot to mention my kickass co-star."

"That's a given." Steve clapped Josh on the shoulder and went off to hunt down the AD responsible for calling them to set when the lights were tweaked.

Josh disappeared inside the studio, stacked up a few specially designed wooden apple boxes the crew used for all kinds of things on set, sat on the top one, and texted Matt.

Do you think she spotted u?

Matt texted back immediately. *Nope*

Good typed Josh *or she'll tie our balls in knots*

Yours, mebbe responded Matt. *In ur sleep*

Screw off wrote Josh, chuckling. *She's got better things to do with my balls in bed*

At his end, Matt was laughing so hard he almost couldn't type back. But he was fairly bored watching Jessie's SUV sit quietly outside the home of Martha Kilfoil, and so he sent Josh a 'long-for-Matt' text. *TMI and don't forget to warn Charles and Dee that Jessie doesn't know I tailed her Steve too if he's joining us for dinner*

Will do said Josh, and that was his last text to Matt until after wrap, as he and Steve got called to set before Josh even had a chance to warm up.

Chapter Fifteen

The first thing Josh did when he got back to his suite was extend a hand to his wife and draw her up off the floor for a kiss and a hug. Jessie, too, had just returned, rather glum, but safe and sound. Josh found her on her hands and knees on the geometric carpet practicing Yoga's cat/cow pose as a warm-up to some gentle Kegel exercises to strengthen her post-birth pelvic floor.

The second thing Josh did was lovingly brush a fingertip over his sleeping baby's pink cheek. Then he started undressing for a hot shower.

"It's so cold I saw a Dalmatian stuck to a fire hydrant," he told his wife. "I'm just about perished."

By then, Jessie was sitting on the arm of the lime green chair, pensive. But something in Josh's voice startled her, and so she looked up in time to see her husband's jeans and charcoal Henley shirt drop to the floor as he made his way into the washroom. She heard him twist on the faucet in the stand-up shower before Josh stuck his head out of the doorway.

"Join me?" he asked, eyes locked on the sleeping baby.

Jessie got up slowly, her eyes flickering from icy pale to cobalt blue and back again. "Why are you so cold? And why do you, in fact, sound like you have a cold?"

"I told you, I'm just tired. A bit chilled, that's all. We shot outside some today. No big deal. It was just a few quick pickup shots Jon needed for episode one."

"So…" Jessie's words were drawn out, but succinct. "The production doesn't own long johns? Or maybe…warm-up coats?" Leaning against the doorframe, she crossed her arms and watched her husband slip off his boxers and the ubiquitous white T-shirt he wore under the Henley. He was also wearing his stylized J pendant, and so he unfastened it, too, and laid it carefully on the counter in the washroom. Jessie stretched out a finger and ran it over the J.

"'Course they do. Just no one thought it was that cold until we got stuck in it."

"So by the time you got the coats you were already cold. Jesus, Josh!"

"So by the time we got the coats we were pretty much on our last two takes."

"What am I going to do with you?"

"I can think of plenty of things." Snuggling up to her, he pulled her close again. His body was indeed cold, still, and Jessie shivered through her top when she leaned into his chest. "The baby's sleeping. Now would be a good time. In the shower, though, I need a good blast of heat running through my bones right about now. And you owe ten bucks to the swear jar."

He started to undo the buttons on his wife's top, but Jessie stopped him. "Get in the shower, babe," she insisted softly. "I'm right behind you. Please just get in and get warmed up already."

"You promise to come in?"

"I'm on my way. Go." She grabbed his shoulders and faced him towards the steam emanating from a few feet away. Jessie undid her top and slipped it over her head, then pushed her jeans down over her hips.

In a moment she was in the shower with her man. They cuddled while the hot water soothed his cold bones and her nagging worry. Josh took the opportunity to ask about the Peterborough relatives.

"Sara was less than forthcoming," Jessie admitted. "Although her husband was sweet." Her gloom disappeared for a moment. "And he was amazing with Emily-Grace and his kids."

"And the boys were…"

"Adorable. Cute as bugs. And get this, the younger one is named for Ren in Footloose. How cool is that?"

"Depends whether you're talking about the original Footloose, or the remake." Josh frowned and ran his fingers through Jessie's wet hair. Leaning in, he brushed his lips against one now-rosy cheek.

"Dork!" She swatted him and winked. "Obviously the original. The director missed a lot of beautiful intimate moments in the remake."

"And your grandmother?"

"Lovely. Absolutely lovely. When I got there she had biscuits made. Like the kind my mom and dad used to make all the time. We sat around the kitchen table and ate them." She paused. "She was pretty emotional. I guess that wasn't really a surprise. She kind of just couldn't stop staring at me. I kept wondering if she could see my mom in my features, or whether she was considering that I looked like the man who ran off with her daughter. She cried, though. So did I. A little. I couldn't help myself."

Thinking about the meeting with her grandmother, Jessie stopped and considered again the older woman's reaction as well as her own. It was their first face-to-face. And Jessie's conception and imminent birth was really the inciting incident that spurred Emily's final climb down an appalling ladder years ago. Unlike Sara, Martha was at the door of her senior's independent living unit before Jessie pulled to a stop outside. It was as if the woman was at the end stage of her life, so she knew to lay the small things aside, to heal, and to let bygones be bygones. The wrinkled face, tiny, arthritic fingers, and stooped shoulders reminded Jessie of George back in P.E.I. His wisdom was lingering and hard-earned. It seemed Martha and he had much in common.

Josh wiped his fingers over a strand of Jessie's hair that was stuck to her cheek. "Was Evelyn there?" He loosened the hair, and bent in for another tender kiss. His heart ached for Jessie's difficult day and he wished he could have been by her side through the reticent sister and the aged grandmother. From Jessie's brief description, he figured he would probably like Kevin. Sara's husband sounded pretty down-to-earth, if he was at least good to his kids and, by extension, to Emily-Grace.

"Yeah. She was fine. She and her mother were tearful old buddies by the time I arrived. Emily-Grace broke down a lot of walls too." Sighing heavily, she lathered soap through Josh's hair. She massaged his scalp just slightly and found herself getting a little turned on at his erotic little purrs of ecstasy as her fingers moved over his skin.

"But not Sara," Josh was saying.

"What?" asked Jessie, refocusing on the conversation and not on the way her hands felt as they passed over her husband's chest. As she moved her fingers lower, he smiled and repeated what he'd said.

"But not Sara. Our baby didn't manage to break down her walls."

"Not yet." Seductively, Jessie moved her fingers even lower. She teased him, lightly running her fingers over the backs of his balls before leaning in for a kiss. "But she will."

"I thought this was a one time trip, Jess." Holding her away from him, Josh studied the intent expression on the hopeful face.

"Maybe just one more," Jessie answered, blinking mischievously. She reached between his legs again and let the corner of one lip turn up. "That okay with you, cowboy?"

"Ahhhh," was his ragged answer. "Maybe one more. But I'm going with you next time."

"Fine," she gloated. "I'll make sure I call Crystal."

"And Crystal is…?"

But Jessie's answer wasn't imminent. She was suddenly rather pre-occupied. And when she slipped down Josh's body, he, too, quickly forgot that he'd asked.

The baby stayed asleep, no one came to the door, and Josh and Jessie took their time enjoying a prolonged snuggle. Then it was time to meet Charles and Dee, Jonathon and Giselle, Matt, and Steve, for dinner.

～～

Jessie arrived at the dinner table half an hour before Josh, who seemed rather relieved at her suggestion that he nap before dinner. She sat alone at the group's table, Emily-Grace in the carrier at her feet. Oblivious to the thinly disguised curious stares of other patrons, she texted Jacob.

I did it. I met my grandmother and my sister

He texted back immediately. *And?*

Grandmother just sad she missed so much, I think. Sister still…broken-hearted. At the whole abandoned thing. I get that. Sux that I'm the reason

U ok?

Jessie poised both thumbs over her phone before answering. Then she typed *Not really. Sara's a bitter woman. With an amazing man and the sweetest kids. But it's like she doesn't see them. Can't get past her own shit, I guess*

Jacob's text came instantly. *U with Josh now?*

She laughed. *not hardly likely. Remember we have a swear jar & ur name is worth double, texting u included*

U suck

He's in our room napping

The lazy cowboy type, huh? Or is it rum runner these days?

Actually Jacob Jessie hit send and then sent a part two of that thought, *I think he's sick*

In Miami, Jacob paused. He read the layer hidden beneath the typed letters on his phone. That layer read simply *remember when Josh lost his spleen? Remember how?*

He'll be okay, Jess. Let him sleep it off. Lotsa vitamin C and ginger tea

I know. It's just a lot today. Old family shit & not much sleep. Makes a girl feel worried & lonely

Ahh u r missing ur Jacob

She laughed, surprised at the tears prickling the corners of her eyes at that. She started to type *Babe just call me* when Matt arrived at the table. He slid into the seat opposite Jessie, eyes dropping to the phone in Jessie's hands, which she promptly let fall to her lap, out of sight. Jessie erased her last few letters, smiled up at Matt, and then typed *got 2 go 4 now call u one of these days k?*

"Hey, Emily-Grace," Matt was saying as Jessie shyly tucked her phone into an outside pocket next to a bib in the diaper bag at her feet, sorry to lose the connection with her best Miami bud.

"She should be good to go to get me through dinner, Matt. I'm getting tired of cold meals."

"Have you thought any further about getting a nanny, Jessie?" Matt smiled affectionately when he reached down and the baby wrapped her tiny fingers around his. Making a few of her adorable *ba-dah dab-bah* cooing sounds, Emily-Grace was rather irresistible to a father missing his own rapidly sprouting daughter.

"Are you kidding me? This baby is everything. I don't want to be without her for one second." Again, Martha and Sara's faces played across Jessie's solemn features. How could either of them have been parted from their own Emily? How could Emily have chosen to leave them? That mystery was still just that—relegated to the image of a very pregnant woman crawling out a second story window down a rickety ladder to flee in the dark abyss of night.

"I don't need a nanny," Jessie grunted disdainfully as the thought of ever losing her child seized her somewhere deep inside and stuck its thorny claws into her abdomen. She wrapped both arms around her belly and looked wide-eyed over at Matt, slumping over as she did so.

She changed tack. "What'd you do all day, Matt?" she asked, putting a halt to the ennui and seemingly constant worry, and granting their conversation a right-hand turn. "Must have been fun. Freedom!" Releasing her arms, she waved them at her sides, teasing him.

His eyes flickered then, and he didn't answer. Jessie frowned, but let it go, because Charles and Dee were just arriving then, all grandparent-ly and huggy and bursting with enthusiasm about their day in Toronto doing the rounds of production company and network execs and, in Charles' case, fitting in a lunch meeting with a hip young sound engineer he was thinking of hiring, while his wife was down the road with Giselle visiting the Toronto Women's Shelter.

For her part, Jessie listened as the older couple chatted away but, inside, her stomach was doing triple axels. She agreed with Sara. She'd hit the jackpot by Jack Deacon's introduction to the powerful Keatings years ago. The image of Martha flitted across her mind—the pale hands, the vague tremor in the woman's voice, the deep wise peace that was not able to completely eradicate an age-old loss and a triple-decade pain. Somehow, sitting here with her pseudo-parents in this luxurious restaurant on the fancy hotel's main floor, just seemed wrong.

Soon, Stephen was at the table too, and it was he who took Jessie's card key and went upstairs to see whether Josh was up to having dinner. Josh was tired and warm, finally—albeit a little too warm—but he made his way downstairs with Steve and brushed his lips over his wife's forehead as he slid into the bench seat on her right. She took his hand and sucked in a breath at its warmth, but he refused to meet her eyes. Instead, Josh pulled his hand away and picked up his menu.

"What do you recommend?" he asked the server quietly, as Jessie met Steve's concerned eyes across the table.

Aside from that new worry and the day's momentous events, dinner was—for the most part—enjoyable. However, when Josh reached into the diaper bag for a bib to wipe a bit of spit off the baby's chin—they had removed the carrier from the floor and placed it on the bench seat next to Josh—he accidentally knocked Jessie's cell phone out when he removed the bib. When he went to pick it up, his eyes landed on Jessie's final text from Jacob, which she hadn't seen, and which read *take care Jess, luv u.*

Josh's relaxed features immediately changed, sliding from a pleasant dinner-table camaraderie to a confused and lung-sucking hurt, especially given the whole-body ache that consumed him this evening, as well as the constant forced effort to remain on speaking terms with Charles and Dee, and even Matt, on some level, these days.

He glanced up at Jessie as he tucked the phone away, but the uneasy surprise on his face registered instantly with her, and she knew it was something to do with Jacob and their earlier texts, because Josh was just now placing the offending phone back in the diaper bag. His lip twitched as he looked away, but the wistful aching sorrow was now imbedded in the liquid eyes Jessie loved. She touched his hand but he pulled away and focused on touching his baby's leg with that hand while wiping at the dribble on Emily-Grace's chin with the other.

Oh fuck, Jessie muttered under her breath. *What the hell did Jacob say?* She decided to ignore Josh's insecurity and mitigate it instead. Shifting her body so she was leaning sideways towards him, she rested her right hand on her husband's thigh. He didn't push her away and, instead, after a moment let his warm hand cover hers, although it took Josh a few minutes to feel up to meeting her apologetic eyes.

Another weird incident over dinner resulted in much bigger and longer lasting consequences. It happened when Charles casually asked Matt a question.

"How did you find the traffic on the 401, Matt?"

Jessie looked up at that, but only out of courtesy. Of course Matt was out carousing during his time off, since she hadn't needed him, nor had Charles and Dee after their fundraising lunch. They were chauffeured by Jonathon's guy Marco, since the old hippie knew the city terrain.

But then Dee fired a shot that accidentally slipped into the wrong net. "I'm sure he was fine, Charles, especially once he got off onto the 115."

It was a slip, because only general questions were tossed at Jessie regarding her trip to see the long-lost family. The group was well accustomed to broaching difficult subjects to Jessie with strategic timing—under cover, away from prying eyes. Dee was antsy to have a conversation with Jessie about the day's Peterborough visit, but she was waiting until after dinner, when they could hopefully meet in Josh and Jessie's suite.

But now, Jessie's eyes narrowed and she sucked in a breath. She stared daggers across the table at Matt. "The 115? To Peterborough, Matt?" She viciously hissed the words out from between her teeth. "Seriously?" Unbelieving, she twisted her head towards Dee, who sat down from Matt with the hapless Stephen in between. Josh was next. Now it was his turn to feel the heat from his wife's blazing eyes. He shuffled in his seat while Dee grunted regretfully, trying to make excuses.

"Jessie, we couldn't let you go meet people you don't know, alone, just you and that tiny baby," Dee was saying, a fork in one hand and knife in the other, both oddly suspended by her plate of crepes.

"You followed me." Jessie was incredulous. Her knife and fork clanged to the table. Her eyes were now on Matt because she was too pissed to look back at Josh. Her words were delivered in a cold, calculating timbre. "You fucking bastard. I'm your boss, Matt. I tell you what to do. And guess what." Abruptly she stood and tossed her linen napkin onto her plate. "You're supposed to fucking listen."

Her piercing eyes darted around the table. She caught Steve's eye. For once he wasn't chuckling, making light of her antics. He looked as upset as Jessie felt, chewing lightly on a fingernail with one elbow leaning on the table, eyes darting from Josh to Jessie to Matt and back again. He held her gaze now, though, and Jessie's belly clenched at the disappointment he telegraphed across the table to her at the way she'd just spoken to someone they all considered a good and trusted friend.

Emily-Grace chose that moment to whimper and communicate her own hunger. Jessie's focus landed on her daughter. In an instant, she reached around behind Josh on the bench seat, forcing him to scoot his butt forward. Jessie lifted the baby out of her carrier.

"You suck, you know that?" Jessie spat, clutching Emily-Grace to her chest. "All of you. You just plain suck." She fixed her gaze on Josh, and then on Matt, and she spoke to each of them in turn. To her husband she said, "Bring the carrier when you come up, please," and to Matt she sputtered, "You sunuvabitch. How the hell could you?"

To the assembled group, she said, "What do I have to do, exactly, to earn your trust? To prove to all of you that I am quite capable of caring for my baby girl? That I can keep her safe, and that I can take care of myself! I—we—don't need a babysitter!"

Wheeling around firmly, Jessie started marching out of the dining room, but then stopped when she realized she didn't have her card key for the suite.

"Fuck!" she cried inwardly, trying to fake-smile through angry threatening tears at the other patrons in the trendy upscale restaurant. Spinning around, Jessie stomped back to the table, where Steve's hand was already stuck out over the table, the offending card key dangling from his fingertips.

"Humphh!" was Jessie's thank you.

"You're welcome," he mumbled, as he eased more comfortably back against his seat.

After she was gone, the table was silent. Dee hung her head. "I'm sorry," she murmured across Steve to Matt, who sighed, averted her gaze, and rested his left elbow on the table while looking towards the right, where a bow-tied waiter was pouring wine for a newly arrived couple.

Dee braced her back against her own chair, and looked at Josh in the red leather bench seat kitty-corner across from her. "We have a pullout bed if you need it, Josh." Her eyes narrowed at the pink cast to his cheeks. "Are you feeling okay?"

"No," he answered. "Not even remotely." He went to slide out of the seat, but Charles gently reached across and touched his arm.

"Sit," he insisted. "We know our girl. Give her some space for the time being. Finish your dinner."

"Are you running a fever?" asked Dee. "You look flushed, honey."

"I'll be fine," answered Josh. "I just need some sleep."

"Take a night off, Josh," insisted Charles. "Jessie and the baby will be okay. She needs to cool down anyway."

"Jessie and the baby have already had too many nights away from me," he mumbled in response, dropping his eyes to his plate. "I'll be fine." But, resolutely, he picked up his fork and poked at the filet mignon on his plate.

In the end, when the group quietly separated, Dee hugged Josh gently. "Come see us if you need anything. I'll drop by in an hour or so to try to talk to your obstinate wife."

Josh looked at Charles. The older man grunted and nodded his assent.

Matt finally spoke up. The only way he knew to handle the sickening thud of Jessie's reaction to what she clearly saw as a major betrayal, was to revert to business. He needed to fill the awkward space with something, anything. But his voice was gruff with emotion. "Let's meet here at eight for breakfast. I'll see the jet is ready for a ten a.m. departure."

And the little group went their separate ways, although Steve accompanied Josh upstairs in the elevator.

"Good luck," he said, after a silent ride. "And by the way, I'm calling Jon. I'm getting a doctor in to see you." Yanking a cell phone out of the chest pocket of his shirt, he held it up in front of Josh.

"Steve, leave it alone, will ya?" Tired, sick, Josh leaned back against the elevator and hung his head. He touched his side, where the old scar remained, a constant enduring reminder of what he almost lost.

"It can't hurt, Josh. Don't be stupid."

"Leave it til morning."

"You're getting on a fucking airplane in the morning."

"They have doctors in P.E.I. I guarantee it." Josh wanted to add *we'll check with Trudy in Vancouver, she knows people in P.E.I., she'll find someone*, but he couldn't muster the energy.

"Jesus, you people and your stubborn pride."

The elevator door whooshed open, and the men went their separate ways.

Steve twisted around and hollered after Josh, "See you at breakfast, Hoser. You better damn well be breathing."

"I might be, if I survive my wife tonight."

Josh screwed up his nose, paused at the door to his suite, and inserted his card key. He twisted the doorknob, and slipped inside.

Chapter Sixteen

The suite's interior was now pale-grey, almost black. It was only light enough for Josh to tiptoe carefully to a sideboard, where he set the room's keycard down alongside the wallet he drew from his back pocket. Only a swath of moonlight in the living area and a muted cerulean glow from one bedside lamp offered Josh any illumination. He had nipped the door closed as softly as he could, since it was Emily-Grace's bedtime and Jessie had about a twenty minute start on him, so she was likely settling the baby for the night.

Starting to haul his heavy body forward, Josh stopped when his wife's dreamlike voice moved softly within the mostly moonlit space...in song. She was around the corner in the bedroom, where he couldn't see her. Unnoticed by Jessie, Josh bent an ear towards the rise and fall of the ballad she was crooning to their infant daughter.

Her voice was almost a whisper, so soft and tender that it broke sometimes when she reached for lower notes. The sound waves were changing slightly, so Josh figured Jessie was moving a bit. He could barely make out the lyrics. Holding his breath, he listened.

You'll remember me when the west wind moves
Upon the fields of barley
You'll forget the sun in his jealous sky
As we walk in fields of gold

She was singing that old Sting song, Fields of Gold—the one she sang for him at his birthday party when she first came back from Scotland, when he was with Michelle and Jessie was still seeing Jacob. It was so ethereal in this space, in the miniscule glow-light, a cappella like that, interspersed with the cherished sweet gurgles of their tiny baby. Emily-Grace, Josh knew from experience, was likely fighting drowsy eyelids as she contemplated her momma's loving eyes.

So she took her love
For to gaze awhile
Upon the fields of barley
In his arms she fell as her hair came down
Among the fields of gold

Will you stay with me, will you be my love
Among the fields of barley
We'll forget the sun in his jealous sky
As we lie in fields of gold

Josh crept forward, resting one hand on the doorframe to the bedroom. He stood still, silent, and set his eyes upon the vision before him. His wife, who so often performed for thousands—or millions, if you factor in television or film—was singing for a single soul…her baby daughter.

See the west wind move like a lover so
Upon the fields of barley
Feel her body rise when you kiss her mouth
Among the fields of gold

I never made promises lightly
And there have been some that I've broken
But I swear in the days still left
We'll walk in fields of gold
We'll walk in fields of gold

At the repetition of those words, fields of gold, Josh felt his feet almost give out from beneath him. He literally almost collapsed. It hit him suddenly—another memory—his recurring dream about an image of fields of gold, about which Josh told Steve the day he moved into this very suite to work on *The Wyatt Boys*. Here he was, standing apart from his wife as a hushed unseen observer, like in the dream, watching Jessie move and sway in her enchanting dance, singing the song the dream brought forth.

Many years have passed since those summer days
Among the fields of barley
See the children run as the sun goes down
Among the fields of gold

As the last words faded, Josh, breathless, moved into the space his wife and daughter occupied. Jessie felt his presence, and looked up. Her eyes were pale, luminescent in the little light available to them at this time. She wasn't angry, as he expected. If anything, Josh realized, she was sad.

Tenderly, he passed his left arm behind his wife's waist, and gently pulled her towards him. He matched his movements to hers, and together they rocked Emily-Grace while Jessie sang the last verse. Josh felt by joining them he could perhaps eradicate the strange nocturnal dream that left him trembling and afraid, with hurting toes and his breath coming in short gasps. He pushed away the thought that the dream featured an older version of his baby daughter—and a toddler son as well.

Besides, he thought, *Jessie is happy in the dream. She is laughing. Joyous, even. And tonight she is cheerless and pained.*

You'll remember me when the west wind moves
Upon the fields of barley
You can tell the sun in his jealous sky
When we walked in fields of gold
When we walked in fields of gold
When we walked in fields of gold.

He reached beneath their tiny daughter and lifted her out of her mother's loving arms. Josh turned, trod softly across the carpet, and laid the child in her travel crib. Jessie approached behind him, wrapped her arms around his waist, and laid her head against his shoulder as he drew the comforter up to the baby's neck. He tucked her in as Jessie did, using the tips of his fingers to poke the blanket just a little underneath Emily-Grace's slumbering body. Lingering there afterwards, Josh pondered where life had brought him, with a baby and a wife in his care.

He laid both hands over Jessie's at his belly, soaking up the essence of her skin, her soul, as she stood with her body pressed against his. It was humbling. With a pang of agonizing remembrance, Josh recalled it wasn't so long ago that he thought he'd lost it all—Jessie, his raison d'etre, his hope for the future, his life.

Finally, he felt her hold on him lessen. One hand slipped into his, and Josh responded to the moderate pull at his fingers, which beckoned him into the other room. Once there, Jessie dropped down onto the small sofa, and patted the spot next to her. Josh sat, sighed, and leaned back, placed his feet up on the ottoman, and clasped his hands above his head. He let his eyes close over.

Jessie lifted his T-shirt and laid a cool hand on her husband's warm belly.

"Josh," she started, a spark of fear alighting somewhere deep in her belly. "We can change our plans. I think you should see a doctor."

Fluttering open his eyes, Josh let his hands float down so one big paw could rub his wife's hand on his belly. He rested the other on her thigh as she sat with one leg under her, half facing him.

"It's just a cold, Jess," was his half-hearted answer. At the distress in her eyes, he added, "I will. I swear. But I'll be fine til we get to P.E.I. Can we drop it for now?"

"So…you want me to drop the doctor-worry thing, but you couldn't drop the Jessie-wants-her-privacy thing."

He sighed. "Jessie, I'm sorry. I am. But in my view there was cause for concern. And as long as we're being honest here, I believe there still is. You really don't know these people yet."

"And how am I supposed to get to know them with Matt breathing down my neck? They'll put up a brick wall between us. They'll never see me as just a normal person."

"Jessie, look at me." Josh took her chin in his fingers. "Little one, I love you more than life itself. But I am here to tell you that you will never be a normal person. Celebrity changes people. And there's no going back."

"Sure there is."

A small *pffttt* escaped from between Josh's lips as he recalled the first time he saw Jessie after her last attempt at being normal. Lavender bobbed hair, a terrified, sullen expression...the aura of weed that surrounded her.

He took a chance, and asked a quiet question. "Do you still wish we'd left you alone? In Edinburgh?" Josh's saddened eyes searched hers.

"What? No! No, Jesus Josh, of course not. Why would you even ask that?"

"You want normal. You don't want this life."

She exhaled. "No, it's not exactly that."

"You like the perks."

"Sure. I do. But at the same time, Josh, it was surreal watching Sara's kids play with Emily-Grace today, and with their dad. They were in this grungy old room, and by that I don't mean dirty, just—you know, an old chesterfield—and they were so happy! I mean, I could feel it, I could feel how genuinely happy they were, all of them. Not Sara, just the guys. Even Emily-Grace could feel it, I know it. I mean, how could you not feel that kind of love around you?"

"Little one, I feel that love around you and our daughter all the time. I can't stand that you have to go back to Miami again in a few days."

"I know Josh, I know people can love one another in lots of different ways, and in different, I dunno, economic brackets, for lack of a better description, but...there was something different about these folks." She shifted her position on the couch and took his hand in both of hers. Jessie searched his eyes, deeply, begging him to understand, to see what she was seeing. "Josh, these kids can go to school. They can hang out at the hockey rink. They can run around, they can do stuff, they can be with their friends without their parents freaking out with worry. They don't have someone like Matt, or Ulysses or Big Dan or Susanne watching them all the time. They don't have people trying to take pictures with their iPhones, hiding behind water fountains to do so, being all sneaky and weird. They don't have to worry about the risk of..."

She ducked her head and studied the comforting way his fingers caressed hers, the gentle way his thumb moved over hers.

"What, Jess? What were you going to say?"

She looked up at him and sighed deeply but couldn't bring herself to speak.

"Stalkers," he said definitively, finishing the abysmal thought for her.

"Or bad people in general," she finished. "People trying to get something from us because of what we do for a living. Which just happens to put us in some weird bubble, for some reason."

Lovingly, Josh let his fingers drift down his wife's cheek. His eyes glistened, their darker flecks lightening in the pale moonlight. "Baby girl," he tried, "you listen to me. What we do is entertain people. The way this world is going, God…school shootings, Syria, Israel…even here on home soil the crap that's been happening, with Mounties and soldiers getting murdered, and the parliament buildings being broken into…well, people need us more than ever. They need an escape. They need your music. And yes, that makes them look up to us—to you. And I suppose that puts us in a bubble. But if I'm going to be in a bubble, I sure as hell am glad it's with you."

Jessie melted, and grinned stupidly at him. "You're killing me, Sawyer."

His eyes lit up at that. "I love you, Wheeler-Sawyer. I'm glad you're not too pissed at me. Although I've been telling myself not to care about how angry you might get over today. No way was I letting you and my baby girl wander off to the boonies on your own."

"So you and Charles and Dee actually agreed on something? I suppose I should be grateful."

"We always agree when your safety is a concern. Or your happiness, Jessie."

"Good thing, 'cuz they know you are the key to my happiness, Josh Sawyer."

Just then, a light knock came at the door, tentative, as if the owner of the knuckles responsible for the sound was afraid the interior occupants might have already retired for the evening.

Jessie put her hand on Josh's lap to stop him from moving. "I'll get it," she said, a sour grimace replacing the brief smile Josh earned from her. "Little late for visitors, isn't it?" But as she hoisted herself off the sofa, Jessie was already lecturing herself for her earlier hot temper. She figured their visitor was somehow connected to that flash of anger, and she fully expected to find Charles and Dee, or one or the other at least, at their door. But when she whipped it open she spied only Matt.

Head down, shoulders slumped, Matt was the picture of doom. He was staring at the tips of his expensive desert boots when Jessie opened the door, but now he adjusted his stance and inhaled before greeting her succinctly and with purpose.

"Jessie. Can I come in?"

Tensing, Jessie moved aside and waved him in.

Josh would have stood to greet him, but he couldn't find the oomph in his bones and muscles to propel his body upwards. Instead, he studied Matt, who was apprehensively pawing at his chin with a thumb and forefinger, agitated and apparently upset. "What is it, Matt?" he asked.

The Keating security chief brandished an arm around the room. "Is the baby down for the night?"

"Yeah," Jessie answered from behind him, as she lifted a hand to stifle a yawn. "Sorry," she murmured. "Long day."

He turned and faced her. "I won't keep you. This will just take a minute."

"No, it's okay, Matt, relax. Have a seat." Jessie removed a throw cushion from the lime green chair so he could sit. She clutched it to her chest and wandered back over to her place on the sofa by her husband.

"It's okay, I'll stand." Matt wiped a hand anxiously over his cheek. "I'm sorry to barge in on you like this. I know it's late and tomorrow's a big day. But I've got something to say."

Suddenly nervous, Jessie glanced sideways at Josh. He caught her look, and straightened.

"What is it, Matt?" Josh asked again, quieter this time, although the low timbre had a definite demanding air.

Matt fixed his eyes on Jessie. "I did what I had to do today, Jessie."

Her shoulders slumped. "I know, Matt. I'm sorry I got angry."

He continued, his usual calm countenance gone, his words instead fired by an edgy, simmering anger.

Then Matt dropped a bomb on them. "I'm not going to P.E.I. with you tomorrow. I've talked to Jon. He's sending a couple of his guys until I can get Dan or Ulysses here."

"Wh-what?" Jessie asked, standing again to face Matt, and releasing Josh's hand in the meantime. "Matt, I said I was sorry. Maybe I *was* just being stupid." She was grasping at straws, at a way to calm him.

"In some ways, Jessie, yes, you were not very smart. But in other ways I understand what it is you wanted today. What you want a lot of days, in fact. And it makes it damn hard for me to do my job." He was facing her straight on, hands on his hips. There was a dangerous light flashing in Matt's usually calm eyes that Josh and Jessie had never before seen.

Jessie was speechless.

When she found her voice, it was a squeak. And it was begging. "It was one day, Matt. One stupid, senseless, dumb Jessie kind of day."

"I beg to differ," were his next words.

Jessie sobered at the realization that Matt was, indeed, telling the whole unfettered unarguable truth. Both knees melted underneath her at his subsequent declaration.

"I'm done here, Jessie."

"Noooo," she whispered, reaching a useless hand out to him, which he didn't take. "You're quitting? You're leaving us? Because I was stubborn today? And because of the Tom Ryan concert that time, in Atlanta, Matt? And because of…" Her eyes watered as she lost her voice and the capacity to speak altogether.

Finally, Josh mustered the energy to stand. He wrapped his warm fingers around his wife's. "We've all made our peace with the McCall bullshit, Jessie. Haven't we, Matt?" He begged Matt to agree, to let Jessie off the hook with at least this one torturous memory.

"It's too much, Josh," was Matt's forthright answer. His voice was muted, which was in some ways disembodied in the dim light. But still, there was enough pale moonlight teasing the small room to allow the three adults present to soak up the angst in each other's eyes. "How are you supposed to protect someone who doesn't want to be protected?"

Neither Josh nor Jessie could find a response to that painful query. They all knew it was the bitter reality.

Matt fixed his solemn gaze on Jessie. "You'll be fine," he croaked. "Good luck to you."

"No," was her stricken response. "No, Matt. You can't."

He kept his hands staunchly at his hips, but let his unhappy scrutiny wander past Jessie and then back again, onto her startling sea-blue eyes that, when they were focused on him, thawed Matt's heart enough times in the past that he could usually see to forgive, and to forget.

Even now he melted when his gaze got caught up in her shocked countenance, but Matt could no longer see to forget. Forgive, maybe. Sure. Eventually. But right now, in this moment, he was pissed. He'd been pushed over the proverbial edge by Jessie's insistent and sometimes insensitive behavior.

Matt was done.

Pivoting towards Josh, Matt actually hurt Jessie further by ignoring her as he reached out to shake Josh's hand. "Good luck to you, too," he mumbled, before wheeling around and leaving the couple standing in the moonlight, shaken and dumbfounded, as the door to their suite *whoomphed* shut behind Matt's back.

"He's my friend," managed Jessie in a dazed whisper. "He can't leave."

"You want normal?" responded Josh, fatigue sinking him fast. "You'll never have normal, Jessie. You couldn't be normal if you tried." He started to move past her towards the bedroom. "And now you've just proven it."

"Josh! What?" Jessie turned to face him, incredulous, overcome with emotion at Matt's stunning announcement and now Josh's obvious frustration with her. "What the hell's that supposed to mean?"

Wheeling around slowly, he intoned with sorrow, "Jessie, there will always be someone who can watch over you—over us. Over our family. Over Charles and Dee. Security can be replaced. But there will never be another Matt."

Staring, she flung her hands out to the sides, then shook her head in disbelief. "What's that got to do with me not being normal?"

Answering her slowly, exasperated, as if she were a child, as if he was tired of explaining things to her, Josh said, "Your little snit at dinner, getting up and leaving like that. Your demands. Your constant nose-snubbing when it comes to letting Matt do his job." He pointed a tired finger at her chest. "You, little one, have been pulling a Kelly Reilly all along. Not all at once, with fire and brimstone, like she's known for. But a Kelly Reilly all the same."

Turning again, he padded over to drop a kiss on his daughter's soft cheek. "Normal, shmormal," Jessie heard him mutter.

She turned to the door and considered going to Charles and Dee's room to ask them to fight for Matt. She pictured the looks on their faces—shock, disbelief, hurt, anger…loss at a true and trusted friend.

Jessie collapsed onto the sofa, hung her head in her hands, and wept.

Chapter Seventeen

"We really left. Without saying goodbye." Jessie was astounded.

Dee affectionately rubbed her girl's arm, and then reached for Emily-Grace, who Jessie handed over with trepidation. Sometimes the child was her security blanket, and right now she didn't feel like letting go.

"Jessie," Dee started, "he's tired. Matt spends so much time with us—"

"With me, you mean."

"Lately, yes, with *Mystic Nights*, honey, but—"

"I get that he misses his family. What I don't get is that even if he's pissed at me, he knows me well enough to know he can talk to me, Dee. At least to say goodbye, for heaven's sake!"

A hostess interrupted the flow of conversation for a few moments as she led Jessie and Dee, and behind them Josh and Steve, to their seats. Charles would be along shortly. He was in an early morning tete-a-tete with Jonathon that would be wrapping up imminently.

Jessie chose to sit by Steve. Recalling the disappointment in his eyes at her behavior the evening before, and after having time to feel truly sorry for her knee-jerk reaction, Jessie needed to clear the air. Besides, they were heading to P.E.I. that day, leaving him behind to shoot some scenes in *The Wyatt Boys* that didn't include Josh, and Jessie had already badly hurt one of her friends. No way was she leaving Steve mad at her too.

At the moment, Josh was fishing in the diaper bag for a warmer blanket to give to Dee for Emily-Grace, since there was a duct nearby conducting cool air towards their table. Jessie wrapped one arm around the front of Steve's belly and leaned on him. He lifted his arm and she scooted underneath.

"I'm sorry," she whispered. "I was being a bitch."

"You don't say," he answered drily. "Matt didn't deserve that. The Peterborough thing wasn't just him, you know. Your whole bossy entourage was involved in overriding your senseless decision to go meet the Jesse James gang alone."

"I'll call him. He'll come back. He just needs a break. From me," she sighed disconsolately.

"He's always had your best interests at heart, Jess. But you don't need me to tell you that."

"No. I really don't. God, I'm an idiot." In truth, she was feeling very sick to her stomach over her part in Matt's exodus from their lives. "What's that old saying?" she asked Steve. "You don't know what you have until it's gone."

"Something like that." They watched Josh tuck the blanket around his baby daughter. "Daddy Sawyer at work," Steve chuckled. "Never thought I'd see the day. Looks good on him."

"It sure does." Jessie's cheeks pinked up at the sight of her man tenderly talking to Emily-Grace, whose animated face and waving, expressive, curled-up fists made her seem absolutely rapturously in love with her daddy. The baby's tiny eyes were fixed on her father as he told her how pretty she was. "She's like her mother. She can't take her eyes off him." She looked up at Steve. "Sometimes you do," she said, referencing her earlier comment.

"What's that?" He glanced down at his friend, snuggled under his arm.

"Sometimes you do know what you have. When it's here." Jessie's thoughts drifted to Sara. She wondered if her half-sister had any clue what treasures she had by way of her husband Kevin and their two rambunctious sons.

Steve squeezed Jessie's shoulders and planted his lips on the top of her head. He brought the two of them back to the subject of their friend. "Matt'll come around, kiddo."

"How can you be sure?" Jessie murmured, eyes wide, hopeful.

"Because I can't imagine how anybody could choose to stay away from you for long. That's how."

"Sometimes I wonder why any of you choose to be near me. Ever." She frowned.

"It's nothing to do with you," Steve joked. Then he took a serious turn. "It's all about him." He nodded at Josh. "We all just want him to be happy." He left unspoken the heartbreaking sadness in Josh's eyes those eighteen months Jessie was travelling the world and then living in Scotland. And before that when she, seemingly unprovoked from their point of view, dumped him by climbing into bed with another actor. "I never dreamed I'd ever see him this happy. Look at him, Jess."

"I told you, neither myself nor his daughter can *stop* looking at him." Her voice softened. "He's so good with her."

At that moment, Dee shooed Josh's hand away. She scolded him. "Josh, you should keep a little distance for a few days. You don't want her catching your cold."

As if on cue, Josh turned his head and sneezed. Pulling a tissue out of his coat pocket, he wiped his nose, then looked pensively over the top of it at Dee, his lips turned down.

Steve hesitated before telling Jessie, "Keep an eye on him in P.E.I. Watch this cold of his." He added, "I guess I don't really need to tell you that."

"He says it's just a case of the sniffles."

"Yeah, well, he would. You're talking about the guy who spent a number of hours in emergency after laying down his Harley and not bothering to tell any of us about it."

"Jon told you?"

"Someone had to."

She wrapped her arms tighter around her friend. "Sometimes I forget what he means to you, too."

"Good motocross partner, you mean?"

"And co-star, I suppose."

Steve grinned. "It's good to hold an old bottle of moonshine in my hand and know Josh has one in his too." Quickly, he fixed his eyes on hers. "With water-diluted coke in the bottles, of course. It's disgusting."

"Must be weird to have to act drunk when you've got addictions issues, huh?"

Steve shrugged. "He says it's not. He never really had a problem with alcohol."

"Just the bad shit," Jessie disclosed sadly. "Thank God he's okay now."

"And that," Steve smiled, squeezing Jessie again, "is why we put up with you, Mrs. Sawyer. Because you gave this guy something—someone—to believe in."

"Well, all of you gave *me* someone to believe in." Peeking up at Steve, she smiled widely, a deeper pink flush spreading across her cheeks.

Holding her gaze, his green eyes were alight.

Josh's voice and the scrape of his chair across from them on the bench seat broke their reverie. "Will you two cut it out? Geez, Jessie, I thought it was just Jacob I had to be worried about." He was frowning across from her as Charles and Jonathon joined Dee in cooing over the baby.

His comment got a laugh from Steve, who finally averted his gaze from Jessie. He left his arm draped across her shoulders, though. It was such sweet pleasure, having the three of them together for a short time, and Josh and Jessie's baby safely close by in Deirdre's arms.

"Sawyer, this girl will never just be yours. She belongs to all of us. To the world, in fact. Deal with it."

Josh smiled at Jessie, then, and she wistfully sent him a loving gaze back. Last night's conversation crossed both minds.

Breakfast ended with hugs and promises to catch up in a few days. As the small group dispersed, Jon walked his son to the elevator. "The dailies are terrific, Josh. *The Wyatt Boys* should get the green light for a few more seasons. Great work. You and Steve have a real chemistry."

Grinning, Josh faced his father. "That's great, Jon. But you need to move the series to the west coast."

"Josh, it's called *The Wyatt Boys* because it's based on the true story of a family and their estate in Toronto. How do you suggest I move it, one brick at a time?"

Laughing, Josh ducked his head and planted both hands on his hips. "I'll see you in a few days, old man."

Jon grasped his son's shoulder. "I mean it, Josh. You are one of the best actors out there today. I wouldn't be surprised to see an Oscar nod come your way for *Freedom Ride*."

"I dunno. Maybe." But Josh's face was lit up full force now. "It took me a while, Jon. But life sure is good. I feel so peaceful these days, for the most part." His headstrong wife crossed his mind.

"I've got news for you, Josh." Leaning forward with a wink, Jon whispered conspiratorially. "It gets even better."

"I can't imagine," was Josh's honest reply.

With a pat on his son's shoulder, Jonathon made his exit with Steve, who, like a boy scout, saluted his goodbye, which left Josh to catch the elevator with the rest of the gang to pack up the last few items for the trip to P.E.I.

Then they were off to the airport, minus one much-loved—and already desperately missed—Matt Kelly.

Chapter Eighteen

Matt's temporary replacements—plural—conducted a meeting once the Keating jet was airborne. The alpha male of the two quickly took charge. Apollo was beefcake solid, with such well-developed coffee-skin biceps bursting from beneath a blue T-shirt that they looked as if they might explode if you stuck a pin in them. His stocky mate, Morgan, a shy twenty-something crew cut blonde of average height, stared at his feet during the chat, apparently terrified to meet Jessie's eye. He mostly listened, punctuating the conversation—which was more like a lecture, from Jessie's point of view—with subdued *yeses* and *maybes,* and only when asked.

"Mrs. Sawyer." Apollo sat across from Jessie in a comfy beige leather armchair, and stared hard in her direction. "Mr. Kelly and I met early this morning. I've been apprised of your itinerary for the next few days and I have a schedule worked out. When your family is separated," he glanced around at the rather downcast folks he was hired at the last minute to watch over, Charles and Dee included, "Morgan will be one party's security. Questions? Anybody?" At the group's glum silence, he continued. "All right. then. So…"

Jessie let his voice fade. She aimed her gaze beyond the window at the blue sky and passing clouds below, and let her mind wander. Apollo seemed capable and organized, but the blonde youngster was obviously cowed by her presence, which wounded Jessie a little. She had a whole inner chat with herself, which consisted of many curse words and reprimands. Squeezing her fingers on her lap was the only way she could keep from inserting the iPhone earbuds and tuning out completely. It was everything she could do not to drive the nails of her right hand into her left.

When Apollo finally vacated his seat to cross the aisle and confer closely with the Keatings, Josh reached into Jessie's lap and grasped his wife's anxious fingers. He turned his head towards the aisle and coughed into his elbow before speaking. Jessie frowned.

"I'm sorry I growled at you last night about the whole Matt thing," he offered sincerely. "I was tired."

"Yeah. And sick." She covered his hand with her left hand. "You were right, though, Josh. I was stupid. I see your side. I see Matt's. I'm the one who is sorry."

"This Apollo guy will be fine. He'll give Matt a bit of time off and then we'll get our friend back."

"Matt's not a friend, Josh."

"Jessie, I thought you said—"

Leaning sideways, she kissed a corner of his soft lips—her tactic to cut him off. She repeated her comment. "He's not a friend. He's family."

At the threatening tears he sensed beneath Jessie's tough veneer this morning, Josh smiled woefully. "Poor Jessie. Still always trying to navigate the corners alone."

"And still messing up. Royally."

She snuggled against his shoulder, legs tucked up underneath her butt on the wide, comfy seat. Josh and Jessie rested in a revised kind of contentment in spite of Josh's need to cough frequently. Emily-Grace was awake for the last part of the trip, but she played happily in Grammie Dee's lap instead of in Josh or Jessie's.

"They're like children with a new toy," Jessie grinned, watching famous producer Charles Keating make silly faces at the baby.

"They're in love," agreed Josh, clearing his throat for the umpteenth time and popping a Fisherman's Friend lozenge into his mouth to cut the scratchiness when he swallowed. "They'll be wanting more babies so they can each have one." He slipped a finger under his wife's thin leather jacket and tickled Jessie, which elicited a tiny laugh before a louder protest.

"Cut it out, Sawyer. Behave. You're in mixed company," she reprimanded him gently as his hand slid higher. Jessie eyed the Fisherman's Friend package that lay on Josh's lap. "Apollo's going to be pissed right off the bat."

"Why is that?" Josh's eyes narrowed.

"Because we're changing his so carefully worked itinerary by stopping at a doctor's office, husband. Before we go anywhere." She fired him a look that left no room for argument and, because Josh was feeling despicably rotten, he didn't try to muster up any energy to argue.

Soon, the jet slipped onto the tarmac at the old Summerside Air Base known to the locals as Slemon Park. Before they gathered their baby and their things, Jessie approached the chisel-chinned super-fit guardian. Coolly, she shoved both hands in her back pockets and rocked forward a bit on her boots.

"We need to make an adjustment in our plans, Apollo. I'm sorry."

Dee overheard, and jumped in. "Jessie, we have to meet the filmmaker in an hour."

Incredulous, Jessie glared at her manager. "Josh needs to see a doctor, Dee."

Apollo saved the catfight from escalating. "Morgan will escort Mr. Sawyer to a doctor. Let's check in at the B & B and do some research to determine who might be available to see your husband."

Josh chose that moment to wander past his wife, baby carrier in hand. He touched Jessie's arm as he passed, but he met Apollo's eyes. "Josh," he told him. He shook his head to accentuate the point. "No Mr. Sawyer. Just Josh."

"All right, sir," Apollo responded with military precision.

Jessie followed Josh out the door and down the steps, chuckling behind him. She looked upward and sent a silent prayer to the indigo blue sky. *God, I know this is selfish, but we need Matt back. Please send him back to us.* She couldn't fathom getting to know a whole new security team, even for one short trip to the east coast, especially a man who was so uptight he insisted on referencing them in formal terms, and a twenty-something kid quite obviously terrified of his own shadow.

~ ~

When Matt arrived home, Julie met him at the door, arms crossed. Her husband was the picture of dejection. It was raining, pouring from the Heavens. Even the spiked hair Jessie liked to tease Matt about was lying flat, as if the gelled strands had given up the fight and were bowing in desolation and defeat.

"You're home early." He hadn't called. All Julie knew about her husband's unexpected trip west was a simple text sent an hour ago from Vancouver International Airport—YVR—that read simply *back in Van, home shortly.*

Matt slid past without meeting his perky wife's steady gaze. Following him up to the bedroom, Julie watched while her hubby deposited his suitcase on the bed and immediately started unpacking.

"Matt? What was all the drama this time?" When he still wouldn't look at her, or offer more than a mumble, Julie took her husband's arm and turned his body towards her. "Matt? What happened?"

Finally, he let his crushed eyes drift up to hers.

"I can't do it anymore, Julie."

"Do what? Security?" She held her breath. Julie Kelly knew what the Keatings—what Jessie—meant to her husband. They were his business, his responsibility, his reason for living (after Julie and their daughter, although sometimes she and Katy felt like a close second). They were his family every bit as much as his aunts, uncles and cousins were. Only much closer. Separating from the Keating-Wheeler-Sawyer world would destroy Matt.

"Security for the Keatings," was his response.

But Julie knew him, and she was well aware of the challenges he faced. "For Jessie, you mean," she stated softly.

He sighed. "It's not just her anymore, Julie. It's Josh now, and Jacob these days a lot too, and…and Emily-Grace."

It took Julie a few moments to find the words to voice what she knew her husband was feeling.

Now, she was succinct and to the point. Her thoughts were spoken in such a subdued tone Matt had to crane his neck to hear. "You're afraid. You're afraid you're going to fail her."

He struggled. His right arm waved uselessly in the air, and Matt sucked in a breath to help him control his emotions. "Again," was all he managed before melting into his wife's arms and letting go of the hefty emotions that held him hostage on the long flight west.

It was only the second time Julie ever saw her husband cry. The first time was the day he came home after reading Jessie's stalking journal after that horrid summer, after Jessie's disappearance.

Julie was a woman who understood pain. And she understood her husband's need to stand by the Keatings. And so, tonight, she knew his loss.

⁓ ⌒

"So what'd the doctor say?" Jessie was breathless. The hockey film meeting was invigorating. First, she'd forgotten how much fun it was to act in feature film projects—they weren't like television, where you were always doing last minute pickups for shots missed in earlier episodes. Instead, you could really relax into your character. And she liked this character a lot! Abby Ryan was a P.E.I. bar singer whose son was missing for the past three years, abducted by his father. In the film, tentatively called *Atlantic Blue*, Abby meets Jordie MacAulay, a semi-pro hockey player who comes back to P.E.I. with nothing to show for the last ten years but a record of pervasive alcohol abuse.

The story was touching, with a real east coast maritime feel, and Jessie could hardly wait to get started.

But now her energy was directed towards her husband, who was sitting on the edge of their big bed in a heritage Summerside, Prince Edward Island, Bed & Breakfast, face drawn and pale with the exception of pink flushes across his cheeks, and a raspy sound to his breathing that grated in Jessie's heart, which skipped a beat at his dejected appearance.

Emily-Grace was, thankfully, asleep in Charles and Dee's room. They'd brought the baby to the meeting, which Charles was co-producing with Jessie, and which Dee was casting. Having Emily-Grace along wasn't Dee's selfless attempt to give the sick Josh a break from the baby—instead it was Dee's effort to keep the baby from catching his cold.

Now, Jessie stepped forward and pressed a palm to her husband's forehead. She lifted his chin so he had to look at her. "Hey. You're worse already."

"It's been hours. Long meeting, I take it."

"Yeah." Studying him, Jessie sucked on her bottom lip. "We came all the way here, Josh. There's a lot of shit to iron out for this production now that we've finally got the green light."

"When are you shooting?"

"Don't change the subject. March. But we'll have to do the hockey shots overnight since the rinks are all in use during the day. Then we'll come back in late May to grab a few early summer exteriors. Fishing boat stuff."

She waited, while he hung his head again. He spoke quietly. "Mind if I skip dinner, Jess?" He wanted to add, "I just need to sleep," but Josh couldn't manage the extra words.

"Josh?" she bugged him. "The doctor? What'd he or she say?"

"She. Dr. Griffin. Nice lady. Took her time. She sent me for a chest X-ray."

"And?"

"Have to wait…for the results."

"And in the meantime?"

"Antibiotics. Chest is a little rattly."

"You're getting sicker."

"Antibiotics, Jess. It'll clear. Just need a little sleep."

At that, he laid down on the bed, on his back at first, but his chest felt laden with bricks, so Josh rolled over onto his side. Jessie reached down and pulled off his boots, setting them on the floor at the foot of the bed. In search of a blanket, she strode over to the closet and yanked it open. Finally finding a cream-colored wool one in the bottom drawer of a chest of drawers, she opened it up and laid it gently over her husband, but he shrugged it away when she tried to tuck it under his ears.

Without opening his eyes, Josh adjusted the blanket to his waist. "Hot," he grimaced, folding his right arm under his head. "Chills earlier, but hot now."

"Did you take anything for the fever?"

"Yeah. Just hasn't kicked in yet, I guess." He neglected to tell Jessie he'd already taken a number of Tylenol this afternoon, four hours apart.

"All right, Josh. Just sleep, okay? I'll bring you some soup or something."

"Not hungry." A loud hacking, choking cough that frightened his already worried wife escaped from between Josh's fire-warm lips.

"Definitely getting worse," murmured Jessie under her breath. Rising from the bed, she wet a washcloth in the bathroom and laid it over his forehead, to Josh's great displeasure.

"Cold," he muttered, without opening his eyes.

"Leave it." Jessie bent down and whispered in his ear. "I love you, Sawyer. Sleep. I will be back within the hour."

Downstairs, she took Morgan aside before they sat for dinner in the B & B's small dining room. The kid was so nervous in her company he could hardly look at her, and instead, as she spoke, he studied the intricate pattern on the floral rug at their feet in the Edwardian furnished room, which was all dark woods and Chippendale cabinets. The wallpaper was also a dark floral, calling to mind Mary Helen and the shelter in Vancouver with its brilliant nature-inspired William Morris designs. Jessie ached to be in Vancouver now, with Josh home in their bed, and Matt close by.

Matt…he would've been right in that doctor's office, she thought. *Gettin' the skinny on Josh and making damn sure he's okay.* She hoped this shy kid had the nerve to butt his way in as well.

"Morgan," Jessie asked, touching his elbow and causing him to jump. "What'd the doctor say today?"

"I didn't talk to her," was his response. "Mr. Sawyer—"

"Josh."

The kid looked up, surprised, and then his gaze disappeared downwards again. "Uh, yeah. Josh went in alone." He shrugged. "I just waited in the waiting room."

"Okay," Jessie said. "Fine." But inwards she was seething, remaining distracted all through their dinner of delicious creamy seafood chowder, chicken cordon bleu, and some sweet potato concoction she couldn't name, but which would have been yummy if she wasn't so worried about her husband.

In the end, Jessie excused herself while Charles and Dee visited with their gracious hosts, a lovely, generous male couple in their sixties.

"Dee," she inquired quietly, bending down by her manager's chair after she slipped off her own, "can you watch Emily-Grace for a few more minutes? Just bring her up when she gets hungry. Please?"

This was unusual for Jessie, and suddenly worry lines creased Deirdre's graceful forehead. "You're that worried about Josh?"

"He's pretty sick, Dee. I don't like it. He's much worse this evening."

"Don't you remember having fevers when you were a kid, Jessie?" At her downtrodden look, Dee sighed and touched Jessie's cheek. "Must not have been much fun for you. Alone…"

"It's okay, Dee. I wasn't always alone." The memory of Sandy dying in her arms broached its horrific head. She shuddered, and Dee winced at the apparent dreadful invasion that crossed Jessie's face, turning her expression dark and sinister.

Jessie shook the fear away, and ached to get back up to her ill hubby. But she wanted to know what wisdom this substitute mother (and now pseudo-grandmother) had to impart. "What about those fevers?" she asked. Wistfully, she added, "I wish you were the one caring for me, Dee. When I was sick all those years ago."

Dee took her hand. "So do I," she smiled sadly. "I was just going to say they always get worse in the evening. Don't worry. He'll perk up. I'm sure the doctor knows what's best."

"Thanks, Dee." Jessie kissed the baby's forehead as the infant gurgled contentedly in the carrier on the floor nearby, and then she nodded at Morgan and Apollo and thanked her hosts before mounting the stairs two at a time.

She found Josh asleep in the darkened room, and so she tiptoed in quietly, and sank into a Windsor Chair at the foot of the bed after pulling it sideways so she could watch Josh's rasping, rattling breaths.

"Don't you even think of leaving me," she ordered him under her breath, as she tucked one foot up on the chair and wrapped her arms around it. "I fucking mean it, Sawyer. Get better. On the double. And that's an order, mister."

She thought of Matt then, and wished he was there so she could just breathe in the energy of his kind wisdom and friendship. She knew he would be able to calm her down and help her think straight. Because right now all Jessie could picture was an eighteen-year-old she loved, staring into her eyes and begging her to help him while he struggled to breathe.

Bending her face into her bent knee, she started counting as Trudy taught her to do when the anxiety seemed too much to bear. "One…two…three…"

Chapter Nineteen

The next day Josh did, indeed, seem a little better. Relieved, Jessie left him with a kiss to sleep the day away while she (and the baby) along with Charles and Deirdre met once again with the local filmmaker, and then were swifted off by Apollo to visit George and Emily at the seniors' lodge on the south shore of the island, in picturesque Clinton. They left Morgan at the B & B with strict orders to keep tabs on Josh and to cater to him if he needed anything. The kid set up a chair outside Josh's door, to the amusement of the B & B's owners, who put a pot of chicken broth on the stove to simmer for the day in case Josh should decide he felt well enough to try some sustenance.

At the lodge, Jessie found George rather sprightly, given his advanced age. They met in the dining room this time to get reacquainted, while Charles and Dee wandered around the halls pushing Emily in her wheelchair. Jessie was as tickled to see her old pal as he was to meet little Emily-Grace. As he offered a finger to the baby, who grasped it with a toothless wide-eyed smile, Jessie watched him happily, and decided that the revelation of his part in her father's demise must have released a ton of weight off the old man's shoulders. He seemed lighter, and even joyful.

In the end, George admitted the reason for his lightness of being. It shocked Jessie so much she was speechless.

"I've been writing to Martha," he admitted gleefully, a light bursting from his gauzy eyes.

When she finally found her voice, Jessie woke up the guy dozing at the next table. "What?! George! She's like…my grandmother!"

"And she's in Ontario. I know," he enthused. "But her emails are so full of life, Jessie. I look forward to them." The frail eyes were sparkling, the almost translucent cheeks imbued with a rosy glow. "Her profile picture on Facebook is gorgeous. That's how I found her."

"Seriously? You're, like, on Facebook?!"

"Say it, Jessie! I'm—well—90. Or so. I lost track years ago, when I turned fifty, I think. You think that excuses me from the likes of Facebook?" Chuckling lightly, he sipped on his tea. "You youngsters are all alike. Us seniors don't stop living and learning just because our bodies crap out on us."

She grinned. "I know. Especially not you, you old coot. Tell Martha I said hi." Narrowing her eyes at him, she queried, "Hey, is she giving away any confidences?"

"Many." That sobered him. He shrugged. "Go see her again. And Sara."

"I plan to," was Jessie's response. She glanced down at her cell phone as a text bleeped at her and the screen lit up.

How's the cowboy?

Jacob.

For once, Jessie wished the text was from Josh, who she hadn't heard from since noon. *He's likely sleeping,* she told herself.

George caught the look. He regarded her curiously.

"It's Jacob," she illuminated him, holding up the phone like a trophy. "He's just wondering how Josh is doing."

"Ah. Yes, and how is that going?"

"What, exactly?"

"Jacob. And this new TV show of yours."

"Oh, George," whispered Jessie. "How I wish you and I lived in the same place. I could use your wisdom." *And Matt's,* she ached.

"And I could use yours." George's rheumy eyes watched her closely. His lips curved up into a broad smile.

"Oh?"

"Well, Martha's a joy, but she's far away. Now Dianne in 107, she's a doll. She was a WREN during the war."

"WREN?"

"Don't you superstars know anything? She served in a women's unit that was part of the Royal Canadian Navy during World War II."

"Oh. That's actually really cool."

The WREN chat started a whole new conversation that, despite missing Matt, and the ever-present worry about Josh, Jessie enjoyed wholeheartedly. Her rapport with George was equal to that of all her *Drifters* friends, as well as Charlie by default, and of course Jacob. She laughed outright when George pointed a thumb in the direction of Apollo, who stood at the entrance to the dining room like some great Colossus, feet spread a hip's distance apart and his arms crossed.

"You'd think that guy was guarding the entrance to King Tut's tomb, instead of a bunch of old has-beens!"

Then it was time to visit with the non-responsive Emily. Jessie left Charles and Dee with George, and she took her mother down the hall to her room. The wheelchair was a new model, recently purchased by Jessie for easier maneuverability and comfort. Turning it so her mother faced her, Jessie eased down onto the bed, surprised to find a clammy sheen to her hands and sticks in her throat, so that her words came out strained. But suddenly Emily was a whole other layer, a stratum of secrets and angst Jessie couldn't possibly fully understand.

Regarding the woman before her now—a living, breathing human being strapped into a hopeless existence, silent and uncommunicative—a whole new dimension opened up. Sara's hurt, angry eyes played across Jessie's heart and mind. She shuddered at the powerful residual effects still resulting from Emily's climb down an old ladder years ago.

"I don't get it, Emily," Jessie thought aloud, with emphasis on the name *Emily* as if it deserved extra weight these days. "I don't know how anyone can walk away from their kid. Even for love of a man."

Josh flashed through her mind, sick and alone while she tried to glean some kind of insight from this non-responsive woman, whose secrets were hidden behind some impenetrable brick wall. She almost choked on the thought of never touching her husband again, of never lying in bed with his hand on her hip and her fingers tucked up under the sleeve of his T-shirt. Of never getting lost in those somber loving eyes again, or having him capture her in his soft puppy-dog gaze, rendering her immobile. Of never again tasting his lips, or clenching her body around him when they made love.

But then…Emily-Grace…she would always be Josh and Jessie's baby, regardless of what the future wrought. Would Jessie ever be able to walk away from a child she created? *No*, she told herself. *Not when she's six, ten, fourteen, eighteen or even thirty-two. If I ever had to choose between loving Josh and my child, or of leaving one behind…*she shook the thought away. Suddenly she was lightning struck with the realization that perhaps this was one reason her mother was silent before her, lost in some deep abyss inside her mind that insulated her from an impossible choice made years ago. And from the loss of the man whose love was apparently worth that choice.

"You failed us," Jessie accused her mother, hands folded neatly on her lap to hide their slight tremble. Sickened, she felt incapable of physically touching this woman, who Jessie saw as a selfish person whose egocentric choices left her daughters vulnerable and hurt.

Jessie knew her grandmother, Martha, had come to some kind of peace, finally, over the years she missed with her daughter. But Sara was certainly holding resentment and hostility close to her chest. They encircled her like ribbons of smoke, curling in and around her ample body, venomous and snakelike.

Did Jessie forgive Emily? Not entirely. Not with these new faces playing across her mind, all victims of a downward midnight climb. Forgiveness no longer seemed black and white. Now, with Sara's physical presence in Jessie's life—and, by marriage and birth, her husband and two boys as well—suddenly there was a whole new dimension to the telling of the Emily Wheeler story and the need to let old hurts go. Because now there was an angry half-sister whose hurts bled onto those around her, in sharp words, angry glares, and an overall bitter countenance.

Here, now, in a long-term care facility on P.E.I.'s north shore, overlooking the river where Jessie's father lost his life, Jessie locked her mother in her vision. Emily was in her childlike place, apparently lost in some memory or fantasy world. Or maybe she wasn't lost at all. Maybe she was just between worlds, in a place that was nothing but blue grey fuzz. Maybe she sang David Wheeler's songs all day…Jessie had no idea where the woman's mind was today. But she knew one thing—it had never really been on her. Nor on Sara, it seemed.

"I'm trying," Jessie whispered to her mother. "I'm trying to forgive you. I understand that it was all too much, in the end. But I have to tell you, Emily. Sara is still that fourteen-year-old daughter you left behind. And you know something?" She gestured to herself, touching her chest as both eyes filled with moisture. "I have a daughter now too. You met her when we came in today. Josh and I named her after you. And after his mom too. Emily-Grace." Her voice softened as she pictured her baby daughter's tiny porcelain cheeks and inquisitive little eyes. "She's something, momma. She's beautiful. And I will never let her down. I swear."

She sighed as her words bounced off the emptiness surrounding her mother. A baby's wail echoed down the hall just as Charles stuck his head in the room on time to see Jessie swiping tears away from her cheeks.

"I'm sorry, Jessie," he said, searching her face for clues as to how this reunion was going. "Little Miss Sawyer seems to need her mommy."

"Oh yeah, sure," Jessie replied, a tiny playful smile lighting her from within. "You and Dee get the fun stuff. Then you give her away when the going gets tough."

It hit her then, what she'd said, and she sucked in a quick breath and reflexively looked at her mother again. "I'll be there in a minute," she breathed to Charles in a subdued voice.

Charles tapped the doorframe nervously before grunting in acknowledgement. As his clipped footsteps faded down the hall, Jessie placed both hands on the arm rails of her mother's wheelchair. Bending forward, she peered closely into the woman's seemingly vacant eyes. "That's what you did," she said defiantly, a tremor in her voice. "You gave us away. Both of us. Her first, then me."

She stood, and smoothed her sweater. "I'm sorry it hurt so bad, leaving Sara behind. Because I can't imagine it didn't. And I'm sorry we lost my dad when we did. But you know something, Emily? I'm glad we had him. For twelve years, we had him. Twelve magical years, Emily."

Please God, she begged, thinking again of Josh. *Let me keep him forever. For seventy years, at least.* Suddenly she was anxious to get the rest of her day underway. Emily-Grace's loud cries echoed that sentiment.

With a raise of her hand, she saluted her mother. And then Jessie banana'd around the wheelchair, and left the room. Outside, she signaled to Jenny, one of the younger staff she'd gotten to know during her visits to the home. "I'm done," she said, fighting the ennui threatening to encompass her like a thick ocean fog. "You have my email. Let me know if she ever needs anything, Jenny."

Forgiveness was one thing. Duty was quite another.

She bypassed the bleached blonde and retrieved her hungry daughter from Dee's arms. Brushing soft lips across Emily-Grace's cottony cheek, she whispered, "You will live a life of roses and sunshine, baby girl. I swear."

Ducking into a comfy blue-cushioned chair, she accepted a light baby quilt from Dee and fed her baby while George and Charles rattled on about the reason behind the small province's nickname for its record-breaking snowstorms of last winter—Snowmageddon. Shuddering as she listened, grateful for Vancouver's pretty cherry blossoms and moderate climate, Jessie reconsidered ever spending a winter in P.E.I.

Then it was time for the little group to take its leave.

"As long as Josh is doing okay, Deirdre and I have an evening at a spa planned," Jessie explained to George. "In Summerside. Mystical Touch. We're getting manis, pedis, facials and massages."

"Can I come?" asked George. "My heels are getting a little cracked."

"You're a little cracked," laughed Jessie as she took the fussy baby from Dee, who had picked her up after the feeding and who was attempting unsuccessfully to elicit burps. Adjusting Emily-Grace in her arms, Jessie swayed gently from side to side, patting the infant gently on her small back. "I'll see you, George. I'm coming back to shoot in March."

"That's months away." He was downcast. "At my age, every day may as well be a year."

"I'll be back," she promised. "Maybe I'll bring Martha. Behave." And then, misty-eyed, Jessie gave him a tender hug, swiveled around, and strode away to the sound of everyone's laughter as Emily-Grace finally released a good belch and, with it, tempered the sadness accompanying yet another parting.

In the car, Apollo assured Jessie that Josh was okay, just asleep, according to Morgan. So he dropped the ladies at the spa in Summerside before running Charles back to their B & B.

They were a few minutes early for the Mystical Touch appointment. Jessie ducked into a treatment room to change Emily-Grace while Dee studied the products lining the shelves behind the reception counter.

Later, after their appointments, she pointed them out to Jessie, and the women left with a bagful.

"Hyaluronic acid," Dee told her. "Magical properties. A very deep moisturizer. They use it on burn victims, in fact."

"They make it here?" Jessie asked, surprised.

"They have a lab out back," Dee told her. "I toured it while you were changing the baby. It's sold under the brand name Quannessence. For Sharon Quann, who gave you that lovely soothing facial!"

"I'm sold, then," Jessie laughed, touching a hand to her cheek. Her facial equaled any she'd had anywhere, and she'd been around the world. "I love coming here, Dee. To P.E.I. This place has some indefinable quality…"

"It's called memories, dear," said Deirdre, patting Jessie's knee.

"It's more than that," Jessie answered, gazing out the window as the car driven by Apollo slithered through slushy snow down Central Street in the small quaint city. She could see the harbor, which was guarded at the southeast entrance by a majestic, charming white maritime lighthouse. "It's the quiet nature of the place. The kindness of the people here. The unhurried pace."

"I doubt everyone's lives are unhurried," cut in Dee. "But I see your point. There are hardly any cars on the streets."

"Certainly not compared to Toronto or Vancouver," mumbled Jessie, who had her hand dangling in the baby carrier so Emily-Grace could grasp it and gurgle peacefully. She smiled at the baby. "What do you think, pretty girl? Want to move to this beautiful island permanently some day? Minus winters, I mean? No Snowmageddon for me!"

Then they were at the B & B, and Jessie forced herself not to tear inside to check on her husband. She wrangled the carrier out of the rented SUV, and followed Dee indoors, where they were warmly welcomed by both of their kind and considerate grey-haired hosts.

Morgan heard the kerfuffle at the entrance to the attractive two-story century home, and he appeared at the top of the stairs. He waved to Jessie, who looked up anxiously as she kicked off her boots and then pulled off her socks to study her new pedicure in the hopes that the UV drying machine at the spa had adequately dried her new cranberry Christmas polish. Satisfied all was well with her toes, she glanced up again at Morgan.

"He's been sleeping most of the day," the shy fella called down to Jessie, finally meeting her concerned gaze. "He took some broth, though."

"Okay," Jessie said, relieved. "Thanks, Morgan." She greeted her hosts, then scooted upstairs, leaving the baby in the carrier at Dee's feet.

He was awake when she entered, but Josh's shrunken appearance dashed Jessie's earlier relief. At her entrance, he hauled himself up against the head-board, where she helped him stuff some pillows behind him to cushion his back.

"You look like shit."

"I feel like shit." His voice was thin and strained, and raspy from coughing.

"Thought you were better."

"Working on it."

"I ordered you to get better."

"That worked so well with Matt. Ordering him around, I mean."

"Huh. Typical man-cold shittiness? I'll let that one go. You get one free pass."

He groaned.

"Tomorrow you see a doctor in Toronto."

"I like this one. She's nice."

"Did she call with the results from the X-Ray?"

"No. Apparently those things take time." Josh raised his cell. "She has my number. She'll call. Or her office will."

"You taking your meds?"

"Yes, sir."

"Eating?"

"Yes, sir. Ma'am. Empty soup. Just broth." Before scanning Jessie's general area for the baby carrier, Josh made a sour face that clearly referenced the tasteless meal. "Where's Emily-Grace?" he queried, punctuating the question with a painful, hacking cough. "Getting spoiled by her coddling grandparents again?"

159

"She's still pretty little, Josh. We don't need her getting sick too. I know—I'll bring you to Miami. That'll dry the sickness outta you."

"How about you come cuddle with me for a bit? That'll dry this old bug up."

Jessie tossed her black marshmallow jacket on the chair from which she watched Josh the night before. She slipped onto the bed and snuggled up to him.

"You're so warm," she murmured. "I'm not liking you being this sick, Josh. Why don't we try to reach that doctor and see what she thinks?"

"She'll just tell me to give the meds some time, Jess. Let's see how I feel tomorrow, okay?" He pulled her closer. "It was a long day here without you."

"Yeah, and you suck at texting, by the way. I need more than the occasional *wanna have sex*. She poked him in the rib. *Not like you'd be up for playing now, anyway. You feel like the inside of a volcano*, she thought.

Chuckling lightly, he told her, "Jessie, I think I can honestly say this is one night when I'm okay to pass on sex."

"Okay, now I'm worried." Burrowing her face in the side of Josh's chest, Jessie wrapped both arms snugly around her husband's waist.

He turned his head away from her and tried to cough again but groaned instead. "I hope the meds kick in tonight, little one," he lamented. "I need to see my daughter. And I'm on the call sheet for tomorrow at three."

"I'll get Dee to call Hilary and one of them will let Jon know. You're going to need some time off, Josh."

"Just give them the heads up, okay? Don't cancel my day yet. You know how insane it is when shooting days need rearranging." He smiled down at the top of his worried girl's head. "I'm planning to rally tomorrow."

"You better." She patted his belly gently and then started removing his belt. "Take off your jeans and climb into bed, big boy. Why'd you get dressed, anyway? Think you were going out on the town or something?" Sliding off the bed, she grabbed his jeans at the ankles.

"Hold up, little wifey." Josh grabbed the waist of his jeans and held on. "Go talk to Dee. I'm gonna get up and brush my teeth anyway. I promise you can tuck me in when you get back."

Jessie paused by the door. "Can I get you anything? More cough syrup or Fishermen's Friends? Empty soup?" She grinned at his cute description of the broth Morgan brought him earlier.

"I'm good. Just come back soon, okay?"

"Josh?"

"Yeah, little one?"

"You sure you're okay?"

He paused, as he swung his legs over the side of the bed. "No," he answered honestly. "But I will be."

Jessie watched him dizzily make his way to the washroom, hanging onto the wall and then the doorframe for support. She tensed, ready to go to his aid, but he managed okay. She went off to find Dee, who would call Josh's manager to see what they could do about possibly rearranging his shoot days.

And I guess we'd better make some calls to Miami, too, she thought. *'Cause I know what my priority is. It's my family. Two people by the names of Emily-Grace and Josh who, right now, need me more than Mystic Nights does.*

She jumped down the stairs, almost skidding into Morgan at the bottom. Just heading out, he was clutching a gym bag.

"Off to work out?" she asked, itching to go along but knowing she was in for the night, with Josh as sick as he was as well as a tiny baby who would soon want a bedtime feeding. Before hitting the sack, Jessie would do some Yoga in her room instead.

"Yeah, I found a gym up the road. Stretch Fitness. Apollo made arrangements for me to get in after staff hours." Morgan's expression changed instantly. "You need me, Jessie, uh, I mean Mrs. Sawyer?"

"Nah." She smiled at his eager, nervous nature. "I'm sure you feel you've done enough babysitting for the day." Jessie cringed at her own reference to Morgan's job that day as babysitting. No wonder Matt was so tired of the Wheeler-Sawyer-Keating menagerie. She touched his wrist. "And it *is* Jessie. Please."

The guy's shoulders dropped as he visibly relaxed. "I don't see it that way, uh, Jessie. Babysitting. I'm sure sometimes the job gets a little more exciting. I'll take the down times when they come. If you guys can use me once in a while, that is."

"Sometimes it does get a little crazy, Morgan," Jessie responded honestly.

"Too crazy, in fact. And I'm sure we can use you again after this trip." She continued around the corner and called over her shoulder, "Have a good workout. I kinda wish I could come."

"I'm going again in the morning." Morgan yanked open the door. The cool air rushed in as he added sprightly, "Six a.m., if you're interested."

"I think I will be," she tossed over her shoulder. "Meet you down here?"

"Yeah. See you then. I hope your husband is on the mend by then."

"That makes two of us, Morgan. 'Night."

And she skipped off to find Deirdre and her baby, and to mess up the shooting schedules of two big productions along the way.

Chapter Twenty

At Stretch Fitness, a cozy white home-shaped gym a mile from the B and B, Jessie wangled her way into a ladies' sunrise metabolic class, which she hoped would lessen her anxiety over the return to Toronto. The early morning squats and lunges were a respite from an increasing nagging worry, providing a desperately needed energy boost. The recent delivery of her baby meant she had to take it a little easy, but despite that, focusing on her body in a healing way with gentle crunches and light weights was a good way to unleash some anxiety.

Jessie'd left Josh dozing; she'd slipped out of bed after a rather sleepless night worrying about him and answering overnight quiet knocks at the door from Dee, whose periodic appearances were not alone—a hungry Emily-Grace was cradled in her arms.

When she returned from the gym, yawning and yanging for a shower before the sweat chilled on her body, Jessie found her husband awake but shaking his head.

"Tell Dee to call it off," he implored her. "Today's shoot. I swear, Jessie, if I thought I could do it, I would. This sucks."

Clutching her cell phone with white knuckles, Jessie fearfully approached Deirdre in the small downstairs B & B dining room. She bent down and picked her daughter up out of Dee's arms, crooned anxiously at the baby, then dropped into a chair by Dee and brought Emily-Grace to her breast.

After dropping her phone on the white linen tablecloth in front of her, Jessie nodded to Deirdre. "Cancel Josh's shoot today, Dee. And tell Jonathon to have a GP waiting at the hotel when we get there."

Dee didn't question the order. She had her own phone in a bag at her feet. Pulling it out immediately, she briskly left the table. Jessie could hear her talking in the front room around the corner of the Edwardian styled Bed and Breakfast. She cocked an ear and strained to listen, but the hushed tones were beyond her reach.

Eyes drifting upwards, Jessie met Charles' formidable gaze. The esteemed producer was frowning deeply, his forehead creased and lips pressed into one pale line. He was hunched forward on his wide chair, elbows on his knees and hands clasped. Silent.

Yeah, you sunuvabitch, Jessie thought, pursing her own lips and fighting back tears as she stared hard back at Charles across the table. Communicating her fear with tortured eyes, she threw bitter silent thoughts his way. *Say what you want about my husband. Curse him, yell at him, fake-apologize to him, I don't fucking care. Just help him. For God's sake, Charles. Just help him.*

As if she'd fired the words telepathically across to him, moving him to action, Charles screeched back his chair and stood.

"I'll get things going now, Jessie. How soon can you be ready to go?"

"I just have to finish feeding this little munchkin," she answered, her voice high-pitched and afraid.

"Make sure you eat something yourself." Charles started to move around the table and head towards the front foyer, but Jessie stopped him with a question.

"Charles? Have you heard from Matt at all?"

Her producer and sort-of father searched her face. "Yes, Jessie, I have. We're making arrangements to have Ulysses take on the role of Chief Security. He flew into Toronto yesterday. He'll meet us at the jet."

"So...?" She left the question unanswered.

Charles softened. He discerned correctly that his girl was already near tears. This news wouldn't help. "He's not coming back, Jessie."

"Oh." Lifting the nursing blanket, Jessie peeked down at her baby, who seemed content. Tossing her head as she struggled to remain relaxed so Emily-Grace could feed well, Jessie let her focus drift back to Charles. Her words were abrupt, fraught with the acknowledgement of her own stubborn past actions. "I really fucked up, eh?"

He kept his feet planted on the Persian rug, but Charles extended a hand to rest on the elegant antique dining table. He planted the opposite hand on one hip and exhaled. "If you want me to lie to you, I will, Jessie."

"I miss him, Charles." The words were thick, hurting. "I—we—need him. What can I do to make things right?"

"You can't," was the answer. "He made his choice. I'm surprised it took him this long, actually." Shifting his feet, Charles continued. "Jessie, Matt's a grown-up. A grown-up who knows he made some mistakes with you—"

"Not like I gave him a choice," she cut in.

"No, you didn't, but still. There were things he should have caught."

"He's human, Charles. Please." Then, as quickly as the thought exited her lips, a new one took its place. "Jesus, Charles. Tell me you didn't fire Matt."

"Of course not! He's more than just security to us, you know that, Jessie. But—" Licking his lips and bringing the hand on the table to his chin, Charles scratched idly before looking back at Jessie. He swallowed before telling her, "But we didn't discourage him from leaving, either. Neither of us did."

"What?" It took a moment for what he was saying to sink in. "So you hung Matt out to dry? You just let him walk away from us...from me. Because of...because I'm worth more to you than he is. Financially. And you had to make a choice."

"Look at you, Jessie," Charles pleaded, his own voice now thick with emotion. "You're sitting over there feeding your baby. A baby that, a while ago, you didn't even want to tell us about. Who now means the world to Deirdre and I, who we consider our granddaughter. Who, if you hadn't chosen to come back from Scotland, in all likelihood wouldn't even exist. How can you sit there and tell me I chose you because you make us money? Do you think we even care about money anymore?" Clearly insulted, he was starting to tremble. "We give back, Jessie. We all do. We couldn't live with ourselves if we didn't. But more importantly, we've had time to grieve the loss of you, and what you've endured in your short lifetime. And we know what to cherish."

His eyes landed on the little blanket, underneath which Emily-Grace was sleepily chowing down. Miniature tan leather moccasins decorated with pink stitching peeked out, the tiny feet inside them moving slightly with their momma's rising and falling chest.

This time, Jessie swiped at a tear. She tossed her curls again, and raised her chin. "And so you chose us. Emily-Grace and me. By not convincing Matt to stay." She didn't add *and so you also chose Josh*. Because in her heart, Jessie knew Josh was not at the top of Charles' list of people to *cherish*, as he so succinctly put it.

"How did you go about it, Charles? Did you and Dee just say 'okay Matt, see ya?' Or was there some discussion about all the ways you figured he fucked up over the years? Or, I know, maybe he went to you and said 'look, you gotta rein Jessie in, she's doing this rogue thing again,' huh? And you stood there fingering your silk tie and told him, 'yeah, well, we can't have Jessie upset, we don't want her going rogue on us but I suppose at the end of the day it all came out okay, so maybe you should just go, Matt. Go, and we won't have this kind of conflict again between the two of you.' Is that how it went down, Charles? Something like that?"

"You want to know how it went down, Jessie? Really?"

She sucked in a breath. Something in Charles' tone scared her before the words were uttered.

He continued, turning his body square on to her and the baby, and leaning over the table so that he was looking down at her. "He got too close. That's what happened. Matt's not stupid, Jessie. All of a sudden he's got you and Josh and a baby to watch out for. And he's made mistakes in the past. Add to that your stubborn, and may I add selfish, insistence on going rogue, and how much he cares about you—*you, Jessie*. He got scared. He walked away."

"With your blessing." Her words were taut, as if they would snap with a whistling *zing* if uttered too carelessly. They were accompanied by quietly rolling tears.

"Yes." Charles straightened, but he, too, had to squelch a tear by pressing a thumb and forefinger against the corner of his left eye. "With our blessing. Me and Deirdre." He paused before leaving the exquisite dining room. "We lost you before, Jessie." Nodding at the baby, he added, "The stakes are higher now. And we are simply not interested in ever feeling that kind of pain again."

As his domineering presence faded from the room, Jessie crumbled. "What about me?" she breathed to herself, to the baby's tiny ears, and to the otherwise empty room. "What about the pain I feel about losing Matt? Doesn't that count for anything?"

Switching Emily-Grace to the other breast, she forced a smile at one of her hosts when the kind silver-haired gentleman wandered in and asked if she needed anything. "Yes," she replied as an ache gutted her belly. "I do. A few things. But unfortunately I don't think they're anything you have on the menu."

Half an hour later, the SUVs were loaded. Jessie escorted her hurting hubby to the first one. She pushed Matt from her mind for the time being, because on her arm now was her dizzy, sick, feverish husband and, for now, he was her priority. She steadied Josh as he eased into a seat, noting with a frightful disdain that something in his breathing seemed to have changed. His breaths were shallow, his attempts to inhale obviously paining him. The rasping was worse, like a heavy old locomotive trying to move a weight larger than it could handle through a stubborn pile of sludge and snow.

"Maybe we should call the doctor here," Jessie tried, hoisting one foot up on the exterior rail of the SUV. "That nice Dr. Griffin."

"I think Charles and Dee are anxious to get going," Josh managed, wheezing painfully. "Let's just get back to Toronto, Jessie. It's only a few hours."

She acquiesced, mumbling under her breath, "I don't really give a shit about what Charles and Dee think." Immediately chastising herself for the wholly uncharitable comment, she reached over Josh's lap to make sure his seatbelt was secure. His eyes were closed, and he was leaning against the seat with his head tilted up and back.

"I'm not Emily-Grace," he said, forcing a small smile.

"No, you're just a *big* baby," Jessie teased rather anxiously. She brushed her lips against his stubbly cheeks. "Luv you, Josh."

"I know," he said, opening his eyes and turning his head to peek at his wife through feverish slits. "Luv you back, little one."

Less than three hours later, they touched down in Toronto. Ulysses met them at the jet with Big Dan in tow. He let Apollo and Morgan go for the time being, and escorted the made-up family back to their hotel in downtown Toronto.

Jon was waiting, a physician by his side.

Within the hour, Josh was admitted to the hospital.

Chapter Twenty-one

"Pneumonia, huh?" was Jacob's contemplative response when Jessie told him. "That sucks. I had it when I was eight. All I remember is going to the hospital and having them strip me down to my nether region while they blew a fan over a big bucket of ice at me." He shivered inadvertently, remembering the exposed feeling of lying almost naked on a small gurney while a busy nurse hummed around him.

Jessie was pacing outside the hospital, near a small entrance over which Dan stood sentinel while she talked with Jacob. "They've upped the antibiotics he was on. He'll be fine. Right?" Drawing a quaking hand over her forehead, she closed her eyes.

"You want *me* to tell you he'll be fine? Sure. He'll be fine, Jess. I was. He's strong, young. He has you in his corner. A new baby…of course he'll be fine."

"Jacob…"

"Come on, Jessie. Chill. He'll be okay." Jacob couldn't keep the worry from edging his voice, though. Not that he was overly concerned about Josh, but Jessie was obviously losing it, what with Matt's recent departure and all. Add to that the gut-wrenching memory of a lonely dark night on a near-deserted road at the bottom of a North Vancouver mountain, an insidious moonlit dagger, and a handgun…

"Jacob…the stats say fifty per cent of all splenectomy patients who get pneumonia within the first two years don't make it."

Jacob paused. "Then good thing he's in the other fifty per cent."

"Fuuuccckkk. Jacob, I can't lose him."

The silence from the other end was unnerving. It was a while before either heard anything but breathing across the connection. Then Jacob offered his thoughts on the subject.

"What is it about him, Jessie? Why are you so sure you can't live without him?"

"Jesus, Jacob! I think I'll hang up now and call my sister for consolation! And she hates my guts!"

"I mean it. I want you to calm down. Take a deep breath and just…think about it."

"You already know. And I'm not in the mood to play 'let's console poor lonely Jacob,' who could have any woman on the planet right about now but who, for some inane reason, keeps chasing the biggest loser on the planet instead!"

"You call me to tell me your cowboy is sick, and you want me to be sorry, well I am, Jessie. Seriously. Pneumonia sucks. I had it once, remember? But you have to stop thinking the worst all the time. And—I'm going to say this even though it'll suck for you to hear it—you would survive if you lost him. You wouldn't be alone. You'd miss him, but you'd survive. So stop thinking the worst. Go hold his stupid hand, and let him know you're there for him. Nothing bad's going to happen, Jessie. He'll beat this."

In a small voice Jessie managed, "I wish you knew that for real."

"I do," Jacob answered. "I do know it for real."

Sarcasm infiltrated Jessie's worried one-word query. "How?"

Copycat sarcasm fueled Jacob's low laugh. "Because, you idiot. I couldn't possibly be that lucky."

"Geez, you're a bastard, Jacob. You know that? A real tried and true certified nutcase."

"Made you smile, though, didn't I?"

"I'm going now."

"You better. Go tell the shmuck to stop messing with his wife's head."

"Heart," she whispered.

"Now who's the bastard?" But Jacob was grinning now, and Jessie could sense it.

She tried to change the tone of the conversation by asking about Michael and Kelly.

"They were great until they heard you're detained in Toronto. Rewrites, y'know? Their surfing vacation in Hawaii is now postponed."

"Ha. Kelly owes me one, anyway, from her self-imposed exile in season one."

"I'm guessing she won't see it that way. Being Her Highness Kelly and all."

"How 'bout you, Jacob? Are you having any fun? Like, maybe getting out to practice your salsa moves? Or are you just doing Zumba alone in your suite to Pitbull's Fireball?"

"Wouldn't you like to know? And you oughtta know I don't listen to Pitbull. I'm more the Hozier type."

"You can't dance to Hozier. Instead, you just suck on salty pretzels and cry in your beer."

"My Cuban-Spanish is improving. Does that count as fun?"

"Ah, are you learning from an actual teacher or just taking an online course?"

"Does the greasy bartender at the Palomino Sound Club count?"

Groaning, Jessie palmed her forehead. Nearby, Dan crossed his arms and waited, eyeballing an old guy with a walker, as if he posed a threat to the anxious woman pacing the hospital's back entrance.

"Jake old buddy, copious amounts of Guinness do not one's Spanish improve. Find a woman, will you? Spend your nights doing the bed boogie instead of gittin' your brannigan on at the local pub."

"The nights are long, Jess. There's lots of time for language lessons, sloshing back the Guinness, *and* picking up women. And for doing the funky monkey after." A pitiful whine accosted Jacob's faraway voice then. "Tell your doofus to get better, will you? Come back so we can spend our nights watching old movies again! I'll spring for the nachos."

"Ah, good ole Jacob, all bubbles with no fizz." Softening, Jessie added, "I'll tell Josh you said so. That he has to get better."

"Tell him I'm moving in on his woman if he doesn't. That oughtta do it."

"Either that or it'll give him a heart attack instead."

"Maybe he just needs a little scare."

"Nah. He just needs me to hold his hand. That's all."

"And with that lovely vision in my head, I gotta run, Jess. I'm meeting the princess and Michael downstairs."

"Crocodile hunting again?" She frowned, remembering Jacob's sharp retort to her on a rather tense day during season one's long shoot.

"Snake wrangling. Rattlesnakes." His grin reached from the depths of Florida to wrap Jessie in a big ole Jacob style hug. "Luv you, Jess. Call me if you need me. Okay?"

"'K."

She paused.

After a bit, Jacob broke the silence. "I really have to go, Jessie. I'm sorry."

"I know."

Muffled sobs brought Jacob to his knees.

"I wish you were here," she moaned.

With a frown, Dan turned away to give her some privacy.

"I am there, Jess. I'm always with you. Always."

"I know, I just mean for real, babe. You know? I could really use a hug right about now."

"Text me lots, Jessie. And call me again later. In the meantime, I am with you, okay? In spirit, at least." *Picking up the pieces as always,* he chided himself for thinking.

"Don't be too hard on them thar snakes. They got families. They got a right to live."

His laugh warmed her heart.

"We're actually going out on some gargantuan yacht with one of the big guys from Hollywood. If I for real see a snake—or a crocodile, for that matter—I'll be the one having the heart attack. Trust me."

"Spoiled little city boy. Grow some balls."

"I've got great balls. Don't tell me you've forgotten them already—"

"Oh, Lordy."

"Go. Hold the cowboy's hand. Tight. I want to win you back the right way, through my own personal charms. Which, for the record, do not include wrassling with either crocs or snakes."

"Yeah, yeah, I know about all your personal charms, Jacob. And, for the record," she echoed him, "I do recall they include a set of very nice balls. I acquiesce."

"Ha," he chuckled. "I knew it. You still want this."

"Always, you doofus. I love you to pieces."

"I love you back. Text me. Tons."

"Bye, Jacob. Thank you for listening." The Eeyore woe was back in Jessie's tired voice. "Hi to Michael and Kelly."

"Hi to your cowboy."

When the connection was broken, Jessie paused, dropped onto a nearby bench, and drew her feet up so she could hug her knees. After a few moments, a big hand dropped onto one shoulder.

"You okay, Jessie?"

A wan smile drifted up to Dan. "I've had better days."

"Shall we go back inside? You're shivering."

"Y-yeah." She stood. "I guess we don't need both of us being sick now, do we, Dan?"

An image of Jacob partying on a yacht in Miami crossed her mind. Rosy sun-kissed cheeks and colorful drinks seemed rather idyllic, about now.

Near Josh's room, Jessie spotted Ulysses conferring with Dee. A new panic seized her, contorting her features with alarm. "Where's Emily-Grace?"

"She's downstairs with Giselle, honey," comforted Dee. "I changed her but she's ready to be fed, I think. She's wailing like a banshee, entertaining the local city folk with an early version of one of her own pop tunes."

"Oh, crap. Already? Time flies with a newborn, huh, Dee?" Eyeing Josh warily from outside the room, Jessie noted with relief that he seemed to be sleeping peacefully. She was torn. She didn't want to leave his presence again, but no way did she want her new baby anywhere near this ward filled with 'who knew what' diseases and emergencies.

Suddenly Jessie had some insight into Matt's feelings. Indeed there was another little body to worry about, a small baby who the world found quite captivating these days. Jessie's whirling mind was painfully absorbed with such thoughts as she motored down the long over lit hall towards the elevator, flanked by Dee and Dan, with Ulysses close behind.

If Matt were just here, too…it physically hurt to think about him, despite the traitorous streak Jessie felt as she glanced sideways at Dan and over her shoulder at Ulysses. The men were 'all about the job.' Matt was a big comfy Charlie Brown blanket.

Shivering, Jessie wrapped both goose-bumped arms around herself. It seemed like all the warmth she usually carried with her was gone, as if the heat afforded by the close men in her life vacated Jessie's body when they did—Jacob and their shared sunny Miami, Matt and his warm enveloping presence, and Josh with the heat of his comforting arms. Charles was still around, but he was more of a frozen chill these days.

As the elevator door slid open, Jessie's shoulders sagged with the heavy weight of physical and emotional fatigue. Then she stepped into the claustrophobic space, disappeared inside, and was carried away.

It was eight that night before the doctor and Jessie managed to co-ordinate their schedules enough to meet. Earlier, she had found a kind nurse who let her into a private room so she could pump milk for her baby, so Deirdre could take the infant back to her hotel suite for the night.

Before Dee left the hospital, Jessie met her in the lobby and handed over the milk, now snuggled into a small cooler provided by the helpful nurse. Smoothing back her daughter's hair, Jessie kissed a tender pink cheek.

"Dee," she said mournfully, "I don't know how I am supposed to do this."

"Do what, honey?"

"Drag this baby all over God's creation in the first few months of her life. Let her go with you. Everything!"

"Jessie, listen to me. Josh is getting what he needs here. He is being treated—he'll get well. Emily-Grace has some constants—her carrier, her travel crib, Charles and I. Her mom. She's adapting just fine."

"She's a good baby, isn't she, Dee? I mean, I've heard stories about colic and that kind of thing…"

"She's an excellent baby, as far as I'm concerned." Dee smiled. "And even if she were colicky and kept us awake all hours, I'd love her to pieces anyway." Leaning forward, she deposited a kiss on Jessie's forehead. "Go be with your husband, Jessie. Your daughter is fine with grumpy old Grampie and me. We'll be along early in the morning."

"Okay. Thanks, Dee. For everything."

"I'm leaving my phone on. Call me if…well, call me if anything changes. And keep Ulysses nearby."

At Jessie's slumped shoulders and forlorn countenance, Dee sighed. "We'll say some prayers for him, honey."

Hummpphh, was Jessie's inward mute response to that…not the prayer part, no. She was planning to do a lot of praying herself. No, it was the notion that Dee—and Charles—would pray for Josh, their not-so-favorite person on the planet at the present time.

Giselle was with the formidable lady, as was Big Dan, who would escort them safely back to the hotel. Both women embraced Jessie before taking their leave. As they wandered towards the exit, they balanced the weight of the baby between them by each grabbing hold of the carrier's handle.

Memorizing the image of the two older women with little Emily-Grace suspended between them, Jessie laid a hand over her heart. The infant was facing her momma, innocent eyes gazing around the busy lobby, curious.

"Sweet baby," murmured Jessie, blowing her daughter an air kiss that floated to the baby on a sigh and a wish. "Nothing but joy and roses for you. Let's get your daddy better and settle down a bit, huh?"

She waited until they were out of sight. Then, with Ulysses at her side, Jessie turned and headed back up to Josh's ward via the elevator. Ulysses set up a perch in a comfy chair outside Josh's room while Jessie met with the physician.

The doctor was a Canadian born Chinese man of about fifty. Apparent confidence and assertive speech made up for his lack of height. He swept into the room with a chart in one hand and a pen in the other, his hips moving in a slightly effeminate manner, but he was all business and that eased Jessie's mind somewhat.

He shook her hand, his grip a little light, but the man's eyes radiated warmth.

"Jessie. Doctor Li. It's a pleasure to meet you. My daughter is 15. She's a big fan."

"Thank you, Doctor Li." Shoving damp hands in her back pockets, Jessie took a breath, which she held suspended for a few seconds before speaking.

When she released the words, they emerged in a swoosh of air and hope. "I'll be a big fan of yours if you can work a miracle on this fine-looking man of mine."

Dr. Li moved to Josh's bedside, and glanced at the chart in his hand. He lifted Josh's fingers and depressed a nail, then settled in to explain to Jessie what Josh was up against.

"The bluish color of your husband's nails when he was admitted suggested immediately that he was low on oxygen. We confirmed this with an arterial blood gas test. The nasal tube you see is providing that much needed oxygen by travelling down through your husband's lungs and into his heart. The heart pumps it to his organs. It also removes waste gas, carbon dioxide."

The doctor studied Jessie to see if she was following. She bit her lip, and nodded. He continued to discuss the various tests—CT scan, bronchoscopy—that helped determine the severity of Josh's pneumonia.

"What about antibiotics? He was taking some, why weren't they working?"

"We made some changes, Jessie. Your doctor in P.E.I. did the right thing starting him on antibiotics, but your husband was maybe sicker than she realized. Given his spleen removal, and the results of today's X-ray, we felt it best to administer antibiotics intravenously. Your husband is a very sick man, Jessie. But he is under good care here, and somehow I feel he's a fighter."

"I hope so. I think so." She aimed her pearl-blue eyes towards the doctor's own dark almond-shaped eyes. She was holding her breath.

"He has a lot to fight for, I think." Dr. Li smiled broadly, hoping to relax this worried wife whose husband was under his care.

"He sure does. We have a baby daughter."

"I heard that. You'll love her until she turns about thirteen. Then you'll wonder who she is." He laughed. "I might take this opportunity to thank you for writing such positive music for those days when Jasmine refuses to speak to us and won't come out of her room. When headphones are a permanent part of her wardrobe."

"Ah. It gets that bad?" Jessie's memory of being thirteen was similar. But she doubted this kind man's daughter was experiencing anything other than ordinary teenage rebellion. At least, she hoped so. No thirteen year old should endure a torment like Jessie suffered at that age.

"Sometimes, yes." The physician regarded Jessie compassionately, a radiant fleck in his friendly eyes. "But mostly it's wonderful. Jasmine can be a handful, but the joy she brings to our lives is immeasurable. You'll see."

"I already see," answered Jessie, relaxing in Dr. Li's company. "Although it's hard to picture my new baby as a snotty teenager."

Dr. Li scrawled a note on the chart in his hands and smiled broadly. "Can I give you some parenting advice, Jessie?"

She had a feeling she would be on the receiving end whether she said yes or not, so Jessie simply nodded. "Sure. Anything."

"Choose your battles carefully. That little maxim has saved me countless times. Here's another—remember who the parent is. Trust me, with these words in the back of your head as your child grows, you'll save yourself a lot of headaches."

"Thank you, Doctor. I'll try to remember those bits of wisdom."

Before strolling away, Dr. Li let his gaze linger on Jessie's bloodshot eyes. "I'll have an orderly bring you a cot, Jessie. Try to get some sleep."

"Doctor?" Jessie finally lifted both hands out of her pockets, and crossed and uncrossed her arms. She garnered a small bit of remaining courage and drove one set of nails into the back of her other hand before she could speak. Then she asked the question she was afraid to voice for fear of what the answer might bring.

"Josh is going to be okay, though, right? I mean…with the spleen thing and all…I mean, he'll be okay for sure, right?"

At that, Dr. Li's eyes softened, but they also took on a slightly guarded look. The businesslike doctor was back, the genial parent side ferreted carefully away. "A lot depends on your husband at this point, Jessie. But like I said, he has a lot to live for."

She swallowed, a bitter dry spit that tasted god-awful. "That's not really the solid answer I was hoping for." A new sheen appeared in the diaphanous eyes.

"Talk to him," suggested the doctor. "Hold his hand. Tell him you love him. Do your part, and let him do his."

"And you want me to sleep?" Slowly, Jessie shook her head from side to side. She grabbed at the cuff on her sweater and started twisting a section around a forefinger. "Not for one second, doctor. Josh will have me in his ear all night, telling him I love him. I'm not giving him a chance to think otherwise. Not for one damn second."

"You won't be much good for your baby, or for him, Jessie, if you don't take care of yourself. Somehow, I think telling him a few times is enough. And maybe a few more times when you get up to pee." He allowed a half-hearted warning smile, but Jessie didn't bite. Instead, she stared at her toes, absently turning one ankle over as she pondered this frightening hospital and the fear it wrought.

Doctor Li started to move past her. "I'll also have someone bring you something to eat. You need to keep your strength up. I'll be around tonight, so you'll see me checking in every hour or so."

"Doctor?"

"Yes?"

"Everyone keeps telling me what I do is important. But it's nothing. You know?"

Dr. Li's lips curved up widely this time. "Tell that to me at nine o'clock on a school night when my obstinate daughter won't talk to me." He stepped towards the door. "I'm glad she has you, Jessie. Especially at those times when I know she thinks she has nobody else."

At his essence, which seemed to flit and hover in the room after the kindly doctor swept off through the door, Jessie whispered, "And I'm glad Josh has you."

She turned to her man, then, who was flat out in bed, a nasal tube delivering the much needed oxygen, and an intravenous administering the strong antibiotic. Raspy sounds were still emerging from his prone figure, and Josh's lungs had a certain gurgling wet cadence to their irregular rising and falling.

Taking his warm fingers in hers, Jessie sucked in a breath when he stirred.

"Hey," came a croak from the bed—a thin, tired voice. Josh's eyes narrowed sleepily. "Don't look...at me...like that. I'm fine."

Inhaling deeply, Jessie replied hoarsely, "You are, you're fine." Trying to muster a smile, she gave up and lifted the droopy fingers for a kiss instead.

"I know...that look," he rasped. "And don't think...I'm going...anywhere,

Mrs. Sawyer. Do you think…I'd shuffle off this mortal coil…and let Jacob…
raise my daughter?"

"He was hoping you would." Her attempt at morbid humor succeeded in
lightening up Josh, but only sank Jessie further. "Babe, please…"

So much for telling him I love him, she thought. *All I can do is blubber.*

"Jessie, I'm…okay. Really. I'm not…planning to go…anywhere." His
words were slow, thick, like honey on a farmhouse pantry shelf in winter.
"Hell, did I tell you…Jon thinks I might…actually…get that…Oscar nomination…the blogs…are…all buzzing… about?" That was all he could manage. The effort left Josh completely out of breath.

Jessie bent closer. "Will you stop bragging and shut your trap, Sawyer?
And yes, I'm fairly certain you will get that Oscar nod. But may I remind you
that if you win you'll still be one gold statuette behind me?"

Josh's tiny smile was her answer, along with a rattly, "Not…for long." He
soaked up the whispery feathery feel of his wife's lips on his forehead, but
wordlessly frowned at the worried pale eyes trying so valiantly to disguise
themselves as playful and strong. A weighty fatigue dogged him, and when
Josh couldn't fight the heavy eyelids any longer, he drifted off with his chocolate eyes buried in his wife's fretful gaze until the sandman won.

Jessie had been bending over her husband during their brief banter. Now,
she dragged a deep armchair closer to the bed, planning to stay by his side,
as she'd told Dr. Li she would, all through the long night. Settling in, Jessie
took in her surroundings. A light cotton coverlet over the usual white sheet
rose and fell with Josh's uneven breaths, covering the broad chest over which
she loved to run her hands in admiration. She pictured herself straddling her
husband, one knee on either side, looking down into those endless brown
eyes, loving the gentle nature of this man whose love she promised God each
day she would never take for granted. Visualizing them together in better
days, Jessie sent Josh strength this way, by picturing the two of them together
forever, in love, raising a family with children yet to come, sharing the ups
and downs of life together.

The steady beeping emitted from a nearby monitor started grating on
Jessie's nerves. Grunting, shifting uncomfortably in the deep chair, she tensed
at its steady rhythm. Aware that it was likely Josh's heartbeat she was hearing,

a part of Jessie was grateful for its constant presence there, but it sounded artificial and she wanted the real thing, available to her when she pressed her ear against his chest. The electronic imitation was unbearable. It had a vicious power, because if it started to slow Jessie knew it would be like some kind of weird marker wedging its way into her brain; a marker she would be powerless to change, to restore to some kind of normal rhythm.

Between the frightening beeping, Josh's rattling breaths, and the invasive hushed tones floating into the room from the hallway, Jessie couldn't settle. She wanted to shut all of them out, to erase their hostile intrusion on her fragile psyche. Bending over, she groped around inside the russet leather bag at her feet. Her fingers landed on the trusty earbuds Jessie carried with her everywhere. Planting them into each ear, and into her iPhone, she leaned back in the chair and allowed her usual healer—music—to carry her to a better place.

The hours were elongated in this weird place. Between dozing on and off, and texting their friends as well as Josh's brother Zach and his sister Kayla, Jessie mostly just told Josh stories and shared thoughts with him she knew he couldn't hear. When she didn't know what else to say, she laid her cheek against the bed rail and started murmuring *I love you* over and over. Jessie didn't dare slip away, in case Josh should…well, she wouldn't think of that. She didn't dare. Dr. Li had faith, and Josh seemed determined to beat this stupid pneumonia, and so Jessie resolved to believe it too.

There was, simply, no other option.

Chapter Twenty-two

*M*att was in the Audi trying to find parking in Pacific Centre's large underground lot when Vancouver's The Peak announced that, after being diagnosed with pneumonia, actor Josh Sawyer had been admitted to a Toronto hospital.

Slamming his palm on the steering wheel, Matt bolted upright and hit the brake. He couldn't care less that the person driving the Mazda sedan behind him had to suddenly stomp on their brake pedal as well. Matt also ignored the heavy-handed obscene gestures aimed at him from behind the Mazda's steering wheel.

Once he collected his wits from every corner of the huge garage, Matt abruptly steered the Audi, which Charles was letting him keep 'as a gesture of good faith,' into the closest spot he could find, which was a tight squeeze between a Porsche Carrera and an old rust-bucket Toyota Camry.

"Leave it to Vancouver," he muttered, eyeing the economic disparity between the two cars, while immediately speed-dialing Magda over at the Keating building on Robson. A sickening gnawing almost choked him. No way would Jessie be handling this latest drama well. At all.

"Hello, Matt," was Magda's sensuous response, spoken in her glamorous 'I-am-gatekeeper-to-Charles-and-Deirdre-Keating (not to mention Jessie Wheeler-Sawyer-and-now-Jacob-Ryan)' manner. "Have you talked to Charles today?"

"No, I…no." Matt studied a stain in his steering wheel; its presence pissed him off because he knew it was there yet he'd neglected to wipe it away. It was a coffee stain resulting from a quick skid and sudden stop at the corner of

Robson and Burrard from a long ago day when he was rushing to shuttle Jessie from one place to another.

So many things I pushed aside and ignored, he lectured himself. Now, though, guilt ripped over him like a tidal wave. He knew Charles was trying to reach him today. He knew it, because he'd heard the ring tones and watched the alerts blaze up on his phone. And Matt ignored every damn one.

He lifted a thumb and forefinger to his forehead and pressed down hard. "I just heard Josh was hospitalized," he said to Magda in a voice he tried to make sound more confident than he felt. "I assume that's why Charles was calling. A…courtesy call."

"Yes." Magda was sorry at the angst she clearly detected in Matt's voice. All of the Robson building minions were shocked when news came through of him leaving the Keating camp. She tried to appease the hurt. "More than that, though, Matt. Charles is hoping you'll take a few minutes and at least give Jessie a call."

Matt pondered the suggestion as Jessie's surely crumpled shoulders and worried eyes flashed inside his heart. "How sick is Josh, Magda?"

"He's in the ICU, Matt. It's pneumonia." She waited. "Will I give Charles a message for you, Matt?"

"No, Magda. Yes. Actually, yes."

"And the message is?"

"Tell him to keep Ulysses on Jessie. At the hospital." *There is no doubt that's where she is*, Matt considered.

Slightly disappointed, and mildly puzzled, Magda agreed. But Matt wasn't finished. "Oh, and Magda?"

"Yes?"

"Book me a flight to Toronto. I'll be at the airport in two hours."

The line was momentarily silent. "Certainly, Matt."

"And one more thing, Magda. Let's keep this to ourselves for now."

"Absolutely. Whatever you say."

Matt hesitated only a second before revving up the sleek sedan and backing out of the tight space. He exited from the subdued semi-darkness of Pacific Centre into a grey misty rain, flicked on the wipers, and turned for home.

"You just got home."

Julie's words weren't really meant to be accusatory in any way, shape or form, but the tension rolling around Matt's brain and tightening his shoulders into a headache-inducing mass of knots colored how he interpreted her message. He snapped at his pretty, petite wife.

"And I'll be home again in a few days." He tossed a pair of leather desert boots into a folding garment bag and went off in search of dress shirts.

"So you need an extra pair of boots? For just a few days?"

Pausing, Matt looked over his shoulder at the open bag, which he'd spread out on his and Julie's bed. Leaving the closet door open, he twisted around and removed the boots. Wiping a finger anxiously across the underside of his nose, he made a quiet *mmphf* sound and dropped the boots on the floor at his feet.

"Maybe you should take them anyway. Just in case," came Julie's careful thoughts as she watched her husband struggle with the prep for a trip he didn't seem to be sure how to handle.

"No," he bit off, and went to move back towards the closet, but Julie took his elbow and turned him to face her square on.

"Matt," she started, eyes searching his. "If you're really doing this…leaving them…then why are you flying back to Toronto? Just get your updates about Josh from Charles, over the phone."

He didn't answer. Instead, Matt looked away from his wife and fixed his gaze on the open closet door.

She tried again. "You're hoping to mend fences." Reaching for his phone, which he'd tossed on the bed, she grabbed it and held it up. "You've been getting texts from him. From Charles."

"If you've read my texts, Julie, you know he's not asking me back. Those are courtesy texts."

"Is that what it would take? For you to get your job back—him asking you? Your stubborn pride's getting in the way, is that it? Because you can call them courtesy texts if you want, but it seems to me they're a friend sharing his worries with a friend. And maybe they're a cry for help."

"You're the one who wants me to mend fences. Face it, Julie, you and I do better with a little space."

"We do best when my husband feels useful."

"In that case, I'm better off without that whole circus," he grumbled, tossing black designer socks into the garment bag. ""Frigging babysitter. An unwanted one, at that."

"Have you talked to Jessie? What does she think? Matt, did something happen you're not telling me about?"

"Julie, there's no room for female jealousy in this equation, if that's what this is. I've got enough on my mind without you wandering off on some strange tangent."

"I know you care about her!"

"Not like that. Never like that. Look, Julie," Matt stopped packing and faced his wife. "I do care about her. I care about all of them. But Charles and Dee are in agreement that I need some time away. I don't know why I'm going back to Toronto. I only know it's not to get my job back."

"Then I know why." Julie laid a hand on her husband's clean-shaven cheek. He placed his hand over hers and waited. "Jessie. That's why."

Matt paused and considered what to say. He blinked and took a deep breath. "I don't know if I can explain what she means to me, Julie. It's not a physical thing. It's more like…I know her, that's all. I know what she's been through, and I know what Josh means to her. There's been a divide between the Sawyers and Charles and Dee over the last many months. They're civil to each other, but there's a wall between them. Jacob's in Miami, and he is Jessie's best friend, next to Josh. Steve's in Toronto, and I'm glad of that, but I feel like…I feel like I need to be there, just to see her, to know she's holding up okay. Which I can't imagine she is."

"You need to end things with her on a better note. Because you were angry, when you left. You left angry."

His eyes widened. "And you know this how?"

Smiling softly, Julie held up her own phone. "She called me from Prince Edward Island. She wanted to know if you got home okay. If you were… okay."

"Oh." Matt shuffled uncomfortably, wondering how to hide his deep emotions from a wife he loved but sometimes felt he barely knew, given their regular time apart. He shoved the heels of both fists into his eyes and blinked again, hoping to quell another impending onslaught of what he felt were unmanly tears.

"You're surprised."

He swallowed. "I suppose so."

"What, you thought it was a one-way street? Your feelings for her?"

"Stop calling them feelings, Julie. You're making it sound like more than it is."

"I don't suppose feelings are always romantic, Matt. But that doesn't make them any less real. Or less painful."

Speechless, he nodded, and swallowed past the lump in his throat.

Tenderly, she bent forward and kissed him. "Why do I feel like the two of you are breaking up?"

"I suppose we are." Matt let his hands land on Julie's small, comforting hips.

"Then go. Tie up your loose ends and let her go with dignity. Then come back to me. Okay?"

"You're not in competition with Jessie, Julie. You never were."

"Tell that to me when you've had time to process life outside the Keating-Wheeler-Sawyer bubble, Matt Kelly. When you're on the outside looking in."

He sighed. "I have a flight to catch."

"All right. I'll see you in a day or so, then."

"You will. I promise."

"Unless…"

Matt placed a finger over his wife's lips. He shook his head. "There is no 'unless.' Josh fought too hard to get Jessie back to give up the fight now. Willpower alone will help him through this."

"What about his spleen? He's more at risk, isn't he?"

"He's getting the best care available, Julie. But…just in case…" Wistfully, he studied her pixie features.

"I know. Say some prayers."

"Light a candle, even, down at St. Mary's."

"I will."

"And tell my girl not to get too far ahead of me in Zelda, or I'll never be able to catch up."

"School's keeping her too busy for video games. She made the gymnastics team, did I tell you that?"

All the things I've missed, Matt thought. "No," he admitted aloud, as he dove back into the closet in search of jeans. "But I'm listening now. What's that going to entail?"

And he packed as Julie dropped down onto the bed, one leg folded underneath, and enjoyed the brief time alone with her husband before he, once again, left her to face a whole old-new drama.

Chapter Twenty-three

"Awww, crap. Didn't we do this already? Like about a year and a half ago?"

It was Steve's voice that woke Jessie from a heavy doze at 6 a.m. She sat up quickly and wiped the drool off her chin to see him standing across from her, hands in his pockets, somberly eyeing his friend's prone body.

"Geez, you like to scare a gal." Jessie shoved away a vivid dream of her with two children, presumably hers and Josh's, laughing as they wandered through a golden field, with Josh watching from the field's perimeter. *Gotta stop singing that song,* she thought to herself, looking muzzily up at Steve through a mist of fog.

Like the appearance of sunshine after a summer rain, the fog slowly cleared.

"Sorry," Steve replied, then nodded at Josh. Jessie had to tilt an ear towards him to hear his half-serious admonition, which was, "I thought I told you to keep an eye on this guy." He spoke in a low tone so as not to wake his *Wyatt Boys* co-star.

"He's doing okay, Steve. He's stable."

"And what does that mean exactly?"

"It means he's okay. The doctor said another twenty-four hours and we should see a big improvement. At least I think that's what he said. I may have dreamed it since I think I was told that around four a.m." As if to accentuate her point, she yawned so widely Jessie thought her jaw might snap.

"You. Go." Steve tried to shoo her away but she shook her head vigorously, large curls tossing from side to side.

"Nope. Not moving. Staying here."

Steve eyed the un-mussed cot behind Jessie, which an orderly had placed up against the side wall, its pristine white sheets and striped blanket untouched. "Then sleep, at least. I'll hold the fort."

"Jonathon was here," was Jessie's response. "For a good chunk of the night. He said you guys were shooting til 2 a.m. Methinks you need as many zzzzs as I do. You sleep."

"I don't have a tiny baby depending on me for survival. Speaking of which, Dee is already up and on the go. I ran into her in the hotel lobby. She was on the hunt for an early breakfast. She'll be here by seven."

"She has to go back to Vancouver."

"She and Charles delayed their plans, Jessie. Stop worrying. They won't leave you here alone."

"What about *The Wyatt Boys*?"

Steve leaned back on the small window ledge and crossed his arms. "Jon did what he always does. After he was here last night, he went home and started rewriting an entire episode. Josh is free to rest and recuperate for as long as he needs." He paused. "And Miami?"

"Well, because of the baby, I wasn't written in a lot anyway. I was supposed to be back by this Friday but that ain't happening. They'll sort it out. Jacob just might have to screw Kelly's character again." A wan smile accompanied that sideways remark.

"You hungry, Jess? You need to eat. I'll do a food run. Whatever you want."

"I'm not really, Steve. Maybe some oj. I think that's about all I can handle right now."

"Coming right up, little girl." Steve started to amble over towards Jessie's side of Josh's bed when she caught him looking up above her crouched head, surprise streaking across his eyes. Then he smiled and let those eyes drift down to Jessie, who straightened, and twisted around to look behind her.

In a second, she was up. Then the tears she'd held at bay all through the long night finally loosed themselves, and flowed one after the other down the exhausted pink cheeks. She crumpled into her visitor's arms as relief torpedoed through her chest and down to her toes.

"Matt!" she moaned. "God, you stupid nerd. You stupid nerd!"

Steve touched her back on his way by. "I'll be back in half an hour," he said to the trembling body. He nodded to Ulysses outside the door, who waved at him with a stifled yawn. The striking black man was patiently biding his time with a Sudoku. Jon's muscled guy Apollo would replace him at eight a.m.

Jessie couldn't take her eyes off Matt, who she had yet to let go of, and who was, at the moment, unable to find enough strength and clarity of emotion to speak.

Standing back at arms length from her ex-security, Jessie studied him. She was humbled to detect the sadness and sorrow in those gentle eyes. "I'm sorry," she disclosed tearfully. "I'm so, so stupid, Matt. I mean it. I'm really sorry."

"How's he doing?" Matt croaked, unable just yet to deal with the 'other' outstanding issue—forgiveness and healing.

At that, the flood started again. Jessie struggled to wipe her eyes, looked down at her toes, and noticed wet spots on her sweater—milk was leaking from her nipples.

"Oh shit," she groaned, flustered.

Matt frowned, and slipped off his navy blue wool blazer. As a father would for a child, he dropped it over the hunched shoulders, fastening the top button after Jessie slipped her arms through the sleeves.

"That'll do until Dee arrives with your baby, Jessie. Emily-Grace will remedy that."

"You were talking to them? Charles and Dee?" The blue eyes were tragically hopeful.

"Not yet."

"You know us that well, huh, Matt? To know where we would be and how we would handle all this, with Josh and the baby."

"I guess I do," he acknowledged ruefully. "Now, about your husband. Tell me what's up."

"We had a scare, Matt. A bad one. That's what's up."

"And now?"

"And now, with you here, suddenly I feel like everything is going to be okay."

Chewing on one corner of his bottom lip, Matt skillfully averted Jessie's gaze by looking past her at Josh, who was still rasping away on the bed.

She caught on and sucked in a breath. In a subdued tone she sulked, "You're not staying."

"Jessie, I don't think we need to have that conversation again. Okay? I just…I couldn't leave you alone. Not like this."

"You left without a hug, even. That was just plain mean, Matt." She was hanging onto him again, as if he might bolt and disappear if she let go of the sleeves of his crisp white dress shirt.

He sighed. "Now it's my turn to say I'm sorry. Can we sit?"

They perched side by side on the small cot. A blonde, ponytailed male nurse strode in and busied himself by efficiently taking Josh's vitals. Watching him exit the room afterwards, ponytail bouncing, Jessie noted with relief that the young man's smile seemed infused with encouragement.

Leaning back against the wall, Matt slipped an arm around Jessie's shoulders. "The problem is," he started haltingly, also visibly relieved, "sometimes I don't know what to do with you."

"Why?" It was a helpless plea, childlike in nature, steeped with a lack of understanding and a need for the world to right itself on its axis again. "You left because you didn't think you could protect me—us—the way I am, so stupid and independent. Matt, I swear I'll behave if you'll stay. I'll do whatever you say."

A heavy weight suffused Matt's voice. "You're right, Jessie. That's a big part of it. I admit it. You scare the hell out of me."

"You're human, Matt. Sometimes shit just happens."

"That's not good enough, Jessie. I think this family needs someone with special ops training. Not a frumpy old retired RCMP officer who has already shown the leaks in his bucket."

"Geez, Spike. You could never be frumpy." Reaching up, Jessie gently fingered the little gelled spikes in his hair. For once he didn't pull away, or yank her hand away. "Even though I gather you took the redeye from Van. Your hair even looks tired. And anyways, Matt, I only want you. You got caught a few times because of my stupidity. That's all."

"No, Jessie. I don't have the skill set you need. Not for a whole family."

"Please. I need you."

He spread out his free arm. "I'm here, aren't I? I'm always only a phone call away. We're still friends, aren't we?"

She shook her head wearily. "No, Matt." She smiled sadly. "We're family."

At that sweet disclosure, his cheeks pinked. He inhaled, though, regained his composure, and continued. "That's another thing, Jessie. I need time with my family. Katy just made the gymnastics team at school, and I'd like to be around to see her compete." Regarding the sad baby blues fixed on him, Matt resisted the urge to tell her about Julie having a moment when she wondered if there was some kind of affair or romantic connection between him and Jessie. He thought, if nothing else, she would find it amusing.

Jessie didn't need to hear it. She was well aware she earned more of Matt's time and affection some months than even his own wife and daughter. Still, even though their connection wasn't romantic in nature, it was still—here, now—undeniable. And it ran deep.

This was a bleak understanding between friends in the midst of a long term parting.

"So I guess me asking you to stay is just plain selfish."

"You asking me to stay is flattering, Jessie. But…"

"But…you have a daughter you don't see enough. I guess I get that part, Matt. I can't imagine being away from my daughter. Ever."

"We'll stay in touch, you and me. If that's okay with you."

"It's everything to me, Matt. Otherwise I'll lose my mind missing you."

"If your husband was awake I'd fill his head with rules. But then again, what'd be the point?" Winking, Matt forced a solemn grin at the woman scrunched under the protection of his arm.

Poking him in the ribs, Jessie forced a chuckle between her lips. Given the sanctity of this new day, and the worries it still wrought, it emerged more like a beat-up grumble.

"I said I would be careful, Matt. That I would try to follow the rules. Write 'em down. I'll make sure the big lug gets them. And enforces them." She snuggled deeper into Matt's side, soaking up the earthy scent of his expensive aftershave. "When he wakes up, I mean. And stays awake."

Turning her head, in her frame of vision she encompassed Josh and the annoying but life-monitoring technology.

"He'll be awake and back on his feet reprimanding you before you know it, Jessie."

"I wish you could promise me that. Like...pinkie swear or something."

"Julie's lighting a candle at St. Mary's." It was a free-floating comment, but there seemed to be a lack of suitable words on this troubling day.

"Julie's the best." An honest verve underlit the powerful statement. "Isn't she, Matt?"

"Damn straight, kiddo. She really is."

"Well, I suppose at the very least I'm glad she gets to have you around more. What will you do for work," she managed to tease between yawns, "take up a security post at a bank or something?"

"Yeah, I'll stand there with a sign. *I used to work for the great Jessie Wheeler.* I'll sign autographs. I'll charge ten bucks each to add to the minimum wage the banks pay."

"Dork. I'm worth more than ten bucks an autograph." She smiled broadly.

"And you wonder why I'm leaving." He chuckled at her upturned lips. "That's it, Jessie. Dilute your arrogance with a smile."

"Touche, Matt! And ouch, by the way."

Their repartee eased into the old comfortable confidence of sincere friendship. At seven, Doctor Li popped his head in and introduced himself to Matt. The day got underway with the increased staccato of footsteps in the hall outside, and soothing orange juice hand delivered by Steve, who forced a carrot muffin into Jessie's hands as well. Emily-Grace arrived none the worse for wear in Deirdre's arms, with Charles following close behind, arms laden with a full diaper bag and the infant's baby carrier.

Jessie ducked out to feed her daughter, looking over her shoulder as Matt offered a nervous handshake to Charles.

"Men," she muttered. "Stupid old pride. Gets in the way every time."

Stopping in the hall before she lost sight of these pivotal people who helped make her world go round, Jessie exhaled and spoke to her baby girl. "Emily-Grace, let me just say there goes one of the best men on this planet. Kind, generous, smart, tough—Matt is gonna leave a big friggin' hole in our lives." Studying him closely, Jessie suddenly saw Matt in a whole new light. She straightened, and whispered softly. "Look at him, little girl. He's as nervous as a barn cat pouncing on the last mouse. And he looks like he might cry. This hurts."

Hanging her head, she started down the hallway towards the private room yesterday's nurse had arranged for Jessie's use when she needed it. "I hope he lets me keep his jacket." Wrapped inside the blue blazer, which gave off a familiar Matt nuance of sweat and spice, Jessie felt safe. Protected.

But more than that, she felt loved.

"And I used to be scared of him. The big ole softy."

She wheeled around one last time to study her old friend.

Looking up, he caught her eye, pausing in his stilted conversation with Charles to watch her go. Nodding at her, Matt felt his smile turn upside down as a deep wrench gutted his belly.

Jessie put two fingers to her lips, kissed them, and sent them floating towards him. Then she forced a smile, hauled open the door to the private room, and disappeared inside.

Chapter Twenty-four

*L*ater in the day, Jessie joined Matt and Steve in a tiny waiting room down the hall. She collapsed onto a seat with a giant *hummpphh* and looked at the guys expectantly.

"What?" Steve asked.

"I need to go to the gym."

"You need sleep," was his determined answer.

Matt studied Jessie closely. Her eyes were red, well shadowed underneath, and she was entirely unsuccessful at stifling regular yawns. But he also noticed she was resorting to some serious hair twisting. Anxiety was getting the best of her. He knew her well enough to know she wouldn't even consider sleeping until Josh was in the clear.

A shadow alerted them to Charles' presence at the door. He eyed Jessie carefully. "What's the news now?" he queried her in his clipped all-business tone as he, too, collapsed wearily into a chair next to Matt. "Has the doctor been in lately?" He had been off with Jon for the afternoon, watching the Toronto crew shoot scenes from *The Wyatt Boys*. Steve had a 'by' from shooting for the day.

"Yeah, he's been in a lot. Doctor Li's great. The hospital brass has been around today too. I suppose they're all curious." Jessie shifted her butt so she could tuck a leg underneath her body. Leaning on the arm of the chair, she inhaled and told the men, "Josh's responding to the new meds. He's a fighter." She met Matt's eye across from her. She was still wearing his blazer; she'd rolled the sleeves up so they rode over her wrists. Jessie telegraphed her wish for him to leave the blazer with her when he left, so she could keep a piece of him around, always.

The object of her scrutiny rose. "I'll have a chat with Ulysses, Jessie. And maybe, if you don't mind, I'll come to the gym with you. I need a run and it's freezing outside. A treadmill sounds like a decent option."

"I'd like that," she admitted, reaching for his hand and giving it a squeeze. "The new security kid, Morgan, goes to a local gym. We can likely go with him."

"Are you sure that's a good idea, Jessie?" Charles' voice was gravelly, tired.

Jessie felt instantly remorseful at her stubbornness in not bringing a full-time nanny on board, since it meant Charles and Dee were picking up the pieces when it came to Emily-Grace's care.

"You're exhausted," he was saying. "And you likely shouldn't be pushing it at this point."

"I'll take it easy, Charles. I swear."

Charles looked up at Matt. An ache creased Jessie's heart when she saw the trust pass between the two men. With his eyes, Charles was asking Matt to keep an eye on Jessie. No words were spoken, but she noticed a slight nod pass between them, which she knew clearly meant 'I'll keep an eye on her.'

Then Matt swung open the door and disappeared into the brightly lit, bustling hallway.

"Steve," Jessie started, switching gears a little, "can you—"

Her good friend cut her off. "You got it, kid. I'll stay with your spoiled, attention grabbing, soul sucking husband." He was sitting next to her, close enough to casually drape an arm around her shoulders. "Don't you worry, little girl," he added sincerely.

"Thanks," she told him, grabbing onto his hand and pulling it tighter around her, and switching her position on the chair so she could lean into him a little.

Charles spoke up. "I'll stay with him too, Jessie."

Both Jessie and Steve were quiet then. They regarded Charles with a mixture of gratitude and suspicion, but in the end they both decided to trust that Charles' intentions were honest. Maybe this latest scare was enough to wizen him up, to bring him to his senses to find some sort of peace with Josh. *Wishful thinking,* Jessie thought.

"Thanks, Charles," she offered quietly. "I won't be long. Just a quick thirty on the elliptical and maybe a few light weights, that's all."

Matt came back to the door then. When he opened it, the noise of the hallway—clanking trays, squeaky footsteps and low conversation—rumbled in. "Morgan is meeting us at the gym, Jessie. I guess we'll swing by the hotel so you can grab a change of clothes on the way?"

He reached out a hand, which she took, and Matt hoisted Jessie off the low chair. Steve and Charles got up as well, and followed them down the hall to Josh's room, where Jessie disappeared inside to whisper her plans to her dozing husband.

"Matt." Charles started to speak, but hesitated. Steve stole quietly down the hall towards a vending machine.

"There's nothing else to say, Charles." Matt was insistent. Crossing his arms, he faced his former boss and good friend.

"She wants you back. She misses you."

"Does she." A nerve on Matt's cheek twitched. "And you?"

"We'll work something out."

"I see." Rotating his head slightly to the right, Matt glanced in at Jessie, who was holding Josh's hand against her cheek. Josh appeared to be awake, albeit sleepy, but he managed to move a hand over Jessie's and was mumbling softly to her.

Charles jumped in again. "There's so much more at risk now, Matt."

"And I fucked up before. Many times. We've been over that."

"It's nothing personal, you know that. Deirdre just needs a stronger sense of security than your limited experience can provide. Ulysses has more training, more experience with technology, and he's got Apollo and this Morgan kid now on as back-up for days like today when Jessie all of a sudden decides to leave her sick husband and go for a run, or whatever the hell it is she does at the gym—that stair climber thing or whatever."

"Elliptical." Matt's tone was dry.

"But Matt…she wants you back. We can find a place for you."

"Just not as the boss anymore, is that it, Charles?" He softened. "Regardless, what she wants and what she's going to get are two different things. For the most part, Jessie and I made our peace this morning. I'll see you."

Jessie joined them then, somber, but anxious to move her body for at least an hour. Although she quickly caught the tension between the two men, besides shooting Charles a silent *f-u* look for his part in Matt's exodus from her security detail, she spoke brightly. "He's awake and telling me to go workout but not to flirt with Dion Phaneuf if he's there. Apparently Morgan says this is Dion's gym. I told Josh he was nuts. I'm a Vancouver Canucks fan through and through, not a Toronto Maple Leafs fan, and he oughtta know that by now."

"He's okay then, Jessie?" Charles' voice was flat, husky.

"No. Dion sucks." Her eyes twinkled with the little energy they had left after the last few crazy days. "Oh, you mean Josh. Ha ha!"

Steve wandered up behind them. "Jessie made a funny." He gave her a push. "Go. I'll tell lover boy some Newfie jokes. That'll scare him back into health real quick. I'll take bets on how long it takes him to tell me to shut up."

Jessie leaned forward and gave Steve a kiss on the cheek. "Luv u," she said. "Thank you. And call me if there's any change at all, okay, Steve?"

"He'll be fine," was his answer. "Don't worry." He looked over at Charles. "So this Newfoundlander walks into a bar…" Steve's voice faded as he stepped into Josh's hospital room, with Charles just behind him. The producer grimaced as he passed Jessie, but he angled his head towards Matt as he walked by. His ex-security chief turned away.

Folding her arm through Matt's elbow, Jessie whistled, a low whistle that only her compatriot heard as they sauntered down the hallway. "I hate to see you two like this, Matt. Come on, make up and be friends again. You're always telling me to choose my battles and take the high road. You should take your own advice."

"Charles is right, Jessie. You need someone with more experience by your side."

"I need my friend with me," she pouted. "I fucking miss you."

"Let's not do this again, okay?" he stated, stopping by the elevator to push the 'down' button. "We've aired our thoughts. Let's just do the gym and have a good day before I fly out again tonight."

"What, you're not even staying twenty-four hours?" She was incredulous. But then Jessie saw something at play beneath Matt's gentle wise eyes. It was pain, and it hurt to see it there, flickering beneath the surface like some steely-eyed Lochness monster, flitting and playing and diving beneath the waves of his usually calm demeanor.

"Honey," she said, biting back her own deep hurts over a situation for which she knew she was in so many ways responsible, "if you change your mind someday…Charles will come around. And you know, he can't," she swallowed because she was about to pull a trump card she knew Matt wouldn't necessarily respect, but it was all Jessie had left in her little bag of tricks at this point in time, and she was feeling desperate, "he can't override me, because without me what does he have? Jacob?" She tried to laugh, but the sound came out tinny and weird. "He needs me," she added in a small voice.

The elevator door slid open and they slipped inside. Matt was shaking his head as he leaned back against the far wall. "What are you saying, Jessie? You'd quit working with Charles because of me? Hardly likely."

"Yeah, Matt. That's what I'm saying." Turning sideways, Jessie took his elbow, then pulled him around to face her. "Go be with your family for a while. But then come back. I don't want to do this without you."

"You'll be fine, Jessie. Ulysses has more training than I do. And his is up to date, not twenty years old. He knows the Aps and all the tech stuff."

Her voice was small, then. She gulped. "But he's not you, Matt. I want my friend. I feel like my arm or leg is missing without you. Emily-Grace feels it too, I swear. And Miami with Ulysses is just wrong. Running with him is like running with a—"

"With a what? A proper security guy? What was he doing, actually running behind you and keeping an eye out for you, or was he chatting you up the whole time?"

"I already miss our running chats." Her earlier sad smile was now completely upended. Jessie slid her hand into his when the elevator door slipped open. They walked quietly down the hall towards the exit to the parking lot, Matt scanning the entire time for any curious onlookers. Like a little kid, Jessie swung his hand lightly between them.

"Well, we'll have a good chat today then, Jessie. And come for dinner when you guys are back in Van, okay? Julie misses you too."

"What else is Katy up to these days?" She stared at the floor as they walked. "Besides her amazing gymnastics prowess, I mean."

He guffawed. "You wouldn't believe it."

"What?" Jessie perked up, removed her hand from his and slipped her arm around his waist. He did the same.

"She's learning guitar."

"Oh, noooo! Tell her to put it away. Anything but guitar. Like…figure skating or soccer or, well, flute's okay, but not guitar! Poor kid."

"Why not guitar?" A bright open laugh accompanied the query.

"Music is wonderful, Matt. It's saved me lots of times, but…well…" Her eyes clouded over.

Matt held open the side door to the hospital so Jessie could walk through. "It's a curse. That's what you were going to say. Music's a curse. Isn't that right, Jessie?"

"Never," she answered him, eyes misty. "It's been my greatest joy. But it says a lot about what kind of person Katy is turning out to be."

His brow wrinkled in curiosity. "Meaning?"

They reached the car, and stopped outside while she finished her thought. He leaned forward and fished his keys out of the pocket of the blazer in which Jessie was still comfortably ensconced.

"She'll hurt deeper, Matt. Music does that to people. It has a power that makes the highs higher and the lows lower. There's no middle ground when it comes to music. It's an ache that lives in you, that can give you the most incredible ecstasy, like, say at a Zumba class when you're just dancing and having so much fun. But then…when things hurt, in your lifetime, music exacerbates them. It makes things worse. Sometimes."

She was speaking in a low, tired voice fueled by fatigue and emotion. Almost as an afterthought, Jessie touched his arm. "You want your jacket back?"

Watching her, Matt considered what to say, how to respond. Finally, he said a simple, "No," to the jacket comment, and then he added, "Well, if the guitar sticks, I hope you'll be around to help Katy sort out the emotional part, Jessie."

"I'm just a phone call away, Matt," Jessie teased, echoing his morning promise. She smiled then, sincerely, hopefully, remembering the doctor's comments about his teen daughter escaping to music when she felt alone or lonely. "Katy will be fine. She has a good dad to give her a strong shoulder when she needs it."

They hugged then, in the parking lot, before Matt shot Jessie a mixed look of gratitude and longing, and circled the car to slide into the driver's seat.

Before Jessie climbed in on her side, a last thought flitted across her mind. *I'm going to miss that shoulder. And that voice. And those eyes.*

"Matt, please," she pleaded one last time when they were seated alongside each other. "I'm begging. You've reduced me to begging. Take a break, but come back."

He hesitated before turning the key. But he didn't answer, with the exception of throwing a sad smile in her direction. Then Matt pulled out of the parking spot, drove to their hotel, and sat in the car aching for a life he knew he could no longer have.

Jessie threw him a worried frown, then ran upstairs, checked on Emily-Grace (and Dee, for that matter), gathered some Lululemon gear and runners, and re-joined Matt for a silent ride to the gym.

～ ～

"I don't like the guy," Matt admitted later to Steve at the hotel bar, where they were celebrating Josh's slow but sure recovery.

"Aw, he's okay," offered Steve as he pushed a bowl of salty pretzels towards Matt. They were sitting at the mahogany bar, their dinner done, their good-nights to Charles and Dee said, waiting for Matt's imminent departure time to creep up on them. Both men were yawning incessantly. A few drinks seemed the only way to keep them awake, even if only by virtue of lifting their heavy glasses.

Matt was referencing Morgan. "Call it intuition," he said. "There's something seedy about that guy."

"Look, Matt," Steve sighed, sitting back. "I'm not going to tell you this is just sour grapes, because you don't need to hear that from me. I'm guessing you're just venting right now, because, for one, all of us are stressed enough over you leaving without having to deal with your 'dour intuition' regarding Jessie's new gym buddy."

"Well, I hope that's all he is, because I mean it, Steve. I'm getting a vibe from that guy I don't like. For one, I don't like the way he stood back and watched Jessie at the gym today. Like she was some kind of candy." He lifted his whisky to his lips and sipped quietly, staring at his dejected reflection in the mirror across from him, behind the bar. A sense of ennui so big it almost doubled him over left Matt slumped.

Steve noticed. He dropped a big paw on Matt's shoulder. "You okay there, pal?"

"Yeah. Yeah. Just tired. I'll sleep all the way home. I'll be fine."

"Everybody watches Jessie likes she's some kind of candy, Matt. You know that. In fact, most guys will quite happily watch any woman in Lululemon pants at a gym, much less an object of curiosity like our superstar girl."

Matt's answer was a low *harumpphhh.*

"Charles should let you take the jet."

"Dee offered. I said no thanks."

"Stubborn old goat."

"Who's a stubborn old goat?" Jessie breezed in behind them.

Steve rotated his stool around to face her. "Damn, girl, you clean up mighty fine." He grinned as he appraised her choice of slim black leggings, low slung suede boots, thigh length floral top, and leather jacket.

She blushed and dropped her eyes to the boots Deirdre had recently ordered for her from some online retailer. "Amazing what a shower and a nap can do for a person. In the opposite order, of course."

"Back to the hospital now?"

"Yep. I'm crashing there tonight. Thanks, Steve, for hanging out with Josh today so I could get some R and R."

"Josh was a picnic. Charles, on the other hand…he makes me nervous."

"I'm surprised he stayed."

"So was I. But he was great. He even did a Starbucks run."

"Seriously? You kiddin' me? What'd you say to him?"

Steve laughed. "Too many Newfie jokes, apparently. He left running."

Matt spun his stool around slowly then. He bit his bottom lip and regarded Jessie carefully. Suddenly, with the weird vibe from Morgan, leaving didn't seem to be such a good idea. Jessie caught the concern and thinly disguised worry.

"What?" she asked him, her voice hoarse.

Matt and Steve exchanged glances. Jessie stomped her foot. Steve pointed at it. "You stomped your foot. You actually stomped your foot! Like a little kid." Casually swiping the back of a hand across his lips, his eyes sparkled merrily.

"Grrr," Jessie frowned at him. "Don't avoid the question. What's up, you two nerds?"

Matt avoided the question wholeheartedly. He held out an arm and Jessie squiggled underneath it, resting both elbows on the bar between him and Steve. "Ginger ale, Jessie?"

"Water," she answered, frowning. "With lemon." She shot Steve a sideways look that said *don't think you're off the hook. I'll get this out of you later.*

They chatted about little things then, odds and ends to fill the uncomfortable last hour before Matt had to leave. In the end, he drove Jessie to the hospital. Ulysses met them at the door.

They said their good-byes in the car.

"I'm not happy about this, Matt," Jessie said, wrapping her arms around him. "I hope to hell you're not, either. Because if you're happy to be leaving me, I will hate myself forever."

"Of course I'm not happy," he confessed, struggling to contain his emotions because he knew if he didn't, she'd lose it. "Just…" He crunched on his lip and cut the sentence off.

"Just what, Matt?" Jessie leaned back and studied him.

"Just…Jessie, the thing about security is, there's only so much anyone can do to protect you. There comes a point when you have to do your own watching and trust your own gut. Okay? You hearing me?"

"Ookkkaayyyyy," she said slowly in response. "Is that your final advice to me, Matt? Your parting gift?"

"I guess you could say that. C'mere."

Their next hug was intense, and finite. Jessie finally pulled away from Matt and, with one last look, slipped out of the vehicle and into the care of Ulysses, who shut the car door behind her and raised a final salute to his old boss.

Matt put the car in gear and moved out of the parking lot, onto the 401, and then towards the airport. But he had a hard time keeping his eyes on the road. For the third time in his life, he wept over Jessie Wheeler. Only this time, it wasn't sorrow for the past.

It was worry for the future.

Chapter Twenty-five

"You are, like, the sulkiest patient. Ever."

It was a week later.

Jessie climbed up onto Josh's hospital bed and snuggled close. "Fussy! What's wrong with green tea? It's good for you!"

"You drink it! It tastes like grass. Which, by the way, is something I've heard you say a dozen times, Mrs. Sawyer."

"Yeah, but you're sick, Mr. Sawyer. And you need to get well. So you need to suck it up and drink and eat stuff that's good for you."

"So make me some chicken soup, little wifey." Josh grinned widely and leaned his head against his wife. He was no longer in the ICU, and was sitting up in bed joking around. Jessie's relief was palpable. Her body sighed into his.

"I can't wait til I can, Josh. I can't wait til we're home again."

"Christmas break is coming, Jessie. We'll have lots of time to chill with our friends. More time than most people will have off."

"I know. That was just me being selfish again. I just got so scared over you." She rubbed his splenectomy scar gently. "Next time, Josh, even the sniffles, you go see a doctor."

"I will," was his honest reply. "And next time you bring me coffee. None of this grassy stuff. We'll save that for Misty."

"Do you want to go there over the holidays? To the ranch? We could ski at Sunshine, in Banff. You could take Misty out for a few rides if you're up for it."

"What about Emily-Grace, if we go skiing?"

"Evelyn's offered to watch her. She's aching for a chance. We'll just do a half day, if you're feeling well enough by then." Craning her neck back so she could more easily see his face, she added, "How are you feeling today, Josh?"

"Like I can breathe without it hurting, finally. No more daggers in my chest."

She grimaced. "It was that bad? Why didn't you say something?"

"Mostly I just wanted to sleep. That's all."

"And you didn't want to worry me."

"I thought the meds would kick in."

Leaning in again, she wrapped an arm around his chest. "Thank God, Josh. Thank God we got you here when we did."

"No more worrying, Jessie. Get out of this claustrophobic hospital. Get Ulysses to take you for a drive or something."

At her hesitation, it was his turn to lean back and study her face. "What? I know that look. It's your 'I-already-have-plans-should-I-tell-him-look.'"

"I do. I have plans. Steve's dropping by here in a bit so I know I'm not leaving you alone."

"You're going back to Peterborough."

"Yep. I am. I need to see them one more time, Josh. Then…who knows?"

"Tell me you are at least taking Ulysses. That you learned your lesson."

"I am not taking Ulysses. But I have agreed to him following me in his own vehicle."

"You still don't want them to see you as who you are."

"Sara doesn't need any more help judging me. At least this way maybe I can win her over."

"By being someone you're not."

"I dunno, Josh. Help me out here. I'm doing the best I can in a weird situation."

"All right. As long as Ulysses is there to keep an eye on you from a distance. I'm okay with that." He changed tack. "What about Matt? Did you manage to convince him to stay, Jess? Or to come back after a break?"

"He says no. But I'm not giving up."

A wail from across the room, where Emily-Grace sat facing them in her carrier on the floor beside a small sofa, caught Josh and Jessie's attention.

Jessie laughed. "Emily-Grace agrees. She misses Matt too." *And Jacob*, thought Jessie inwardly.

"Apparently." Josh crooked his left elbow and placed it under his head so he could prop himself up higher to better see the baby. "A tiny baby and she's voicing her opinions already."

A louder wail moved Jessie to action. Sliding off the bed, she headed over to pick up her daughter. "She's been voicing her opinion a lot lately. I guess she's a little out of sorts."

"How has Dee been making out with her?"

Jessie shrugged, and moved her hips from side to side to rock the baby. "She's been doing okay. But I know she and Charles are pretty beat. Giselle's been helping out. It'll be nice to take Emily-Grace for a drive and let Sara's boys spoil her."

The object of her attention let out a great roaring cry. Jessie's forehead wrinkled in consternation. "Huh."

"Maybe she's wet," Josh tossed in.

"I'll check her," responded Jessie, wandering back to the sofa to lay her baby down and see if a new diaper might help. "But she's been like this since I picked her up from Dee this morning. I think she just misses her momma and daddy." She proceeded to remove Emily-Grace's little leggings and then her diaper. "No, she's fine. Just being cantankerous, that's all."

"She's afraid you're going to send her back to Charles."

"Shhh, Josh, don't say things like that," Jessie scolded, eyes glinting, unable to hide her amusement. "He's great with her."

"Good thing. Cause he's not great with everybody."

"You're too hard on him." Scooping Emily-Grace up in her arms, Jessie crossed the room and perched her butt on Josh's bed. She held the baby so her daddy could make silly faces at her, but she didn't let Josh touch her. No way was Jessie taking any chances on Emily-Grace catching anything. In fact, just thinking about it made Jessie antsy to get her out of the dreary hospital.

Josh caught the look.

"Go," he said. "Break my heart."

"You'll be discharged in a few days, Josh. Then you can have her as much as you want."

His instant frown stopped her from continuing. "You'll be going back to Miami."

"Only for a week to catch up on the scenes I'm missing right now. They were good to move my stuff to the end of this episode's shoot. Then I'll meet you back here and we'll fly home to Vancouver together for the Christmas hiatus."

More cries from their baby daughter had Jessie respond by shifting Emily-Grace to the other arm. "Geez, I hope the car ride settles her down."

"Me too." Josh touched Jessie's arm. "Go. But text me every chance you get."

"Okay, Josh. I will." Pausing, she studied him. "Thank you. For getting better. I need you." She touched the baby's head. "*We* need you." Bending forward, she brushed her lips against his. "I'll text soon. I swear."

Once the baby was dressed and Jessie had her own warm puffy black North Face jacket zipped up, she saluted Josh and spoke loudly over the baby's increasing wails. "I'd better get her out of here before they kick us out. I'll be back around dinner, okay?"

Josh was frowning. "Are you sure she's okay?"

"Well, something's bugging her, that's for sure. I don't think she's sick, she seems okay. Just temperamental. Mad at us for screwing up her schedule."

"I guess." But Josh was worried—and not just for the baby.

Jessie smiled at him. "I know what you're thinking, Sawyer. But it's fine. I can handle her. Emily-Grace and I are a team."

She blew him a kiss and was gone.

Thankfully, Jacob's soothing ballads granted Emily-Grace a twenty minute rest. But then nothing could calm the baby down.

"Not even Jacob's soothing voice?" Jessie begged her, turning the volume up a few notches in the hopes the music would somehow work its magic on her daughter. She pulled over twice on the way, once to try feeding the yowling infant in the back seat of the running SUV, which was completely unsuccessful, and once to change her and walk with her. By then she was twenty minutes outside of Peterborough, but Jessie was aghast at the notion of wandering into her grandmother's home with a screaming baby. She considered Sara's place, mostly because Sara was not 89, like Martha, and also because her half-sister had two young boys, so maybe she'd be able to deal easier with a howling infant in her home. But Sara was not really welcoming to Jessie, even via the few texts sent this morning to co-ordinate the visit. So Jessie was at the end of her rope when Ulysses finally left the vehicle he parked fifty meters away at the rest stop behind her, and wandered over.

He held out his arms. "Give me the baby, Jessie."

She did, begrudgingly, but Jessie was losing it. "What is it with babies?" she asked him, bewildered. "I thought they were fine with just, I dunno, sleeping and shitting at this stage."

"I don't know," was Ulysses' unhelpful response. "They're a mystery to me." He juggled the newborn, trying to hold her but totally unsure just what to do. Uselessly, he stared at the wrinkled eyes and flailing wrists.

"You're a lotta help," Jessie grumbled, silently wishing he were Matt. "You need a good woman, Ulysses. And some babies of your own." She tried to get the baby to take her finger, but the little fists were flailing. "She's frantic about something." A friendly poke or two at Emily-Grace's bunting was also futile. "If you were your daddy, I could read your mind. But I'm not there with you yet!" She looked up at Ulysses, a determined panic in her eyes. "Gimme that screaming bundle of joy. I think there's a sister I need to drop in on!"

Twenty minutes later, Jessie, too, was fighting tears. The incessant howls of her baby were a mental strain for which she was not prepared, each cry jostling her nerves to the point of implosion. Finally, she wheeled the SUV to a frantic stop outside Sara's pretty townhouse.

Sara was inside drying dishes when she heard a vehicle pull to a quick stop in her driveway. The boys and their dad were at a Peterborough Petes junior hockey game, and Sara was cursing Jessie, wishing she were with them, but she had agreed via text to meet her half-sister one last time at their grandmother's that afternoon. A *good riddance* charitable visit, she thought. And she only agreed because she'd watched the news reports about Josh's pneumonia and hospitalization, the cameras catching shots of Jessie going to and fro from the hospital, and Sara had *some* compassion for the girl's downcast, worried face.

And that poor baby, being hustled here and there and left with someone who isn't even her real grandmother... Sara was rather disgusted, just thinking of it. And part of her…well, she admitted to herself that a tiny small part of her actually wished Jessie would have called. Sara would have gladly taken that beautiful baby in, and kept her in a consistent, warm environment where she could take regular naps and get on the kind of schedule newborns need instead of being hauled here, there and everywhere.

Now, though, as Sara recognized the fancy SUV and the frazzled woman jumping out of it, fear leapt in Sara's chest. *She's supposed to be at Martha's,* was her first confused thought. Tossing her dishtowel over the sink, she jogged to the door, which she threw open with vigorous gusto. The storm door stood in her way; she opened it, too, and stood outside hanging on to it, not noticing that the thin layer of snow on the ground was seeping into her slippers.

"Jessie?"

The singer stood wide-eyed, dancing frantically from side to side, swiping at unshed tears. Sara heard the baby screaming. The *neighbors* heard the baby screaming.

"She's got a set of lungs on her." Suddenly Sara was smiling, just a teensy bit. In a way, she felt a sense of pride in Jessie, for doing this momma thing alone. Lots do, but the thing is, *she* didn't have to.

"I can't get her to stop crying, Sara. She's been at it practically all morning. Fussy at first, but for the last hour…" She shook her head. "I tried feeding her, I changed her, I…I'm at a loss." Anxious eyes were trained on her half-sister. "I think she might be sick."

At that point, Sara allowed a tiny bit more compassion to weave its way into her heart. Given Jessie's history…and a very real worry regarding her husband's pneumonia and his exposure to the baby…again, Sara allowed a tiny curve to raise her lips into a small smile.

"I doubt that, Jessie," she said by way of comfort. "But I think I know what the problem may be. Bring her in."

Relief washed over Jessie. "Thank you," she said. "Thanks, Sara."

Moving to fetch the carrier from the back of the SUV, she stared at her daughter in utter confusion and frustration. "What's the matter, beautiful girl?" she begged fruitlessly. "Tell momma. Momma needs to know so she can help you!"

Sara held the storm door open so Jessie could make her way inside. As Jessie kicked off her boots, Sara bent down and undid the baby's carrier harness. She picked up the little writhing, wailing body.

"I bet you've got a sore belly, Emily-Grace," she surmised, standing, before looking over at the baby's momma. "She's likely fighting some colic, Jessie. Gas. Let's run her a warm bath and see what we can do to soothe that sore little belly."

It was over an hour before the two women finally got the baby settled. As Emily-Grace's cries turned to sad little whimpers, they took seats in Sara's living room with cups of tea at their sides.

Jessie rocked her daughter to sleep in a cozy squeaky old rocking chair. Grateful, she allowed a small smile to filter off in Sara's direction. "Thanks, Sara. You're a miracle worker. You've got the touch."

Waving her off, Sara couldn't help but feel a smug satisfaction at her own patience and success with the wailing baby. And there was a certain light freckling her eyes at the thought of Jessie the sister, not Jessie the superstar, sitting here sharing a cup of tea, her baby drifting off to sleep in her arms.

"I was picking on Josh this morning for turning his nose up at the green tea I brought him," Jessie was saying. "I might have to get some of this—it doesn't taste like grass. He might be convinced to go for it."

"It's a chai blend one of my friends brought us from Japan. It's my favorite." Sara tucked her feet underneath her and checked her cell phone. "Two-one for the Peterborough Petes at the end of the second."

"Do you usually go to the games with them?"

"I do. We're a hockey family." Sara shrugged. "Rink fries. You can't beat 'em." She swung their conversation around. "How's Josh doing?"

A sigh from her heart to her toes was Jessie's response. "He got through this one, Sara." The pale eyes wilted.

"He'll get through them all, Jessie." It was bizarre to find herself in this position, comforting the half-sister Sara neither wanted nor told herself she needed; the half-sister Sara herself envied far too long for all the wrong reasons.

"He might not, Sara. I know that he might not."

"You really love him." Sara said this as though she was surprised a kind of true love actually existed.

"Yeah," Jessie replied, astounded at Sara's evident wonder. "'Course I do. He's my husband. I love him like crazy."

Uncomfortable, Sara picked her teacup up off the nearby end table. She fidgeted with the cup, twisting it around a few times until she decided which hand to drink it with, and then she settled the handle in between a thumb and forefinger. She lifted it to her lips while Jessie regarded her, a mixture of astonishment and wisdom soon resolving across her features.

"Sara?" she asked bravely. "What about your husband?"

"Hmm?" Avoiding Jessie's gaze, Sara twisted her teacup again.

"Kevin. You love him, right?"

A sudden state of high alert left pink pinpricks on Sara's cheeks. "I don't really think about it." She looked up. "Not everybody has what you have, Jessie. Real life isn't some Hollywood romance."

"Why the hell not?" Jessie sighed. "Look, Sara. When I met Josh I was engaged to Charlie Deacon. We got engaged, like, an hour before I got hit with lightning over Josh, in fact."

"That's so weird," Sara cut in. "Charlie Deacon." Shaking her head, she tried to clear the cobwebs taking root there.

"Huh? What? Oh." Once again, Jessie forgot about her life—that everyone knew about it, for one. And that people were regularly cowed by her fame and by those she knew who were also victims of fame. She continued, talking softly so as not to wake the finally resting baby. "He's a good guy, Charlie. He really is. He is still one of my best friends. But there was never any real magic, you know? Then when Josh came along," her face lit up, "boom. Lightning. Like I said. Didn't you and Kevin ever have the lightning?"

"Give me a break." Sara got up and took Jessie's empty teacup from the coffee table where Jessie set it. She started into the adjoining kitchen and rested it on the countertop. "We met at a bar. I was out with Crystal, and he sat down next to us because the place was packed and there was room at our table. We got drunk and we danced and we had a good time, so we caught a few movies and had sex." She shrugged, and turned to face Jessie. "We had kids, we go to hockey, we go to church. We run to soccer in the summer."

"And you have sex."

"Ha!"

Jessie's nose wrinkled up in consternation. "You don't have sex? What's the point of being married?"

"Like I said," Sara muttered, cheeks flaming. "Not everyone has this magic you speak of, Jessie. And after a while, things just sink into some kind of normal, you know?"

"But you never had it? The magic? That...desperate need for someone? That electric tingly ache that, when you're near him, drives you around the bend? Like...so if you can't at least touch him, like drop your hand over his belt or run your fingers over his forearm, you feel yourself drying up inside? With a hurt so bad you think you'd rather just die than live one more day without him?"

Sara laughed outright. "You sound like some character in one of your films, Jessie! Some stupid—forgive me—cheap romantic comedy."

"Hey, I've done some good stuff too, you know! But who doesn't like a good love story? And Sara...I'm not a character in one of my films. I'm real, I'm here, and I need to tell you...I'm in love. And it is like that."

Silence prevailed while Sara's eyes darted around the room. Jessie could see the old tape playing there, on rewind, running over the last twelve years with one man. "Well then, I guess you're one of the lucky ones," was Sara's final response.

"D'ya ever think...Sara, just hear me out." Jessie started cautiously as Sara struggled with the reality of her life, the everyday hurts that still challenged her when she woke fraught with anxiety at three a.m., or when she had to get out from underneath warm flannel sheets to start yet another tedious day. "I'm just wondering...Kevin seems like such a good man. Maybe you *do* have what I have. But you just aren't seeing it."

Sara's silence continued. She stared at a wet spot on the coffee table. But she swallowed, and listened. *Crazy. It is actually kind of amazing, having a sister to talk to...for once...if I can just ignore the truth of who said sister really is.*

Jessie added carefully, because she knew she was skating on thin ice with this nervous half-sister of hers, "You need to remind yourself sometimes. To grab his belt and pull him towards you. To touch his arm. To...have sex. I would think that would be easy, knowing he's the father of your two gorgeous kids."

"Maybe some of us are grounded in reality, Jessie, worrying about stuff like bills and how we're going to get those new skates Mark needs, cause he's growing like a bad weed these days. We're not living in your pampered little world."

"My pampered little world, as you call it, is a curse sometimes, Sara. And even with my new baby, I feel like I never see my husband."

"I guess we both have prices to pay for the lives we're living, then, Jessie." A hot red flush spread across Sara's neck. She forced herself to speak more calmly. "You are solidly entrenched in a world I will never understand. See, you ask me why I'm not having sex with my husband, and my question to you is, why would you choose to live a life where you never see your husband? And you with a new baby? How long do you think that kind of relationship can last?"

Tears pricked Jessie's eyelids. "I know, Sara. I know we are living and working in a tough business."

"The women alone who must be after your husband…and I'm not talking about fans here, I mean, who's he spending time with on his new show? Cast, crew? He must get hit on all the time!"

"I trust him."

"Not just him. What about you?"

"What about me?"

"Aren't you working with an ex-boyfriend? That Jacob guy who sings that hit song about Scotland?"

Jessie swallowed. "Well, yeah." Her voice was thin. "But Jacob and I are friends. We're over that shit."

"Are you."

"Come on, Sara. We're talking about you here. You should be just as worried about women hitting on your man as I am about women hitting on mine. And men, too, may I add, just for interest's sake. At least in my crazy corner of the world."

Sara guffawed, loud enough to startle Emily-Grace, which Jessie noted. She prayed the baby stayed asleep. "Why would I be worried about anyone hitting on Kevin? He's not a sexy movie star! He's just some ordinary looking guy who works in a lumberyard."

"Because he's a good man, Sara. And women see that. And sometimes, men succumb to the idea of breaking out of the normal, especially if they find a woman willing to give them the positive attention they don't get at home."

"Pshaw! Kevin would never cheat on me."

"I'm not even sure you can call it cheating if he's not getting it at home…"

"He's married, for God's sake!"

"Then treat him like he's married! Minus the nagging part! Sara, if you and Kevin have some sort of agreement where both of you are comfortable where things are at, great. I'm happy for you. But don't go telling me you wish you had what I have, and then ignoring the plain fact that it's right in front of you!"

"I never said I wished I had what you have. We're not talking about material things here."

"What? Oh." Jessie's eyes clouded over. *Of course that would have to come up. Again.* She fingered her engagement and wedding rings before switching tactics. "You didn't have to say it, Sara. I see it. In your eyes. Although just for the record, you did, last time I was here." She held out the pricey engagement ring.

"What?" Sara squeezed her empty teacup tighter. Outside, a vehicle rolled into the driveway and its driver cut the ignition. Martha and Evelyn, likely, who she'd called earlier and asked to come here. Sara didn't move. She needed to hear the rest of what her half-sister was trying to tell her.

"I see it," Jessie offered softly, genuine compassion and feeling in her kind eyes. "I see the *want* there, and Sara? I see the *need*. And I see the loneliness." She allowed a tiny smile to break through. "You see? We are sisters. And we have more in common than you might think. I was lonely, too. But I found peace, and I found joy. With a man I love. You have a good man, and an amazing family. But you know what I think, Sara? I think you just need a little reminding."

Chapter Twenty-six

That night, back at the hospital, Jessie told Josh about her conversation with Sara while they ate chicken soup she, Sara, Evelyn and Martha all contributed to making. She was blown away by the woman's ability to comfort Emily-Grace, a baby who, by the time of her arrival at Sara's door, was hysterical. Yet Sara was so efficient, so lost in efficiencies perhaps, and in worry, too, that she was unable to find and appreciate a joy she had access to but couldn't see.

"And Kevin is such a good guy, Josh," Jessie was saying, giggling all the while, as Emily-Grace cooed happily in her carrier by the sofa in the small room again. "You know what he did when he got home?"

"Since I don't know the man, I can't even begin to guess, Jessie. Suppose you tell me?"

Josh was happy too. His wife was radiant. The visits with her long-lost family seemed to be going well, Steve had been in for a visit that day, making Josh laugh the whole time, and Josh was feeling better. Add to this the fact that the nerve-wracking Keatings were back on the west coast, and Christmas break was approaching.

Josh was positively cheery.

In high spirits too, Jessie jumped in exuberantly. "Well, they were all asking about our lives, you know, security and all that crap, and I finally admitted y'all wouldn't let me come to Peterborough completely on my own." She held up her hand, palm facing Josh. "I told them it wasn't my idea, y'see, but they all just laughed. And when I admitted there was a good-looking black man somewhere outside in a Honda CRV, they all growled at me!

213

In a good way, of course. 'Cept maybe Sara, who was pretty quiet. Anyways, Evelyn insisted we bring Ulysses in and at least give him a cup of tea. So Kevin grabbed Mark and Ren and off they went down the street and, sure enough, they found the car and Ulysses patiently waiting inside, sucking back a Starbucks and doing a Sudoku."

"And they gave him tea?"

"Yes, despite his caffeine coffee rush, but you should've seen the look on his face, Josh, when he came inside. As if he was terrified I was going to start screaming at him or something. He stood there in the entryway and watched me, at first. But I told him to come in. And of course I felt—I feel—like shit, for leaving him out in the cold in the first place."

She glanced out at the hallway, where the topic of her conversation was deep in discussion with Morgan, who was trading shifts with him. Jessie planned to go to a gym with Morgan (with Giselle and Jonathon kindly offering to watch Jonathon's granddaughter for a couple of hours). Dan, who was taking advantage of the increased security during shift-trade time to go off to dinner, was in charge of Josh's room today, to protect him from overzealous reporters and fans. Susanne was in Vancouver with Charles and Dee.

"At least you let him go with you. Speaking of which, Jessie, are you taking Ulysses to Miami? Or Dan?"

"I want Matt." The jubilant mood sucked its way out of the room real quick. "Call him."

"I will."

"Otherwise?"

"Ulysses, I guess. He'll want to come to scout things out some more."

"Since he's the new chief, huh?"

"Something like that." She shrugged, and steered him around another corner. "So Josh, after Christmas I agreed to do a little show in Peterborough."

"What? How little?" His eyebrows narrowed conspicuously.

"Small. Like at a fire hall or something, I'm not sure, they've got a place in mind. There's this little boy who is sick. He's only three. He's been in Sick Kids here in Toronto since September with some lung issues the doctors can't seem to solve, and the family needs money to help with expenses."

"We can give them money, Jess. If you think it's legit. And if it's close to your grandmother's heart." Josh was subdued. Sick children were one of their spoken and committed causes. Both spent time with children when and where they could—in pediatrics wards, in cancer wards, at fundraisers, although Josh acknowledged even now, silently, that this was a painful pursuit for his soft hearted sensitive, compassionate wife.

"I tried that, Josh. They wouldn't go for it. Although I plan to donate, anyway. They're taking donations at the door."

"They just want to hear you play."

"They didn't ask me. I offered."

"Uh-huh. I see. You want to play for them."

"That's part of it. But the little guy's the biggest part. Josh, I can't even imagine if one of our kids got sick…this past week has been scary enough!"

"We promised ourselves, Jess. For better or for worse. We're survivors, you and me. Whatever life throws at us, we'll deal with it. Together."

"I'm glad. To have you with me on this crazy journey, I mean." She scuttled closer, laid down on the bed, and rested her head beside his on the snowy pillow.

Since Emily-Grace seemed to be settling okay, they drifted off to sleep for an hour, hand in hand. When the baby woke, Jessie fed her, regretfully kissed her lonely husband goodnight, and went off with Morgan to drop the baby off to Jonathon and Giselle. A gentle stint at the gym was next, under Morgan's shy guidance.

Two days later, Josh was discharged from the hospital, and Jessie left him at the hotel under orders to take it easy, although he'd promised Jon he would try to do some easy scenes during his recovery. Jessie flew to Miami, did her thing, flew back to Toronto to collect her husband, and they spent a deliriously happy Christmas with their new baby at home, with a one week side trip to the ranch in Alberta to get some skiing and horseback riding in.

Evelyn did babysit, Josh and Jessie cuddled and, for a time, life was once again magical in the Wheeler-Sawyer camp.

Chapter Twenty-seven

"Ren. Hey, Ren. C'mere."

Sara's littlest guy scrunched up his nose and paused. One of the big kids was calling him over. This never happened. And it was one of the scarier big guys. It was Dugey MacIsaac, who everyone knew would fight you over anything. Like last summer at the soccer field when Mark was playing, and Ren was at the playground with Jed Lawson and Mike Jebsen playing color tag while their older brothers were losing badly against the East City kids, and Dugey gave Mike Jebsen a bloody nose just for sticking his feet in crushed pop cans and walking around on them.

Acting all hot, Dugey'd said before he cornered the kid on a yellow slide and shoved him to the ground, and then pounded him three times, once as a warm-up, once to get the blood going in his nose, and once more to entertain the masses gathered to watch, their bloodthirsty cries of 'hit him again' still echoing in Ren's ears.

Ren never went to the playground during Mark's soccer games again. Even with Jed Lawson, who was big enough to deal with bullies their own age, but not tall enough yet to fight off the hulking Dugey MacIsaacs of the world. Ren wouldn't even consider going again with Mike Jebsen. That kid was marked now, like a sacrificial lamb just waiting for the big slaughter. The first bloody nose was likely just a warm-up, in the opinion of the entire fourth grade at Saint Catherine.

So, today, the first day back at school after Christmas, Ren's heart crashed to his toes when Dugey MacIsaac called him over. The older boy was casually leaning against the brick of the school, a knowing sneer twisting his fat lips

216

into a sinister grin as he watched Ren almost tiptoe over the snow towards him, his boots crunching over the crisp footprints made by students earlier in the day during lunch and afternoon recess. Dugey had a cell phone in his hand, one of the newer models, in a neon blue case that actually matched Dugey's brand new Snowboarder jacket.

Ren only went over because there were lots of parents around, and his dad was expected any moment now. And because when Dugey MacIsaac called you over, you damn well went, or there'd be hell to pay the next day at school when you were strolling down the hall with your friends or playing 'defend your snow fort' on the playground.

When he got three feet away, Ren stopped trudging and forced himself to look at the big sixth grader's work boots. Ren's winter snow boots were Mark's hand-me-downs, and his snow pants were faded and torn at the knees. His coat—another Mark special—was patched on the elbows, just like the threadbare coat of that old hobo they saw in the Disney movie on TV last week.

He was also wearing one of those funny trendy crocheted hats with animal parts on it. This one had a red zebra mouth and black ears that stuck out of the top. When Ren wore it, Mark refused to be seen with him. But the boys' Aunt Jessie sent it to Ren for Christmas, along with two new vintage dinky cars—a pale green woody station wagon and an old fashioned ambulance, which looked amazing on the plastic townscape spread out on the floor of their room. And Ren liked Aunt Jessie. A lot.

Besides, although he would never admit this to Mark, he liked the hat. It was funny, and Ren had a thing for exotic animals from Africa. He and Jessie even watched a nature show together during her last visit, while she was sitting on their old couch feeding her baby. And she didn't cringe when the lion pounced on the deer and ripped it apart. So he wore the hat.

He swiped a finger up and shoved an itchy strand of hair inside it. Then he forced his apprehensive eyes up to meet Dugey's, to find the older boy leering at the zebra ears.

"Shit, Baby Lawrence, you got dumbass ears growing out of your head."

Ren knew better than to respond. He swallowed and remained quiet, though his heart was pounding out of his chest. He was glad he'd put his knapsack on, because half the time he just carried it dangling from one hand after school while he waited for his dad. But today he was hoping he could find some decent snow for snowballs, and he wanted his hands free, although the snow wasn't looking good—too crispy—and having his hands free seemed like a good idea for defense, about now.

"That's the stupidest hat I ever seen. Suits you, though, Baby Lawrence. Animal hats are for babies." Dugey studied the hat. "I don't even know what kind of messed-up animal that's s'posed to be. What is it, a dog?"

Gee, thought Ren. *It's a zebra. Haven't you ever seen a zebra before? It has stripes!*

Dugey got bored with the hat. He had more important things to discuss with this puny kid. He turned his cell phone around to face Ren. "Look. You ever seen titties before, Baby Lawrence?"

Eyes widening, Ren gulped. "Noooo," he croaked. *And I don't want to, either.* He resisted looking at the screen thrust in his face.

Glee lit up Dugey's long features. This Lawrence kid was definitely a tittie virgin. This was gonna be fun. Grabbing Ren by the shoulder, he yanked him forward, then twisted the kid around and shoved the phone in front of him again. He shielded the sun's glare with his hand.

"Look. I'd say they're like your momma's but she ain't pretty like her sister. But they're probably close. So here, have a look at your momma's titties, Baby Lawrence. Or at least as close as you're gonna get."

Ren didn't want to look at the screen. But Dugey MacIsaac had a grip on him, still. And he knew there was no chance of freedom, today or ever, if he didn't do what the sixth grader said. So he looked.

Instantly he recognized the face of the woman on the screen, the one naked except for panties, lying back on a big bed, her back arched and her hair messy, with one hand on a breast and one set of fingertips inside the panties. Her eyes were looking directly at him, and Ren didn't like what they were saying, which seemed to be *look at me, I'm a bad girl.* He felt sick, like he'd just seen his mom's private parts, 'cause Dugey said Aunt Jessie's were like her sister's, and Aunt Jessie was Ren's mom's sister. And the woman in this picture was Ren's Aunt Jessie.

"Get an eyeful, Baby Lawrence." Dugey shoved Ren's head in closer to the screen and used his opposite thumb to scroll to another naked photo, and yet another.

A sickening ripple, like the one Ren got after he heard his mom yelling at his dad one night and thought they were getting a divorce, and got so scared he climbed into Mark's bed, coursed up his legs and through his belly. Swallowing to keep the bile down, Ren started gulping and gasping, like a fish with no water around it to give it life. He didn't really understand what he was seeing, but he knew it was bad, and that it was dirty. Tears wanted to leak from his eyes, but he was scared Mark or some of Mark's friends from the big boys' hockey team might see him, or worse…his dad might see him. And Ren didn't want anyone to see him cry.

But when Dugey MacIsaac finally let him go, with a hard shove and a diabolical laugh, the tears did come, although Ren used a woolen mitten to quickly wipe them away. He saw his dad's old truck pull up to the curb where all the kids' parents got them after their day at school, and he climbed in just after Mark, and stared out the window all the way home, not being his bubbly self like usual, when Mark always had to tell him to shut up.

Ren waited til he was out of Dugey's sight before he pulled the zebra hat off his head. At home, in the room he shared with Mark, he took the pale green woody car and the ambulance off his city road map. Roughly, he tucked them behind the baby books still on his bookshelf.

Chapter Twenty-eight

"Jessie, I don't want you coming out here anymore. And that includes for the fundraiser." Sara's voice was trembling, her futile attempt at remaining unemotional and in control failing her dramatically. She was in her car, pulled over in the Peterborough Canoe Museum's parking lot, alone. She'd almost made it to work at Boston Pizza when her cell beckoned her. The thought of not taking the call crossed her frazzled mind when she saw Jessie's name displayed on the screen, but in the end her blood pressure skyrocketed, so she hit the green phone icon, yanked the steering wheel to the right, put the car in park, and left the engine idling.

She barked into the phone before her shocked half-sister even had a chance to respond to the first comment. "Ren won't want to see you either. He got a little, let's say, educated, in grown-up shit yesterday at school. He's devastated. It took me an hour to find out what was bothering him. And when he finally caved, he cried. Like a baby, Jessie."

"And this has to do with me because…?" But Jessie already knew. Someone, somewhere, spilled the beans about some aspect of her wayward past, to a kid who might've really liked her if he had the chance. The old self-loathing kicked in and sucked the life out of her. Jessie was calling from Miami to check on the final plans for the fundraising concert, but an angry mom wasn't what she expected to find on the other end of the line, especially after she and Sara seemed to be finding some middle ground in their relationship, finally.

Sara softened, but only a bit. Her heart was still racing. Sure, Jessie was her half-sister. The same blood flowed through their veins. And the woman was a superstar, a singer and actor deeply loved the world over, albeit partly for a tragic past that spared her no pain of her own.

"Jessie, Ren's nine. He's nine. And he's my baby. But yesterday at school one of the older boys got on some mobile porn site and there you were. Worse, the kid told him it was like seeing his mother naked." She choked back a sob, which pissed her off for showing any kind of weakness in Jessie's presence, even on the phone. "He didn't need that yet, Jessie. About you, whom he worships, or should I say worshipped, past tense. Or about life in general. He should have been able to stay a kid just a little while longer. You know?"

The anger that, since last night, was tumbling around Sara's hurt heart and causing her head to feel like it was caving in, reached a pinnacle point. But it didn't explode, instead it imploded, and came crashing through Sara in volcanic waves, from the inside out. She sucked hard so it would stay buried, and she held her breath while her body shook. She couldn't speak.

The line was silent for a minute as Jessie digested the painful news. Alone in her suite in Miami, with the exception of her beautiful slumbering daughter, whose innocence she swore to protect before the baby was even born, Jessie shuddered. Sweet young Ren, named for a tenacious kid in a beloved classic eighties dance movie, exposed to his first breasts via risqué photos on a porn site…photos of her. Jessie was sickened. She could tell by the gasps for breath on the other end that Sara was devastated too. What mother wouldn't be?

"How'd the kid know, Sara? That you and I are connected…" She hesitated, and then since all she was getting from Sara were sniffs, Jessie just said, "I'll let you go." A quaking finger tapped *end* on her phone. She hung her head in shame but had to get up almost immediately and bolt into the bathroom to throw up. Picturing Ren's sweet face, his innocent eyes puzzling over her erotic image on the screen, she knew, although he wouldn't fully understand, that a good chunk of his childhood was just erased—*wham, bam, thank you ma'am*. Just like that. *Kapoof. Gone.* And Jessie was responsible. That's what she, Jessie Wheeler, brought to Sara's family by reconnecting. Shame, and more loss of innocence.

A knock at the door shocked Jessie out of her stupor enough to make her crawl out of the bathroom. On hands and knees, stifling choking sobs, she pulled herself up by grasping a nearby sideboard. Looking through the peephole into the hallway, she hesitated before turning the lock and opening the door. The visitor was Jacob.

Right now what Jessie needed was someone to tell her she wasn't a total fuck-up, because right now a small baby was sleeping nearby, and that baby needed her. Also on Jessie's mind were friends, and a therapist—with a cozy tawny striped cat—who'd been teaching her to stop shutting people out when she needed them. She looked up at Jacob with heartsick eyes and trails of black mascara running down her cheeks.

"I'm such a fucking idiot," she whimpered, hanging on to the door with one hand and slouching halfway over her belly with the other.

"Jessie—what the hell?" Jacob stepped in immediately, and shoved the door closed behind him. "What happened? Where's…" His anxious eyes darted around the suite, searching, wondering. They stopped at Jessie's disheartened expression.

"The baby's fine, she's sleeping. It's Ren, Sara's youngest kid. He got a dose of reality, thanks to his fucked up aunt and her nude photos. So now Sara pretty much hates me. Even more than before." Her sorrow was complete. The pained eyes searched Jacob's. *Please help me. I can't stand it.*

"C'mere." As always, Jacob didn't disappoint. He wrapped both arms around his friend—the woman he would love forever—and drew her body to him. She sighed into his warm embrace, her body shaking as she let this new ache be known. Jacob's eyes misted over too. He couldn't help it—when she hurt, he hurt.

"Jessie," he finally pleaded, drawing back and placing both sets of calloused fingers over her soft cheeks, "those pictures are not who you are. They are who you *were.* Caryn was a bitch for releasing them like that. And…I hate to say this, but like it or not, you knew they would likely make their way to your sister's kids at some time in their lives."

"Yeah, but why now, Jacob?" she wept, absently hooking both thumbs over the thick black belt at his hips. "For one thing, I kept my visits quiet. No one in that city should even know I was ever there. Or who I was visiting, or what my connection is to Sara."

"Who knows about your upcoming appearance at the fundraiser?"

"A few people, I guess. Some police, technicians. Maybe a few folks involved in the fundraiser itself. The boy's family."

"Enough for someone to have said something."

Groaning, Jessie agreed. "Apparently. Just my fucking luck."

"That'll be ten bucks."

"Oh, stop," she moaned, shaking him in jest, but his comment lightened the new agony this latest revelation unleashed, and Jessie's lips turned up just the tiniest bit. "That poor kid," she lamented, before landing on the couch with Jacob beside her, his hand in hers.

"Yeah, like seeing your boobs would be the worst shock of anyone's life. Especially if they're the first sets of knockers you've ever seen," Jacob grinned, lifting her knuckles to his and brushing his lips gently over them. "I feel sorry for the kid because, let's face it, it's all downhill from here."

His hearty laughter filled the space when Jessie started hitting Jacob with a cushion from the sofa.

"Sssshhhh, you'll wake the baby! Jacob, stop! Quiet!" Shoving the cushion in his face, she straddled him, then removed the cushion and placed a hand over his mouth. After a moment, her singing soul mate settled, and rested his hands on her hips as she faced him. Jessie saw his eyes change; saw them flicker now with light, while his smile faded and the pouty lips parted, just a little—enough. Jacob's breathing changed too. It quickened.

Frowning, she placed a hand over his heart. It was racing.

"Stop," she whispered, slipping a hand inside his ubiquitous plaid shirt, over the white T-shirt he wore underneath. "Stop looking at me like that."

He sucked in a breath, a deep one, then looked away as he removed her hand from his chest, where it burned a hole right through his aching heart. Ruthlessly shoving her off his lap, Jacob spoke gruffly. "Then stop fucking touching me like that. Jesus, Jessie."

Now her afternoon was truly toast. But once Jacob paced the room a few times and peeked in at the blissfully sleeping baby, he ran a finger over one lip and then the other, before turning to look at Jessie.

She was crouched on one end of the sofa, slumped over, her back to him right now, and she was silent, hiding inwardly, disgusted and sickened with herself, clutching the cushion to her chest as if it were the only thing holding herself together. Jacob didn't know it, but she was thinking *I don't know what Josh sees in me*. It was only a momentary lapse into self-pity, because

Trudy was teaching Jessie how to navigate such precarious waters, but it was genuine at the moment, fraught with self-loathing and fueled by the sad eyes of a small boy who, yesterday, apparently took a hard knock on the harsh realities of life.

So Jacob didn't get the entire gist of Jessie's angst then, but he knew her well enough to understand the general feel of it, and so he approached her from behind and sat on the arm of the sofa with one lazy hand looped around the drooping shoulders.

"I'm sorry," he muttered. "That was my fault. I know the boundaries." Josh jumped into his head, and he was instantly remorseful. The guy was doing his best to trust his wife, and here was Jacob wanting to hold her, to soothe and comfort her. To…Jacob immediately shoved that thought away.

A small voice broke into his thoughts. "I thought you were seeing that grip, anyway. You and me can't cross that line, Jacob. You need to settle down with her, maybe."

"We're just fuck buddies," he offered lightly, trying to lessen the tension now suffocating them in the spacious suite. "Which means I can see other women."

"Lovely. How wonderful for you." The sarcasm fired from between the pretty pink lips was biting.

Jacob gazed down at the top of Jessie's head. "I love that it drives you nuts. Me with other women, I mean." He took a breath. "Some day you'll come back to me, Jessie. When your cowboy's star rises too high and he succumbs to how easy it is to put it in some other woman's pants."

She sighed. "Nice. Thanks for that lovely visual, Jacob."

"Just tellin' it like I'm seein' it."

She let her eyes drift up to him. "He loves me, Jacob. Josh will never hurt me that way."

"I hope not, Jess. But that time in season one when you screamed at me, about circling the tank…you should know I will always be circling the tank. Your tank. I'm here for you. I'll always be here for you."

"I don't deserve you." She looked away.

He barely heard her, because she was now facing away from him, but Jacob got the idea of what she was telling him.

"It's the other way around, Jessie," he murmured back, lovingly running his fingers through her hair, which she was wearing loose today, kind of messy but with big curls at the ends. "I don't deserve you."

She took his hand and ran her lips over it, then pressed it against her cheek and closed her eyes, soaking him in. She wasn't entirely sure what Jacob meant by that comment, because he didn't have her, but in the end she decided he was referring to their friendship and the success he was now enjoying at the mercy of Charles Keating.

What she didn't understand was that he was telling himself he truly did not deserve her, and that's why he didn't have her. *But some grand day, maybe...* Jacob wouldn't give up. He knew where he stood now, and he wanted to be trustworthy. He had a willing woman to meet his desires these days, which was helpful...but what Jacob wouldn't give to slide himself inside this woman at his side now even just one last time, to hold her close and feel her clench and sigh around him, to suck him dry and wrap her arms tightly around him while he came...to become one with him again, in a way more profound even than their connection through music.

Sure, Jacob would always be second...for now. Until the day Josh fell from grace again. Not that Jacob was a doomsday seeker, no, he knew how much that would hurt Jessie if it should ever happen, and he didn't want to see that kind of pain in her eyes ever again. But...if it should happen—and heaven help him, but Jacob knew the Keatings sensed it coming too—well, who better to pick up the pieces than the man who loved Jessie from the first time she picked out the bridge on that difficult song while they were sitting around a Scottish campfire under the watchful stony eyes of freedom fighter William Wallace? Who better to pick up the pieces than himself, Jacob?

He could not imagine anyone loving Jessie more than he did. He bent now, and gently kissed the top of the unruly locks. Then he stood, stretching, for the reason he was there in the first place was to go on a coffee and tea run.

"Tea?" he asked. "I was on my way to Starbucks when you so ruthlessly kidnapped me."

"Sure," she whispered, the light eyes still pained. "Chamomile. Thanks."

"Jessie," he started, eyes twinkling again, "the kid will be fine. Another year or two and he will realize he won the lottery by seeing your boobs first.

And he'll be showing them to all his friends, who will be jealous 'cuz he actually knows you."

The cushion got tossed again, and its corner caught Jacob in the eye. He started laughing as he backed out of the suite. "I'll leave the tea outside the door, okay? I'll just knock and make a run for it. Okay with you?"

But he didn't. It was a day off for the two lead actors of the raging hot popular *Mystic Nights*, but Jacob's sex buddy was working, cutting shadows and shaping light for other cast at the moment, so he went back to Jessie's with his Guatemalan drip coffee and her tea, and he had dinner with her and played with the baby while they ran lines for tomorrow's shoot. They planned to snuggle up in her King-sized bed after Emily-Grace dozed off. The hotel had recently added a classic Jimmy Stewart film to its movie line-up, so they were poised and ready for a quiet night.

While he was thinking about hitting 'play' on the remote, Jacob watched Jessie carefully place Emily-Grace in her travel crib. He was leaning against the backboard of the bed, ankles crossed, munching on nacho cheese Doritos while she gave the baby one last tuck.

"Hey, Jess?"

At the baby's crib by the foot of the bed, Jessie touched the back of her sleeping daughter's cheek lightly. "Mmmm?" She turned to smile at him, and he ached to always see that lovely tender expression light her eyes. She was in a good place here with her small child, despite the absence of the baby's father at the present time.

"I was just thinking about the first time I went with my dad to his place."

"Oh?" Jessie stretched and yawned, tucked the baby's blanket a little tighter around her pink sleepers, and made her way over to the big bed. She crawled up on her belly and rested her chin on folded hands. "What about it? Was it awesome?"

"I dunno," he answered, thinking about what to say. Jacob pointed the chip bag towards Emily-Grace's crib. "Just…something about seeing you with her reminded me." He sat up taller and adjusted the pillow behind his back. Jessie reached into the Doritos bag and pulled out some chips, which she munched on while he talked.

He continued. "It was like this—we smoke a little weed on the way down, in the jet, so when we get there I am, you know, hungry and tired. So he shows me to a guest room and it's huge. It's nothing fancy, I mean it's nice, but pretty normal, really. I drop my stuff on the bed and go looking for him because he tells me to come down and he'll get his cook to make us something to eat."

He glanced down to see if Jessie was following. She grabbed a few more nacho chips.

"And?" Her luminous eyes locked into his thoughtful cobalt blues.

"Well, the house is big. It's one of those old white antebellum Civil War mansions, with Georgian columns out front and a big verandah stretching all the way around it."

"This is his house in Virginia? That's the one?"

"Yeah, he goes there when he wants to chill, to hide away, you know."

"I know."

Grinning down at Jessie, he touched her cheek. "Not all of us want to drive on the wrong side of the road."

"You hardly drive at all." She narrowed her eyebrows. "We should work on that. Get you a new Mustang or something."

"Listen," he said, letting her take the Doritos bag from him. "I'm talking about my dad here!"

"Okay," Jessie said, munching happily.

"Well, I go looking for him downstairs and when I find him he's in this big room with lots of books in shelves on the walls. There's a huge, and I mean huge," he opened his arms wide to pantomime the size, "fireplace in the middle of the far wall. And he's staring at something above it. My dad. He is sitting in this big old fashioned chair facing the fireplace and he's staring at this...well," he said, swallowing, lost in the surreal memory of that day with his dad, "it's a painting, actually. And the painting...well, it's of my mom."

Jacob looked down at Jessie again. She stopped eating, and just silently watched him.

"It's cool that it's my mom, that he has this huge painting of her, and she's beautiful, Jessie, I mean really gorgeous. Like...long blonde hair, a wide, blissful smile, and she's wearing this flowy dress." Again the hands moved expressively, to needlessly show Jessie where the skirt would be. "So I can see why he likes it, she's so beautiful..." His voice faded in remembrance.

Jessie touched his thigh, which drew him back to her. "Of course she's beautiful, Jacob," she breathed. "She's your momma." She was thinking about how special it was to be sitting here with him while he shared an intimate story about his visit to his dad's place.

After grinning wordlessly to thank her for the compliment, he went on. "Well, it is kind of a shock for me to see the painting, in this big room with books everywhere all around it, and not a lot of light. It's early evening by then and the room is kinda getting darker, and he's sitting there staring...I don't know, I guess me being there gets him all reflective, you know. Lost in memories. At first I don't think the great Tom even knows I'm in the room. But then..."

He let his gaze drift back to Jessie. "There's this other thing." Uncrossing his ankles, Jacob shifted onto his belly so he could lie by his friend, his face close to hers. She rolled onto her back and held his hand while he talked, the Doritos forgotten.

Jacob cleared his throat and changed his tense, as if he was no longer there in the room, as it seemed he was before, but is now simply reminiscing. "Well, in the painting, my mother was holding a baby. Like, close to her, in her arms, but the way she was gazing at that baby, and the way the baby was looking at her..." He couldn't finish. Jacob exhaled slowly and laid his head on his folded arms.

Jessie scooted onto one side and rested her head on her folded arm on the bed. She wrapped her right arm around his elbow and rubbed that hand over his forearm.

"Babe," she started haltingly, "I'm guessing that baby was you?"

"Well, yeah," he answered, turning to face her. "It was. It is...me. And so when I realized that, I guess I made some sort of sound, because the old man, he all of a sudden turned around and looked at me. And we couldn't say anything, you know, I was just standing there wondering why the hell this man who is my father has this painting of...not just her...but the two of us, I mean, me too, up there on his wall all these years, larger than life, and..." He sighed and dropped his right ear to rest on his folded arms so his and Jessie's faces were only inches apart. "And never came to see me."

"Oh, honey," she murmured softly. "He had his reasons. No one just doesn't come see their kid for no reason."

"Well, I asked him, actually. I asked him why."

Jessie removed her arm from around Jacob's, and she tucked his hair behind his ear in a soothing over-and-over motion while he bared these difficult truths to her.

"He said he couldn't. That's all."

"What'd *you* say? To that, I mean," she wondered.

He shrugged. "I just told him I had to have all my birthday parties at pizza places and sliding hills, 'cuz my grandfather always lost it when there was too much noise around, like with little kids running around. And that, uh, well that I got 'most sportsmanlike player' once at a hockey tournament, and that I got my first guitar in grade eight. That it was a flea market guitar and that I learned how to play it from a cool music teacher at school. I told him those kinds of things. And that when I was little I liked chocolate milk with my food, and that my grandmother always gave me ice cream when I got home from school, with dribbles of chocolate on the top that she let me put on myself."

Jessie chuckled quietly at him. She was still touching his hair, twisting a strand now around her finger, her left cheek still lying on her folded left arm.

"What?" Inhaling, Jacob kept his gaze focused on the diaphanous eyes he trusted and loved.

"You played hockey. I still get a kick out of hearing that."

He managed a small smile then. "Til grade five."

"You were 'most sportsmanlike player.'"

"Yeah. And I went home all proud and my grandfather told me they only give 'most sportsmanlike player' to the kids that suck at hockey."

"Did you?"

"Did I what?"

"Did you suck?"

He laughed, a low rumble that started in the back of his throat. "Probably. Yeah. I guess I probably sucked."

"Good thing you got that old guitar, then."

"Yeah."

"Vancouver Canucks woulda never picked you up."

"Not likely. No."

Tenderly, Jessie leaned forward and brushed her lips against her musical partner's fuzzy cheek. "I'm sure he knows what he missed, Jacob, having that painting to stare at every day."

"Why would you torture yourself that way? Hang that painting there but never go see your kid?"

"It was too much for him, honey. He's a songwriter. We all live on a deeper plane where the hurts are worse than most people's."

"That's not enough. Like…get over yourself, Tom." He rolled over onto his back and stared at the ceiling.

Wistfully, Jessie watched him, wishing there was some way she could take away all of Jacob's hurts.

He had a little more to say on the subject. "When I get up the guts, I'm gonna ask him what happened. Why they split up." A pause drifted between his thoughts. "There was one thing I sorted out from that painting, though, Jess." Jacob's voice was quiet, reflective.

She didn't answer. Instead, Jessie waited.

Twisting his head, he looked at her. "I must have come from love."

If there was ever a moment Jessie wanted Jacob back fully and completely, that was it. Her eyes glistened as she watched him sort through difficult feelings he somehow found the capacity to wrap up in one tidy bundle—that he was conceived from an incredible love shared between his mother and his father. He was not the result of a fly-by-night fling between a singer and some love struck groupie. And he was looking at Jessie now with his little boy look, like he was still the kid who spent every birthday wondering whether his father even realized it was his birthday. He was all innocence and vulnerability now, lying on his back on Jessie's king-sized bed, with her and Josh's baby lost in sweet slumber close by.

Jessie wanted to climb inside his soul and love the hurt away.

She thought of hers and Matt's conversation during last season's *Mystic Nights* shoot, when she asked him if it was possible to love two people at the same time. Jacob saw the complicated feelings skitter across Jessie's face, and he reached for her, but he was a gentleman, and so he simply took her hand and held it.

"I know," he whispered. "It's okay, Jessie. I get it."

By then her throat was all tense and filled with lumps, and her eyes were trying not to leak. She nodded a sincere *thank you*.

"Jacob," she adjusted her position a little as she pondered what to say, but he placed two fingers over her lips and shook his head.

"No," he said. "Just no."

But it was a hard day, or at least parts of it were—not all, since Jacob was a safe place for Jessie so many times, but still, she couldn't help herself. She scooted her butt over so she was closer to him, and if she couldn't love him the way she sometimes still wanted to, well then at least she could breathe him in. So Jessie laid alongside Jacob with one leg over top his, her arm draped over his stomach, underneath the plaid shirt, with just her baby finger tucked under the waist of his jeans, and her nose buried in his hair.

A heavy sigh accompanied the ache for her friend, and for her faraway husband. Jacob's chest, too, rose and fell in its own sweet, sad, longing echo. He laid his left hand over her right, and gave it just a little pressure, not too much, but just enough so he could feel her against him. His right hand, which she was partly laying on, unearthed itself and scooted up under her top over her back, pressing Jessie's precious body closer so Jacob could feel her soul as it tried to climb inside his.

I love you, Jessie was telling him silently, over and over and over. *I love you so much*. And although it was a non-sexual love between them these days, because it had to be, because of her love for another man, tonight she wished for more. Tonight she wanted to push her right hand further beneath the waistband of Jacob's jeans, and tonight she ached to once again hear him moan with pleasure. Instead, Jessie inhaled the green apple scent of him, and willed herself to behave, for her sake, for Josh's sake, but—especially—for Jacob's sake.

Because in the end Jessie knew, as she had always known, that Jacob would be the one who would really get hurt if she ever stepped over the line tonight, if she succumbed to her desires and easily moved her body on top of his, and slipped both hands up underneath his shirt, and lowered her lips to his chest; and then tongued him lower, and even lower, until he arched his back underneath her and grabbed her cheeks between his palms like he always did when she went there in their shared past, so he could watch her play between his legs, his eyes lost in perfect agony as she sucked and teased and licked while his breathing grew shallow and he begged for release.

She moaned, slightly, emitting just the tiniest little warm breath that Jacob felt light his neck, and she moved, too, just a bit, but enough for him to feel what she was feeling, and Jacob thought I could have her now. *I know I could have her now. All it would take is me moving her hand a little further down, or turning my head so my lips meet hers.* He felt her press her hips gently against him, the slight movement followed by another ragged, tiny moan, but, with a willpower he had to fight for, Jacob stilled himself and didn't act on it.

"Jessie," he murmured instead, "Jessie." That was all, just her name, but it was enough. He felt her still her body beside him—or half on top of him, actually—before she pulled her right hand out from under his and moved it up Jacob's body to rest in a safer spot, on his chest. His neck was wet—her tears, which brought up hot tears of his own.

I want you, he was crying to himself then, but it was followed with *but I want all of you.*

And more than anything, that's what stopped Jacob that night. That's what kept him from acting on a thought he'd had many times, which was *I won't hesitate to take her if I get the chance.* He knew all they would succeed in doing if they made love would be open new wounds and create hurts that, in the end, would likely be big enough to destroy all of them—himself, Jessie, and Josh too, but mostly...

A gurgle from the direction of the baby's crib completed that thought for him. Jacob had opened his soul to Jessie that night. He told her what it was like for him to be raised without his father. He'd seen the pain in his father's eyes the night they lingered to gaze over the painting in Tom Ryan's library. And no way did he want that for any other child or for that child's parents.

But at the same time, there was a warm body sobbing quietly next to him. Why, he wasn't sure. Because of how much it hurt to love two men at once? Because of remorse for what Jessie may have done if Jacob helped ease her into it? He didn't know. But there was one thing Jacob was sure about. And that was that this moment—with Jessie's body trembling against him, and his soul luxuriating in the sweet, simple closeness of her, was sheer, honeyed, perfect bliss.

A tiny smile lifted his lips, and Jacob turned his head slightly and brushed those same lips against Jessie's hair.

"I love you back," he whispered. He completed the thought with a silent *and one day when you can be all mine, you will be.*

They lay together and breathed each other in until both grew heavy with fatigue. Sleep took them to its dusky corners until sometime in the early dawn, when Jacob's dreams of lavender and music and hope faded. In the wee hours of early morning light, he turned onto his side, tenderly tasted the soft, welcoming lips of the woman he loved as carefully as he could manage without waking her, and then he slipped away.

Chapter Twenty-nine

*J*acob finally got a break in shooting. Much to Josh's dismay, he landed in Toronto with Jessie on the Keating jet. On the plus side, Charles and Dee did not exit the sleek jet when Jacob and Jessie disembarked. Ulysses, however, was in tow. Emily-Grace was in her mother's arms, her empty baby carrier in Jacob's, which struck Josh funny.

"Hey, sexy," Jessie called to her husband before extending one palm and steadying his cheek for a kiss. "Missed you," she murmured lovingly into his neck.

"You better have," Josh said, staring hard over her shoulder at Jacob, who, with Ulysses, was at this moment trying to stabilize the baby carrier in Dan's black Lincoln SUV. "Couldn't leave the riff-raff in the sunshine state, huh? Had to drag the dregs with you?" He was only half teasing.

"It was a last minute decision, Josh. He's got a break in his schedule and we're hot and heavy writing for my new album, so—"

"Hot and heavy?" Josh frowned. "Seriously?"

"Dork." She swatted him lightly, coloring as the heavy memory of the Doritos night washed over her features. "We just don't want to lose the momentum, Josh. Besides, he can play with me at the fundraiser for the little boy in Peterborough this weekend." Her eyes were dark when she mentioned Peterborough. She had filled Josh in on the less-than-desirable welcome she expected there, though, so he erased the muzzy hot fog from his mind for the time being. They would deal with the crappy stuff later.

It was January 14th, the day before the Oscar nominations were to be announced. Josh was already biting his lip nervously, and the twitch in his cheek was rearing its unwelcome head every few minutes. He was not interested in sharing the moment with Jacob, should it be a good moment, or— a bad one. Nor was he particularly interested in the trip to Peterborough on Saturday. He wanted to do his part for the ailing child, but meeting Jessie's relatives would undoubtedly be unnerving. It didn't help that whenever Josh's life and associated nerves were ramping up, Jessie's little love-struck sidekick seemed to always be along for the ride.

Still, Josh was thrilled to have his baby daughter close again. He lifted her out of Jessie's arms and grinned stupidly down at the rosy-cheeked cherubic face. "Hello, beautiful," he whispered dreamily. "Is your momma treating you okay?"

By the baby's quick smile, he figured Jessie was doing just fine. Looking up at his wife, he commented on that one bad ride to Peterborough. "How's the colic these days?"

"Virtually none," Jessie replied, visible relief easing the tension from her shoulders. "She only has the occasional attack. Thank God. It must have been my nerves that first time, on the Peterborough trip. I was a mess, Josh. I was so scared."

A solemn pout on the pretty lips almost had Josh on his knees, but he licked his lips thoughtfully and tucked the accompanying delicious thoughts away for later. For now, the gang was expected for dinner at the new home Jonathon and Giselle had purchased after hearing the news *The Wyatt Boys* would be shooting at least one more season.

Dinner was fun—Josh and Jacob dried the dishes while Steve washed. Jonathon, since it was his home, was recruited to put things away. Jessie and Giselle took advantage of the boys' generosity, and gratefully played with the baby.

Later, back at the hotel, Emily-Grace wasn't the only member of the Sawyer clan looking forward to bedtime.

After the baby was dozing in her little girl world of sugarplums and fairies, Jessie crossed her arms, leaned her butt against the bathroom vanity, and watched her man foam-talk while he brushed his teeth.

"I swear, Jessie, I know the reality of this whole Oscar thing. I know what's important in life, and that awards are just, I dunno, some weird icing on the cake. I can handle it if my name's not called tomorrow, but at the same time I sure as hell hope it is." Josh spit, and pondered her serious stance as he rinsed his toothbrush and shoved it back in a drawer before slamming the drawer shut. "What? I guess it doesn't have the same glory for you as it does for me." He seemed a little sad at that thought.

"That's not it, Josh. Of course it does. I want your one little Oscar to sit up there dwarfed by my two." She laughed and covered her face when he frowned, coiled up the towel, and started swatting at her. Finally, she grabbed it from him. "Ouch! Stop hitting me! You nerd!" Then she continued, pulling him closer with her end of the offending towel. "It's just that I wish you were around back then. So you could have shared my Oscars with me. You want the truth, Josh?"

"Always, little one." The deep brown eyes were lit from within as he placed one hand in front of the other on the rolled up towel and slowly drew her even closer.

"The truth is…" Forcing a smile, Jessie lost herself in her husband's vibrant sensual gaze that was now, at this moment, brimming with unspoken erotic suggestions. The fizz settled a little upon Jessie's disclosure. "The truth is, that night was one of the loneliest of my life."

They stood there, the coiled white towel between them, each hanging on to one end, their hands not yet touching, but still, that electric connection between them. Now, the brown eyes were solemn, their flickering intensity adapting to the new earnest feelings coursing through Josh's veins by deepening. Josh allowed Jessie's comment the moment's grace it deserved before he finished his hand over hand movement to end with both hands on hers. Now, he searched her baby blues in the realization that, although he'd been married to this woman for over a year, and they had a child together, there were still so many fields yet to be plowed in her psyche, in her soul. There were still so many unknowns about her—about the troubled past, about the years of loneliness, about the years of pain.

"It's not a big deal," Jessie was saying as Josh adjusted to this new knowing. "Everyone was busy, you know? Doing their thing. Charles and Dee were swamped with tons of little details and we were all getting our hair done and our nails manicured…running all over the city…"

"And Charlie?"

"He was there, at the last second, but…well, you remember Charlie then. He was never *really* there." She lifted the hand she loved and brushed soft lips against her husband's knuckles. "No matter what happens tomorrow, Josh, know that I will be with you always. I hope you get your nomination. But whether you do or don't, whether you get your Oscar this time or down the road—and I know you will, one day—I will be with you always. Always and forever, remember? I don't ever want you to feel again, for one day in your life, the way I felt that night."

"What did I ever do to deserve you?" he murmured lovingly. "You are a dream, Jessie. You and our beautiful baby girl. One big surreal incredible dream." *Maybe that's why I keep having that weird dream about the golden fields,* he thought. *Because I think of them that way—as a dream. That's gotta be it.* He exhaled slowly and took the towel from Jessie's grasp.

Josh had already removed his T-shirt and left unbuttoned the top button of his jeans. He was in bare feet and, from Jessie's rather close inspection, quite adorable to rest one's eyes upon. It was still a thrill to rest her fingers upon his chest and feel his body tense at her touch in delicious anticipation. Their baby was growing, healthy—and thankfully, at this moment sleeping peacefully—and they had only recently resumed their much desired intimacies. They were used to being tired, and knew to treasure the moments the universe gave them to just be together—alone. So they took advantage of this night.

Josh kissed her first, a slow, lingering, burning caress of his lips against hers. He placed his hands at her hips, and sighed when he felt her own small hands land on his biceps. He moved one hand up then, and placed a palm on her cheek. She covered it with her own hand, interlacing her fingers in his.

"How much sleep do you plan on getting tonight, Oscar boy?" she asked him, a dreamy need telegraphing itself from Jessie's pale blue eyes.

"Well, Oscar girl, I suppose that depends." Josh let his kisses land behind the pretty ears, and on the graceful neck he loved to adore from afar when she was on stage, which was made all the more pleasurable because he alone had access to this lovely waif; only he—well, maybe Jacob sometimes, he thought irritably, pushing that unwelcome thought away the instant it attacked him—could ease her hurts and love the pain away.

"On what, exactly?" The object of his admiration was teasing him, as she moved her hands down to rub him through his jeans. He didn't even try to stifle the ragged moan that escaped between his lips at her touch.

"Oh, I suppose it depends on how much sleep you intend to get tonight, little one."

"Sleep, schmeep. I'll sleep when I'm dead." Jessie unzipped him then, and slid a hand inside her husband's jeans. "This is without a doubt much more fun than sleep."

"Being with you is everything, Jessie," was Josh's breathy response as his legs melted and his breathing quickened. "You're all I ever want. Ever."

"Say that when Oscar is on your shelf and women are throwing themselves at you," she teased, rubbing him a little harder with one hand and moving the jeans down his hips with the other. "Not that the whole Josh Sawyer frenzy hasn't already started. But even now, you know if you get that nomination that all of a sudden Hilary will have you everywhere while you chase down that little gold statue."

He couldn't help but smile at that, but inside, Josh knew Jessie was—and always would be—his partner, his touchstone, his soul mate. The mother of his children. No way would he be stupid like Charlie, who he knew, despite the man's obvious love for his wife and their daughter Stella, would always regret the reckless things he did to one day lose Jessie forever. No, Josh would not make the same mistakes. Nor would he let his jealousy of Jacob get in the way. Even that night, drying the dishes at his dad's grand new home, he, Jacob and Steve had a lot of laughs, some even at Jessie's expense, which she got a huge weird kick out of.

No, Josh knew Jacob would always be in the picture. Was he worried? Not really. But he wasn't stupid, either. He'd always have one eye open as far as Jacob Ryan was concerned. But in the meantime...he was married to this amazing woman, and her hand was down his pants at this very moment. Which made him want to return the favor real quick...

Josh had his arms around his wife super fast, then. He lifted her off the shiny tile floor and carried her around the corner into the suite's bedroom. Setting her down by the bed, he grasped Jessie's white peasant top at its bottom hem and pulled it up over her head. He let his fingers tease her under her bra before he undid that, and he gasped at the pleasure his body found simply by pressing his skin to hers.

Soon, he enticed her onto her back on the bed. Josh found himself in that glorious abyss between pleasure and desire, in total ecstasy over the realization she was his, body and soul, that they were here together, and that they were husband and wife. It was not something he would ever take for granted, and neither would she.

Slipping off her jeans, he grasped her hips, and his first taste of her left both of them wanting and gasping. Later, he would tease her that she likely woke their neighbors with her unrelenting moaning and groaning, but she just laughed and swatted him playfully. No way was Jessie stifling the pleasure this man wrought—he was her everything—her light, her rock, her soul.

When making love to his wife, Josh no longer thought much about Deuce McCall, or the way Jessie once shouted at him about her crazy orgasm with Jacob (and Katrine, apparently). Instead, these days when he slipped inside her, he simply clasped her to him and loved her. And tonight was one of those perfect dreamlike times after an absence, after a perfect evening with friends (and family!) and after watching their baby settle into a faraway nocturnal world of honey and roses, when the timing was perfect, the feeling of love mutual and desirable, and when their lovemaking was elevated to the point where simply living in the world was an immaculate wonder.

When they finished, Josh and Jessie held each other for extra-blessed moments, because this was a time to cherish; it was a time in which to breathe in the glory of a perfect instant in time and, above all, it was a time to bear witness to the joy of God's coupling of two once-very-lonely people. Josh tented Jessie inside his arms and rested his head on her shoulder. She pressed her fingertips into his skin, into the muscles there, into his hot sweaty flesh, as if by osmosis they could become one.

Then, they slept.

A few hours later, at 5:15 a.m., neither got out of bed. Instead, Jessie groggily reached for her iPad, which she'd placed on the nightstand the evening before. She poked the power button and opened Safari. Selecting a bookmarked site, she let Josh rearrange the large pillows to cushion their backs.

In nervous anticipation, they waited for the live Oscar-nomination broadcast to stream.

"It doesn't matter," Josh whispered to her, entangling his fingers in Jessie's while breathing warmly on her neck. She snuggled into him and hoped her man would not be disappointed today, because Jessie knew Josh had already spent enough years lost in the muzzy veil of disenchantment and frustration. This was his time, and *Freedom Ride* was his key to the highest level of reward in his chosen field. He deserved the win; hell, it was justified. He'd taken a serious fall during the shoot, laying down his bike like that and ending up with a visible reminder, a tiny scar on his cheek that she, even now, loved to run her tongue over when they played in bed.

She held her breath.

Steve and Jon must have been riding their cell phones. They must have thumb-typed CONGRATULATIONS before the announcement was even made, because their sincere accolades were on the screen on Josh's phone the instant the Best Actor nominees were announced.

He didn't text them back. Instead, Josh and Jessie leapt up and did a Cuban Zumba dance on the bed for the next five minutes, until they woke their baby, who adamantly protested her parents' vociferous exuberance. They woke their long-term neighbors, too, who were a senior couple always excited to text sneaky pics of the celebrity couple to their grandkids, and so who didn't really care. But the baby was instantly hungry, so her raucous cries succeeded in getting at least Jessie back to earth rather quickly as she went off for a pee and then settled in to feed Emily-Grace on the lime green wing chair, one leg folded underneath her butt while Josh took calls from Jonathon, Zach and Kayla.

Surreptitiously, Jessie watched her own phone's small screen as she basked in her husband's glory. He paced the room while rubbing a hand excitedly through his hair, occasionally kneeling down in front of his wife to kiss her and the baby, while he chatted exuberantly on the phone saying things like, "I know! It's crazy, it's surreal!"

There were no texts, no calls, and no emails from either Charles or Dee until much later that day. When the message finally did come, it was an email, and it was from Deirdre, who wrote simply, *Flying in tomorrow at 2 for the evening fundraiser. Give Josh our best. Sounds like you are going to the Oscars. Kisses to Emily-Grace.*

Mmmpphh, was Jessie's huffy response. Would she ever be able to amend or heal the distrust Charles and Dee felt for Josh after the whole Caryn thing? Josh almost died—he could have died, from the pneumonia that even now marked him with a pale countenance. He was the father of Charles and Dee's grandchild, in a manner of speaking. Their deliberate distance from him did nothing to ease Jessie's own reticence around the power couple. She didn't bother emailing back.

After lunch the next day, Jessie and Jacob took a run out to Peterborough for the fundraiser's sound check. They kidded and joked all the way out, with Ulysses joining in to occasionally mediate. Josh would drive in later with the Keatings, followed by Jonathon and Giselle, who would have Steve with them. Jessie was rather relieved she wouldn't be in the vehicle with Josh, Charles and Dee, but she secretly hoped they'd somehow be able to mend some fences. After all, Dan, as driver, would be able to provide a neutral voice if it were needed.

Her hopes were quickly dashed. When Dee arrived, her flashing eyes were the first to transmit the lack of success during the drive. What was worse was that the group was joining Jessie and Jacob at Martha's home, as her guests. Jessie's usual clan was meeting her extended long-lost family for the first time.

Even during the introductions, the hostility was barely disguised, which made Jessie angry and defensive and rather glad to be connected to a whole new set of *real* family, despite the angry glares she was receiving from Sara at the moment, and the low-slung glances courtesy of young tow-headed Ren.

Childish spoiled woman, Jessie thought of her manager uncharitably, while Dee purposefully raised her aristocratic chin and glanced in a rather hostile fashion around Martha's small seniors' unit.

A caterer had laid out food so Jessie and Jacob could stay in and thus keep their appearance as much on the down low as possible, and their Ulysses-led security—with cooperation by Big Dan, Apollo and Morgan, and awareness given to the OPP, the Ontario Provincial Police—was intact. The singers didn't need anyone else spotting them before the event, which was mostly an auction with intermittent entertainment. Jessie and Jacob would appear last. Which left lots of time to fight.

Dee started it.

"Is this Belleek?" she asked Martha first, her nose in the air. Martha had two pieces of the cherished delicate eggshell-thin Irish porcelain—a tiny square vase and a cream and sugar set.

The sweet Martha responded with a hunched over, "Yes. They were a gift from my late husband." Jessie's heart melted at the love in the woman's eyes. But Dee just nodded. She was a woman with many expensive gifts from her husband. But it wasn't something she usually flaunted. Today, she seemed primed and ready for a battle, and it seemed to have its roots in the ride up from TO, although Jessie quickly began to realize its roots were, in fact, much deeper than that. In truth, they seemed to be about, well…roots. The family kind.

Dee's response to Martha was a quick, "Oh, Charles gave me a Monet for our last anniversary." At Martha's confusion and surprise, she rather expediently added, "You know, *dear*. The French artist. Pastel palettes? Water lilies?"

"I know who Monet is, dear," returned Martha smartly, unable to keep disappointment from edging her voice.

At least she has the composure not to accentuate the dear in the nasty way Dee did, thought Jessie, stunned at Dee's wholly mean-spirited manner. In Martha's home, for God's sake! She glanced at Evelyn, whose eyes narrowed at Dee before she sent a questioning look back to Jessie.

Jessie looked at Josh and wondered wildly *what the hell did y'all fight about in the car?* Besides a quick brush of his lips on her cheek, and a moment for her to suck in his warmth and energy, he hadn't met her eye since arriving. And Charles was just eyeing her with a disappointed frown.

Dee's mean streak continued as she dolled around the small room judging Martha by her collectibles, which mostly consisted of card-store figurines. "I suppose you have some Royal Doulton tucked away somewhere," she half-smiled, only one corner of her lip turning up, which left her looking about as heartless as she was managing to quite aptly sound. She grazed a fingertip over one particularly poorly made porcelain ballet dancer, whose dress was a maudlin red and yellow and whose face was so poorly painted the lips bled onto the chin. Then she had the audacity to pick it up and frown openly.

"My daughter Emily gave that to me when she was seven," piped in Martha, hobbling towards her guest upon noticing Deirdre's blatant disapproval. "It was my first birthday gift from her." Martha retrieved the gift and placed it delicately back in its place of honor where, unknown to her guests, she'd only just recently put it after digging it out of an old box in her basement.

Already hostile Sara entered the fray, despite Evelyn's attempt to shush her. "I suppose you have a lot of those kinds of gifts too, Mrs. Keating. From your...oops. Pardon me. I forgot. You don't actually *have* a daughter."

At that, the men in the room sucked in a collective breath. Deirdre Keating, the lion lady, had just been quite adequately verbally attacked by a woman who, although they didn't know it, wouldn't even consider inviting her to *her* home. For lots of uncharitable (and low self-esteem) kinds of reasons. Namely the sagging chesterfield. Sara hadn't even considered the porcelain...um, er...lack thereof.

Deirdre didn't have the nerve to look at Jessie at first. But when she did, she found on the girl's face sheer disappointment and disapproval instead of the sadness she, for some inane reason, wanted to see.

Dee rolled back her shoulders and dove in further.

"In a manner of speaking, I suppose you could say no," she returned. "But I've considered Jessie my daughter for many years now. Since she was twenty, in fact. And for my last birthday, she took me to Paris for a mother-daughter soiree. I suppose this year we'll take my grand-daughter as well."

"Jesus, Dee," sputtered Jessie finally, fists clenching. "Can we possibly not do the drama queen thing tonight? We're here to try to help a little boy, remember?"

To everyone's utter horror, Sara blatantly ignored her. "You go, girl," she spat off to Dee. "The two of you just leave good old Emily in her wheelchair in that snowy redneck wasteland people call P.E.I. That's about what she deserves, anyway. I can see Jessie did much better by fluttering under your golden wing all these years." She crossed her arms.

Horrified, Jessie took a step closer to the women with the intention of trying to stop the bleeding, but Josh grabbed her bicep and, when she glanced back at him, he shook his head. *Let them play out their little who's-Jessie's-real-family drama*, his eyes telegraphed to her. Behind him, Steve and Jacob were trying not to meet anyone's eyes, but Jessie's flashed to Jacob, which Josh caught. Jacob telegraphed *we'll laugh about this on the way home, Jess, let it go*, but Josh looked back over his shoulder and glared at him, which erased the pouty smile rather quickly, until Josh steered his eyes away again.

Jessie cocked her head at Jacob as if to say *seriously, Jacob? This isn't exactly the time to make light of the situation.*

She was even less impressed when Josh gave her a disdainful look and dropped her arm rather menacingly. *Oh, so likely that's what the hostility in the car on the trip up was about. Groan. This group is a bunch of children.* Jessie fired her own hostile look to Josh, then.

Emily-Grace decided she'd had enough of these supposed grown-ups and their childish ways. She didn't care about the value of the porcelain in the room. She just wanted her momma, and so let out her first anxious *feed me* wail.

No one moved. The baby was in the kindly Kevin's arms. Moving protectively in front of him, Sara slipped her arms under his. She lifted Emily-Grace and rocked her gently, keeping spiteful, narrowed eyes focused on Deirdre the whole time.

"Kilfoil babies like this," she said to her, emphasizing the *Kilfoil*. "They respond well to the swaying motion." Sure enough, Emily-Grace settled for the moment, and even offered a smile up to her doting aunt.

Deirdre was incensed. Jessie could see the blood pressure visibly rising in the woman's face, an unattractive deepening red blotch forming high on each cheek. *Oh shit*, she thought. *This can't be good.*

But then she looked closer at Dee and was quite surprised to see a wet sheen coating her manager's eyes. The knuckles were white, clenched tightly by the sides of the Donna Karan blazer and skirt that together, Jessie suddenly realized with surprise, was known to be Dee's favorite outfit. This was the woman who took her in and believed in her when Jessie was rescued from a homeless existence on the streets of Vancouver's Downtown Eastside. This was the woman who made her a star. This was a woman who, every day, wished Jessie was something she was not—her daughter. And now, this evening, Dee was rallying her defenses in order to protect herself from the truth, in this place where she felt what attachment she had with Jessie might be threatened.

In fact, one thing Jessie now clearly understood, was that Dee—and Charles, too—were both afraid of losing her. Not just to the surprise Peterborough family, but to Josh as well. Yes, there was a time when Dee at least, and maybe Charles a little, felt Josh was worthy, but that time was passed. Were the Peterborough clan worthy? No way. Even the city itself felt working class, with its interminable train tracks and smoky factories.

So rather than ease the minds of the Kilfoil branch of the family by aligning herself with them, Jessie made a critical error, in Sara's mind. She tried to rescue Dee, who most folks in the room didn't think was worth rescuing.

She took Emily-Grace from Sara's arms and gave her to Deirdre.

The room went stock-silent before reverting back to its before-drama buzz. And then it was apparent something was missing. It was the friendly truce Jessie established with Sara the day she landed at her door with a virtually hysterical screaming infant.

Sara packed up her family—a quiet, subdued Ren *I'm-not-talking-to-you-Jessie* in front of her, her hand on his shoulder—and vacated the tiny middle-class dwelling, which left Kevin apologizing to Jessie at the door, and Martha wisely focusing on serving the men. It had long been her experience that feeding gathered menfolk was the way to many victories or, in this case, at the very least to some kind of ceasefire.

Humbled at what Jessie told her by her simple action, Deirdre behaved for the rest of the evening. She helped Jessie with Emily-Grace—the changing and the rocking—and afterwards, when Josh took his baby from her for a welcome before-sleep cuddle, she ducked her head and dried dishes for Martha.

Upon leaving Martha's home, Jessie slipped her hand in Deirdre's. "So. That was as much fun as rubbing salt in an open wound."

"That's what it felt like." For the powerful woman, this was quite the admission.

"You started it, Dee." Sure, she helped her, but Jessie wasn't leaving Deirdre any room to behave that childishly again—ever.

Dee helped her understand. "I wasn't exactly in the best mood when I arrived."

Sighing, as they stood in the driveway, Jessie swung their hands in between them while Charles supervised Josh's placement of Emily-Grace's carrier in the back seat of the Lincoln. "What did my husband do now to upset you?"

"Your *husband* just signed on to another year of *The Wyatt Boys*."

Wrinkling her forehead, Jessie said simply, "Well, yes. He's the lead. Did you think Jon would kill his character off after season one?"

Dee was silent.

"Jesus, Dee," Jessie stammered. "Seriously? You didn't think Jon's show would get a second season, did you? So who're you really mad at? Josh or his father?"

Spinning on her heel, Dee faced Jessie as Charles and Josh looked up and over curiously. The suddenly elevated voices were renewed cause for concern.

"Jessie, your husband has just been nominated for his first Oscar."

Well that's a good thing, flitted across Jessie's mind. *She said 'first'.*

Dee continued. "You are in Miami most of the time, while he's in Toronto." The woman's expression softened. "Your baby is coping, but all this travel is exhausting, even to watch from the sidelines. And now this…" She waved an arm at Martha's home. "More travel. Driving, which you mostly insist on doing yourself, despite the fact that it's going to get out tonight that you have family connections here. Suddenly everyone's going to be at risk, including that nice woman getting into Dan's vehicle as we speak."

Jessie looked over to see Big Dan and Evelyn helping her fragile 89-year-old grandmother into his large black SUV. The woman was smiling up at him, sweetness and kindness emanating from the wrinkled face. *My mom's mom*, Jessie thought as a weird feeling traipsed up her spine and across her chest, almost choking her with the realization that the woman was frail, old…but she was hers. Her grandmother. By blood. And now the world would know. Would it change Martha's life, Sara's life? Ren and Mark's life? Maybe, on some level. But surely not in any remarkable way, at least once the fizz ran out of the entertainment news story.

She shuddered momentarily, and let her gaze drift back over to Dee, who was preparing to unleash another rush of emotion.

"Jessie," she insisted, "it's not even so much the baby I'm worried about."

Jessie cut her off. "It's Josh. And me, I suppose. Because of what happened. The photographs."

"And the Oscar nod. And no Matt around to pick up the pieces."

"You and Charles can share the blame on that count, Dee. As well as the whole 'me in Miami' shtick. Besides," she added. "I have Jacob." It was a whisper, and Jessie sucked the words back the second they were unleashed.

"Exactly," replied Dee and, without looking at him, she sent Charles a one-finger notice that they just needed another minute before climbing into the car. "And Josh has…" The words faded into oblivion.

The men leaned against the hood and waited patiently. The other vehicle waited too, idling quietly, its passengers shifted somewhat now that the little Sawyer family wanted to travel together. Jonathon and Giselle were already at the fundraiser.

"Catfight," muttered Steve to Jacob as they sat in the second car watching the women in their heated discussion.

"Yep," Jacob agreed. "CIP."

"What?"

"Catfight in progress."

"Hmmm. AAK."

"Huh?"

"Alive and kicking."

"Oh. Yeah."

From the front seat they heard Martha say wisely, "G2G B4 MNC."

"What?" both boys echoed at once.

Dan answered the first part, "Got to go before…" He grinned at Martha and raised his eyebrows.

She peeked in the rearview mirror and met Jacob and Steve's pleasant, questioning eyes. "Got to go before mother nature calls. Texting changes quite dramatically after you reach eighty." She held up her phone. "I just heard from Sara. Jacob, you and Jessie are on in thirty minutes."

Outside, while the boys in the second car were having a laugh and embarking on a 'tech for seniors' conversation with Jessie's grandmother, Jessie was awaiting more bullets from Dee. Finally, with no response forthcoming, she spoke for her. She was still holding her hand, as if she was afraid Dee would run and avoid the thought both knew was prevalent on the older woman's mind.

"Josh has…? What, Dee?" Jessie picked up Deirdre's earlier unfinished thought. "Did Jon say something to you? About Josh…like…on set or something?" She couldn't imagine going through that fear again, the fear of seeing him with Caryn at Revolver and…wondering…her stomach seized and she wrapped an arm around her belly.

"No, Jessie, no…not…anything real, at least. But no shortage of women who wouldn't hesitate, if that door should be opened for them. Are you prepared to handle that?"

Incredulous, Jessie almost lost it. "What do you mean, am I prepared to handle that?"

"Don't play innocent with me. You know exactly what I mean, Jessie!"

Josh was close enough to hear…but wise enough to straighten but not interfere. He and Dee already had that heated discussion in the car and he wasn't about to dive in there again, although he watched Jessie carefully for signs of rescue, should she need it. She didn't. But she did look over at him, and was calmed by what she saw in his eyes.

Trust. Love. And a simple unshakeable faith…in *them.*

When she met Dee's anxious eyes again, she chose to be the adult in the conversation. "He won't cheat on me, Deirdre."

The impact of using her manager's formal first name resulted in the desired reaction. Dee was suddenly solemn. "And if he does?" She didn't turn to look at Josh, but later, when she was reliving the conversation, she would take note of his silence and quiet observation at a time when she thought he might in fact lose it.

Jessie shrugged. *I'll deal with it.* Then her mind drifted to *hmmm, so that's what they were talking about in the car on the way here. No wonder everyone was in such a funky mood when they got here. I thought it was the usual Josh and Jacob thing.* She was starting to calm down a bit when Dee's next words read her mind and choked her.

"Word from Martinique has it that you and Jacob spend time alone in his room. In Miami. Or he spends time in yours. Overnight."

Closing her eyes, Jessie finally let go of Dee's hand. "We hang out, Dee. Sometimes."

"In my day, men and women only spent time in hotel rooms to do one thing."

"Uh huh. Let me guess, you couldn't wait to tell Josh." *Who is listening. Right now.* An icy nausea gripped Jessie's belly as a cold, clammy sweat travelled up her core. "You're driving a knife in between us, bringing up this shit, Dee. You know that, right? Although maybe that's your intention, huh? Couching your so-called fears in some Mizz 'I'm-so-worried' act!"

"You two need to know what you are up against now, with this Oscar nomination and all the press we'll have to manage for him. And for you, by association."

"Jesus, Dee, is that what else this is about? The extra workload for you? Don't worry, Hilary's got Josh covered!"

But again, no response was forthcoming. Finally a dim light appeared across Jessie's pale eyes, dancing over them as a new dawn alights a dewy day. "No. That's not it." She pointed a finger at Dee. "I know what you're really pissed about. You're pissed because I'm doing TV, which by the way both of you seemed downright joyous about at the time I started on *Mystic Nights*, but Josh did a film—"

"Which he made when he deserted you in P.E.I."

"And he's nominated for an Oscar while I sit around and flirt with Jacob, who it seems you and Charles perhaps think is more worthy of my affections than the man I married."

"Not more worthy, Jessie. More…trustworthy. There's a difference."

"Ha! Trustworthy? How can you, in one breath, accuse him of sleeping with me, and then in the next breath call him trustworthy?"

"Because, Jessie, it's…" But Dee was stuck, silenced by the truth, which Josh and Jessie both now clearly understood. Her and Charles' affection for Jacob was not entirely about *Jacob*. It was quite substantially also about *Josh*. In the negative sense.

"God," Jessie gasped. "You all make me sick. You and your twisted way of thinking."

She wheeled around and grabbed her husband's steady hand.

Disheartened, Josh shot Dee a sorrowful look before following Jessie into the back seat of the SUV, on the side opposite her so the couple could flank their small daughter. The Keatings followed quietly afterwards, crowding into the front seat with Ulysses.

Apart from the baby's adorable *bah-dah-dab-bah* gurgles, it was a silent ride to the fire hall, where the fundraising concert for a young boy was already well underway.

Chapter Thirty

Sara had decided to snag seats at the back of the hall in case she decided at the last minute to sneak her family out. It wasn't a problem—the place was packed. As she and Ren learned the hard way, sadly there were some who knew Jessie and Jacob—and Josh, by association, those folks hoped—were in the city, although most didn't, or at the very least absolutely did not believe the rumors. And there were the wise observer types who wondered why the hell there seemed to be a hefty security presence at a fundraiser for a very sick three-year-old boy.

In their assigned makeshift green room, before Jessie was beckoned on stage, Josh knelt before her. She was seated, abstractly tuning the Gibson. He reached up and plucked a guitar pick out from between her teeth, where she was resting it temporarily while she adjusted the guitar in her arms.

Startled, she met his eyes. His were somber.

"I'm not worried," he said.

"'Bout me or you?" she asked, grabbing the pick back from him and shimmying her butt closer to the edge of the plastic chair she was sitting on to tune.

"'Bout either of us."

"Nothing has ever happened with Jacob."

He raised his eyebrows.

"I mean recently," she added, exasperated, blushing. "Geez, I do get tired of this."

"Dee has a different view of the world, Jess."

"Harrumph. You're telling me." Pausing, she tuned an E string, and looked up from the Gibson to her husband. He was watching her patiently. "What? What aren't you telling me?"

Shifting his weight to the other knee, Josh grimaced. "I'm getting old," he groaned, rubbing one knee. Then he said, "Martinique. That's what I'm telling you. Dee knows what it's like to be away from her husband. And what can happen when you're separated. Not just…the Charlie thing. With you. The *Charles* thing. With her."

"What? Martinique?" As awareness bloomed across her cheeks, Jessie snapped her head over to the right where Dee and Charles were engaged in what appeared to be a heart-to-heart. Charles was trying to get his wife to hold his hand but she was refusing, instead crossing her arms like a petulant child and shaking her head from side to side. "Well, yeah, Matt said something about Martinique and Charles when we were out for a run in Miami one day. Not now though, right? I hope?"

"Not recently, apparently. A long time ago. When he and Dee were first married."

"Okay, well as shocking as that is, it's old news, Josh. They've obviously mended their broken upscale pressure-treated cedar fences."

"Yes, but that's what's been triggering her lately. Apparently. Notwithstanding all the other stresses and pressures she's under these days, with guilt over Matt's departure, and me in the hospital and this new-old family of yours…running out to redneck Ontario to sing for little boys you don't even know…"

"Harsh, Josh," she yelped at him. "It was bad enough with you being sick. I can't imagine what it would be like if it was one of our kids." She gulped back the fear.

"I know," he agreed, "I know, Jessie. And you wouldn't be you if you didn't do this for this child." He touched her cheek with his fingertips. "I just think Dee is losing it a little. There's too much all-over-the-place and not enough control. Especially without Matt. I think she's only now realizing how much he did for all of us. Seems to me she's feeling like a ship without a rudder. So she's lashing out at everything that scares the hell outta her. That she can't control."

Jessie deflated then. Her shoulders relaxed and her lips turned up in a smile. "My God," she murmured so only he could hear, although Jacob caught the love and tenderness passing between them as he tuned too, over in the far corner, while he leaned against a plywood countertop. "And you wouldn't be you without trying to understand someone who constantly launches missiles at you. Why doesn't everyone out there see what I see when I look at you?"

There was no need for words then, for once again the old Wheeler-Sawyer magic ignited. Jessie bent forward and, leaning over her guitar, staunchly kissed her husband on one bristly cheek, and then she let her lips trail down to his. Silently the couple shared an intimacy no one else in the room could have intruded on had they wanted to. The familiar bubble was in place. And it was not about to burst.

Although some in the room would have relished the opportunity to strike up a match and set the intangible thing on fire, despite the close proximity of hoses and skilled firemen. Indeed, Jacob's heart plunged when he beheld the tender kiss, yet he knew there was something sacred here; he had always known that from the first time he saw Josh's ring around Jessie's neck. But it was still surreal, in a way, to bear witness to the great love between the two. He struggled with his hurting heart before forcing his eyes back down to his guitar.

Dee spied the kiss, too, and its impact on her heart was pain. It was nothing more than a simple knowing, for as much as she and Charles shared what both considered a long and faithful—for the most part—perfect love, she was cautiously aware of celebrity pitfalls. And—the higher you went, the further you had to fall. Sure, Jessie was wise enough to see through Dee's cracking veneer to spy seeds of truth, but ultimately both of the Keatings just wanted a final peace for Jessie, a happiness she could count on.

The fear wasn't so much Josh as what might *prey* on Josh and, if the worst were to happen, his ability to remain aloof and indestructible.

Still, neither Dee nor Charles could help but be touched by the genuine intimacy they saw at play between the Sawyers now, nor could they deny the sheer bliss in Jessie's new-mom-mega-travel tired eyes.

A nervous voice interrupted the quiet picking of strings on Jacob's guitar and the touching moment shared by Josh and Jessie.

"We're ready for you." Clearly, as the volunteer stagehand's eyes swept the room, he was referring to the hangers-on who would not be watching the show. Steve, grinning at his good friends, gave Jessie the thumbs-up as he grabbed hold of Emily-Grace's carrier. Josh kissed his wife one last time and whispered a quiet *luv you*, and then he stood and followed the others out of the room.

Jessie was alight with her husband's good grace and wisdom when she heard a chair *scrreeecchhhh* up behind her.

"You two are absolutely sickening," offered Jacob, a lazy sardonic twist to his pouty lips. "Disgusting. I'm disgusted."

"Get a grip, Jacob, we've been married well over a year. We have a kid. No sleep, no sex. Honeymoon's over." But the baby blues were shining, misty even, and Jacob—for some inane reason he didn't understand—was happy for Jessie.

"Come on, girl," he commanded. "Let's make our own magic."

And soon they were on stage, two of the world's most popular singer-songwriters of the time, in a small fire hall in downtown Peterborough, Ontario, for a crowd of three hundred and fifty, which soon ballooned to five hundred and then to a thousand.

For the young Lawrence boys, Ren and Mark, seeing their aunt up there on stage while the audience lost their minds over Jessie's humbling appearance was a defining moment of their young lives. They were only starting to understand celebrity and fame, and music too, and this concert delineated music for them forevermore, in a way that made it sacred and not just a tool with which a very few made a whole lot of ridiculous money. Ren's dad had talked to him about the sketchy pictures. And somehow the music seemed separate from the dirty way they made him feel. Somehow it helped him heal.

For Kevin, the show was magical, but mostly because of what it did for his wife.

Sara and Martha watched Jessie and Jacob's thirty minutes of music with, first, trepidation, and then with a slow longing for the years they missed, and then with earnest heartsick survivors' grief for what was irretrievably lost, and now was found. Which was appropriate, since one of the songs the couple sang towards the end of the set was called *Take Me Away*, and it was one of Jessie's old signature pieces. It was a song of loneliness and heartache, and it sucked the breath out of Josh, Steve, Charles and Dee every time they watched her perform it. Even Josh acknowledged—only to himself, of course—that he was glad Jessie had Jacob on stage with her to help get her through that song. Many of her pieces reflected her angsty past, but tonight this one was on the hot seat even more profoundly.

Because...*she changed the lyrics.*

And Josh immediately recognized this gesture as a message to the Peterborough folks, as well as to Charles and Dee.

You sneaky little thing, he thought, as a subtle smile broadened across his face. *Music is your language. Well done. I hope they're listening.* He glanced over to Dee and saw her take Charles' hand. They were.

Was Sara listening? Was Martha?

The kids were. Everyone in the audience was. The interesting thing, Josh noticed, was that Kevin was watching his wife. And something was happening there. Kevin was suddenly panicking, it seemed—his face was flushed and he seemed unsure about something, about what to do, perhaps. He was twitching, moving slightly, reaching out and then drawing back.

Josh's eyes went to Sara. Jessie's half-sister sat frozen, unmoving. Loss flowed through her eyes—loss of a mother at age fourteen, loss of knowing a sister who she only just now was beginning to understand...loss of innocence, loss of self-esteem, loss of hope. And now, on stage, the girl who was the result—not the cause, although sometimes Sara got that mixed up—of a confused and scared mother's quest for love, was singing to her.

The song was, of course, a Jessie Wheeler special, a ballad in three-four time that blamed no one, not even Emily Wheeler, for all her misplaced actions that hurt both Sara and Jessie deeply. It was an elegy for a lifetime of lost sisterly love, and it was an ode to a grandmother whose spirit and lust for life must have been irrevocably diminished the moment her pregnant daughter climbed down a midnight ladder and abandoned her family.

Then it was too much.

Martha raised her chin and stayed focused in the moment, maybe because she had a hard-earned wisdom after all these decades, or maybe because she'd made her peace with the world, in these, what must be her final years.

But Sara, instead of searching for peace, over the years had done the opposite. She piled brick upon brick of stifling anger and indignant stinging ache around her soul, and she buried herself deep within the hallowed walls.

And now, tonight, the bricks were being loosed—they were coming down. Jessie's presence on stage and her song to Sara were working loose the binding around her heart, around the bricks. They were unraveling years of pent up agony from abandonment at the hands of a misguided mother. From financial stress, from the distance she created between herself and her husband, and between her and her children, too, by virtue of always focusing on immediate requirements instead of on the simple gift of spiritual and loving *time*.

She crumbled.

Kevin tried to catch her, and so did Evelyn, but in the end it was Martha, the Kilfoil rock, who grasped her granddaughter's hand and held it, steadying her. Fully attentive, under the Wheeler spell they sat, while Jessie, with Jacob's help, spoke to them her own tale of loss and then, too, of being found, clearly (at least to those who were paying attention) referencing the Keatings.

She knows her power, Josh was thinking, *and she's using it.* He caught Steve's eye. His friend, too, understood, and he was clearly in awe. Jessie's power on the stage, live, in front of them, never failed to impress either guy. And it never would, even in the tough times to come.

There was another thing about Jessie—when she sang, she did so with everything she had. That always took her to a place beyond the forum where she found herself singing, beyond the people watching, and beyond the music. Tonight was no exception. When the final note of the ballad was played, Jacob sat in watchful silence for he, too, had disappeared to a place beyond the song, and even though he came out of the spell first, he knew to wait for Jessie to exit it too. He recognized the moment when she broke out of it, as did Josh, Steve, and the Keatings.

Evelyn seemed to realize this. But Sara did not. Her gasping breaths and struggle to get a grip were not heard, but they were seen by some, eventually even by Jessie, who stood on stage frowning towards one of the last rows of the small hall, the trusty Gibson a shield she white-knuckled at her side.

Then a voice tickled her ear, and a beloved breath warmed her neck. It was Jacob, murmuring to her, telling Jessie to go. He took the Gibson from her, and Jessie dropped down the few steps of the stage and made her way cautiously down the aisle alone to her half-sister at the back of the fire hall. Vintage fire hose decorations and years of faded fire chiefs' portraits lined the tall walls; under stoic posed eyes, Jessie's tentative steps to an uncertain reception were crisply monitored.

She stopped in front of Sara, who was not standing, like everyone else in the space.

Instead, Jessie's half-sister was gulping for air, almost hyper-ventilating in fact, with two scared boys and a terrified husband—who never saw their mother and wife express this kind of emotion—at her side.

Unsure, Jessie knelt before her sister.

"Sara," she managed, through her own building emotion, "it's not too late. There's a lot of living left in both of us."

Peeking up from beneath the crumbling brick, Sara gasped, "We're from two different worlds, Jessie. Don't you see? We lost each other the moment our mother met your father."

"I'm weary, Sara. I'm tired. And I need my sister. Stop fighting me."

A tremulous voice cut in from Sara's left side, where Martha bent to eye-ball her two granddaughters. "Well, there's not much living left in me, girls. So let's stop wasting time. THT!" She waved an arm to accentuate that final point.

"What?" Jessie and Sara asked in unison.

She'd said it loud enough that Steve and Dan, in the row behind them, overheard. "THT," called Steve over the exuberance of the crowd, who were stomping their feet begging for an encore, "Think happy thoughts!"

Eyes sparkling, misty in the semi-lit space, Jessie smiled at Sara. "Okay?" she asked, tentative. "Can we at least be friends? So we can say good old Emily at least did *something* right?"

Lips trembling, Sara hesitated before she grasped her husband's hand and nodded. A glimmer of hope lit her suddenly buoyant eyes.

And with that, Sara and Jessie stood and hugged each other genuinely for the first time in their lives. Relieved and excited about the possibilities for real kinship in the days to come, Jessie tossed her curls, and got on with the business her life expected of her. She leaned between Martha and Sara and wrapped grateful arms around her husband in the row behind them, kissed him (to the welcome delight of the rapidly growing crowd), and then she twisted around and slapped hands all the way back to the stage.

The surprise appearance at the fire hall did not end until Ulysses got nervous and shepherded Jessie and Jacob off the stage. They drove back to Toronto immediately afterwards, leaving Morgan and Apollo, along with local OPP, to watch over the homes of Martha and Sara in case any curious strangers decided to peek in their windows in a search for the visiting talent.

Jessie fell asleep on the way back, her head on Josh's shoulder. This time they were in the front and Charles and Dee were in the back, so Dee could hold Emily-Grace's little hand. Before she dozed off, though, Jessie heard Josh whisper in her ear, and she smiled.

His words were simply, "Sleep well, little one. You did good."

Not that what he said would have mattered—his husky voice was enough. His presence was enough. He was her constant, her hope and, occasionally, when she missed him, her sorrow. He was the glue holding her together.

He was her everything.

She peeked beneath fatigued eyelids to spy their fingers entwined around each other, nestled comfortably on her lap. The feel of his skin on hers was reassuring; he brushed a thumb over and over the back of her hand.

She'd just left a room with many people she loved dearly within it. In the same room.

Jessie almost felt complete.

And she was happy.

Chapter Thirty-one

"She came to me one day when I was standing in the garden wishing it was spring. It was winter, I recall, because there was snow on the ground. And we were freezing. But things heated up, and…I guess both of us knew nothing would be the same from that day on. So we stood there and shivered, until finally your grandfather's car pulled in and we either had to face his questioning eyes or avoid him altogether by vacating the garden. So I trucked off inside, and your mother went home."

Martha was seated on the lime green wing chair in Josh's bright suite. She and Sara were there, and Evelyn was on her way up—she'd gone on a coffee and tea run after the little group arrived in Toronto. They were there to hash over the events of the night before, to be briefed by Ulysses on some security and privacy issues, should the need arise (regarding both their families as well as Jessie, Josh and Jacob), and to find some peaceful common ground regarding Emily's actions more than three decades earlier.

Josh was on set filming and Jacob was, surprisingly, with him, with Steve as a buffer. Jonathon had invited Jacob, hoping he would consider taking on a guest role. Josh was less than impressed, but amenable to the set visit, given Jessie's visitors for the day. And any chance to keep Jacob away from Jessie…

So far, at the hotel, Sara was silent, but her wide eyes spoke volumes, and she was unable to stop wringing both hands. Jessie had a feeling if Sara spoke she would likely start and not stop, like one of those Energizer bunnies—once they get started, they go on forever until the battery wears out. Indeed, Sara's eyes were red and swollen. It seemed last night's melty tears must have

259

lasted for a while. Studying her, Jessie wondered how she felt this morning. Was she exhausted, spent from her emotional night? Was she still angry?

So weird, Jessie thought from her perch on the ottoman facing the two women—Sara was kitty corner to her, on the sofa—*music has the strangest power.* Here, today, she was being given some sort of reprieve from the old family angst, and it was definitely a direct result of last night's appearance at the fundraiser. The tension was, at least partly, gone. Now it was time to talk. To *really* talk.

Martha continued, her tremulous aged voice as steady as it could be at 89, her mind sharp as a tack, her memory, seemingly, clear. But then again, how do you forget the last dramatic months with a daughter you would likely never see again?

"Any time we talked after that, it was all accusations and threats...a lot of 'how could you's' and 'don't you dare's.' She wanted to leave Mark but she knew he would never let her take Sara. And Sara, frankly, was being a bitch to her mother at the time." Searching Sara's eyes, Martha reached across the small space and took her hand. "But there was a reason for that. Wasn't there, Sara?"

Jessie watched quietly, arms loosely folded across her belly, shoulders slightly slumped, knees and toes turned in. There was a closeness inherent in the two women she was only just getting to know. The way Martha touched Sara affected Jessie deeply. Her grandmother was 89. But for Jessie...all those years alone...from the time her father died...there were so many lost years because of stupid Kilfoil pride. There was so much pain.

Sara turned her sad eyes to Jessie. "Our mother...we were close. She was...good to me. We didn't have a lot of extras but she put me in figure skating, and in dance...she came to all my practices, she watched the ice shows... we went shopping, we had movie nights practically every Friday. But...my dad...he wasn't a part of that. She and I were one, and he and I were one. She and him..." She shook her head. "I'm sure they loved each other, but it wasn't a Hollywood love struck kind of love, you know? It was...well, whatever it was, it didn't give her what she needed. So when she met David... your dad...well, I guess she thought it was real. I have to admit, Jessie, all these years...I wondered whether it was real. For her and him. Or was it just a temporary lust thing."

Now that Sara was talking, Jessie remained silent. She didn't want to stem the flow. She herself had things to say, but they could wait. Dee had the baby in her suite down the hall, despite her own anxieties of not being included in the unscheduled surprise meeting, and the boys would be on set until three, so Jessie was left free to focus on the truths being unleashed here today.

"I happened upon them…together…my mother and your father. I was barely fourteen. I had no idea."

"Ohhh." It was an inadvertent slip. Jessie couldn't help herself. The impact of that simple statement…a fourteen year old stumbling upon her mother with a man other than her father…at such an impressionable age…well, that would knock any daughter flat.

"She was supposed to pick me up from skating. She was never late. She always came to the practices, until…well, I guess until she had a better place to go. So this one time she wasn't there, I went looking for her. I was still in my skating dress. First I just went out to the parking lot, thinking she was maybe waiting in the car, although she never did that, but I didn't know… I went back inside and called my dad, but he didn't know where she was. And no, he didn't know anything about her affair at the time. That was a hard secret to keep, which made me hate her even more, having to keep it." The fingers clenched into knots on Sara's lap.

Jessie noticed the white knuckles, and she wanted to reach out and offer Sara a touch of comfort, but…not knowing what she would get back, a scream or a yell, maybe…the end of Sara's telling…she didn't risk it. This was too important. She waited.

A huge deep intake of breath seemed to steady Sara's resolve to get this out, at any cost. She continued. "I went down the road in my short skating dress, my skate bag hung over my shoulder because we didn't have those fancy ones the kids drag behind them today. With my boots and tights… I must have been a sight. I thought I was cool, at the time, because I was a skater, and I could do stuff, you know, axels and flips and lutzes and double toes and double loops…and I was just getting my double flip, I was so close, in fact I kind of cheat-landed one that night, and I was excited to see mom, to tell her. I couldn't believe she wasn't there to see it." Looking up, she stared hard at Jessie. "She was my biggest fan."

Ouch, thought Jessie, slumping a little further. *I used to have one of those… my dad.* The reality of a few million super fans didn't even cross her mind. What were those anonymous faces compared to one person who loves you so much—who knows *you*—sitting in the stands, or even in your living room, watching you practice a skill you love as you fine tune and hone it? *My mother was never really my fan*, Jessie pondered, confusion flecking her eyes. *I wondered why.* Regarding Sara now, hearing her story, answered that question. Finally.

"She was in a coffee shop. With him. They were holding hands, which I couldn't believe they were doing in public. Yes, Peterborough is a city, but it's a small city. People knew her. People knew him. They knew my dad. She was taking a huge chance, and I didn't get it. I didn't get any of it." The sour memory came rushing back hard and furious now. Sara's words tumbled over each other like snow in an avalanche, threatening to bury her.

"I remember just standing there in shock and total disbelief—could this be my mother? And who was that man sitting there with his elbow on the table, leaning his head in his hand, staring into her eyes obviously completely love-struck by her, by my mother? She was laughing, telling some stupid story, about me for all I knew. Her back was to me and so I could only see his face; they were sitting in the window, but she was waving her arms around the way she always did when she was excited, and by the way she was throwing her head back I could tell she was happy. There was real joy there, which I never saw at home. I never saw that kind of joy in her."

Sara quieted for a moment, wrinkling her brows, as if that realization was hitting her now for the first time. She looked up at Martha, and then over at Jessie, whose fingers were now covering her mouth. Tears glistened in Jessie's eyes. Awestruck, this telling of her mother and father as lovers early on in their relationship floored her.

Sara went on. "And then he spotted me. David. Your father. He was wearing this, I don't know, some kind of brown leather aviator jacket, the kind with big pockets at the chest. Tom Cruise must have made the movie Top Gun around the time, because those jackets were all the rage then. He had sandy brownish hair, which I remember was kind of messy. He was nice looking, Jessie, but what I remember most, when he saw me standing there…" Sara choked back a sob. "Were his eyes. Pale blue. Icy." She reached a hand fruitlessly towards Jessie. It hung in the air between them, a fairy-like wave of a hand recalling something long past that still had the power to cave in one's soul. "Like yours. You have a lot of him in you. Don't you, Jessie?"

Jessie's voice was throaty, gruff. "Well, I guess you have a lot of her in you."

Haltingly, Sara's lips drew back in a small wistful smile. Her gaze stayed focused on Jessie. "When he spotted me, it took him a second, but then I saw him notice the skating dress, and the way I must have been looking at them through the window, so he straightened and I guess the shocked look on his face telegraphed to my mother that I was there. So she turned and saw me and I guess I took off. The rest is kind of a blur. I remember her screaming at me, and I know I went back to the rink but I didn't stay there. I hid…for a while…in one of the rest rooms. I dumped my skate bag in the stands and I hid. Eventually I caught a ride to my grandmother's." She looked up at Martha, the pain a brand new layer in the forty-something eyes. "And I never skated again."

Martha spoke up. "She was a mess when she came to us. But she wasn't talking. We didn't know what was wrong that night. Not until afterwards. I suppose you knew," she said to Sara, "exactly what your grandfather would have thought."

"I soon found out, didn't I, Grandma?"

Again, the closeness between the two women saddened Jessie. Martha was lovingly moving a strand of hair back from Sara's cheek. Swallowing her own angst, Jessie recoiled, and shimmied back a bit on the ottoman.

"When Sara's dad finally found out, it was Emily who told him. She admitted the affair later on the same day she told me. She wanted to leave him but he wouldn't hear of it."

"He loved her," Sara whispered, big eyes misty. "And I…hated her. She destroyed everything. I never went to the rink again until I went there with my kids for hockey. I disconnected from school, from my friends. I…married the first man who asked me." She choked back sobs. "And when I heard about you, I hated you too. You were me, you see? You took my place."

"I never took your place, Sara. From what you just told me…I never had any of that with her. To me she was detached, most of the time. But I get it now. When she looked at me…she saw you."

Sara's eyes acknowledged this, and transmitted a mute *thank you*. Then she asked, "What were they like—our mother and David? Together, I mean? Was it real for them? The whole—love thing? Or was it just an illusion. A 'grass is greener on the other side' thing."

"What were they like?" Jessie repeated, sitting back and pondering the question. "Do you really want to know?"

Sara paused before answering. She looked at her grandmother for assurance that the answer would be the right one. After all these years…

"Yes," she said. "I do."

Exhaling with a slow *pfffttt*, Jessie considered what to say, how much she thought this woman, suddenly a fourteen-year-old abandoned child again, could handle. She started slowly.

"Our mother was bitter, edgy, not affectionate for the most part. Not to me. You got the best of her, Sara." She took a chance, and laid a hand over her half-sister's. To Sara's credit, she didn't pull away. "David…my dad… was amazing—gentle, musical, loving. They were so connected I felt like I was in the way sometimes. The way she would look at him… she never looked at me like that." Jessie took a breath—fuel for the next trying admission. Her words were subdued, although she fought the toughness of them by letting one side of her lips twist up and by intently meeting Sara's apprehensive gaze. "When she looked at me, it was like she was waking up from a dream and I was the nightmare. Now I think maybe sometimes…she wanted me to be you. Now I understand why she was so unhappy with me."

She let her eyes drift around the room, but Jessie wasn't seeing anything except her life as a child in Prince Edward Island. "There were no figure skating lessons for me. I wanted to…my friends skated…now I know why, Sara. Mostly I just learned guitar from my dad. We lived in a rural village, so good ole David and Emily I guess weren't too keen on doing much driving into town. They were in their own little world."

"So she was happy."

"With him…to a point. But he wasn't a money earner. He was a dreamer, with his head in the clouds. There was a lot of worry. There were a lot of tears. I suppose I understand those now, too. Better, anyway."

Sara shook the memories dusting over the slide show in her mind and asked, "What's it like having the Keatings…as your sort-of parents?"

Jessie stiffened. To her, Charles and Dee were sacred ground. How could Sara ever even begin to understand what the Vancouver power couple had done for her? Were still doing for her, despite their perhaps understandable aversion to her husband? That they were not just some wealthy elite? That they were from a world with pressures Sara could never fully appreciate?

But she tried. She started slowly, pondering each word before speaking it out loud. "What do you need to know, Sara? They saved me. I don't know where I would be today if Jack Deacon didn't deliver me to their doorstep. Probably dead. I suppose that's where."

Evelyn chose that rather sickening truthful moment to arrive with a tray of coffee and tea from the indie café down the street. Rather than tiptoe around during the awkward silence after Jessie let her in, she tossed her gray ponytail and plopped her slim physique down next to Sara on the sofa. "What'd I miss?"

Down the hall, Deirdre was pacing. Charles had the baby, and was carrying her around to the various pictures in the room, showing her all the details—boats, flowers, and cityscapes with the CN Tower featured prominently. He was talking baby talk, which was starting to annoy Dee, who sniped at him as she silently wondered how things were going in Josh and Jessie's suite. Finally, she slipped her feet in new beige Christian Louboutin sling back pumps, and rested a hand on the door handle.

Charles stopped his baby talk long enough to call out behind her, "No, Dee. You're not invited."

"The hell I'm not. Josh is working. And someone has to ensure Jessie doesn't soften up and give away the farm." She whipped open the door and stormed down the hall. Her knock was more tentative than the nervous jealousy ping-ponging around her brain, though.

Jessie answered, almost relieved, and certainly not surprised to see her manager standing there, arms crossed and eyes uneasy. Standing back, she waved Dee into the room, wondering how long Charles would be okay with the baby on his own. The women on the sofa squished over and made room. Everyone watched Jessie as she regained her seat on the ottoman and sighed deeply.

"Where were we?" she said to no one in particular. "Oh, yeah. Evelyn was asking what she missed." She glanced at Dee as if to say *good timing*, and accepted a tea from Evelyn's tray. "I tell you what I miss. Coffee. Geez Louise."

"Breastfeeding doesn't last forever," Sara muttered. "Before you know it they're eleven and nine, and have no interest in your breasts."

"Um humn." Jessie stared at the floor and studied her toes.

Evelyn picked up the conversation with a smirk. She knew the story about Ren being rather ungraciously shown his aunt's breasts on the schoolyard. "Not their mom's boobs at least, huh, Sara?"

Sara shot her a nasty look before glancing at Jessie who, she knew, had reason to be more upset than anyone over her very public nude photos. A look to Martha broke her heart, though. At 89, Martha was spritely and aware. Too aware. She was now watching Jessie with tears freely flowing down her cheeks.

"Grandma?" Sara hunched her comfortable girth forward on the sofa and reached for her grandmother's hand.

Martha squeezed and released Sara's hand. The distance was just a little too far for comfortable hand holding at this juncture. She trained her tired eyes on Jessie. Dee cocked an ear and listened carefully. The woman's voice was old and crackly, and she didn't want to miss a thing.

"Jessie, sweetheart. I need to say something to you, and this seems like the right time."

On the ottoman, Jessie straightened. She met the old woman's eyes, biting her lip before letting her gaze drift over to Dee, who she knew was not the rock everyone thought her to be. Jessie ran a finger over her top lip and then over the bottom one before allowing her sea-pearl eyes to wander back over to Martha. "I'm listening." She spoke softly, with a cautious absence of feeling. It was good, all of them finally at some kind of truce in a common space, but it was draining.

The woman whose daughter ran away with her lover by climbing down a rickety ladder in the middle of the night, never to lay lucid eyes on her mother again, spoke quietly. "I want to say how sorry I am. For letting you down."

"Mmphhff," Jessie mumbled. "The way I see it, you didn't have much choice, Martha."

"We knew where you were. We knew about your father…being killed. We did nothing."

"Why would you?" But Jessie was back to staring at her toes.

Dee noticed she was also driving her right fingernails into the back of her left hand. "Jessie," she said, a note of warning in her voice. Jessie looked up at her, and followed Dee's downward glance to her hand. Rolling her eyes, she removed her hands and sat on them instead.

Martha kept on. "When Evelyn got word to us you'd run away, we should have done something. We should have gone to the police, or registered you with Child Find or whatever it is you do when a teenager leaves home. But we didn't. It was like you didn't belong to us. And my husband…" She shook her head. "Your grandfather was a good man, Jessie. But he could be a mean bastard when he wanted to be. I couldn't bring myself to do a thing, except imagine you in my head and wonder where you were."

Finally, Jessie looked up and met her grandmother's eyes. "I didn't even know you existed. The only family I knew I had was Evelyn, with the exception of a mother who I now realize probably never really forgave herself for… for leaving Sara behind. So she never fully accepted me. And when Evelyn didn't help me when my step-monster…" She gulped. "Well, when my mother's new partner climbed into my bed and everyone just turned the other cheek," she was whispering now and, watching her, Dee was sick to her stomach, "I just considered myself alone. No family. You know?"

She glanced at Evelyn, who was also rather heartsick now. The aunt's eyes were remorseful, wistful. But she was silent.

Deirdre wasn't. Even her cheeks had pinpricks of anger dotted throughout. "This is what I mean, Jessie. You owe these people nothing. Where were they when some dirty old man was hurting you? Where were they when you were hiding under some random guy's backseat in exchange for sex on your way through the border down to Charleston? And where were they when Sandy was murdered in front of you?"

"Oh, Jesus," moaned Jessie. *That stupid Shawna Coupland interview. My life is a fucking open book.* Dee had known some of this anyway. But they'd never spoken of her trip south that was, yes, just another exchange—sex for a ride. *These people…they're nice,* she caught herself thinking. *But maybe I need to let them go. Yeah, I've got money. I've got fame, for what it's worth. But Trudy and Josh and me—and maybe Jacob—know how worthless I think I really am. They know that will never change. And these people don't deserve worthless old me.*

Emily-Grace flitted across her mind. How would she ever save that little girl from…herself? A tragic flicker swept over her face. Dee saw it, and flinched, because she knew from experience what came next. And Jessie didn't disappoint. A hard cast came over her eyes, and she straightened noticeably. She removed her hands from underneath her bum and folded them in a very ladylike, graceful manner, in her lap. She raised her chin, which was a move Dee herself took some credit for instilling in her girl.

"Sometimes," Jessie said, "I think about everything. Now, I mean. Now that I understand more, like that you knew all along I existed. And I do wonder, Martha. I do wonder why no one ever came looking for me. Because the thing is," she swallowed, "all of you are such nice people. And you have all the things I wanted…all the things I could have had…but now will never have."

Lifting her chin further, she studied Sara, who was watching her with a mixture of horror at the tragedies in Jessie's life, and respect for surviving them. "Hockey practices…a husband who coaches the kids…no one staring at you all the time thinking *that whore*…kids who go to regular school… all those things…you don't know what you have, Sara. I told you before and I will tell you again, it's staring you in the face. Love from a good man is staring you in the face. Yet you push him away. Sex is a gift you give someone, Sara. It's not something you hold over your husband's head, like a goddamn reward for good behavior. And it's not…." She groped for the words. "It's not something you should take lightly, either. Or give away. Or sell for a ride south." Her glare in Dee's direction told her exactly what she thought of having that comment released into the air here, today. "And it sure as hell isn't something someone should take from you when they have no right to."

Eyes drifting back over to Martha, she watched the old woman fight years of pent up guilt. The angst raced up and down her face like demons fighting over her soul. But Jessie just shook her head. "I lost so much, Martha. And I don't fully understand why no one cared enough to look for me. But in the end…I got the most amazing gift of all. Gifts, actually. So if that helps appease your guilt, than take it and run with it. You have my blessing." She was crumbling now, too, the mask flaking off like sand on a beach's drying sandcastle.

The old woman was sobbing. But she spoke through her tears. "Josh, you mean. Your husband."

"And my daughter. And I could care less if the three of us move to a jungle in the middle of god knows where. They're all I want right now. I'm working on making my peace with the other stuff, with what Sara has...and doesn't even know she has, because she's too damned angry and blind to see...and what I will never have. Josh loves me and he *knows* me, and I feel safe with him. So you see, it was all worth it in the end. And if changing a part of my history would mean losing him, and Emily-Grace..." She shook her head. "Then I want no part of it."

Martha reached across the little divide and grasped one of Jessie's hands. "I'm still sorry, Jessie. We were all so angry...for so long. We were so angry and hurt we could barely function. And this girl here," she gestured towards Sara, who was sitting in shocked silence over Jessie's public little lecture on sex, "was devastated. At everything her mother did. For love, supposedly. We couldn't see past Emily's treachery to the child she gave birth to."

"You know something, all of you?" Jessie looked a little wildly around the suite. Even Dee waited in mute silence, sandwiched between Evelyn and Sara on the small sofa so she appeared less formidable than usual. Finally landing at Sara, Jessie voiced her last few thoughts, the ones that froze all of them until Dee finally cracked the chill and rather graciously— at least for her, in this company—suggested they all go down to the dining room for lunch.

"It's worth it," were the words that brought the room to ice. "Love. It's worth it. What Emily did...what my mother did...they were magic together. She and my father." Crushed, she searched Sara's piqued face. "I'm sorry for what she did to you. And not only because she left you, but because now I understand that by leaving you she deserted me, too, before I was even born. But watching them together...Sara, sometimes, like I said, they didn't even see me. I'm not sure you get it. I'm not sure any of you get it. And this is the one thing all of you really need to know." Her voice was pitchy now, high, as she tried to make her point heard. Now the words were punctuated, each floating there in the room all on their own, and all spoken in the exact same fairy-tale wonder. "They—were—magical. And-they-were-my-childhood."

She stood. "And once they were gone…once *he* was gone…him, yes, David Wheeler, the man who stood at the bottom of that godforsaken rickety ladder you all can't stop talking about," she was crying openly now, "once *he* was gone, it was over. The magic just disappeared, poof…" Holding out a hand, she snapped a finger. "Until…" This time her eyes were focused solely on Deirdre. "Until Josh walked into Charlie's Club, messed up on god knows what, as alone and lonely as me. Sandy, too, he was magic at one time. But we all know how that ended."

A chill ran up and down her legs, and she shuddered. "This isn't going to end, just so all of you know. Josh and me. And Emily-Grace. We are a tight little unit, and I forgive all of you for everything you're doing and thinking and for everything you've done and thought for all these years, and I am choosing to live in the moment. And if any of you want to be a part of that, then you are welcome and you are invited in. The past is the past. All I ask is one thing. Stop being stupid. Sara, love your husband. Evelyn, stay in Peterborough for a while. Be with your mother. Deirdre, I have enough love for everyone. So let me love who I want to. And that includes my husband, by the way. We don't need yours or Charles' judgment hovering over us like some diabolical bad wish."

She turned to Martha to deliver the coup de grace. "And Martha? Grandmother? Take a trip. To P.E.I." She leaned over the old lady in the wingback chair, each hand on an arm of the chair so she enveloped Martha. She stared long and hard at the lines on the woman's face before continuing. Her demand was a release for all of the Kilfoil relations in the room. Again the words were punctuated. "Go—see—your—other—daughter."

At that, Jessie headed to the door, her ice bomb hanging in the air. Her final words were delivered flippantly over her shoulder. "I'm going to rescue Charles from what is likely now a very hungry baby. Chat amongst yourselves."

And then she was gone, the door coming to a close behind her with a loud *thwunk*.

Behind her, no one moved until Dee's invite to lunch was spoken.

They'd all just been schooled. And they were humbled. Because this was one time Jessie Wheeler did not deliver her messages through music.

Yet, in some ways, the messages delivered on this day were perhaps some of Jessie's most important messages of all.

Chapter Thirty-two

*J*essie's last trip to Peterborough for a while was for two hockey games—she got to see her nephews play. Ulysses drove. Josh, Steve and Emily-Grace were also part of the entourage, as was Sophie, who flew in from Vancouver the night before. In the stands they cozied up to Crystal, who Sara got a huge kick out of since it was the only time her super social friend was ever rendered speechless, sitting next to three TV stars in one fell swoop, and all.

Part way through the Zamboni's run around the ice between Mark's second and third period, Jessie laid her hand on her husband's lap and motioned for him to let her by. Ren was doing his usual puck hunt around the rink. Pensive, Sara and Josh watched as Jessie made her way around to the far end of the ice surface and caught up with the little guy.

As Jessie approached, she spied a loose puck underneath one of the seats. Bending over, she picked it up and handed it to Ren.

Wordlessly, he accepted it. Then he aimed his big eyes up at her.

Jessie dropped into a seat. "You ever gonna talk to me again, Rennie?"

He fiddled with the puck in his hands, outlining the Peterborough Petes logo with the small forefinger of his right hand.

Jessie tried again. "I'd really like it if I could fly back to Vancouver knowing you and me were friends."

A small voice accosted her, but the child didn't move. "We're not."

"Can you tell me why?"

A heavy sigh was his response.

"I know you saw my pictures. I think they scared you."

He was silent, but since he seemed to be listening, Jessie continued. "Ren... have you ever done something you thought was okay at the time...but you were sorry for later?"

At that, he looked up. His eyes drifted over the seats, to the area where his mom was sitting, and then down to the ice surface, where the Zamboni was motoring away, leaving trails of shiny wet ice where before there were zigzags and scratch marks.

"Sometimes," he said, in a tiny voice.

"Well, that's what I did. I made a mistake. But it was a long time ago. And I'm learning to forgive myself for it."

She waited, to see if he had anything to offer, but Ren was still quiet and thoughtful. He started picking again at the puck in his hands, his head down.

"The thing is, Ren, I'm hoping other people will learn to forgive me for it too."

"I think my mom has."

"I think she has too, honey. But I think she would like for you and me to make up."

"Why, because you are babysitting me and Mark tonight?"

"That's part of it, I think. She doesn't want to leave you home with me if you're unhappy." Leaning forward, she whispered conspiratorially, "But won't it be nice for your mom and dad to have a nice dinner at a fancy restaurant, and go to a movie together? And be able to relax and be happy?"

"What are we gonna do?"

"Ah. I thought you might be curious. Well, I think the boys want to go skating on that rink your dad built in your backyard."

"Do they play hockey?"

Jessie laughed at the idea of Josh, Steve and Ulysses playing hockey. A sweet pang accosted her heart at the thought of Jacob on the ice with her nephews. She figured he could handle a game or two, if he was around. To Ren she said, "I don't think they do. But I bet they would like to learn."

"I can teach them. But Mark would be better on the rule stuff. He knows them better than me." Casually, he shrugged his shoulders. "Well, some of them, anyway. I can teach them about what 'offside' means. And how to drop the puck, that sort of thing."

"That would be really nice of you, Ren." Smiling at him, Jessie couldn't help but reach out and tousle his hair, which was a little mussed up from his earlier game. "What do you say, Ren? Can you and me be friends?"

Ren thought of Dugey and what he would think if he knew. Running a few quick nine-year-old pros and cons around his mind, he decided he would just keep his Aunt Jessie a secret. Dugey didn't play hockey. The grade six bully wouldn't be around the rink. He would never know Ren was friends with his aunt again.

"Okay," he agreed, still a little nervous but hoping for the best. He thrust out the puck Jessie gave him a few minutes earlier. "Would you like to keep this? After all, you found it."

Surprised at the emotion that immediately clawed its way to the surface at her nephew's simple gesture, Jessie nodded, and swallowed back tears. "I would, actually," she said. "I'd like that very much. Thanks, Ren." She took the puck and fingered the pockmarked rubber lightly. "Maybe someday I can come back and see the Peterborough Petes play."

"We can get pizza," Ren decided, as he turned and started looking for more pucks. "Tonight. Sometimes we get pizza after the games."

Following him around the arena, Jessie listened to Ren chat about the things that were important in a nine-year-old boy's world. She felt her heart bursting. Her husband and daughter were well, Sara and Martha were starting to feel like, well, family, and Sophie and Steve were holding hands on the other side of the rink. Things weren't perfect with Charles and Dee at the present time, and Matt's absence was still sorely felt, and Jacob was still a lonely soul whose presence in Jessie's life was complicated and sometimes painful. But for now, there was a whole blessed Saturday in front of herself that included people she loved, there were new skates freshly sharpened and waiting for them at the Lawrence household, and tonight there would be pizza and popcorn, and maybe board games. And, Jessie knew, for sure there would be a lot of laughs.

When she and Ren made it back to their family on time to see Mark's third period, they had four newfound pucks between them. Ren turned his back and leaned against Jessie for the remainder of the hockey game, and they swapped stories about his vintage dinky cars and about a blonde girl at school named Lucy who it seemed was a dancer, and who dressed as a Dalmatian for last Halloween.

Alongside, Josh listened with one ear cocked towards the little boy and his wife. Idly wondering whether he and Jessie would have a son of their own someday, he focused on his wife's happy responses to her nephew's storytelling. At one point, Josh draped an arm around the back of her seat, and then found himself drawn into the conversation. Ren's generosity was in overdrive—the little boy also made Josh a recipient of another stray Peterborough Petes puck. The spell was magical, and apparently Sara felt it because she, too, watched Jessie with Ren more than she focused on her older son's game.

That night, with two exhausted boys asleep in bed, a baby asleep in her carrier, and Steve and Sophie putting on jackets after being rousted from their cuddle on the couch, Jessie said temporary good-byes to her half-sister. Josh and Ulysses had already gone out to start the Lincoln and position the baby seat inside, and Steve and Sophie were close behind, so Jessie had a quiet moment to thank Kevin and Sara for trusting her rowdy gang with Mark and Ren. But it was hard to find the words.

In the end, it was Sara who spoke first. She took Jessie's hands between hers and smiled sadly at her. "When I first agreed to meet you, I expected a circus, Jessie. A superstar. I didn't expect to truly find a sister."

"I hoped," Jessie blushed, smiling warmly. "I really hoped. And I'm glad. I can't tell you how glad." She leaned in for a hug. "Today was one of the happiest of my whole life, Sara. Emily did something right."

A cloud washed over Sara's face. "I guess she did. But I wish she'd done it differently. I would have liked to have known you a long time ago."

"Same," was Jessie's teary response. Letting her gaze drift over to Kevin, she couldn't help but notice that one of his arms was draped around his wife's waist. Grinning, she posed a question to him. "As soon as your own hockey season is over, will you bring the boys to Vancouver to see the Canucks? I promise to let you know when the Leafs will be playing them." At his hesitant look, she added quietly, "All expenses paid. And it's not charity. Let me do this for you. Please. Suck up that stupid Kilfoil-Lawrence pride."

"Mark and Ren would love that." Kevin pulled Jessie into a genuine embrace. "Thank you," he said. "For everything."

When the sleepy entourage was on their way back to Toronto, he took his wife in his arms. "She's just lovely, Sara. Like you. A good mom and a sweet person."

"I haven't been…" But Sara couldn't finish. In front of her was a man she felt like she was seeing for the first time. There was something about watching Josh and Jessie together—the way they gazed at each other in silent understanding, the way they leaned on each other, or grazed their fingertips across each others' cheeks when they thought no one was looking…the way they randomly pulled each other into an embrace and brushed their lips across each others' foreheads, the way they stood in silent wonder at the beautiful child they made; all of these things were an education to Sara, she was a quiet observer, but she took notice. And now, she took notice of her husband.

Kevin was a good man. He was a hard worker, a great dad, a good husband and a run of the mill kinda guy who just happened to adore his wife, as was evident now in the way he, too, was studying her. Sure, he was balding on the top, and he was not a high wage earner. But she and the kids were fed, clothed and housed, and what else really mattered?

"Kevin," Sara started, but she didn't get to finish because their magical day was already being christened with a magical night, that started with a gentle kiss. Sara had a new-old sister in her life who she was quickly learning was someone with a great capacity to love. And Sara, too, had a new-old husband in her life. He was the same man she married years ago, who gave her two amazing boys, but when Jessie left that night amongst her clan of tired family and friends, Sara's marriage began anew.

Chapter Thirty-three

*P*erched at her home desk with a tray of fruit within snatching distance, and one leg tucked under the other, Jessie called out to Josh, who was scrolling through emails on his computer.

"Listen to this. It's a Facebook message from George." She giggled, reading the email to him as he rotated his chair around to face her.

Sorry I haven't written or called. Martha and Sara arrived three days ago and we've been busy up to our eyeballs. There were tears of course when they saw your mother for the first time, and I can say I think Emily recognized them. She couldn't stop staring at Sara, and yes, she was one of the three women with tears. Sara is doing fine. She is as lovely as you are, albeit I think she is more thoughtful than you as she brought me homemade chocolate muffins. They left this morning with promises to visit again soon which is fine by me although my lady friend down the hall is not speaking to me at the moment. I guess we had one too many wheelchair races that didn't include her.

Jessie sat back and laughed. "George musta been some ladies' man in his heyday, huh, Josh? He goes on to say they were considering moving Emily to Peterborough until they got to P.E.I. and saw the place. And met him. Now they think she is happy where she is." She sighed. "Crazy that she had an emotional reaction to Sara. But still...all those lost years...all that anger... all that lost time."

Watching her, Josh realized one thing—he did not ever again want to lose time with his wife. The silly things they argued about were never worth growing apart over, nor were they worth spending time not talking to each other. He resolved that whatever the future brought, it would have to involve forgiveness and love. Otherwise twenty years would pass in the blink of an eye, and when they did, he wanted to be able to say he loved well, and was loved well.

"We'd better get ready, little one," he said now to Jessie, as he stood and stretched out a hand to pull her to her feet. Grasping her shoulders, he turned her to face him square on. "I was wrong," he added apologetically. "About your family, I mean. They're really great people."

"Hmmm? What was that? Did the famous Josh Sawyer just admit to being wrong?" Pale eyes sparkling, Jessie adopted an insincere frown and crossed her arms.

"Uhhh…if you think I'm saying it twice, you're delusional, Jessie."

"I think you need to apologize the proper way, Sawyer." Wrapping both arms tightly around his neck, Jessie pressed her body to his and inhaled his musky Josh scent of spicy aftershave and, today, the outdoors, since he just came in from shoveling a small overnight dusting of snow from their driveway.

"The proper way…well, I suppose I could be convinced, Wheeler-Sawyer."

"Sawyer. Today it's fully Sawyer."

"Well, Sawyer, we'd better make it a quickie since we have a jet to catch to L.A. in about two hours."

"What, the great Josh Sawyer wants to hurry sex in favor of getting to the Oscars on time?" Her mischievous pixie smile did a 180. "The world is off its axis."

"I could rethink that."

"I think you should." Brushing her lips against his, Jessie peeked up to meet her husband's contented gaze. One hand reached down to his waist and undid the button on his jeans.

Josh lit up. "Oscar, smoshker," he grinned. "The Oscars can wait."

Their detour in the bedroom was accomplished just on time, for Emily-Grace awoke just as Jessie exited the shower, and Ulysses arrived a short time later, hurrying the family into his Audi for the trip to the airport. In L.A., they would meet up with Josh's brother Zach and his wife—and Josh's manager—Hilary. The ceremony was a few days away, but there were arrangements to be taken care of, and press appearances and interviews with the *Freedom Ride* folks, so it would be a busy few days.

In L.A., Jessie sat back and soaked up her hubby's radiance. Josh's joy was her joy. She was reaping the benefits of sharing life with a happy man, and a beautiful child created by their love. Surely the future would, if not erase all the pain of the past, at least help mitigate it.

～～ ～～

When the Academy Award ceremonies were over, and the hoopla and exhilaration complete, Josh had his own gold statuette to keep Jessie's company on their mantel at home.

Back home, as a new snow globe powder lightly flaked over them, she stood in their driveway and pressed her lips to his. Jessie wished Josh well in Toronto, where he and Steve had more episodes to shoot before wrapping their first season of *The Wyatt Boys*. Then she climbed into Ulysses' sedan and flew to P.E.I., with Charles, Dee and Emily-Grace for company, to make the long awaited hockey film, which she would intersperse with the last few episodes of the *Mystic Nights* season two shoot.

At one point, over an evening meal at the Summerside B and B after a long day in production, Jessie rather arrogantly spoke to Charles and Dee. "I told you so."

"Mmmm?" Dee absently asked as she rocked Emily-Grace. "About what, honey?"

"About everything," said Jessie. "My family's fine. Awesome, even. And Josh is doing amazing. Everything's great."

A sudden silence in the Edwardian dining room stopped her from saying more. In the back of Jessie's mind, an unwelcome rumbling notion percolated and took hold. It seemed somehow to shadow Charles and Dee's unspoken thoughts.

I...don't trust happiness.

Shaking the unsolicited, intrusive darkness away on a shiver and a prayer, Jessie lifted her baby from Dee's arms, and left the room.

～～ ～～

In April, around the time *Mystic Nights* and *The Wyatt Boys* were finally wrapping for the season, Jacob and Jessie reconvened at the Robson Studio. Josh was still in Toronto finishing his last episode, with plans to attend the production's wrap party before heading home the following weekend. Jacob and Jessie were putting the finishing touches on her album—they'd already shot a surreal music video to accompany the first single—and were digging into quinoa salads on the big comfy couch in the corner of the studio, when Matt popped in.

Jessie didn't hesitate—she caught her breath and jumped up for a hug. "What'd we do to deserve your esteemed presence, Sir Matt?" Thrilled to see him, she was vibrating. "Coming back?"

"No, Jessie…not coming back. I…well, I took a new job. You might be seeing me around a bit, though. I thought I should drop by and tell you in person."

"Huh. Well." Crossing her arms, she faced him, pondering what said 'new job' might be. "Does this have anything to do with *Mystic Nights*?"

"It does, actually." Adjusting his stance, Matt raised his chin.

Jacob tossed in, despite a mouth full of Quinoa, "He's taking Michael's job."

"Oh. Uh-huh. You knew, huh, Jacob? Thanks for the heads up."

"Don't act like it's a surprise, Jessie. You knew Michael went back to singing full time. Over the hiatus, he and Kelly are going out on the road."

"Kelly, huh?" Jessie let her thoughts transmit to Matt over some unseen wire. Her eyes paled even more as a tiny light dimmed.

Matt's were firm, but something in his gaze was different too. The single-minded purpose he'd always had before seemed to be missing. Now there was just a lonely aura in its place. "I wanted to tell you myself. In person," he repeated, as if he was at a loss for any other words.

"So you're good enough security for Kelly and Michael, but you're not good enough for the 'great Jessie Wheeler.'" Her arms remained crossed. Pouting, Jessie turned one foot over sideways.

"It's not like that, Jessie," was Matt's even response.

"Then what's it like, Matt?"

He didn't answer. Matt waited for Jessie to come to the reason on her own.

"It's Charles."

"Not so much Charles, Jessie."

"Deirdre, then. Still."

"Yes."

"I thought she was having second thoughts, Matt. When did they become such over-protective shmucks, anyway?" Jessie heaved out a great breath and leaned back against the wall next to the arm of the couch. She put one foot up behind her but left her arms crossed. At Jacob's inhale, she air-palmed him. "No. I don't need you to remind me, oh Sir Ryan."

"I'm sorry, Jessie," said Matt, genuine loss shadowing his face. "But at least this way we can still be friends, right? I'll see you around set. And…kid…it goes without saying…if you ever need me…"

"I know, Matt. Thank you. But Kelly? I guess at least I'm glad you get to hang out with your brother. Michael's amazing."

"Of course he is. He's my brother." Matt was smiling then, if a bit tragically, but he opened his arms wide. "C'mere," he demanded. "One last hug before I hit the skies for Miami."

She acquiesced, bitter defeat in her countenance and the word *traitor* flicking around her brain. Still, Matt's familiar scent of hair products and expensive leather warmed her heart.

After their sweet hug, Jacob stood and shook Matt's hand. "We'll miss you," he offered with sincerity. "Stay in touch."

"Yeah, I will, thanks," Matt replied, before backing slowly away. He glanced behind him at the sound of low voices. A couple of technicians were wandering down the hall towards them. One last lingering sad smile was thrown in Jessie's direction before he waved, swung around on one shiny heel, and took his leave.

Jessie dropped back down and picked up her quinoa dish. She played with her plastic fork, dipping it into the salad and flipping its contents over and over. "He was rushing so he wouldn't have to run into Charles. Wasn't he, Jacob?"

"I guess. Yeah."

"It's funny, because just when one part of your life gets going really well, another part goes all to hell."

"Sometimes," Jacob agreed.

"I just wish everyone could get along all of the time. And I don't get what's going on with Charles and Dee lately. It's like ever since Josh fucked up with Caryn, and then Emily-Grace came along, they've just gone a little too far with their defense by creating a lot of offense, if you ask me."

"You've been watching too much hockey." Jacob shuffled back and leaned into one corner of the couch. Hoisting his booted feet up onto Jessie's lap, he set his empty dish down on the floor by the couch.

"Or maybe I've been watching too much Team Keating."

Regarding her thoughtfully, Jacob tossed in a question he knew would throw Jessie for a loop. "Do you think you'd ever leave them, Jessie?"

He was right. She froze, her fork now poised in mid-air. "No. Never. Why, would you?"

A cool shrug was Jacob's answer. "My dad thinks Charles' stuff is too over-produced."

"Not like it's hurting you."

"Don't look at me like that. I'm not going anywhere. My dad's from a different generation. He likes a more pure sound."

Charles made his way into the room then, a white Starbucks cup in his hand. By the subdued expression on his face, Jessie and Jacob knew he had run into Matt along the way. He tapped Jacob's leg so the singer would make space on the couch for him.

"Ten minutes," he said. "I need to catch my breath."

"You saw Matt." Jessie frowned.

"In a manner of speaking."

"He was your friend, Charles."

"Wife trumps friend," he grumbled.

"I'm sorry," whispered Jessie, shooting Jacob a nervous sideways glance that said *geez, I hope he didn't hear us.* "Although I thought maybe Dee was coming around. She seems stressed without Matt around."

"Harrumph," was Charles' initial reply. Then he said, "With regards to the sorry bit, that makes two of us." Charles took a sip of his hot beverage. "Referencing Dee, you're right, but she doesn't want to take him back as top dog. Only as a minion. And his pride won't let him go there." A heavy exhalation expressed his true feelings about the run-in with his old good friend. "I've tried to talk to both of them more than once but it hasn't been a cakewalk. And now…well…it seems final."

"Three." Jacob bent over and picked up his empty dish. "With regards to the sorry bit." He rose, strode to a nearby compost bin, and dumped it in.

Turning to face them, he rubbed his palms together in anticipation. "Let's get this track sorted, Jessie, so we can get your over-produced album out to the masses." He grinned mischievously at Charles, and draped an arm over Jessie's shoulders when she got up to join him.

"Humph," was Charles' response.

"So I guess Morgan and Apollo are officially Keating team security now, Charles?" Jessie asked. "Along with Ulysses, Dan and Susanne, I mean."

"Morgan is. Susanne will only fill in as a backup when needed. Her hockey player is her top priority these days. As for Apollo, I'm not sure. He's got a good gig with Jon in Toronto." Sensing an unease, he glanced up at Jessie. "Why? Is that okay?"

She shrugged. "Morgan's so quiet."

"Does that make you uncomfortable, Jessie?"

Jacob knit his eyebrows together in curiosity as he watched her respond.

"Nah," she said, shoulders drooping as she stared at her toes. "Probably better that way. This way I won't get to know him. He can stay security, and that's it. No more making friends with my protectors. Blah. Don't take this the wrong way, but Dee kinda sucks right now."

"She means well, Jessie. You know that. So do I."

"Yes, Charles, I know that. And, when all is said and done, I take responsibility for losing Matt more than anyone. But I miss him like crazy."

"It's the hair," Jacob decreed, trying to lighten the mood. "Spike." He grinned at her nickname for their good friend. "You won't be able to pick on Morgan that way or he'll curl up in a fetal position and cry like a baby."

"Half the time I'm scared Morgan will curl up in a fetal position when I say his name, Jacob." Grimacing, Jessie reached for her Gibson.

Charles jumped in. "Should I replace him, Jessie? If having Morgan around is not working for you…"

"Nah. Like I said, it's likely better this way. He seems good at the security part, at least."

"He came highly recommended from Jon."

"Fine, then."

"Fine?"

"Fine. Can we just get to work?"

And so, as Matt made his way out of their lives by heading towards Miami, the Robson Street crew got the rest of their session underway, and Jessie buried her lonesome thoughts in music.

Chapter Thirty-four

Fifteen months later…

$\mathcal{M}$organ was humming as he made his way into the studio in Toronto where Josh was wrapping a film with the director Joss Whedon. It had been a good shoot overall, but tonight was the end of 28 grueling days. Still, it was one of those shoots where everybody got along and so the vibe was positive, despite early mornings and long days. Ashley, Carter's quiet live-in girlfriend, was one of those folks—Joss Whedon, like most successful film folks, often brought his tried and true crew with him from project to project, so Ashley was on the shoot, which meant that Carter was around a bit too.

Morgan liked Carter a lot—the guy was quiet, thoughtful, amicable, friendly…in fact, Morgan liked Carter better than he liked Josh. Over the last few years working on the Keating security team, under taskmaster Ulysses, Morgan had learned a lot about Josh. He had access to a lot of his and Jessie's private moments and, although Morgan never seemed quite able to make the leap from staff to friend, he got along okay with them overall.

Usually Morgan was assigned to Jessie when she travelled, and lately, she'd been travelling a lot, promoting her latest album with a 65 city tour she'd just wrapped. The gal was exhausted, flat out. Her husband joined her a lot on the tour, and Jacob Ryan was along for some of the cities, but in the end, Morgan was her constant. And he'd gotten to know Jessie as well as he, a tall, shy, quiet guy, ever got to know anyone. He knew his role and he never crossed it. But he was around, a lot, and over time he grew fiercely loyal when it came to Jessie Wheeler. He was her workout partner, her eyes, her ears, her shadow. So maybe that was why whenever any other guy was around her—Josh included, and even Jacob—Morgan found his heart racing and his senses on hyper-alert. When he asked himself why, he told himself he wasn't crushing on her, no, it was never that. Instead, it was more of a protective thing—she was under his care and watch more than she was under anyone else's eye, because Ulysses had Jacob, Josh and Emily-Grace to watch too.

So she was his. She belonged to him.

Tonight, Morgan was a little grumbly because he was assigned to Josh for the wrap party since Jessie was back in Vancouver sleeping off the tour, and because Big Dan, who was supposed to do this gig, just got married and so he was off on his honeymoon in Cancun.

Still, Morgan caught himself humming as he walked down the hall towards the bevy of excited voices celebrating the end of another sure-to-be-great Joss Whedon sci-fi flick. He had a great job—he admitted it. And he'd lucked into it just because a friend on the crew of *The Wyatt Boys* had heard Jonathon McCloud was looking for a big buff guy to do some last minute security for Charles and Deirdre Keating. So how could he not whistle now?

After tonight, Morgan had a few weeks off. Then Jessie was going back to work, on a film in Atlanta—some period film about the American Civil war. Since Josh would be between films then, he was going with her. Just thinking about having Jessie's husband around all the time, Morgan had a sick taste in his throat, a metallic taste that hurt sometimes when he swallowed.

He liked Josh okay. But *he* was Jessie's protector. He was her shadow. And he didn't like what he saw now when he turned the last corner in the studio and spotted the person in the world with the most capacity to hurt Jessie doing something Morgan knew would hurt her.

He caught Carter's eye. Carter tried to catch Josh's eye. But it was too late. The damage was done. Josh was leaning against one of the sets, in a darkened corner, with his hand on the hip of one of the girls from the make-up department, and he was obviously 'into' the conversation. The woman, a pixie blonde, had laid her hand over his, and the two were having some kind of deeply animated conversation that precluded either from looking up, until Carter finally grimaced, left Ashley's side, and gave his friend a light shove.

Morgan was close enough to hear what was being said. He stood stock still, unsure what to think, except that when he left Jessie she was completely fatigued, handling a lively 21 month old—on her own, still, with only Dee's help during the tour, and the occasional sitter—and here was her husband, flirting openly with some ditsy blonde.

What Morgan heard Carter say was, "Josh. You've got eyes on you."

Josh flipped around then and met Morgan's unforgiving eyes. He stood straighter, and let his hand fall from the woman's hip. Then he gave Morgan a look that said *asshole*, narrowed eyes and all, and he left the woman's side with an apologetic half-smile and trudged off with Carter.

That was all. The rest of the party was fine, in fact Morgan had a good time himself despite the uneasiness between him and Jessie's husband. And he noticed with a sense of smug satisfaction that although the young woman tried more than once to get Josh to herself again, Jessie's husband didn't take the bait. Morgan credited himself for that. Sure, he was a goddamned hired babysitter at times, but he felt he saved Jessie tonight from certain heart-ache, merely by his presence.

The wrap party was on fire until five a.m. Stifling a yawn, around dawn Morgan deposited Josh at the airport with a quiet good-bye, after which, with wrap party adrenaline still pumping, he drove to his gym and did a circuit on the weights and a half hour on the treadmill before going home to grab a few daytime zzzzs.

Later, off schedule and still tired, Morgan trolled a few buds to see if anyone was up for a drink. Pensive when he met up with them at a club near his apartment, he couldn't get over the fact he was now on break for a few weeks. Seemed like his right arm was missing. Unsettled, unable to relax, Morgan just shrugged when his friends caught the vibe. They teased him until his wife Nadia walked in, and then all eyes were on her.

In her mid-twenties, an air of utter confidence preceded Nadia's entry into the bar, and it almost superseded her dark-skinned beauty. Of East Indian descent, her skin glowed with the oil of some exotic plant. Mysterious dark eyes landed sensuously on every man in Morgan's company, and each wilted just a little in turn. She had an aura that read *I get what I want*, yet underneath that aura was a lingering ennui of loss that one could only see upon either close inspection or a private audience.

Morgan's friend Peter pulled back a stool at the bar for Nadia. She accepted the gesture with a small smile at him, then sat with her back straight and one knee tucked gracefully over the other. With a feathery wisp of manicured nails, she adjusted her halter top so each breast sat in it exactly the way she wanted it to—perfect half moons rounding out of the top of the sexy halter.

She sat half facing the bar so that she could eavesdrop on Morgan's conversation at the table beside and below her. He was almost oblivious to her arrival, but the other men were not, so it took a moment for the conversation to regain its earlier focus and passion. Nadia perked up when she realized who the topic of conversation was—Josh Sawyer. Every woman in North America perked up when his name came up.

Sipping on a Perrier with lemon, she listened.

"It just pisses me off, that's all," Morgan was saying. "Jessie works so hard and she idolizes the guy, and they have this beautiful little girl, yet it's nothing for him to flirt with other women."

"Does he sleep with them or just flirt?"

"How the hell should I know? He had his hand on her hip. It looked open-ended to me." Morgan didn't bother disclosing the fact he'd had eyes on Josh all night and into the wee hours of the morning, and that nothing further had transpired. Nor had anything, ever, with any woman, as long as Morgan was around the guy. Still, he felt like rubbing Josh's name in dirt, so he added, "Anyways, I was with Jessie on tour the last few months. I haven't been around Josh. So I have no idea if he sleeps with other women or not. But put it this way—Jessie wouldn't likely know if he did. It's not like he'd blast it from the rooftops."

"Uh, Morgan, it's not really any of your business," Peter said from his perch beside Nadia at the bar. A white guy from the east coast, he was a part-time bartender on the hunt for a better job, a house, and a wife, in that order. He was the product of staunch Roman Catholics from Nova Scotia, which made him throw the novel 'Trinity' at the wall when he read it at eighteen. He'd never set foot in church since the day he left Halifax. Yet his beliefs were irrevocably intertwined, and occasionally at odds, with his upbringing; he couldn't condone Josh Sawyer's behavior if the guy did sleep around, but he would defend to the death the guy's right to live his own life.

"You're too involved with these people, Morgan. Jessie Wheeler's your boss, not your family. And it sure as hell doesn't sound like she's your friend," he dictated.

That comment earned Peter two fake bullets right between the eyes. Morgan sat taller while his sensuous wife Nadia looked on wordlessly. "Yes, she's my boss. And she's amazing. She doesn't deserve that asshole." A small twinge of guilt wound its way up Morgan's gut at that vociferous proclamation, partly because in all the time he worked with Josh and Jessie, Josh had never really provided any fodder for complaint. Generally Morgan found him easygoing and kind to Jessie, but always there was this protective barrier Morgan put around his charge. He thought of himself as some kind of bulletproof plastic wrap that guarded her constantly. Nothing would get past Morgan's impenetrable barrier, and hurt Jessie. Nothing. Especially the man she loved most on the planet.

Sucking back his beer, Morgan tipped up the bottle to get the last few drips. He pounded it on the table.

A lilting voice jarred him out of the angry bubble in which he was wallowing.

"Of course he sleeps around. He's Josh Sawyer, for God's sake. He can have any woman on the planet." It was Nadia.

"I just wish they'd split up. They're hardly ever together anyways." Morgan raised his left hand and beckoned the bartender to get him another beer.

Peter wrinkled his nose in curiosity. "Why would you want them to split up? So you can have her?"

"No, Jesus, Peter. I don't look at Jessie that way. She's my boss, like you said. No, I just don't ever want to see her get hurt. That's all. And he has the capacity to hurt her. I feel like we're all just waiting for it to happen, you know, or for it to become public, at least. He pisses me off. I'd like to teach him a goddamned lesson. He acts so damned perfect all the time. But I saw his hand on that woman's hip. I'd like to catch him in the act."

"Then why don't you?"

Morgan's head jerked towards his wife. "Why don't I what?"

"Catch him in the act."

"Sure, I'll just go find Miss-Joss-Whedon-Make-up-girl and send her off to Vancouver."

"Hmmm," was Nadia's vague response. But she stewed about it until they left the bar in an hour, when Morgan slipped into the passenger seat of her old Mazda so she could drive them home.

In the car, she spoke quietly. "Let's set him up."

"Sure. I'm up for it." Morgan was still sulking but he was feeling his beer and only half listening. A wide yawn stretched his strong jaw to capacity.

"I know how," Nadia offered.

He turned then, and studied her as she navigated a busy intersection. He waited.

She smiled at him, all perfect teeth and red lipstick to match her liquid nails. "It's easy. We break him down first. And then we go in for the kill."

"And then what, Nadia? He has a big fight with Jessie, then they kiss and make up."

"Or…"

"Or what?"

"Well…I've always wondered what it would be like to be some famous guy's woman."

Throwing back his head, Morgan roared. "Good luck with that! I told you, they're head over heels in love. Even if he does sleep around, he's never giving up Jessie."

"He will if he has no choice."

"And you plan to orchestrate that how?"

"I told you. We break him down first. We destroy him. And then I move in."

"And we destroy him how?"

"You said it yourself. His biggest weakness is Jessie. Remember what a mess he was when she went missing?"

"Yeah, such a mess the asshole had another woman within the year."

"Exactly. You get Jessie, and I get Josh."

"I don't want Jessie. Not like that." Morgan's voice was small. "I want you."

She harrumphed. "You and I need a pick-me-up, Morgan. Lots of couples have open relationships. Having Josh Sawyer in my bed could add a lot of spice to our marriage." A delicious shiver travelled up the backs of her legs.

"Duh, and how do you propose to get him in your bed?"

"You'll introduce me."

"You're my wife! So, uh, I just say hey, Jessie, this is my wife Nadia. She thinks she can spice up our marriage by fucking your husband, is that cool with you?"

"As if they know I'm your wife! You've never taken me to any social functions with your elite little tribe, Morgan! You've never even offered!"

"Because I'm always either travelling with her, or in Vancouver, Nadia. There hasn't really been any cause for you to meet them."

"And no one's never asked about your wife?"

Picturing Jessie's businesslike relationship with him, Morgan frowned and exhaled slowly. "Nope. They're not interested in my personal life. None of them. They don't care. It's all just work to them."

"So we'll say you are my stepbrother, then. I'll be your stepsister. I'll use a different last name. No one will be any the wiser. It'll all just be a game, a sex fantasy game. It'll liven up our own relationship, Morgan, you'll see."

"I don't know, Nadia. We'd be playing with fire."

"If you love me, you'll do this for me, Morgan. Let me try, at least. A real life fantasy…"

Letting her words drift off, Morgan stared out of the car window and watched the Toronto streetscape slide by. A homeless guy pushing a cart slid by, muttering hopelessly to no one.

Nadia's purr and an elbow in his ribs drove Morgan back to the nefarious topic infiltrating the small sedan. "You want him out of the picture. You said so."

Hesitating, Morgan waited before stating flatly, "It'll kill her."

"She'll rally. They all do eventually when their men bed other women."

"You're not a nice person, Nadia."

Nadia smirked. But she had one last thing to say to her husband as she pulled up in front of their small apartment building.

"Didn't you say they could use a nanny?"

Chapter Thirty-five

When Josh got home around six that evening, he found his wife asleep in their big king-sized bed, their little girl curled up into her belly. He stood at the door to the bedroom and gazed upon them, memorizing every feature of Jessie's body as she lay on top of the covers—the curve of her back, the way her hair drifted onto the pillow in waves, the delicate arm around his little daughter's body. Emily-Grace was equally stunning—golden hair, *just like in my dream*, he thought, catching his breath. He half wished her hair was red, or raven-black even, but no, it was blonde like his was as a child. And she was porcelain doll beautiful, all sunshine and roses and happiness, the much-loved child of two people who lived and breathed for their daughter, and who enjoyed every hiccup and smile from that cherished baby doll face.

He moved slowly into the room. Josh knew Jessie was exhausted after her tour, in fact he'd been quite worried about her over the last little while. He had been in touch with Deirdre on a regular basis when he couldn't fly to whatever city they were in, which drove him nuts because Dee was always hitting him over the head with *well you should do this*, or *don't do that*. In the old days Josh would have just called Matt, but their old friend was busy now watching over his brother and Kelly Reilly's tour. Josh could have called Ulysses, but the guy mostly left that Morgan kid with Jessie, since Ulysses was also responsible for Jacob and often had to fly between cities himself to co-ordinate security for each singer. Morgan seemed fine, Jessie didn't mind him, Josh knew, but he always seemed a little awed by her, and although Jessie found him dependable, Josh always felt a little unsettled by the guy.

Steve had told him one day while they were eating lunch on *The Wyatt*

Boys that Matt felt the same way. That stumped both men, but when Josh brought it up to Jessie she just laughed and told him he was jealous. That Morgan was just painfully shy, that's all, but he sure knew his way around a gym, which she appreciated since Matt was gone.

Morgan. *Harrumph.* Yeah, it sucked last night having the guy walk in and spy Josh with Helene from make-up. Not that anything was going on, it was just loud in the studio after their final wrap, everyone was drinking beer and laughing, and someone had turned some music on which blared in and around the cast and crew as they blew off steam after the tough Joss Whedon shoot. So he was leaning into her, yes; and sure, maybe he shouldn't have rested his hand on her hip, but it wasn't anything sexual. Did Josh like to flirt back with the women who flirted with him? Sure. He enjoyed the attention. And he got a lot of it. But he didn't sleep around. He had a woman in his life who he'd paid a hard price to get. And no way was he going to fuck that up.

Laying down behind his wife and small daughter, he laid a hand on the hip of the only woman he would ever love. Josh's body sighed into hers, and he felt her stir and nudge her backside a little his way. He smiled, just a little, and breathed into her ear, "I love you, Mrs. Sawyer."

She rolled over to face him, wiping a tired hand across sleepy eyes. Instantly Jessie came fully awake and moved her body upwards to lie on top of her husband. Emily-Grace snored lightly on the bed near her parents.

"Oh God, are we really here? Together? Are we home?" Jessie was smiling broadly at Josh now. She moved so that both knees straddled him, and then she took his hands and moved them at ninety-degree angles over his head so she could pin him down and nuzzle her favorite parts of his cherished body.

"We are, little one," was the answer Jessie longed for all these long months without her husband by her side. "And I'm coming to Atlanta with you, so we've got, hmmmm, how much time together before *Mystic Nights* and *The Wyatt Boys* start again?"

"Almost four beautiful months, that's how long. So…after Atlanta we do P.E.I., and then the ranch in the fall?"

"Whatever you want, little one." Forcing a hand out from under hers, Josh swept some stray locks of hair back from his wife's face. She took advantage of the movement and brushed his cheek with her fingers.

"How was the wrap party?"

"Another five a.m.'er." He yawned to accentuate the point and they both laughed.

"Did you bring dinner home with you?"

"Sushi is downstairs waiting for you to wake up."

At her frown, he laughed. "Kidding. I got Noodle Box since it's kind of a ritual. Although I did get sushi for the little princess over there. How long has she been sleeping?"

"Only about half an hour. We were at La Casa for a bit this afternoon and she was going around the garden with her grammie, studying all the ladybugs and flutterbies, as she calls butterflies."

"Then we have some time…?"

"We do, Mr. Sawyer. Come with me." Jessie slipped off the bed and took her husband's hand.

Josh checked his daughter first to make sure she was safe on the bed—no weird blankets tangled around her or any other such hazards—then he followed his wife to the guest room across the hall. When they made love, they were celebrating the sweet joy of being together in a life that often tore them apart.

It was perfection, and the result, nine months later, was a gorgeous baby boy.

$\mathcal{A}$t took Morgan and Nadia more than a year to implement their plan. All the while, Morgan played dumb around Jessie, but his mind was reeling. Could he go through with it? Nadia told him it was just a game, that it would end fine. But in time Morgan realized she wanted more than an ending *for her.* No, she wanted this charade of hers to be a beginning that would 'fairy-tale last' forever.

He wanted that for her. Morgan wanted to see Nadia happy. Life had not been easy on her. They got pregnant at a young age, and money was always tight. When their child turned five, cancer took him. He died with Teenage Mutant Ninja Turtles action figures splayed out across his hospital bed, some of which Morgan placed in the casket for the burial. Nadia never spoke of the child—her main reminder of her and Morgan's son's existence was a small tattoo of his name and age over her left breast—*Darin5.*

With the boy's death, something inside her broke. Darin was Nadia's raison d'etre in a harsh and often unforgiving world. She changed. She hardened. The sweet Nadia with whom Morgan shared sacred vows became a bitter old woman at the ripe old age of twenty-one.

Morgan sometimes went to children's hospitals with Jessie, and he often found himself incapable of speech. Jessie thought it was endearing that first time, when he had to leave her to duck into a kid's bathroom and puke. But Jessie knew nothing, really, about him. So how could she know he was mourning his son, a child whose existence wound in and around Morgan's soul every day, with whom he played Ninja Turtles up until two days before the child was stolen?

So now, as Morgan slowly became aware that his wife's little game was now becoming a big game, he bit his tongue and said nothing. He told himself it was all for Nadia. But he knew it meant more than that to himself. He wanted Jessie. To sleep with? To make love to? No. He would be terrified to even touch her! And he knew she wouldn't want him like that. But to watch, to study, to love from a distance? Without Josh nearby...now, that he could do. To Morgan, that would be paradise.

The game started three days after Emily-Grace's third birthday. The children—and there were two now, because David Sawyer was now six months old—would be a part of the puzzle too. But Morgan knew they would be fine. He and Nadia went shopping just yesterday, and got all kinds of toys for them. They bought coloring books and puzzles for Emily-Grace, and baby blocks for David to chew on. They even got some pajamas and a few changes of clothes for the kids, and for Jessie too, which Nadia got a kick out of because she bought them at Giant Tiger, where she was pretty certain Jessie never shopped a day in her life.

Under a made up name, Nadia rented a small one and a half story beige clapboard house in Langley, only a few kilometers from the old *Drifters* set. The landlord didn't give a shit about the place, and he never checked up on them since they paid him a full year's rent in advance. *Money well spent,* Morgan thought as he installed a one-way mirror in the basement of the home. *By virtue of paying me, Jessie's paying for her own new little apartment.*

It was easy to set things in motion, because Morgan was Jessie's right hand man, her 'someone-to-watch-over-me.' He knew where she was at all times. He had flown Nadia out to Vancouver for the weekend, and they were ready. The first thing they did was scrawl a note to give to a kid. The second thing they did was prepare an old beat-up silver cargo van, by throwing a mattress on the floor in the back and tossing balaclava masks in the front. The third thing Morgan did—not Nadia, she was too detached to feel any more emotion than adrenalin that it was finally happening—was puke until he was dry. The fourth thing they did was wait.

Jessie was at ROAM, on the UBC campus. She had the two children with her, and she was waiting for Josh. They'd said a hasty goodbye that morning, a quick brush of his lips against hers, with plans to meet at ROAM around four after Josh's day on the set of his latest film, which he was shooting at SFU (Simon Fraser University) on Burnaby Mountain, a good half hour or more from where Jessie was waiting.

Morgan wasn't shadowing Jessie that day. Ulysses was fairly relaxed about her and the kids living their own lives in the city when she wasn't working, so Morgan was supposed to be back in Toronto enjoying some time off before heading to Miami with Jessie for another season shooting the hot *Mystic Nights*.

Baby David wasn't the easygoing infant his sister was. He was colicky and discontented much of the time, although he seemed to be growing out of it at the ripe old age of six months. Today he was betwixt and between, mostly okay because of a good nap in the black BMW SUV, but still a little out of sorts—enough, at least, for Jessie to succumb to bouts of frustration. At ROAM, she held and rocked him. Eventually he quieted enough for her to grab her cellphone when it rang. It was only three-thirty. Josh wasn't expected until four.

Jacob's voice greeted her. "Hey, you."

"Jacob! Are you in Van?"

"Nope. I'm in…what city am I in? I think I'm in St. Louis. I swear some days I just don't know."

"What are you doing in St. Louis? Your tour's over, dingbat." Still juggling the baby, Jessie reached down to her daughter at their small round table, and she handed the child a red crayon, which Emily-Grace took with gusto, her little pink tongue sticking out as she wrapped pudgy three-year-old fingers around the fat crayon and made great swirling motions on her paper.

"I'm doing the dad thing for a bit."

Jessie's ears perked up. "You broke up with your latest flavor-of-the-week," she intuited.

"Yup. Didn't I once tell you I have yet to meet a woman whose PMS I can even remotely tolerate? Well, this one's I couldn't tolerate at all."

"Did you try chocolate?"

"Yup."

"Salt? You know, chips. Pretzels."

"Affirmative."

"Massages?"

"She didn't want to be touched."

"Hmmm. I see. Are you okay?"

"Sure. I guess. I will be."

"I'm sorry, Jacob. I know you were hoping you and this girl might work out."

"Hey, Jess…?"

"Yeah?"

"Do you remember that time a few years ago when we were in your room in Miami and Emily-Grace was still pretty new…and I was telling you about my dad's painting of me and my mom?"

"Yeah. I remember that night." Jessie's voice softened. *How could I forget?*

"I felt like…I felt like you wanted me that night. That we could have somehow changed things between us that night."

Sighing, Jessie puckered her lips before answering. "I know that you knew, Jacob. That's why I had to stop having you over at night. That and the fact Martinique was spreading her tentacles all over the hotel spying on us."

"Sometimes I wish…"

She cut him off. "It wouldn't have worked, hon. Between us. It would have destroyed what we have. Including this little boy monster's chance at life, if Josh ever found out." Since David seemed to be settling, Jessie lowered herself into a chair and took a sip of her now cooling mocha.

On Jacob's end, he was reclining back against the arm of a couch in his dad's dressing room while his dad was on stage. He had one arm behind his neck and was leaning his head on it. "I wish I had taken you that night, Jess." He was talking in a subdued tone now, in case any hangers-on should be clinging to the doorway on the outside of the room. "I wanted you. And I had the chance. I should have gone for it."

"It wouldn't have changed anything, Jacob. It just would have destroyed things."

"One night…that was all…we could have walked away from each other after."

"One night would have turned into two nights and then three…and I would have found myself in love with two men." She caught her breath.

The catch in her voice was distinct. Jacob sat up. "But you are in love with two men, Jess. I know you are."

She didn't answer. The last few years were magical, with Josh, with their children, with her music and Jessie and Josh's regular TV series gigs and scattered film projects. Even the P.E.I. film had gone to Sundance and jump-started a career for the P.E.I. filmmaker. Was Jacob a part of the magic? *You bet*, Jessie reminded herself. But she had managed to keep a respectable distance, yet maintain a solid, close friendship. She knew his call today was fueled by ennui, loneliness, maybe a sense of despair after this latest break-up, and probably more than a little weed.

"Babe," she said, because she always called him that when she was feeling he needed a tender voice in his ear, "you will find the right woman some day. I swear it."

"What if I already have? And lost her?"

David chose that moment to start fussing again. His baby voice was so loud Jessie and Jacob could hardly hear each other. She laughed. "Do you want this? Huh? This kid's a colicky little bastard. An adorable, loving, sweet, colicky little bastard." She tweaked her baby's small pink lips and he smiled. Glancing down at Emily-Grace, Jessie gasped. "Honey, you only color on the page. Not on the table. Oh, shit."

Jacob's next words were dry. "You and your cowboy still have that old swear jar?"

"Ha. Funny guy, are we now?"

Just then a subdued freckled kid of about nine pulled on the plate glass door of the café and made his way inside. Standing at the entry, he looked around before heading over to Jessie's table, where he stopped and stared nervously up at her. Startled, she met his flickering eyes.

"Hey," she said.

"What?" asked Jacob from the other end.

"No, not you," answered Jessie. "There's a kid here. He's handing me a note." Eyes narrowing, she looked down at the note. "Thanks, kid," she said to the boy, who peeked at Emily-Grace's drawing before he wandered away. "Hmmm."

"What?" Jacob said again, yawning in St. Louis.

"It seems to be from one of the AD's on the set at SFU. Not someone I know. It says Josh is running late so can I meet him at this new place downtown. Says she wrote the note because his cell isn't charged and he's already hit the road. Huh. That's weird."

"What's weird?"

"Well, why would this AD send a note? I mean, why wouldn't she just call the café and tell Chris or Zev to tell me? Or call me on my own cell, for that matter. Although I suppose Josh wouldn't even know my actual number to tell her. Technology. Humph."

She flipped over the note. "Oh."

"What?"

"Geez Jacob, what are you, a broken record? There's writing on the other side. It just says 'sorry for the note, my brother lives in the UBC area, his kid's a real fan and I thought it would be fun for him to meet you.'"

Juggling David over to her other arm, Jessie was silent for a moment. "Kid didn't seem like much of a fan," she muttered. Easing the phone between her shoulder and ear, she started using the now-free hand to pack up her daughter's crayons. "All right, Jacob. We'll have to finish this conversation another time. It'll take me at least twenty minutes to get to this new café, which is on…" She glanced at the note. "Apparently it's somewhere near Cambie and Main, there's an address. I guess I'll be GPS'ing this one. Geez Louise, seems like there's a new café to check out just about every damn day in this city. Someone on set must have told Josh about this one. You gonna be okay, babe?" Folding the note, she shoved it in a pocket in her jeans.

A heavy sigh was her barometer for Jacob's feelings at the moment. "Sure. I will be. But I miss you."

"Honey, I'll see you in Miami next week. In the meantime, hugs hugs and more hugs from little 'ole me. Who isn't worth the time you spend dreaming about. Okay? I get PMS too."

"Yeah, but Jess…your PMS I can handle."

She laughed. "That's cause your memory is messed up from all that weed." But inside, she agreed. The time they had together, in Scotland, and then in Vancouver, was surreal. If you factored out the engagement ring Jessie wore constantly around her neck in Scotland, and the fact that Josh was on her mind—and in her heart—24 / 7. "I'll see you real soon, Jacob. Cheer up, babe. And...I do love you. You know that, right?"

"Do I detect a wistful tone to that voice?" Already sleepy, hearing those magical words from Jessie was sending him into sweet slumber. Jacob grinned.

"You do. Always. Sweet dreams, Ryan."

"Luv you back, Jess."

"Bye."

"Bye."

After she disconnected, Jessie demanded her heart stop its fluttering. Yes, she would always love Jacob, but right now she was feeling a little annoyed with her husband for making her pack up their two children again and travel downtown to some sketchy area of the city she hardly knew. So she was feeling a little more pre-disposed than usual towards Jacob's sweet overture.

She shook him off. David was really wailing now, and other patrons in ROAM were starting to send her hard looks of annoyance and disapproval.

"Sorry," she waved to an older lady who obviously didn't watch *Mystic Nights*. "He's a colicky little—" She bit her tongue and offered the lady her best *I-know-it's-annoying-but-it's-driving-me-crazy-too* smile. She placed the baby in his carrier and then packed up her daughter's things. Taking Emily-Grace in one hand, and the carrier with David in it in the other, she stopped by the cash to offer a quick explanation about her hasty departure to Chris, who she knew would be wondering why she was leaving in such a hurry, barely touching her mocha. Then, the diaper bag slung over one shoulder, kids in tow, Jessie headed to the SUV.

On Cambie, she drove up and down in the busy traffic searching and searching for this new café, cursing her husband, but the GPS took her to a back alley with a dead end. Parked there, she stared at her cell and, with David screeching bloody murder now, and his sister holding her hands over her ears screeching, "Top, Dawid, top," Jessie texted Josh's cell, hoping he'd charged it in his truck. She didn't know Nadia, wearing a wig, had paid off a PA to pilfer it for her, telling the kid it was a practical joke.

Jessie was starting to panic. The GPS was telling her she was at her

destination but, glancing around, she could only see large industrial gar-
bage bins and a few graffiti'd back doors.

"Damn it, Josh," she mumbled half-heartedly, putting the SUV in gear
and starting to back the car up. "I'll just go home, then. You're bound to end
up there at some point."

The corner of her eye caught movement somewhere behind the SUV.
Through the rearview mirror she saw a silver cargo van screech to a halt
behind her, angled in a way that made it impossible for Jessie to continue
backing up.

Eyes widening, her heart rate picked up.

"What the hell?!"

She tried to maneuver the SUV anyway, but there wasn't enough room to
go anywhere. When she saw two balaclava clad figures emerge from the van
and start striding quickly towards her, though, Jessie lost it. "Oh fuucckk,
this can't be good. Kids, hang on!"

Twisting frantically around, she started backing up quickly, smashing
into the van and pounding the lock-all-doors button on the driver's side door
as she did so. At the last second, with the sinking realization her vehicle was
trapped, Jessie grabbed her cell from its resting place on the seat opposite,
and speed-dialed her always 'go-to guy' when things got rough, even though
he wasn't her regular security anymore, and hadn't been for ages now.

He answered immediately. "Jessie?" Matt asked, surprised but happy to
hear from her.

"Matt!" she was already screaming. "Matt, there's a van…blocking us
in…we're in trouble! I've got the kids, Matt, help—"

Matt's knees buckled when, through the line, he heard the horrific explod-
ing sound of a window shattering. Jessie screamed wildly. Then, as Matt
sucked in a frantic breath, and his heart crashed to the ground, the connection died.

Chapter Thirty-seven

Josh landed at ROAM with a hop, skip and a jump. He cherished this time of his day, when he got to meet his wife and their two kids at a coffee shop or restaurant, or just at home. Seemed they were always separated, so these days, when both he and Jessie were in Vancouver, were blessings to be treasured. Today, Josh knew his wife would be anxious for him to help with David, the fussier and more needy of their two children.

Strawberry muffins were on his mind when he bounded down the steps and into ROAM. Shooting had gone well that day. Josh was pleased with the director as well as with his own performance, and ROAM was known for their fresh homemade muffins. He rubbed his belly in anticipation.

Chris, the lean barista with the cool tall-ship tattoo and Buddy Holly glasses, eyed him quizzically. He leaned an elbow over the espresso machine and said, "Hey, Josh. You looking for Jessie?"

Josh looked around. ROAM, this time of year when the patio wasn't used much, with the exception of on a rare sunny day, was a small café. Jessie and his children were nowhere in sight.

"Well, yeah…" he responded, disappointment fringing his voice. "Guess she got tired of waiting, huh?"

"Actually," Chris said, furrowing his brow and rubbing his chin, "some kid came in and handed her a note. When she left, she said the note was a message from you telling her to go to some café downtown, that you were running late."

Josh shuffled his feet and stared at the barista he'd known for more than a few years. "You serious, Chris? I didn't send Jessie any note. I mean, I would

303

have texted but I couldn't find my phone after being on set. Which was weird because…because I always leave it in my jacket pocket. But it wasn't…it wasn't there."

He knifed a hand through his hair the instant Chris clued in that Josh was clueing in that all was suddenly not right in Wheeler-Sawyer world. "Can I use your phone? I need to use your phone." Josh was already grabbing for the young barista's phone, which was sitting by the cash, but when he got it he stared at it fruitlessly. "Jesus, Chris, I don't know anyone's actual fucking numbers. Jesus, this can't be good."

"Who do you need, Josh? Ulysses?" Chris snatched the phone back and selected a contact name. "Here." He handed the phone back to Josh and answered his questioning look with a shrug. "Ulysses insisted we have his numbers in case…" He swallowed. "Just in case. Here's the first, it might be his landline…"

Blinking, Josh nodded in gratitude. A curious *hello* reverberated in his ear. "Ulysses?"

Ulysses answered with a casual, "Hey, Josh. I thought you were Chris the barista. Wondered why he'd be calling me."

"Uh, Ulysses…" Josh glanced at Chris again before heading outside so he could talk without disturbing other patrons or without them clueing into his increasing anxiety over the whereabouts of his wife and two small children. "Look, uh, Ulysses, I don't want to push the panic button here, but… Jessie was supposed to meet me at ROAM with the kids, and she's not here. And the thing is," he was pacing now, still running a hand through his hair, over and over, "there's this story about some fucking sketchy note, and—"

Ulysses cut him off. "Josh? Okay, relax, I've got to call you right back, I'm just getting a call from Matt, uh…which is weird…" On his end, Ulysses was staring at an incoming caller ID. He, like Jessie, had not been in touch with Matt in a while.

He put the phone back to his ear briefly when he heard Josh saying loudly, "I don't have my phone, Ulysses, it's gone missing. Just call me on this number, it's Chris' phone, right away, okay man? I'm at ROAM. And I'm starting to freak out here."

"Okay, Josh, hang on, I'll get right back to you, I should take this call from

Matt. Back to you in two." Ulysses tapped on the incoming call and his old boss' voice came on the line.

"Ulysses, where's Jessie?" Matt skipped all formalities. He was standing on the tenth green of a golf course in Virginia with Michael, who was now staring at him in curious bewilderment.

While he listened, Matt jumped into the cart he and Michael were using to steer around the course. Michael bounded in opposite him just as Matt floored the thing and careened crazily back to the clubhouse, pissing off a lot of golfers on the way and narrowly missing getting beaned by one angry putter whose green he traversed rather rudely.

Ulysses' response was quick and to the point. Discerning the urgency in Matt's voice, he leapt up from his home's sofa, where he was relaxing with his iPad opened to the Vancouver Sun. "Not where she's supposed to be."

"She just called me, she's in trouble. She got cut off." Matt closed his eyes at the terrifying sound of the SUV's window shattering, and…Jessie's bone-chilling scream. "I'm calling the police. She has the kids. Where's Josh?"

"Oh, fuck," he heard Michael groan beside him.

"Josh is at ROAM, where Jessie's supposed to be. He just called, he says someone passed Jessie a note and she left, thinking it was from him. It wasn't."

"Call Josh back and meet him somewhere, get him somewhere safe, Ulysses, take him out to Coquitlam, to my old RCMP partner's house on Madore. Gary used to always be part of my back-up plan. Charles has the address. Tell Josh to lay low for now, 'til we find out what the hell is going on. And Ulysses?"

"Yeah."

Matt screeched to a stop at the clubhouse, and, with one eye on Michael, he vaulted for his vehicle, his brother close behind with both sets of golf clubs in tow.

"I'm on my way."

~ ⁓ ,

And so it was that Josh was standing outside ROAM on a borrowed cell-phone when he got the news that he was to go to a safe house, per se, in nearby Coquitlam. But he couldn't go right away. He sank to his knees instead and found himself gasping for breath as Ulysses' words started to sink in.

She called Matt. She was in trouble. She got cut off. He's calling the police. She has the kids. She has the kids. She has the kids.

～～

What do you do when your world suddenly starts spinning out of control? You can try to outrun it, to stay out of the fray the best way you know how, or you can give in to despair.

And if you choose that option—despair—or if it chooses you…you just might end up on the ride of your life, struggling with everything you have in you to hang on while some strange version of the world spins you faster and faster in a direction you neither recognize nor understand.

When the love of your life and your two children suddenly and inexplicably disappear, you can't help it—you get sucked into a downward spiral. Because a part of you disappears as well.

You are shattered.

You are wrecked.

And you…are broken.

～～

The End.

～～

Hello!

I cannot get enough of Josh and Jessie…and Jacob.

Thank you for continuing along the *Drifters* journey with me. I hope you are enjoying Josh and Jessie's story as much as I love writing it.

I have a favor to ask—writers like myself depend on ratings and reviews from readers to help spread the word about our books. If you feel so inclined, please take a moment to visit Goodreads and Amazon (if you've read this on your Kindle) to rate and/or review my books. Also, any word you can help spread through social media is very much appreciated.

Thank you so much!

Susan

www.susanrodgersauthor.com

Facebook: search **Susan Rodgers, Writer**

Twitter: **@srbluemountain**

www.bublish.com

email: **fatcat@pei.sympatico.ca**

About the Author

Susan Rodgers' first novel *A Certain Kind of Freedom* was a Finalist in the Writers' Federation of Nova Scotia Atlantic Writing Awards for unpublished manuscripts. Her short story from the novel of the same name, published in two anthologies, has received rave reviews, as have the Drifters novels, Susan's all-time favourite books to write.

Owner/Operator of Bluemountain Entertainment, Susan is a 'Diploma With Honours' graduate of Vancouver Film School. She produces mostly documentary style client films and short dramas with plans to one day shoot a Feature Drama based on the novel Atlantic Blue.

Formerly a Museum Curator, in winter Susan lives with her partner Steve and her striped cat Oliver (Lucy Maud Montgomery once said the only good cat is a striped cat) in Summerside, Prince Edward Island, Canada. In summer, she hides in a small trailer in Darnley, P.E.I., where she writes novels, paddles kayaks, and crafts sandcastles on the beach. She makes frequent trips to Vancouver to visit her son Christopher, where she enjoys life in the hippie city while listening to great music and sipping on good espresso.

Books by Susan Rodgers

Drifters series:
A Song For Josh
Promises
No Greater Love
Riptide
Whispers of Home
And Then There Was Silence
Let the Music Cry
If I Could Sing You Home

Other:
A Certain Kind of Freedom
Seasmoke
Atlantic Blue

Feature Screenplays:
The Story of Jack & Emma
Atlantic Blue
Beautiful Jane
They Were Dreamers (adapted)

Short Stories:
S12
A Certain Kind of Freedom
A Gentle Peace

www.ingramcontent.com/pod-product-compliance
Lightning Source LLC
Chambersburg PA
CBHW060550030726
47498CB00005B/1336